Dance on Fire

Also by James Garcia Jr.

Seeing Ghosts

The Dance on Fire series:

Dance on Fire
Flash Point

Dance on Fire

James Garcia Jr.

DANCE ON FIRE

Second Paperback Edition

ISBN-13: 978-1479156290

ISBN-10: 1479156299ISBN

Publisher: James Garcia Jr.

Editor: Natalie Owens

Cover Illustrator: Maria Zannini

For my two boys: Riley and Rian.

"I can do all things through Him who strengthens me."

-Philippians 4:13

Table of Contents

Sunday...1

Monday 6

Tuesday 63

Wednesday..103

Thursday 153

Friday..203

Saturday 247

Epilogue 359

Author's Note...374

Author's Bio 375

"It is a perpetual statute throughout your generations in all your dwellings: you shall not eat any fat or any blood."

-Leviticus 3:17

"And any man from the house of Israel, or from the aliens who sojourn among them, who eats any blood, I will set My face against that person who eats blood, and will cut him off from among his people. For the life of the flesh is in the blood…"

-Leviticus 17:10-11

"But about the resurrection of the dead-have you not read what God said to you, `I am the God of Abraham, the God of Isaac, and the God of Jacob'? He is not the God of the dead but of the living."

-Matthew 22:31-32 NIV

SUNDAY

PROLOGUE

May 4, 2008
11:59 p.m.

The great beast paused in the dark and sniffed the cool spring air as if welcoming in the fragrant bouquet from a glass of fine wine held below his nostrils. Hands casually held inside the pockets of a brown leather coat, long single strands of his dark hair leaping and dancing in the light breeze, head held slightly elevated, he breathed deeply so as not to miss a single delectable whiff.

After all of these many years, he was close now. Before, he simply had a sense of it; perhaps one might call it a fool's hope. Now he could smell it, taste it.

He was very close indeed.

The breath within him now spent, devoid of any flavor; the beast released it and stole another.

Cold, penetrating eyes pierced the moonless night as he was on the move again strolling languidly eastward, as if in a hypnotic trance, through the peach orchard. Had he already become intoxicated by the scent? Perhaps not the blood that led him, but what the blood was telling him. His eyes swept across his field of vision obscured as it was by the trees' thick canopies. With each additional step, more of the approaching town was revealed—multi-colored light, the spectrum of sounds, the differing shapes of buildings. Looking was unnecessary, however. At this moment, he was as finely tuned to the world around him as he had ever been before. Ahead, where the small town met the open country, and where the clues had led him to, a coyote prowled cautiously, desperately searching for a morsel. To his far left was laughter. Actually, it was more like

1

giggling—the squeals of drunken hyenas, intoxicated with the blood and flesh of their kill. Although in the case of these young men, much too young to drink, It was Budweisers that they were killing. He could actually detect the faint sound of the beer sloshing within the long-necked bottles held in the hands of these who probably thought themselves safely undetected among the rows of the raisin vineyard. This night, at long last, after much searching, longing, nothing could escape the beast's notice.

He paused yet again, this time kneeling low to the earth that lay below his heavy riding boots. Though quite minimal, the scent of blood was now sweet and heavy in his flaring nostrils and parched throat, awakening a deeper hunger within him, as if that could be possible. The sensation seemed so new to him. It felt so virginal, like that first bumbling attempt at lovemaking; that first night away from home; that first bloodletting.

Yet, it was none of these. It was the sweet taste of revenge. The beast would have to salve that hunger with something else tonight, he knew, and perhaps tomorrow as well, but not for very much longer.

Claw-like fingers dug slowly and confidently at the ground until a tiny leg emerged. It was followed by another, and then a shriveled face. They stopped digging and wrapped themselves around the tiny head, where nails all too similar had recently gripped and snapped away the last of the cat's life. Without a thought, the beast pulled the corpse from the shallow grave. He did not need to search for the wound that had drained the last of the creature's life, but he did. He *longed* to see the wound. How could he not? Was this not what had been driving him, filling his days? And now, he would do nothing but enjoy it to the fullest.

He bent the pathetic little neck back until there was an awful crack. His expression showed little knowledge of the sound of it. When he found the matted place where cold lips such as his had drank, when he could see the bite that had drawn the blood, he brought it quickly to his mouth and blew away the dirt with a sharp blast of dank air. Now he did the unthinkable. He licked the wound, long and slow, like a lover would the breast of his beloved. Then the great beast smiled a horrible thin smile as he looked up from it.

"At last," he whispered, nonchalantly dropping the dead cat and gazing up toward the small town before him. He spoke as if to the entire population. "Nathaniel," he declared, gritting his perfect white teeth as he did. "I have you at last. And when I am through with you the insignificant souls of this place shall gladly hand you over to me!"

The vampire immediately headed off into town, setting events into motion.

*   *   *

Kingsburg, California. It is a rural community in the heart of the San Joaquin valley, the richest agricultural valley in the world—so states the city's official website. Incorporated on May 11, 1908, it has a population of over eleven thousand and lies twenty miles south of Fresno, nearly halfway between San Francisco and the city of angels.

This is the home of Sun-Maid, the largest and most well-known raisin plant in the world. The gold medal Olympian Rafer Johnson was raised here. The actor Slim Pickens, who rode a nuclear warhead in the film, "Doctor Strangelove", was born here.

The Swedish Village, the signs read and the police cars and police badges proudly proclaimed. The style of the buildings' architecture, the baby blue and yellow colors of Sweden, as well as the frequent sighting of the traditional dress from one or another of the downtown business owners, further testify to this. Signs at various points along the city limits greet strangers with the

3

Swedish Word: *Valkommen*. It means exactly as it sounds, which is "welcome".

Every third weekend in May thousands of people converge on Kingsburg for the Swedish Festival. It is a time when nearly the entire town puts on its traditional dress and a show for the weekend, with the highlights being a dance around the May Pole on Friday night and a pancake breakfast and parade on Saturday. This year marks the forty-third annual celebration and the town's centennial anniversary.

The festivities were set to begin in ten days.

MONDAY

May 5, 2008
4:18 a.m.

"*Are you sure* you're not going to get in some sort of trouble for this?" the young man asked for the third time. His shift at the glass plant began at 6:00 a.m. In the meantime, he was visiting his new girlfriend.

"No, Jeremy," Kingsburg Police Dispatcher Lainie Bishop answered. "Will you please relax? We're just talking! You're over there, I'm over here, and nothing is keeping me from doing my job. Now let it go!"

"Kingsburg, one-five-nine."

"See," she said, taking her hands away from her lap and presenting them to him, palms up. "I'm doing my job." Lainie put one foot on the thinly tiled floor and pushed off, spinning her chair back around toward the microphone and keyboard which was her charge. She keyed the base microphone. "One-five-nine, go ahead."

"Ten-ninety-eight, Draper Street doors."

That was shorthand police talk. The Dispatcher was being informed that the task of checking that all of the businesses along Draper Street were secure was accomplished. There had been no doors found unlocked, nothing amiss. "One-six-one and I will be ten-twenty at the fourteen hundred block of Draper." More Police talk; very official.

"Ten-four."

"Has CPS arrived to pick up that minor?" the officer asked, still official-sounding, but less serious.

"That's a negative, one-five-nine," Lainie responded professionally, although the question had been far from it. It was an inside joke.

"What minor?" Jeremy asked, but not before his new girlfriend had released the microphone. CPS was an anagram for Child Protective Services. Jeremy was freshly nineteen years old, while Lainie was five years his senior: a fact which lent itself to much ribbing and sarcasm toward the woman by her co-workers. On her end of the line, she sighed quietly. On the other end, down on Draper Street between Marion and Smith Streets, laughter erupted.

"You," Lainie answered, dropping her head dramatically into her left hand as if in defeat, her short blond hair falling forward. She couldn't hear the laughter now or see the faces twisted in glee, but she could certainly envision it quite easily. She looked back meekly at the young man, slightly embarrassed for him, but mostly for her. He wasn't the one who had to work with these guys.

After having introduced Jeremy to some of the members of the swing shift who had found him visiting her, some of the officers had begun volunteering to return before ten o'clock and drive the "boy" home before curfew. Others had been less charming. Lainie just knew that Officer Browning, the jerk partner of the voice on the other end of the radio traffic just now, had been the one to plant the pacifier in her lunchbox tonight.

"Please, Jeremy," she asked. "Don't say anything while we're miked."

"Ten-four." Officer Mancuso completed the conversation, still snickering about Jeremy's pubescent-sounding voice coming over the airwaves.

"Man, Nicky." Mancuso's partner began the tired argument. "I'm tellin' you, football is boring without Dallas kicking San Francisco's ass!"

"Mm-hmm!" Officer Nick Mancuso grunted, stepped near a yellow and green fire hydrant and spat a small wad of greenish, yellow phlegm into the street. It made an ugly unmistakable splat which he tried to ignore. He could not see the small mass in the dark, but had heavily evacuating his nose and throat for two days now, so he could well imagine it. The cold in his lungs was getting worse, he knew. Just exactly how he had

8

caught a spring cold, he still could not figure out. He had no allergies to speak of and was hardly ever sick. Yet, here he was. Sure, it was 50 degrees outside and the Graveyard Shift in a small town where nothing ever happened. However, dressed as they were in multiple undershirts, a Kevlar bullet-proof vest, black clothing and twenty-five pounds of equipment clipped to their belts, one could hardly tell.

Officer Lawrence Browning was the younger of the two and he sounded the part. Brash, often unthinking, he many times uttered an insensitive and stupid comment, realizing too late his mistake. They had been partners now for eighteen months. Eighteen *long* months.

Mancuso stared at him incredulously. "And yet it seems to me that we kicked *your Cowboy ass* the last time we played! Do I have that right?"

"When was that?"

"Funny you can't remember!" he added sarcastically. He half-choked on another piece of phlegm that suddenly broke loose, catching it quickly in his mouth before swallowing it by mistake and evacuating it, too.

Officer Mancuso was almost six years older than his partner with five more years of experience. He was five-feet, eleven inches tall; black hair; thin build. His partner was six-feet, four inches tall; blonde hair, blue eyes, muscular and fully prepared to call his own number on fourth-down and goal with a long two yards to go for the winning touchdown. Though both men hailed from California, Browning looked the part, while Mancuso looked as if he had just emigrated from New Jersey. He was 180 degrees from the type of character that Browning was. Quiet and reserved, he was often accused of being shy or introverted, a notion which could not be further from the truth. Instead, he was a people watcher. Where others might lose themselves in a daydream, the detective within him was always analyzing others. While waiting for his wife in the Fashion Fair Mall up in Fresno, he would pass the time by studying the faces and mannerisms of everyone around him.

Mancuso reached into his shirt's left breast-pocket for his pack of Winstons and offered one to his partner, which finally shut him up. Browning quickly accepted a cigarette from his partner and leaned close while Mancuso fished around his patrol car keys in his right pants pocket for his San Francisco 49ers lighter. When he had it, he lit Browning's cigarette first and then his own. He hoped that the sight of the 49ers emblem and colors would not set his partner off again.

Browning's eyes lit up just like the tiny flame when he saw the hated team come just inches from his nose.

"Look…" He attempted to pick up the argument where it had been left off.

"C'mon, Larr!'" Mancuso quickly interrupted before exhaling cigarette smoke into the cool early morning air. "Don't you ever shut up? No wonder Alicia left you!"

Browning took a long drag and then pointed his cigarette at his partner. "Cold shot, Nicky. Alicia split 'cause I didn't make enough to support her decorating habit." He paused. "Besides, I think she likes her men a little more...feminine."

"Oh, hell!" Mancuso turned and spat again. "Here it comes."

"No, seriously!" Browning continued, undaunted. "Have you seen that guy? What a wuss! You know, to tell you the truth, I'm not even sure he had a..."

"Well," Officer Mancuso quickly cut him off before he was given the graphic details of the man's genitalia. "I've met him before. I thought he was a nice guy."

Officer Browning took another long drag and then grinned as he blew it out. "See, that's why you're not allowed near the junior high!"

Officer Mancuso raised his hand before his partner's tanned face and thrust his middle finger upward in playful response.

"Oooh, Baby!" Browning went into his undersexed collegiate freshman girl imitation. After having spent so much of the past eighteen months together it was quite possibly the only skill that Officer Mancuso could identify his partner having.

"You're a sick man, Larry."

"Pardon me, Officers." A voice suddenly appeared behind them out of what had once been an alley but was now a small picnic area between Gino's Italian Eatery and the Apple Dumplin Antique shop.

The police officers spun. Mancuso lit his heavy Mag-lite flashlight, while Browning ripped his police issue Glock 22 from its holster and pointed the .40 caliber weapon in the direction of the voice.

"Gentlemen!" the man shouted weakly, offering his empty hands out before him to demonstrate to the men how unarmed and quite safe he truly was.

Mancuso's flashlight bathed him in artificial light. He was a Caucasian male, standing at least as tall as his partner with straight long dark hair, probably black, framing a fair-skinned face. He had a better than average build, wore a long brown leather coat, designer jeans, and large motorcycle riding boots to match.

"Put your frigging gun away, Larry," Mancuso whispered, reaching out with his free hand and nudging his partner.

Browning immediately lowered his weapon. "What did you expect me to do, Nicky? He scared the... You know you scared the shit out of me, sir!" Browning berated the man.

"I apologize for it, gentleman," the man said with an embarrassed grin as he lowered his hands and carefully approached. "It was...inexcusable."

"You're damn right!" Browning continued his assault. "You might get your ass shot off one day!"

11

"Thank you, Officer. I will keep that in mind."

"Give it a rest, Larry." Mancuso ordered, turning off his flashlight. "What can we do for you, sir?"

"I wondered if you might allow me one of those cigarettes?"

"Sure," Mancuso answered, reaching into his shirt pocket for the Winstons. "It's probably the only way to keep the blood flowing this early in the morning."

"Ah, but my dear Officer," the man began, taking the offered cigarette, "there are certainly more ways than this to keep the blood flowing, as you say, on such a beautiful and perfect night."

"Got that right!" Browning said, still visibly trying to calm down. He tossed his spent cigarette behind his partner and into the gutter. "I know exactly what you mean."

"Do you?" the man asked, turning in Browning's direction, seeming genuinely interested.

Mancuso shook his head as he fished around inside his pants pocket for the lighter once again. If the stranger did not entirely guess where Browning was headed, *he* certainly did. *Sex!* It was the only thing Larry Browning *ever* had on his mind. He just wished that his partner would be more selective in deciding when to mention it. Locating his lighter, he raised it to the man's face and attempted to ignite it.

"Oh, yeah!" Browning continued. "There's nothing like an all-nighter to get my blood flowing."

Suddenly, as if it were the most amusing thing that he had ever heard, the stranger threw back his head and roared with laughter. It echoed loudly around the rest area, the sound reverberating between the brick walls. It did not dissipate immediately, but seemed to hover there just like the Tulle fog that blanketed the Central Valley in the winter.

At first, Browning joined the laughter, as if thoughts of a pair of long firm lightly tanned legs locked around his waist teased his perverted mind. However, they soon faded. For something quickly and decisively ripped any pretty images from his head. There was something about that laugh that caused everything about the morning to suddenly feel much cooler than it was.

Mancuso snuck a glance at his partner, whose face drained of color as if he were just a simple child again, and not a graduate of the Police Academy and Fresno State University with a degree in criminology. And now, for Mancuso, bringing the cigarette lighter to life seemed all but impossible for him to manage.

"Allow me to assist you," the man said, no longer giggling but using a tone that dripped with mocking amusement. He casually took hold of Mancuso's hand.

Officer Nicholas John Mancuso shuddered at the touch. He had never experienced any winter like this man's fingers. They felt cold and lifeless. He remembered one night during his first year while training with the Fresno County Sheriff's Department, when they had responded to the ranch belonging to an elderly male who hadn't been heard from in four days. This man's flesh was just as dead as Mancuso's first corpse that he'd found lying in a heap on the bathroom floor.

On the man's first attempt, the lighter came on. Both officers jumped as it flickered to life. "There we are," the man said with a smile and then leaned close to the dancing little flame to light his cigarette. "You see, that was no trouble at all."

Mancuso and Browning *did* see. *They saw the impossible.*

Mancuso looked deeply into the man's eyes—they were black and cold and lifeless. They looked like a shark's eyes right before it bites into you.

This man standing before them, still clutching onto Mancuso's wrist, was dead as well, with unblemished skin that appeared as smooth as a white satin sheet pulled tightly over a bed in a suite at the Ritz Carlton.

13

Only this was no bed, but a grown man's face with holes cut out for eyes and a mouth. And gleaming teeth.

Mancuso was still thinking of that shark when he beheld the vampire's incisors. Browning must have thought the same thing because he quickly went back for his gun. He got it as far as the top of his holster before the man's free hand sprang like a trip-hammer, cutting through the air between them. The attacking hand never seemed to get close enough to the weapon, but it obeyed him just the same and leapt out of the officer's grasp. Browning stood there dumbfounded, his empty hand held high as if he carried some new prototype invisible blaster, and was preparing to use it to vaporize this creature standing before them.

Mancuso's heart sank. His eyes followed after the fleeing Glock as it skipped into the shadows of the former alley.

He still had *his gun*, but not the necessary courage.

"Now I've done it!" The man flicked the unsmoked cigarette into the deserted street in disgust. "I must once again apologize for my behavior, gentlemen. It seems that I have a flair for inspiring fear in the hearts of men." He paused briefly with a sigh. "Ah! All is not lost. As we were discussing before I made a most incredible mess of things, I agree that there are indeed other, more splendid ways to get the blood flowing, as it were."

And he roared with laughter again.

4:57 a.m.

The figure moved effortlessly southward, down the west side of 21st Avenue just north of Riverside. He seemed to glide along the sidewalk as if moving on skates. The navigation wasn't easy considering how the massive roots of the old Magnolia trees caused large sections of sidewalk to jut here and there; their thick leaves littering the neighborhood like some extravagant minefield alarm system were one to be stepped upon.

It was easier to navigate only if one had been here before. And he had.

A sign upon a white picket fence down Riverside Avenue read: **Caution**. Area patrolled by Basset Hound. The figure turned its direction and allowed the slightest of grins, but continued on his way.

The morning was a bit cooler than it had been, considering summer was well on its way. The slightest of breezes could be felt every few steps. The figure kept his head tucked half hidden within the drawn up collar of the trench coat; however, like a turtle peeking outside his shell. It was unnecessary. Both the canopy of trees and the early hour kept out whatever light might have otherwise been present and concealed him well enough.

But one could not be too careful.

He stopped. There, two houses further across the old street, was movement. He waited, ensuring that his presence was yet undetected. The hour was getting late, he was extremely well aware, and very soon people would begin to invade the waning night's last moments and the inherent danger they brought would drive him back into the shadows for another day. Finally, the hunt was on and he began to pursue what would become his last meal of the day.

He was across the street and up the immaculately groomed yard in no time at all. He passed directly before one open-curtained window and then another as he went, but there was no light present within, so he continued on his way, undeterred. He came upon a gate. He gently placed his hands upon the wooden door but never took hold of the latch. Instead, the figure slid his hands up to the top of the fence and scaled it as silently and effortlessly as a snake. A long mane of shoulder-length dishwater blonde hair spilled out of the trench as he went over.

The first window he came to there in the yard behind the house held his prize. The window sat above a row of four foot tall yellow rose bushes. He crept toward it carefully, but easily, as a ghost might, hovering over the ground, soundlessly. He had *years* of experience.

From beyond purple lips, the vampire's fangs pushed eagerly out of his mouth, anticipating the warm rush of young blood. At the foot of the bushes, the vampire stopped and reached for the window's ledge. Cold fingers gripped it tightly, followed by the other hand and other fingers as he leaned forward and peered into the young boy's bedroom. He saw youthful brown locks of hair which curled and surrounded a nice pink neck, no doubt warm. The boy's headboard was against the window, so he was facing the other direction and would never know what hit him. The vampire surveyed the window frame and the old bronze latch intended to prevent access from the outside. He smiled at the old rusted mechanism which probably held fairly well in 1931 when it was first installed.

It wouldn't even stop a poor thief, let alone me, he thought. *Had I sought to gain entry, nothing would stop me.*

Immediately, like the bar on a mousetrap that suddenly springs into action, crushing the mouse's neck, he reached down behind the rose bush and took hold of the cat that he had followed into the yard. It had just lay down across the decorative walk-on bark and had closed its eyes for its latest nap, never suspecting that it was being hunted until it was too late.

The vampire strolled across the yard, away from the child's window toward the safety of the shadows. The quite startled, thin and undernourished tabby cat hissed weakly within the clutches holding it captive, and then sank its teeth into the skin of the vampire's left thumb. It fazed him little.

"Poor creature," the vampire whispered, feeling every one of the animal's thin ribs. "You have not tasted an adequate meal in quite some time, have you?"

He was reminded of Southern California now which he had just recently abandoned. There had been a great many types of animals there with which to take a meal. There had also been a great many types of human animals on which to feed, most never to be missed, had that been his desire. It was not. The place had been nicknamed the city of angels. It still made him laugh. It had been his experience that man outnumbered the vampire there, but just barely.

Wanting to remain on the move, however, and wanting nothing to do with his own kind—with their violence and upheaval and dissention—he'd left. With as long as it had taken him to find two small meals, and both cats, he wondered how long it would be before he was forced to move again.

It was painfully obvious, as he soothingly stroked the cat's back, that this animal and he had much in common. He, too, had had very little in the way of nourishment this night. Standing there before the slumbering child's open window, the vampire felt lonely. It wasn't a particularly new feeling for him, but one he usually felt coming. Neither he nor the cat belonged anywhere. So, while whispering softly and tenderly into its ears, gently caressing its ragged and matted fur until it closed its tired eyes, the vampire quickly snapped its neck and put it out of its pitiful misery. It was a maneuver that he had perfected.

The vampire kissed the top of the dead cat's head. He held it to his breast as if it were his dead child for a time before feeding on it. When he had drained it of most of its blood, he buried what little was left in the flowerbed between two of the rose bushes.

Before he took his leave because of the fast approaching dawn, something urged him to steal one last look at that young boy in the window. He turned deliberately, as if another part of him, the *part* of him in charge of archived memory, knew what was coming and hoped to spare the *whole* from some great emotion. When he took his glimpse, the feeling that overtook him was one of great sadness.

Cimpulung, Romania
July 13, 1737.

The young boy awoke with a start to the horrible sounds of hell unleashed upon the earth. The commotion knocked him half out of bed.

Wolves!

That was his first thought as he awoke to find himself scrambling free of the covers and onto the safe neutrality of the middle of his bed. He had seen them before, so he knew what they sounded like. His father had had to scare them away from their home many times. He spun to face the glass-less window behind his bed, bracing himself for the sight that he fully expected to see should he be brave enough to push back the shutters. He could already visualize the ravenous beasts throwing themselves against his bedroom window, hunting feverishly for a way inside to get at him. He could picture them very clearly already gathering themselves into a mad frenzy. However, the din had ceased just as quickly as it had begun.

The boy waited. His lower lip quivered nervously as he stared sullenly at the foreboding shutters, trying to ratchet up the courage to push them open.

Just to take a peek.

His eight year old heart pounded thunderously within his small chest. Other than the sound of his quick and rapid breathing, the cottage and property was deathly silent.

Now he began to doubt.

Cautiously, only after making quite certain that whatever had occurred beyond his window was completely over and was not about to start anew, he crept back along the length of his bed. Hand over hand, he crawled; knee rubbing against knee. Absently pulling his old blankets out of place, dragging them with him, he inched forward. It was a snail's pace, but eventually, he made his way back to the goose feathered pillow that he had known his entire life.

Taking a deep breath, the boy took one final move forward. Cautiously, still summoning up that courage, he reached out slowly with one small right hand. There was no latch or lock on the shutters, so he simply pushed.

The boy looked.

With the absence of moonlight he could not see very far. He craned his scrawny neck and could see a little further now. The yard appeared empty.

Straining his eyes to see as much of the yard as he could, the boy tried to calm his racing heart to attempt to picture how it had appeared during the day. He and his mother had stolen some time to play beneath that very window in between chores while his father had toiled in the field. He was having trouble with this, however, because of the fear that he still could not shake. Hidden below the surface—behind the silence he could not trust—was *something*, he was certain of it.

The boy tried to inch further, placing both hands upon the walls of his room while he poked his head outside. He was careful not to fall out.

He could not see or hear any wolves. There were no animals of any kind, or signs of any type of struggle. The boy furrowed his brow, crinkling his nose in the process, as he attempted very hard to understand what it was that could have pulled him from his sleep.

That's when it happened again.

The poor boy's head whiplashed around as the sudden sound seamed to leap out of the darkness at him like a monster, worse than any wolf. Once again, he heard the sounds of the wild.

It wasn't wolves. It was his mother, letting out a horrible, bloodcurdling scream from her bedroom next door.

4:58 a.m.

"You're kidding!"

"It's true, Candy!" Jane Lynch reassured. "I heard the whole thing!"

"Wow! What I wouldn't have given to see that," Candace said through rapid breaths, jogging alongside her good friend of more than twelve years. They had been running every day before work, except on Fridays, since January. The last name in the office pool had them giving it up by June 1st. It was the two hundred twenty-five dollar pot which helped to keep the women motivated.

"I know. I couldn't believe how lucky I was."

"Then what?" Candace asked excitedly as they swung left at the Citibank Building from Lincoln Street onto Draper, onto what the locals referred to as "Main Street" and was the very heart of town.

The decorative red bricks beneath their running shoes were set at an angle now, seeming to turn with them, or in the very least used as a marker to keep them on the course. The Citibank sign before them was also an LED display that gave both time and temperature. It flashed 5:01 a.m. and then 49 degrees Fahrenheit, but neither paid it much mind beyond a cursory glance. This would be the coolest day of the week, and it was cold enough already without having to see actually how bad it was. They just kept up their pace and continued on their way. Shade trees and large blue celebratory banners hanging from blue poles lined the course now on the right; a Mexican Restaurant, pizza joint and other shops on the left.

"He told her everyone was complaining. She hadn't done a thing since they'd been sleeping together, marching about like a queen, treating everyone like she was the new CEO after a hostile takeover."

"Ain't that the truth?"

Jane continued. "She said some B.S. about how she never realized she'd been doing that. She'd be better from now on..."

"Sure, now!"

"But see, by this time, he's not even listening. It's over. She doesn't know it yet."

"Wow!" Candice exclaimed as they jogged from cement sidewalk back to brickwork.

On the right, a tree planter area bordered the next intersection. Most of the streets throughout Main Street were decorated in similar fashion. This particular one contained shrubs, flowers and other greenery kept very well groomed by the Model Drug Pharmacy which was located across from it.

"I haven't gotten to the good part."

"What?" Candice asked as they crossed Smith Street and continued west. Their usual route took them westward through town where they would eventually cross Draper at California Street and then head back for home. The two friends lived one block from each other and both worked for a large payroll firm in town. They were more like sisters than friends.

Their footfalls reached the sidewalk once again, bringing them across the entrance of the Bank of America. They paid little attention to the police cars that sat silent and unoccupied on the street.

"Her jaw literally dropped when he told her she was fired!"

"Wow!" Candice exclaimed once again as they reached their normal rest stop between Gino's Italian Eatery and Apple Dumplin Antique store.

It was here that they allowed themselves ten minutes to rest. The area extended its entrance on

Draper to the alley that ran behind the restaurants and shops. A sign had been recently erected pointing the way through to the historic old jail that sat behind the newly refurbished Fire Station. A large orange Swedish Dala Horse statue stood before them as if guarding the site. In fact, it wasn't to dissuade, but to invite. Two stone tables and two wood benches encouraged visitors to stop and sit for a while. There were small trees in stone planters, and one fully grown shade tree and four screens installed for holding back the squelching 100-plus degree summer days which arrive all too soon.

"Stupid vacation days! Always happens! Take a day and someone either quits, gets caught with someone in the copy room, or gets fired." Not that the copy room had ever been used for anything other than the occasional mild flirt session.

Jane continued her workout by jogging in place while Candice leaned over, feet spread apart, her hands on her knees to catch her breath beside the Dala Horse. "Then security came in and handed her stuff already boxed up."

"Shoo!" Candice winced with surprise, waving a hand across her face to do away with two flies that had suddenly materialized before her face.

She stood upright and stretched her back, raising her hands behind her head. She took a step and a half into the area as something caught her eye. Her left hand went immediately to her mouth and her eyes ballooned as what she was seeing was being made clear. Jane didn't see it, nor could she hear the faint whimpering over her own labored breathing.

"Then Jack points at the open door in his office and tells her…" Jane continued, still running in place, slipping into a bad imitation of their boss's voice. "'Call my wife! She's had two lovers herself this millennium.'"

Candice reached out blindly with her right hand and squeezed Jane's left arm, her other hand still frozen against her mouth as if sealing a crack in a dam. It was all that she could do. Never in a million years could she have found the words to describe to her friend the horror that was displayed there in the former alleyway, now all ornate brickwork and tree planters, cement tables and mutilated policemen.

"Hold on," Jane attempted to continue, glancing down the street, oblivious to the grizzly scene behind her.

It was not until Candice dug manicured fingernails through her friend's sweatshirt that she seemed to understand that something might be wrong. She just had no idea how horribly wrong it was until Candace suddenly yanked her forward to share her find.

"What's gotten into you, Candy?" she demanded and then fell silent.

Before them, in the very heart of the space, stood that solitary tree. It poked its canopy between two screens and into the nautical twilight. Before it grew a shrub in a stone planter surrounded by rail ties. A police officer was in that planter as well. At least part of him was. Jane froze.

"Jesus!" she whispered, stepping back in shock.

Candice Gutierrez never heard it.

*   *   *

Police Officer Nick Mancuso didn't hear the woman either. He was long past the ability to hear or see or feel anything. His only salvation was that he had been long dead by the time his head had been wrenched free from his neck and impaled atop a corroded metal spike. It stood there as some grotesque warning, but for just what, no one could yet know. Above the head, shoved violently through the screen, there hung the rest of him. His outstretched arms reached limply forward just as welcoming as that Dala Horse or the "Valkommen" banners that preceded it. The photo was framed by the famed Kingsburg water tower that rose a hundred twenty-two feet high above. In 1985, it had been transformed into a giant coffee pot, decorated with floral motifs in red, blue, yellow and green.

Now this city was being forever transformed.

* * *

Jane looked away before the first wave of vomiting struck her. It splattered hard atop the sidewalk, but Candace couldn't hear that either, thankfully. She stood transfixed by the eyes seemingly staring back at her; the frozen open maw, screaming in silence.

5:24 a.m.

Barbara Lopez' eyelids were closed tight; however, her eyes beneath darted to and fro like a worm that burrowed beneath the earth but could not decide in which direction to travel. Deep in REM sleep, she was looking at nothing and yet seeing much. She wore a white sundress and stood in a large open meadow. Thin, tall trees to her left looked like a small remote island surrounded by a sea of flowers that hid her feet and stretched as far as the eye could see. She surveyed their beautiful shades of pink, white, and yellow, lifted nearly two feet into the air on stalks of flowing green.

She glanced up, reluctantly. Was she hearing something now as the cool breeze pushed everything, making the stalks dance and the flowers sway? A voice was speaking to her, calling out to her, but she could not make out any words. She felt soothed as if she could hear the calming voice of wisdom itself. There appeared to be someone standing in the shade of the trees ahead, not that the sun was very warm, though exquisitely brilliant and directly overhead in the cloudless blue sky. Was that who was calling? She began to walk towards the figure.

Who the shaded figure was, she could not tell. At this point she could barely make out anything except that there definitely was a rather tall someone leaning against the trunk of a tree. Whoever it was had yet to see her approaching. If the person did know, then he or she was ignoring her, at least for the moment. Her initial thought was that it was a male, and as she grew ever nearer, that intuition proved accurate. It was definitely a "he" and he was watching the flowers at his feet, his hands linked behind him.

She heard the voice once again, but this time more clearly than before. It was an old voice and clearly not coming from before her but from behind. She pirouetted in the midst of the flower sea. No one was there. With the sky so blue and the sun so bright, with nothing preventing her from seeing a mile in all directions besides the cluster of trees behind her, there was simply no way that anyone could be speaking without her being able to locate him. She turned back. The figure continued to disregard her presence there.

"Nathaniel, Nathaniel!"

For the first time, Barbara could understand what was being said only to find that she was not the one being called. Something else occurred to her as well. A first name repeated was the calling card of someone very wise indeed. She immediately looked up to the heavens. God did that. When He called anyone throughout the Bible that was how He did it.

Since Barbara was not the one being called, she did not take it as a disappointment that she could not see the owner of the voice, nor His shadow. She looked back to the figure ahead. *Nathaniel?* It was an old name. These days everyone was Nathan; maybe even Nat. In any case, Barbara appeared not to be the only one that Nathaniel did not acknowledge.

"Nathaniel, Nathaniel!"

Again, the figure before her did not seem to hear. She stood her ground for a while, waiting to see what might happen. When nothing did, she began to grow frustrated. Why she did what she did then simply made the situation all the more curious.

"Nathaniel!" Barbara yelled.

The figure before her in the shade of the flowery meadow suddenly looked up and found her.

5:29 a.m.

Kingsburg Police Detective Michael Lopez opened his eyes gingerly to the pre-dawn light of his bedroom and yawned. Half-way through this, he stopped and jerked his head from the pillow. He looked up at the clock on the dark oak dresser across the room. He already knew what time it was.

He had heard women speak of their biological clocks, how they ticked away unmercilessly, reminding them of their age and the little time that was left for realistic childbirth. He was sympathetic to this concept because he had one of his own. Unlike a woman's, however, which silently ticked off the time like some great internal stopwatch, making its unfortunate way to 00:00:00, *his* actually *kicked* to remind him of its presence. *His* was a frigging control freak, bent on driving him insane, ringing mere moments before the real alarm clock on the dresser just to see him leap from the bed and fly across the room to turn it off.

Oh, they had tried living without the alarm, but that damned internal clock of his, no longer having a reason to wake him, didn't. Everyone had been late that day.

He and Barbara had also tried for a while living with the alarm clock near their bed, but neither had been able to keep themselves from falling into the trap of turning it off and falling back to sleep.

26

The problem had nothing to do with scaring the children, particularly the twins, or with waking them up at all. The problem here was a case of ownership. With Barbara being a stay at home mom, naturally the arrangement centered upon him working and her predominately raising the kids. But that was after six-thirty, not before! *He* was the one who needed to be up early since being promoted to detective grade; the rest of the house was content getting up when they were used to getting up. If he woke up the kids, again particularly the twins, it was solely his responsibility and absolutely no concern of Barbara's. At least that was the deal the way it had been reported to him.

Realizing his fate, Michael tossed his bed sheet into the air and leaped for the alarm. Sometimes, as the saying goes, it is better to be lucky than to be good. This morning, however, Michael was too late.

The alarm sprang to life as 5:29 became 5:30, just as his fingers made contact with the alarm button. He clicked it home in disgust and waited, holding his breath.

Familiar with the game, Barbara woke but did not move a muscle. She didn't even blink. They both waited in the first light of the day like psychics in Pompeii just milliseconds before the eruption. There was nowhere to go, nothing to do but wait for the ground to shake and the peaceful blue sky to fill with heat and ash. At 5:32 Michael considered himself lucky.

"You're a lucky duck, Michael," Barbara whispered.

"You don't have to tell me, babe," Michael answered his wife with a childish grin, still listening for the slightest peep from down the hall as he approached her side of the bed. "What'd I win?"

"You, my dear, have won the lifelong love and affection of your wife."

"Wait just a minute," Michael kneeled and rested his elbows upon the bed. "Didn't I have that already?"

"Theoretically."

"Theoretically? Sweetheart, I'm shocked!"

"Michael, love," Barbara purred as she stuck her finger out from beneath the covers and motioned him closer. He leaned forward. "If you want me to think of you in a day or two when I get off my period, I suggest you let me go back to sleep before the twins *really do* wake up!"

"Well," he smiled. "With a proposition like that, how can a guy refuse?"

The telephone rang. Michael had it off the cradle before it finished the first ring.

"Hello?" he answered.

He glanced down at his wife with one ear turned to the receiver and the other on the nursery. She was listening in that direction, too.

"Detective," the voice on the other end of the line began. "It's Bishop."

Lainie Bishop was the graveyard dispatcher. She was barely out of college, and one of the sweetest girls he knew. This morning her voice was obviously troubled. Normally, as young and naïve as she ought to be, she was confident and polished. Right this minute it sounded to him as if these were uncharted waters.

"Detective Jackson needs you downtown at 1448 Draper. It's bad."

"What is it?" he asked.

"Kingsburg, one-six-eight," an electronic-sounding voice in the background interrupted them.

"Go ahead, one-six-eight," Bishop quickly answered. "I'm sorry, Detective. It's been a rough morning. Just call Jacks." And then she hung up.

It must be, he thought as he replaced the phone.

"What's wrong?" Barbara asked.

"I don't know," he answered, still staring at the phone. "Bishop said Jacks wants me downtown."

Michael could still hear the buzzing sounds of a busy dispatch center ringing in his ear. And now he

28

could hear the twins starting to cry. Both parents sighed, neither one blaming the other.

Nineteen minutes later, Michael was fully dressed. Barbara was still in bed, though now sitting up and no longer alone. The twins were there; one teasing as if he might attempt his first crawl, the other wriggling about on her back.

Barbara stretched and yawned as he entered the room. He waited for his window of opportunity—the moment when her arms were raised their farthest and her breasts were pushed together and almost coming out of her pretty peach nightgown. *She could use a warm shower*, he thought to himself but acted as if he hadn't noticed. It was here that he started to make his move.

"Don't even think about it, Detective!"

Barbara suddenly opened her eyes and stuck her left hand out before his face, putting a halt to his impending advance. She was now the tiny, innocent field mouse in a silly cartoon, suddenly rolling onto her back and ripping out a hidden rifle with a scope on it, the word ACME printed on its side in bold black letters, and blowing away the hawk just as it extended its talons for her at the bottom of its dive.

"Don't flatter yourself, sweetheart," he lied. "I was just waiting for you to finish your stretch so I could give you a big hug."

"Yeah, right!" She slipped into their son's voice. "And monkeys might fly out of my butt!"

Michael dropped his head into his hands before looking up again. "I'm really worried about you, Barbara."

She laughed.

"Have you been watching that 'Wade's World' with your son again?"

"It's 'Wayne's World', you big dummy!"

"Whatever."

"You're showing signs of your age."

29

"Who, me?"

"Yes, you."

"Naw! The Lord and I made a deal..."

"It's not the Lord who makes the deals, sweetie," she giggled. "I think you got the wrong guy."

"Very funny!" Michael said, making a sarcastic face and nodding. "No, really, we made a deal. I stop saying the "F" word and He stops aging me."

"Oh, boy," she laughed. "I'm surprised you don't have more gray hair in your head than you do, making a fool-wager like that!"

"It wasn't a bet, dear."

"I know," she said. "Because you'd lose!"

"What do you mean?" He leaned back as if insulted.

"It's your favorite word. It's right up there with the word "yes" when it comes out of a woman's mouth. The race is so close; it's a photo-finish!"

Barbara leaned forward and grabbed her husband's hands, pulling him close before he could mount a comeback. She kissed him long and deep like Superman making Lois Lane forget his identity. When she was through with him, she pushed him away dramatically as if she were sending him off to work with a bang.

Acting obedient, Michael turned around and began walking out of the room. He stopped at the doorway and looked back at her. "Sweetheart?"

"Yes, Dear?"

"Brush your teeth!"

Before she could react to what he had said, Michael leaned down in a crouch and started to rock from side to side, waving his fists around in some dimwitted, "I got you" kind of celebration.

Barbara silently waited for him to stop his childish dance and then raised both of her fists into the air and mockingly flipped him the bird using her non-middle fingers. Michael laughed at the sight and then turned and walked away.

On his way out he peeked inside his eldest child's bedroom. Ten year old Jerod was that rarest of child. If questioned, neither mother nor father would have been able to recollect the last time that their son needed to be awakened for anything. Even for vacations or day-trips to Dodger Stadium, Disneyland or Pismo Beach, he had always been the first one up. This morning was no exception.

"'Morning, Son."

"'Morning, Dad."

Jerod was still in bed, but he had already thrown back his bedcovers and was just lying there, staring up at the ceiling with his hands behind his head. It was early yet, after all. He usually got up at six o'clock which gave him plenty of time to dress, eat breakfast and then head over to his buddy's house down the street where they always met to play PlayStation 2 before Steven's mother took them both to school. Steven Harris was the son of Judge Judith Harris, and he knew that Jerod liked to call her Judge Judy after the famous television judge. Whenever she heard him, the judge threatened him with contempt that would promptly begin at the stroke of midnight, August 15, 2016 on his eighteenth birthday. She didn't let him have all of the fun, however. She liked to ask Jerod whatever came of the search for his mother like the Jerod on the television series, The Pretender. A show that he had never seen, but now knew all about thanks to her. She promised to equip him with all of the seasons on DVD.

"I'm going to work, Kiddo, so you take it easy and have a good day, okay?"

"Okay, Dad."

"Who's got the trophy now?" he added with a wink.

"Steven!" Jerod said without a moment's hesitation, suddenly animated. "He had me by two scores! But in the fourth I got a pick and then forced a fumble on a sack to jump back in it!"

"What happened?"

"Extra point!"

"Missed it?"

"Missed it!"

"How do you miss an extra point on a video game?" his dad asked incredulously.

"Heck if I know! But if I had that weasel on a fantasy team, he'd be out! It was a chip shot!"

A moment later Michael was walking toward the driveway to his unmarked dark gray Ford Crown Victoria—which might as well have been marked "Detective" in large block letters as inconspicuous as *that* was. He climbed inside and cranked on the ignition. Immediately, the sound of radio traffic overwhelmed the turning over of the large engine. Seemingly, one voice was jumping over another, as if that were possible. Lopez called his partner's cell phone. It rang several times before his obviously agitated partner answered, "Jackson!"

Mark Jackson had been Michael's partner for as long as he could remember. He was more than a partner really, but perhaps the best friend that he had ever had. They shared not only their working hours together—whether during the day in the office or around town, or during the night on stakeouts—but they'd taken small vacations together and shared much of life's great events: two weddings, and the births of Michael and Barbara's children. Other than his family, Michael had never felt closer to another human being. Those who were old enough to remember the artist loved to refer to the both of them as Michael Jackson, playfully dropping the word "and" between the two names.

"Jacks, it's Mike. What the hell's going on?"

Michael could hear buzzing there, too.

"Mike," his partner said without hesitation or greeting, "we've got two dead cops!" And he did not wait for the information to sink in before continuing. "I need you here now! This is like the fall of Saigon down here! Rodriguez, watch where you set that! I want you and all of that equipment within the path of contamination. I catch anyone outside those limits, I'm gonna' have their ass! Mike, are you comin'? I need you!"

Without using his seat belt or checking his mirrors, Michael pulled out into the street and quickly accelerated. A cop in a film or television show might have taken the time to consider a great many things during these first unsettled moments. He might have already taken into account his character's motivation; or perhaps made some last minute change in his head to the scripted dialogue before making his delivery. Unfortunately for him, this wasn't Hollywood; this was reality. In reality, this was Kingsburg, and in Kingsburg the only things that got killed were the occasional dog and a great many cats.

"Mike, are you still there? Are you on the way?"

"Jackson, I'm on my way."

5:59 a.m.

In another part of town, another phone was disrupting the peace of someone's morning. By the third ring her blue eyes sprung to life. The first thing that came into the mayor's view was the bright red digital numbers on the fancy contraption on the nightstand before her. It was a dual phone and alarm clock with two alarm settings, which was no longer necessary in her house. Not since the divorce. It played CD's and had both AM and FM radio capabilities with a fairly strong antennae. It seemingly could do anything. By the fifth ring, she wished that it could answer itself. Of course it could, but that was not what she had meant. By the sixth ring it dawned on her that her alarm was about to sound as well. As she reached over to interrupt that seventh ring, it did that very thing.

33

"Peterson!" she answered, unable to disguise the agitation in her voice as she struggled to turn off the alarm at her bedside.

"Ma'am," said the apologetic voice on the other end of the line.

"Yes?"

"I'm sorry for waking you…"

"Don't be ridiculous," she snapped, unintentionally. She quickly regained her composure, none too proud of having shown showing weakness. "Of course I'm awake. It's Monday morning, for heaven's sake. I'm always early rising to begin a week."

"Of course."

"Now, what do you need?" It was an easy question, a safe question. She still had no idea who she was speaking with. She covered the phone quickly while she yawned. That last glass of Berringer White Zinfandel was still with her this morning.

"Your Honor, something terrible has happened."

"Go on."

"I came in early to put out some displays in the store window…"

Councilman Johnson! She sighed with the realization. He was the only member in City Hall who owned a business.

"…and when I looked out the window I realized nearly the entire block had been cordoned off."

Careful not to let him hear that she was still in bed, she sat up slowly and simply allowed him to continue. Of course, nothing was going to be able to prepare her for what she was about to hear.

"I couldn't see anything from where I stood except for the gray blankets. It looks like someone's hanging their laundry out in the heart of town. The place is crawling with cops, both uniforms as well as plainclothes. One guy looked like he was wearing pajama bottoms! They're not letting anyone anywhere near…"

"David," she interrupted loudly. "Did you say the police are hanging blankets on Main Street?"

She was awake now, by God. And not only that, gone was any thought of pretense. Before her mind could wrap itself around what she was being told the thought of cash registers slamming shut began to sound in her ears. There were yet a few details to finalize, some very minor tasks to perform, but suddenly it sounded as though the Swedish Festival, her first one, might be in big trouble.

"Just what the hell has happened?"

"Madam Mayor," the councilman said. "Two police officers were found murdered this morning on Draper Street."

6:42 a.m.

Detective Michael Lopez brought his car to a halt at the intersection of Marion and Draper Streets behind what appeared to be every squad car that the city of Kingsburg owned. His first thought was that in all of the excitement he had mistakenly driven into the Kingsburg Police Department parking lot, or perhaps the back lot at Universal Studios on what should have been a closed set and certainly not the small town he had lived in since the time that he was five.

The heart of Main Street was effectively shut down. Faded orange barricades and yellow **CAUTION POLICE** tape stretched across his view from the old city hall building on the north to the WestAmerica Bank to the south. Down the street, the scene was repeated from the Bank of America building to the former clothing store turned musical instrument store. It was a great rectangle that none were being allowed within and he was more than a little proud. Great care was being taken to preserve the integrity of the crime scene. In the great metropolitan cities in the country—Miami, New

York, Chicago, San Francisco, Washington D.C., Seattle, and Los Angeles—this kind of police procedure was commonplace; however, this was Kingsburg. This was a hamlet compared with those great cities. So far, it seemed, his little town was getting it right. The trick, of course, especially now that he and his partner were being passed the baton, was for that trend to continue.

Though it was still relatively early, onlookers were growing in large numbers outside the cordoned area. Obviously, the early morning jogging group had been first. Of that particular demographic, most now clutched coffee and donuts, this being infinitely more interesting than exercising. They had since been joined by the small business owners, who were much less excited by the developing scene since their bottom line depended upon cars and customers being able to drive and park in the now restricted area. Inside, uniforms were engaged in all sorts of activity from basic crime scene investigation to pedestrian control to just plain old standing a post. This morning, however, the word "uniforms" hardly seemed to apply. At first glance, there appeared to be few who had actually been afforded the time to put on a uniform due to the nature of the emergency.

As he reached the caution tape and prepared to enter the largest and most important crime scene he had ever witnessed, his thought was: *And I may need every one of you!*

"Mike," a grim-faced sergeant in faded jeans and a dark blue t-shirt which read, **POLICE**, greeted him behind an old and tightly clenched jaw. Joe Chavez was his name. If Michael respected anyone on the force, it was him. He had always been a great friend and mentor, more than once going out of his way to take care of him, especially since Michael had made detective. Actually, he was more like the father Michael never had, his own having died when he had been very young. He respected him dearly.

"I've never seen anything…" Joe's voice cut out.

Michael glanced at the scene laid out before him, allowing his trained mind to begin disseminating the rough data. Halfway down the block on the south side of the street, blankets had been hung from caution tape that stretched tightly between two trees, keeping what lied within from being seen by anyone on the outside. Michael's partner was there, he noticed, already thick in it. By the look of him, Michael needed to hurry along and join him.

Michael looked up into the sergeant's face as the names of the dead worked their way inside him. Everybody knew who had been working the Graveyard shift last night. Kingsburg was a far cry from the big metropolis of Fresno where it might be nearly impossible to even have met everyone in the department. In Kingsburg, not only did you know everyone intimately, but you also knew who they knew intimately.

Michael nodded at the sergeant and began to walk away. He heard Joe Chavez exclaim under his breath: "I wished to God that I'd never seen it."

"Lopez!" the chief's voice came resounding from his right as he made his way to the heart of the scene. He recognized it immediately. He slowed his pace just a moment, allowing the man to catch up to him.

"I'm sorry I didn't get here sooner, Chief."

"I'm just getting here myself," he said. "What have you heard?"

"Not much. Two dead. Browning and Mancuso." He glanced up at his superior. "I can't believe it."

The chief grimaced and looked into his eyes. "Yeah," he said simply.

When the two men joined Detective Mark Jackson, he was waiting for them. He was dressed in a gray sport coat, solid red tie, black slacks and shoes. He wore his curly black hair short and still sported the closely trimmed beard that he had grown during the winter.

Jackson held out his hands to stop them momentarily. Glancing around him, he addressed the small group of police officers, firemen and the three members of the ambulance crew that had arrived some moments ago, all on their own. No one had thought to call anyone in a rescue capacity.

"You men," he began. "Harry, Carlos, you, too. Some of you guys don't answer to me, but I would like your cooperation. We're going back inside there, but I don't want anything to happen while our attentions are divided. Fall back and maintain crowd control while we wait for everybody to arrive. We've got Travis County Sheriff's Crime Scene Investigation Unit on the way. More of our own are still getting here, and whoever the hell else needs to be here." He held out his hands to motion them back. "Please."

"Philips, Guerra, Alaniz," the chief took over. "You heard the man. I want containment here. Everything looks good so far. If we're going to figure out what happened here and catch the sonofabitch, we need your heads in the game. Alright? Let's go."

Immediately, the men fell back and went about their jobs. Even the E.M.T.'s quietly turned and started back closer to the ever increasing number of bystanders. Soon those numbers would include teenagers on their way to the high school. No doubt many of those wouldn't even make it to school, and that would go unpunished today, perhaps even the entire week. Nobody in the Department had time for truancy pickups now.

"Chief, Mike," Mark Jackson said without looking at either man. "Prepare yourselves."

And with that he quickly walked over to the spot where the blankets overlapped one another, parted them with his right hand and entered. Michael paused, allowing the chief to enter first and noting that his experienced partner did not give propriety a second thought.

"Jesus," the chief said as Michael stepped through the blankets and nearly bumped into him.

He put a hand out, catching the man's shoulder, and quickly balanced himself so as not to knock him over. Michael had to sidestep the man before he could see what had given him pause.

The first thing that he saw was Nick Mancuso's mouth gaping open. Michael put a hand to his breast as he could feel the horror wash over him. Impossibly, there was very little blood anywhere. At first glance the spike appeared to be relatively blood-free, nor was there any visible pooling in the planter below.

To the left was the rest of the police officer. Detective Jackson gave his chief room to kneel before the headless body. What remained was still hanging above with its great open wound facing north, the spine visible to any who cared to look for it. Its legs haphazardly trailed its torso. Both arms appeared to be broken. There was now a small blue tent covering the headless body, shielding the view from any potential news helicopters.

"Browning's back here," Jackson told them. He stepped carefully to the right along the path of contamination and walked over to the body of the second police officer. "He got off easier."

Michael and the chief followed suit. Officer Larry Browning's unbruised face appeared peaceful and serene, as if he were simply asleep. He lay on his right side with his back to them. It felt akin to standing over a deceased brother. In point of fact, both Mancuso and Browning were brothers to them all, or in the case of the chief—sons. As they hovered over what was clearly the worst crime scene in Kingsburg's nearly one-hundred years, Michael—and undoubtedly the others with him—never bothered to take the time to either ponder the historical significance or mourn the fallen. There would be time enough later to mourn these men. For now, the

39

only way to concentrate on the task at hand was to catalogue them as bodies, evidence, clues.

"He hardly has a scratch on him," the chief said, thinking aloud.

"I've been waiting for Fresno County to get here before poking around him too much, but that's been my conclusion as well. He's as white as a sheet, so I can deduce great blood loss. I just don't see where it went unless it is beneath him. I haven't moved him."

In the distance, someone called out. "Chief O'Donnell?"

"Yes!" the chief shouted back without looking up. There was no response. He finally turned, his voice growing loud with impatience. "What?"

Still, no one answered.

"Christ!" he muttered to himself, rising to his feet and moving quickly to the blanketed area. Michael's gaze followed him. He stabbed the place where the blankets overlapped with his left hand and pulled one aside. "What?"

"I'm sorry, sir," said one of the plainclothes officers, barely more than a cadet, really.

"If I have to ask you one more time what the hell you want, I'm going to bust you down to washing police cars! Do you read me, damnit?"

"Yes, sir," came a terrified response.

Clearly this kid didn't wish to bother the chief anymore than the chief wanted to be bothered.

"Good." The chief moved to turn back only to be bothered again.

"Sir, it's the mayor. I stopped her from coming to see you, but *she* started threatening me, too."

The chief turned back, quickly glancing over the young officer's shoulder until he spotted the Honorable Katherine Peterson. She had been selected the city's first female mayor.

Just six months ago.

She was dressed in a tan pants suit. Her blonde hair was up in a knot behind her. She stood with her hands clutching police tape, looking as if she were giving him thirty seconds to invite her inside or she was coming in whether he liked it or not. He had so much to do, but knew instinctively that he would get to none of it done until he had granted her an audience.

"Shit!" he muttered to himself, but not before he quickly turned back toward the blankets behind him so she would not be able to read his lips or note his reaction.

"Yes, sir," the young officer sarcastically agreed with his boss's assessment.

The chief glanced back to the man's eyes and allowed a minor grin to reach his face. The poor boy had been caught between the proverbial rock and a hard place, having to choose who to tick off: the Department or the City. Nice choice.

"It's okay," he nodded in a newfound respect for the officer. "Good job. Get back to your post. I'll go see her over there."

"Yes, sir," he said, acknowledging the moment only with his eyes. He turned and headed back to the exact spot he had been standing before his world began to get politically hot.

"Lopez, Jackson," the chief called out, but did not wait to hear a response. "I gotta' go see the mayor."

6:45 a.m.

Barbara Lopez hugged Jerod briefly and watched proudly from the dining room window as he made his way across the street toward the Harris' house, which was on the corner. The twins were on the floor in the living room feebly attempting to roll over, not yet mastering the art of crawling. They were relatively quiet now, but that would not continue unless she fed them

41

soon. Usually, she was able to get her shower in while Michael was still home, but that was obviously out of the window now. Today, she would have to adapt.

At least she did not have to face the day without coffee. That, other than the fact that she loved Jerod dearly just because he was her son, had been today's real reason behind her hug: he had made coffee. He had also offered to watch his brother and sister for his mother so that she could take her shower, but Barbara knew how much he loved to play video games with his best friend, Steven Harris, so she simply sent him on his way. *But I'll sure enjoy that coffee!*

Bless that angel!

She bent over the nearest baby and scooped her up. "Come on, sweetheart," she said soothingly. "Let's go get some 'ummies."

It was their pet word for "yummies"; itself another pet word for food. It saw its first use ten years before with Jerod, along with a dozen or so other silly words. It had seen its reemergence this past summer when Michael and Barbara brought home twins.

10:40 a.m.

Barbara glanced up from her Bible to the forty-two inch widescreen Sony Grand Wega across the living room. She had been attempting to do her daily devotional, but found herself hopelessly unable to. It was the third local news brief this morning, and second this hour, and although the reporter did not seem to have anything fresh to report, the young anchorwoman just kept "going back out to him". The picture on the screen was a shot of their little town, a town that she had known since she was eight years old, yet she could hardly recognize it. Were it not for the large blue lettering at the bottom of the television screen which read: *Breaking news...Kingsburg, California*, she might

42

have surfed on by on her way toward something interesting on the Food Network or HGTV.

And on top of that, she just could not shake the feeling that she was forgetting to do something, or perhaps neglecting some item of importance that deserved some thought.

When the telephone rang, it startled her as if she were about to discover that she had been left a widow by the man she had sent off to fight in a foreign land. She knew her Michael was not one of the dead because she had caught a glimpse of him earlier this morning at the scene during the first bulletin; however, that revelation did little to curb the great feeling of dread that she'd begun to feel since hearing the news.

It had never crossed her mind that it might be the school. She quickly got up from her chair at the dining room table and grabbed the handheld off of its charger.

"Hello."

"Yes, Mrs. Lopez?" the voice on the other end of the line asked.

Barbara thought the person sounded familiar, but could not place the older lady's nasally-sounding voice.

"Yes, it is."

"This is Dorothy Elms from Reagan Elementary School."

"Oh. Hello, Mrs. Elms. What can I do for you?" She went back to her chair. Momentarily forgetting about the rehashed news coverage, she stared at the nearest wall and subconsciously pictured the woman on the other end of the line.

Had Barbara been the mother of one of her son's friends instead of *his* mother, she probably would have immediately jumped off the handle at the notion of being called by the school; however, Jerod was a great kid and model student, so she took it calmly.

"Well, you see it's kind of a funny thing...I mean, it's certainly not amusing. Heavens, no! It's horrible! Simply horrible! Especially with the poor dear thinking it was..."

"Mrs. Elms, you've lost me," Barbara interrupted. "What's this all about? Has something happened to Jerod?"

"Forgive me, Mrs. Lopez." Mrs. Elms took a deep breath and started again. "It seems that poor Jerod caught word of what happened to those police officers this morning and he, well, the poor dear thought his father might be one of them."

"Oh, God!" Barbara sighed, putting her hand to her head. "I never even considered Jerod finding out about what happened! Dear, Lord!" Her eyes dropped onto the New American Standard before her on the table. The words were a blur.

"Now, Mrs. Lopez, I assure you we've tried everything we could think of short of calling you to make him believe that his father was not among the dead; however, we are having one whale of a time. I saw him myself during the live news coverage this morning, but Jerod still will not believe it. That is why I have called you. Principal Davis and Nurse Biekert hoped that you would be able to dispel any horrible thoughts that he might have to the contrary."

"Yes, thank you. May I speak to him?"

"Indeed you may, Mrs. Lopez." the woman answered. "He's coming right now."

"Thank you."

"Oh, and Mrs. Lopez."

"Yes?"

"Jerod *is* a fine young boy."

"Oh, thank you..."

"This news has just been so terrible for him," the old woman added. "Poor dear probably never even considered that his father's job could be dangerous. Tragic. Tragic."

Barbara did not reply to the woman's final words as the telephone was handed over to her son. Inside, the principal's words continued to reverberate. *Perhaps none of us thought that.*

Her thoughts went out now to the girlfriends or wives of the two slain officers, and also to their families. They did not have the luxury to think of the what might be's or the could be's; they were living the real life nightmare of, *Good morning, but someone very close to your heart is dead today. Sorry!*

Jerod was speaking into her right ear now but she did not yet decipher his words. A finger dallied between her lips while she put herself in her son's place, imagining him staring up into her eyes and asking the painful question: *Where's Daddy?* After all, weren't police officers just the cute keystone cops in children's books that helped little boys and girls find their way home? Weren't they?

They were when I was a girl, Jerod. Not anymore.

"Mom?" Jerod said sharply, pulling her out of her daydream. His voice sounded so small today.

"Hi, sweetie," she said quickly, attempting to sound strong for him. She wasn't doing a very good job and she knew it. How would she have sounded if it really had been Michael? How would she have been strong for her son? Or for any of them, for that matter?

"Dad's dead, huh, Mom? I knew it. They won't tell me..."

"No, sweetheart."

Barbara tried to catch the water and push it all back inside the hole in the dam before the whole thing gave and flooded the entire village. She had done a lousy job, both in trying to reassure Jerod that everything was alright, and also in the fact that she never had that little talk with her son like she had always meant to. Maybe all of them should have discussed this.

"Two officers who worked last night while all of us were asleep were..." She paused. She hadn't prepared what she might say.

"They were what, mom? Murdered?" Jerod answered for his mother.

Jerod sounded so young still, and yet his words were so mature all of a sudden.

"Yes, Jerod. I'm afraid so. But neither one of the men was your dad, honey. I promise."

"Are you sure, Mom?"

Inside, perhaps Jerod believed all along. Maybe he just needed to hear the person he most trusted in the whole wide world tell him that everything was alright with his Mom, Dad and the universe.

"I'm sure, sweetie," she told him. "I'm sure."

"Okay, Mom."

"Hey, Sweetie?" Barbara said. "Do Mom a favor and put Mrs. Elms back on the phone."

"Okay, Mom."

"Yes, Mrs. Lopez."

"Mrs. Elms, I think Jerod's probably had a little too much excitement for one day, so I'm going to come and pick him up."

"That sounds fine, Mrs. Lopez. It is so lovely to see him smiling again."

"Thank you for calling, Mrs. Elms."

12:40 p.m.

"Ready, Mike?" the coroner asked as he came walking briskly down the tiled corridor of the Fresno County Coroner's Office.

There was little sound of his footsteps striking the white flooring thanks to the cloth boots covering his shoes. The city of Kingsburg and her needs had drastically reduced his forty-five minute lunch to eleven minutes. He made no effort either to complain about it or to draw attention to his sacrifice as he swallowed the last bite of what appeared to Michael to be a hot pastrami sandwich.

"As ready as I'll ever be," he answered with a slight grimace as he watched in disbelief while the man only partially chewed his meal and forced it down in large gulps like a shark that feared larger sharks in the vicinity might take it from him.

It had been many years since Michael's last autopsy. Though he had been preparing himself during the last half hour for the sights and sounds *and smells* that he would be exposed to, he could in no way even think about food. Maybe not even for the rest of the day.

The doctor stopped as he prepared to lead him down the remaining corridor to the autopsy lab. Michael stiffened.

"Sorry," he said, quickly wiping his hands on his lab coat.

Without another word, the coroner motioned him along.

Michael swallowed hard as he followed the coroner into the lab. He had hoped that he could be strong during the autopsy; however, after the incident with the sandwich, he had begun to doubt it. As the lab door closed behind him, his nostrils were immediately flooded with the *blessed* scent of hospital antiseptic. His stomach cramped ever so slightly, just enough for him to notice.

Not now! Michael addressed his stomach under his breath. *We haven't seen anything yet!*

He closed his eyes and swallowed again.

Michael stood before the bodies of two men that he had numbered as his friends. Both were covered in drab green sheets. He knew good and well that there was a jagged gap between the sheet covering Mancuso and his neck, but from where he stood he could not see the damage, thankfully.

To his relief, years of training began to kick in, providing his mind with other details to evaluate and reflect upon that were difficult to accept no matter how many times he went over them. It was back to another point that he and Jackson had discussed earlier in the day: they could not fathom how two outstanding veteran

Peace Officers could have been butchered, seemingly without a fight.

Neither man attempted to radio in during their attack, Michael reminded himself, *so whatever happened, happened fast. The dispatcher last heard from Mancuso at 4:18 am. Neither man got off a round. Browning's weapon had been found in the crime scene near his body but scuffs on the gun indicated that it'd been taken from him and thrown clear. They had to have been taken by surprise*, Lopez thought, *because Browning was the quickest shot in the department.*

Michael knew Larry Browning well. During March qualifying, he had been the fourth best shot, but first in the secret quickest draw contest which had been held the night before.

What could possibly have happened?

"Ok, Detective," Doctor Bettencourt announced as he reentered the lab, pulling Michael from his thoughts.

Then, as if alone, he walked over to the nearest table, the one containing Mancuso's body and head, and thoughtlessly yanked off the sheet.

The coroner stepped on a small button next to his right foot, turning on the florescent light above the table as well as a microphone which hung near where he was standing. At his right, an aluminum tray was adorned with a collection of sparkling clean scalpels of various sizes as well as an assortment of other miscellaneous surgical tools. Michael reopened his eyes just in time to see the coroner reorganize his cutting tools.

"Doctor Russell Bettencourt, May 5, 2008," the man began. "The subject is Nicholas John Mancuso, police officer. Caucasian male. Let's see…" He glanced over at his clipboard which hung on the edge of the table on a tiny hook. "Two hundred and eight pounds, five ounces. Five feet tall from protruding spine to toe…"

Detective Lopez' eyes blinked steadily during the initial moments of the autopsy, his way of trying to cope with his squeamishness. The first incision had yet to be

48

made, but he was already sick. The question was not whether or not he would be able to make it until the end, but rather, *how much longer* he would be able to hang on.

"...neck torn open. Carotid and jugular severed. Crushed vocal cords and trachea." The Coroner felt down to the right shoulder. "Dislocated right shoulder..."

It was not the sight of the body that did Michael in. Rather, it was who the body had been just hours before. It was not as if this were the first time that he'd seen the ugliest of human remains. He had worked many a car accident in his career, two suicides, one death by misadventure and one murder. The idea that this particular bit of human mutilation still wore the same shield as he, and the fact that both it and its owner now lay before him, well-lit and directly under his nose, aided to compound the problem.

"Compound fracture of the right radius. Broken right wrist. Fingers missing on right hand; distal phalanges crushed on both fore and middle fingers, middle finger also crushed middle and probably proximal phalanges..."

As Michael's eyes roved across the horror, forced to further download into memory inch by terrible inch, he became increasingly submerged, almost hypnotized by it.

"Detective Lopez?"

The coroner reached across the body on the table before him and waved his right hand across his field of vision. "Detective Lopez?"

With a start, Michael swore, using what his wife had claimed just this morning was his favorite word. It seemed so long ago already. He shook it off with a sign while the coroner waited.

"Jesus, Doc," Michael warned in a voice just above that of a whisper. "Don't do that."

"Sorry, Lopez, but I thought you were going comatose on me there. Are you alright?"

"Yeah," he answered, wiping his brow absently.

"I'm going to begin cutting now, Detective. Are you sure you want to stay?"

Michael glanced down at the man he had known while more images downloaded. Images that he had yet to see, but already could vividly picture. He had seen enough.

"To tell you the truth, Doc," he began as he looked back at the coroner. "I don't think so. Just let me know what you come up with."

"Get in line," he said with a wink. "I've already taken calls from your new mayor, my mayor, and missed the call from your chief while on the phone with my boss." He stopped with a pregnant pause. "Not a problem." Clearly, he felt the political heat. "As you can well imagine, I plan to take my time with this subject. It shouldn't take too long, however." He glanced down at the body and then looked back at Michael with a look of anguish. "Much of my work's already been done for me."

2:35 p.m.

After being spotted immediately thanks to Pelco Security cameras and buzzed in by the dayshift dispatcher, the chief of police yanked open the front door of the relatively new police station and acknowledged no one as he hurriedly went about his business. He had been chief now for sixteen years, well longer than the rookie new mayor, bless her pointed little head. The day's events, however, had him feeling as if this were not the case. He had had opportunities to move on to bigger cities earlier in his career, and now, more than ever, he was glad that he had never done so.

Typically, the biggest problem he had ever faced was unrest during the week when the Kingsburg Vikings met up with their arch-rival Selma Bears on the football

50

field in the fall. There had been a string of churches vandalized during the previous year which proved frustrating for a time until the day that fateful tip had been called in. Yet, certainly nothing like what they had woken up to today.

As he headed for his office it wasn't to make some phone calls, or to address some piled up paperwork. Instead, it was to grab a moment's peace while he did his level best to make sure that his tiny police department didn't find itself overwhelmed. He loosened his tie and removed it completely as he walked, unbuttoning the first button on his light blue Van Heusen dress shirt. He was still wearing the sport coat, but not for much longer. Dispatcher Susan Reynolds had followed him and seemed to be saying something, but he quickly waved it off. He sighed as the door engaged the frame.

"Tired?" the voice of the person seated behind his desk asked, interrupting his peace.

His desk sat on the right side of the office, facing east. He knew the voice. He had already spoken with the woman once today. Something told him that the two of them were about to become very close for the foreseeable future, whether he liked it or not.

"Your Honor," he said simply, slowly turning around as if he had expected her all along.

"You can drop that, 'your honor' crap right now, O'Donnell! Don't you ever send me away again from a crime scene! I'm the mayor of this town. I don't care who you voted for."

"I get the sense you're angry," the chief began. "Am I way off base with this?"

Without looking her direction, he headed toward the row of chairs placed in front of the desk. It was typically where his guests would be seated, but he was too tired to argue why he had to take one of these instead of the more comfortable leather chair behind his desk. To his left, the south wall was adorned with a set of what most who visited the chief referred to as antique swords. They were US 1860 Calvary Sabers, actually, with fullered blades and leather spiraled grips. They had been in the family for four generations. The accompanying steel scabbards were mounted there, as well. The chief did not glance their way, but knew that they were there should he need them.

The mayor remained seated behind the chief's desk, her hands folded atop duty rosters for the upcoming week. However, those schedules were all blown up now.

"Do you know what this would do to the Owedish Festival?" she said after a measured pause. Even she recognized what it would sound like.

"Yes, Katherine," he answered, before sitting down. He turned and faced her finally. "Of course I know what time of year this is. Do you think I'm an idiot? I have been doing this awhile, you know." The mayor raised one hand in hope of interrupting him before he got any further, but he continued, oblivious to it. "I've been working the festival since I was a cadet. I was coming to the damn thing well before that. Hell! I used to carry a baritone in it with the frigging marching band!"

"I get it!" The mayor stood now, her voice climbing as well. "But damnit, this is huge. We need to solve this thing and catch the bastards responsible before…"

"We? Is it *we* now, Katherine?" Chief O'Donnell demanded to know, incredulously approaching his occupied desk. His voice was rising now, too.

She slammed her hands on the desk, knocking everything there in disarray.

"No," she snapped. "But my phone has been ringing off the hook all morning. I haven't been able to think since yesterday. I've got councilmen attached to my hip, business owners banging on my door because you've got half the city behind caution tape, and vendors calling from as far away as Denver wondering whether or not we might be thinking of canceling. This is the frigging centennial year!"

"Yes, I know that, Your Honor," he matched her tone for tone. "And I'm sorry. My day hasn't been exactly tickles and giggles, either. I've got a police department that has rarely heard of a murder case, let alone worked one. Some of these guys haven't seen a corpse since the Academy. I've got two detectives and no CSI's to work it. I've got to rely on a host of others and hope to God that all of the different jurisdictions don't 'F' it up!"

The chief glanced behind him in the direction of the door. It was a solid door with a simple name plate, carrying his name and official title. He could visualize some of his braver employees hovering there, attempting to listen in on the conversation. It would not have been difficult up until now. He turned back to the woman behind his desk and lowered his voice.

"And to top it all off, I've got you breathing down my back, making it that much harder to do exactly what you're asking me to do, which is to identify and locate the outstanding suspects."

The mayor started to react, but he put out his hand.

"Please, Your Honor," he asked her. "Let me do my job. This department may be a bit green when it comes to murder cases, but we'll get it done. The first thing you're going to see is a much larger police presence, which, thanks to the festival, you were going to have anyway. It'll just start a bit sooner.

The mayor stared at the chief for a moment, then took her hands from his desk and stood. A flash of guilt passed through her eyes as she stared at the mess she'd made—discernible enough for him to notice it— but it was quickly gone. He waved it off. Things unsaid hovered between them; however, in the end, she simply walked slowly around his desk and headed toward the door.

53

For his part, Chief O'Donnell wondered whether he might have said too much. Was it necessary to confess how difficult the situation was, or to paint it as so precarious? He moved behind his desk and began to reorganize. He fixed everything where he thought it might have been prior to her disturbing it, but even he wondered how important it was in light of the day's events. He grabbed a few folders that might have been moved, but dropped them back down again.

The mayor grabbed the doorknob and pulled open the door, but stopped and looked back. The chief glanced up to meet her gaze.

"Alright," she said simply and took her leave.

4:12 p.m.

The phone on the desk rang. Michael grabbed it quickly.

"Kingsburg P.D., this is Detective Lopez."

"Mike," a familiar voice spoke. "It's Russell Bettencourt."

"Hey, Doc," Michael replied. Jackson was at his desk across from him. He looked up immediately. This had to be the autopsy results that they were expecting. "What have you got?"

"Well, I just completed both posts. I faxed a preliminary report to you because I know how important this is. I'm still awaiting some toxicology results, but no one expects anything to come of them. Mancuso was sick with Influenza, about five days worth I think. Other than some over the counter, that should be all we find there."

There was a strange pause.

Michael waited a moment, not sure of what was happening. He glanced up from his notes that he had been taking. A fax was probably awaiting him down the hall, but it was an old habit to jot everything down. He

54

glanced at his partner who opened his hands as if to receive something from him.

"Well?" Jackson asked. Michael shook his head and frowned.

"Doc, are you still there?"

"Yes, Mike." But that was all that was said.

"Is something wrong that you're not telling me? As you can expect, I don't have a lot of time for games here." His voice was not loud, but firm.

"I appreciate that, Detective," Doctor Bettencourt said, his voice growing impatient as well. Perhaps it was fatigue or stress. Michael didn't know, and did not have time to guess. "Look," the doctor continued, finally. "I called you because something's bothering me, and I don't really want to write it down. I've got a reputation to think about and I don't need anything—"

"Doc," Michael interrupted. "I don't know what you're talking about. Will you just spill it already?"

"There was not a drop of blood left in the bodies," the doctor said at last.

Michael recalled the crime scene and the pool of blood collected in the soil of the planter where the head adorned spike had been affixed. There had been very little blood loss from Officer Browning; just obvious broken bones and contusions. With that in mind, total blood loss concerning Browning did not seem plausible.

"Doc, I don't remember any great blood loss with Browning."

"There wasn't."

"So how could that be?" Michael asked.

"I saw the pictures," Doctor Bettencourt continued, not hearing the detective. "We've got over one hundred, and not one of them shows any substantial blood at all. Yet, I'm telling you, there's no blood left in this guy."

"Great!" Michael said. "The guy I need to fill in the blanks is going blank on me."

"Listen," Doctor Bettencourt tried to continue.

"Next you're going to tell me that you found tiny bite marks on their necks!" Michael said aloud what he was thinking out of frustration. His partner stared at him transfixed.

On the other end of the line: silence.

"Doc?" Michael sighed, lowering his voice.

"Yes?"

"You haven't answered me."

"I know that."

"Is that what you don't want to put on the report? Bite marks? They had vampire bite marks on their necks?"

"Mancuso didn't."

8:36 p.m.

The car glided methodically like a child sleepwalking onto Roosevelt Street. Michael pulled up alongside a curb. He sighed as he looked up to the house and turned off the car's headlamps. The outside light above the front door and the driveway flood lights were on, highlighting the yard. Ever since his appointment to the rank of detective, coming home to outside lights was bad news. It meant that he had put in well over twelve hours. Those types of days had been extremely rare, but not completely unheard of. Today, he could feel it. He almost wished Barbara hadn't turned the lights on for him because it just made him feel that much worse.

The detective eyed his dark surroundings through blurry tired lenses as he walked around the unmarked police car to the sidewalk, then up the cement path which led up to the house. He yawned three times between the Crown Victoria and his castle. Rubbing his eyes with his right hand, fingers in one eye and thumb in the other, he futilely attempted to bring life back into them for the five minutes he felt he could reasonably give his family before his systems shut down for the night. It was 69 degrees already, but he did not notice.

Michael yawned one more time upon stepping up to the front door. Only by sheer force of habit was he able to get the key to go into the doorknob and open the door.

"Hi, honey!" Barbara smiled warmly and genuinely as she rounded the corner of the hallway to greet her husband. Her smile faded. "Boy, you look awful!"

"Thanks, I love you, too!" he moaned.

She laughed and then embraced him. "I *do* love you. Come on in here and take a load off."

Michael followed his wife into the dining room and then into the living room where he headed immediately for his recliner. He groaned happily, eyes closed as he allowed himself to be swallowed up in the chair's comfort.

"I've been waiting all day long for this!"

"I bet you have, sweetie." she said softly, sitting down in front of him on the arm of the couch which was just four feet from his recliner.

"How are Robbie and Rebekah doing?" he asked just before a wide yawn swept over him.

"Well, Robbie's been trying to sleep all day," she began. "You know how he is." Michael grinned. "But Rebekah kept waking him up. He wasn't a happy little camper at all."

"How 'bout Jer..?" He started to ask, but something caught his attention behind Barbara. Jerod was asleep on the couch. Barbara followed Michael's gaze, turned and gave her sleeping son a look over. "Looks like it's past both our bedtimes, huh?" he smiled.

"He was trying so hard to stay awake so he could see you." Barbara turned back to Michael, "He didn't have a very good day today."

"He didn't?"

"This morning at school, he found out what happened. He thought that one of the dead officers might be you."

"Oh, shit!" Michael sighed.

"Yeah," she agreed with the assessment. "The school had to finally call me because they couldn't get him to believe them that you were fine. I talked to him over the phone and assured him that what had happened occurred before you had even left the house this morning. After that, I just decided to pick him up and bring him home."

"Good," Michael rose from his recliner and quietly walked over to his son.

"We had a pretty good day together."

"Next time, come pick me up, too," he whispered.

Barbara smiled. "Are you going to take him to bed?"

"Yeah, then I'm going to bed, too."

"You don't want any dinner?" she asked.

"No, I haven't been able to eat since this afternoon."

Michael put his arms underneath his son and picked up both him and the blanket he was wrapped in and carried them down the hall to his son's bedroom. Barbara turned the light on ahead of them so all he had to do was get him into his bed. Once inside, Jerod began to stir.

"Hi, Dad."

"Hi, Son," Michael smiled. "How'ya doin'?"

"A little tried." he muttered.

"Just a little?" Michael grinned as he tucked his son into his Dale Earnhardt Jr. sheets and bedspread. They were new. When Junior got his new number, Jerod got new bedding.

Jerod smiled.

"Jerod, did mom talk to you about what happened today?" he asked, sitting down across the 88's which denoted Earnhardt's car.

"Uh-huh."

58

"So you know that sometimes my job can get kinda' hairy, right?"

"Mmm-hmm."

"Okay, good," his father continued. "Now, what happened today was a terrible thing, but not something that happens all the time. Dad's been a police officer for a long time and nothing like this has ever come close to happening to me. If you're careful and smart, if you always follow the rules and let everybody know where you are and what you're doing at every moment, then nothing should ever happen to you. You see, what happened today was a case where...."

"Michael?" Barbara was trying to get his attention now.

"Huh?" He turned around.

Barbara was wearing her black nightgown, the one that always seemed to do wonders for him. Of all the gifts he had given her over the years, this was the one that *he* had gotten the most mileage out of. It was doing things to him even now, even though he was too exhausted to act on them. He looked her over *(he couldn't help it)* once more before he realized what it was that she was doing. From the doorway, she pointed silently over his shoulder toward Jerod. He turned his head and glanced down at their son. He was fast asleep.

Michael sighed and dropped his head. *Smart kid.* "He's got the right idea," Michael said, rising as quietly as possible from the bed. He joined his beautiful wife at the doorway. Together they stole one last look at their son and then turned out the light.

"We've got a wonderful family, Michael." Barbara whispered as they walked hand in hand into their bedroom.

"I know, sweetheart," he whispered back, putting his arm around her waist and pulling her close. "I know."

TUESDAY

May 6, 2008
4:36 a.m.

The old man's shadow seemed to outrun him momentarily as he moved from directly beneath the bright streetlight to the darkness just beyond it. His pace was near-perfect: his breathing rate was as steady as it would have been under hypnosis; his heart beat a strong, rhythmic cadence, unstressed by the pounding of the jog; his muscles and joints, relaxed.

He was relaxed. Why wouldn't he be? This was his neighborhood, and he had run this exact route a thousand times, perhaps to the very step. Had the route not been asphalt there might have been a visible path worn into the ground. The William H. Benton Memorial Trail, they would have called it. Large pretty signs would have been posted every mile, denoting the precise route. So, of course, he jogged through the silent streets, confident and proud as if the trail was marked right that minute, and he was still alive to enjoy its celebrity.

William H. Benton picked up his pace as he neared the end of his run. All that remained was to run the third side available of Rafer Johnson Junior High School, named for the famed Olympian and former resident. After that a quick left turn on Wilson Way and he'd be home.

A sweep of cold breeze whipped past his ears suddenly as he turned from Stroud Avenue onto 14th Street. He reached up with his right hand and gently pushed the longer than usual blend of black, but mostly gray, hair from his face. As soon as he lowered his hand though, the breeze pushed the hair right back.

I've really got to get this trimmed, he thought as he attempted in vain to push it back in place.

As he continued on the trail, the cold, whipping air grew stronger. Absently, he pulled the zipper on his navy blue jogging top all the way up. He was reminded of the vacation that he and Geraldine had taken in Alaska eight years earlier. Everything had been beautiful until the flight attendant had opened the Alaskan Airliner's doors and it was time for them to disembark the plane, and that was only the tunnel between the plane and the actual airport. They hadn't even stepped out into the naked air yet.

To him and Geraldine, two people who seemed to appreciate the desert more than the mountains, Alaska was brutally cold. Just like this.

Suddenly, the cold morning air was a barrier. It was as if someone had just opened a mystical portal into the North Pole, allowing the great arctic winds there to flow freely here. His smooth jogger's pace crumbled away immediately. His legs pumped laboriously, trying to maintain their original pace as Mother Nature beat against them. He huffed and puffed with each step; his exhales were suddenly a white fog, shielding his eyes from the track.

Then something seemed to whip by his left ear.

At first, he thought it was simply another blast of cold air, but it was soon followed by another going in a completely different direction, and then another. Each time, he thought he could almost hear some kind of squeaking. Or was it giggling?

He quickly glanced over his shoulders as his body grew more exhausted with the struggle, but there was nothing there. What was more, when he looked back, the giggling was suddenly in front of him. Now behind him again, but still he could see no one there.

Each step got worse than the previous one; his New Balance running shoes were suddenly full of lead. His body wanted, *needed* to stop but he could not. The sound was almost inside his ears now, pushing him well into panic. His heart was a million miles away from the steady, contented pulse of before. It was no longer a jog, but a dead run.

It was then that whatever was playing with him was no longer content to do so and attacked.

Benton struck the asphalt hard. His body rolled several feet before coming to an excruciating halt in the gutter. It was there that all sound stopped. Conscious of this, he rolled onto his back and listened, waiting. He knew that he was not alone. Moreover, he knew that there was nothing that he could do about it.

"Please," he spoke at last. "Don't hurt me."

From high above, there came a giggle. This was unmistakable.

"Who are you?"

"Would you believe, a friend?" the voice teased.

Benton most certainly *did not* believe the confident, unfriendly voice which seemed to hover over him, daring him to rise to his feet. But he was a successful man who had built his career and reputation on facing and meeting every challenge, so he did his best not to falter before the voice.

"Please," the voice spoke again. "Rise!"

Benton looked up, surprised at the sound of the command. Having caught his breath, his exhales finally began to thin enough to allow him to see the man behind the confident voice above him. Just before he was able to get a good look, however, the man spoke again.

"Did you not hear?" the voice asked, incredulous.

Although the voice had never been very soothing, there was now a definite tremor of turbulence to it. Benton noticed the difference with a faint chill up the length of his spine.

"Look," he began, rising slowly to his feet. "I don't want any trouble. I'm just on my way home."

"You were."

"Yes, I am," he calmly answered.

"No," the voice repeated, dryly, as if growing bored with the interaction. *"You were."*

Benton took a step backwards at the words. He moved to turn, the world spinning momentarily as he did so.

Two steps.

Four steps.

Eight steps.

He glanced over his right shoulder. There was nothing or no one there.

He yanked his head back around, slamming into someone very large. He braced himself for the impact with asphalt or cement, but it did not come. The earth spun again, but he did not fall. Someone had him by the arms and spun him around further. He made a face to protest, looking deeply into the man's eyes for the first time as his fingers bit into the sleeves of his sweat top and then deeper still into the flesh beneath, pulling him closer to give him a better look. They were black eyes.

"Let me go!" Benton shouted.

His attacker leaned into his face and sneered, opening his black eyes wide. Benton felt his face drain of color.

"Have you anything else to say before I make you my dinner?" he asked clearly, daring him to action.

Benton said nothing. He couldn't. He managed to part his lips as if to speak, but found himself completely immersed within the colorless regions of his attacker's hypnotic eyes, unable to do anything but let loose a long string of foamy spittle. It dribbled down his chin and onto the top of his sweats as if he were a child.

"I am *so* delighted," the vampire grinned. He released the man, but rested his cold, long-dead fingers upon his warm, flushed face. "I do hate these games!" And then he pushed his hands together.

Benton's skull gave in, killing him instantly.

There was a moment of exquisite silence for the vampire before the blood came, like some madman's twisted orgasm. When it came, it was beautiful. The hot, red blood exploded free from every orifice, whether natural or new, including the sockets where there was nothing left of the old man's eyes. The vampire allowed the blood to splash over him and the street only for an instant. Then he snapped back the man's head like a squashed piece of fruit and quickly drained what was left by placing his mouth upon the great wound in his neck and drinking.

5:09 a.m.

The scent of blood was strong in his nose tonight, he realized as he maneuvered through the shadows along the intersection of 14th and Ventura Street. As always, in every neighborhood that he visited, he left both house and occupants undisturbed, leaving no visible trace of his presence there. All Nathaniel needed was his meal.

Nathaniel watched the cat further. This morning, though extremely desperate, he had followed this particular cat for half a mile. The animal appeared well-fed and comfortable, yet did not seem to pay allegiance to any particular house or specific neighborhood.

We are a lot alike, you and I, Nathaniel thought as the cat continued on its way, cutting across a well-manicured lawn and heading north. Two blocks away was Rafer Johnson Junior High School.

Growing more impatient with each subsequent step, Nathaniel filed the thought away for further consideration and started after his prey. So close that the vampire suddenly tasted salty blood, he hesitated. *What's this?*

Like the animal, the vampire thought that it was his hunger which seemed to flood his senses with the scent of blood, long before he had even taken a hold of his meal. However, Nathaniel realized that this was not the case.

The vampire suddenly stood upright. Unaware of the invisible menace above him, the cat jumped a foot into the air with the sudden movement as the presence was made known to it. It went scurrying across three yards, trying desperately to catch up with its legs, and didn't stop until it had disappeared in shadow somewhere across the street. Nathaniel ignored it. His senses were already too deeply immersed in what he could not yet see. He began to walk in the same direction the cat had fled, but now it wasn't the cat that he was after.

Tonight, Nathaniel had been planning on shedding a little blood. Somewhere near, however, a lot of blood had already been shed.

It only took Nathaniel a moment to locate the source of the disturbance to his senses. After he had, he wished he hadn't.

The body was lying in a heap beyond a chain-link fence twenty feet into what Americans would have referred to as a soccer field. Nathaniel leapt onto the fence and vaulted over it in short order, but approached the remains with a great sense of foreboding. He did not realize it then.

Nathaniel moved carefully, making certain that he was alone, that the monster responsible for the atrocity before him was indeed long gone. An upraised nose tasted the light breeze to check for predators, but could detect only the victim's blood. The vampire started to kneel down before the remains, but stopped in mid-descent, startled, and bolted back upright.

The vampire was not horrified with the violence below him. He had seen much of what a beast or man could do to a fellow human being. He had seen carnage, brutality, rape and war. For as strong as man could be, he knew full well what little effort was actually required to render man undone. There had been nothing new done to this poor fellow that could have shocked him: the strength and extreme prejudice necessary to obliterate the old man's skull. Clipped to the body was the front page of the latest edition of the Kingsburg Recorder. On it was a note that had been left for him.

In blood.

Hello Nathaniel.

Nathaniel knew the signature because he had seen it before, although certainly not recently. He had hoped that he had seen it for the last time, yet here it was in bloody splendor. He recognized the strokes made not with a finger but a very large fingernail; more similar to a claw, actually. And it was in that moment that he realized why he had found himself plagued of late by flashbacks of a time long thought forgotten.

He turned, surveying the area of the town about him. He felt alone presently, but generally speaking not nearly as alone as he would have originally hoped. He checked the breeze, but it was still too difficult to taste anything with all the blood in the air tonight.

As it wafted around, his mind began to wander off without him again.

Cimpulung, Romania
July 13, 1737.

It happened again.

The boy jerked his head around. Once again he had heard the sounds of the wild. His mother had let out another awful shriek from her bedroom next door.

"...father forgive me, have mercy on my soul who giveth life, who art in heaven hallowed be thy name...," the boy heard his mother uttering somewhere within the darkness of the room as he ran inside. He couldn't see her, nor could he understand her. He could hear her voice, but recognized nothing of her panicked ramblings.

The young boy listened *beyond* his mother; however, there was nothing else to hear. And suddenly, he felt cold. He looked up from the dirt floor, trying to see if he could find his mother.

The boy shuffled his feet forward.

From somewhere below, his mother let out a whimper as he stepped accidentally upon her hand. Yet, she didn't pull it away, nor did she falter in her incessant muttering. She hadn't even felt it.

Secure that she was safe, although quite out of her mind by the sound of it, the boy continued forward through the dark for the window. Having found his mother, he now wondered where his father was, although he didn't stop to look for him. He was sure that he was near. He seemed to feel him.

"B-b-boy!"

The boy stopped immediately at the sound of his father's voice. His first impulse was to breathe a sigh of relief; however, now that he had, he was even more afraid. Something was wrong. His father's strong, proud voice was gone. What he now heard was weak and broken and almost...defeated.

"Father?" he cried. He knew better than to sound afraid; Father didn't like to see weakness. He wouldn't allow it, in fact. A slap always accompanied weakness. Yet, his vocal cords failed him and the plea came out pitifully, much like a small child's; much like his own would.

"Stay back!" his father cried out, ignoring his own credo of strength. In fact, he had very little strength at all. He could barely speak. It was almost beyond him now.

"Father!" the boy screamed, stepping forward, sensing what he could not see.

Two large red eyes were there to greet him; red with bloodlust.

The wild dogs! The boy immediately made a move to flee. The original panic had returned as well, however, the fear holding him unable to move.

"You would do well to obey your father, lad!" the eyes spoke to him suddenly.

The boy fell backwards as if a strong wind had just flown into the bedroom, assaulting him through the open windows. He tripped over his mother's outstretched leg and hit his head and shoulders hard on the dirt floor. She didn't feel that either. She wasn't dead. Not yet. She was still muttering prayers to herself, but madness had almost completely wrapped itself around her. A moment or two later and she would be.

The vampire came out from behind the drapes of darkness and stood over the boy. The boy witnessed the attack as shadow suddenly hovered over him, blocking out the open window before him. Fear grabbed his heart in a good tight grip and slowly began yanking it out of his throat an inch at a time. He was hyperventilating, a sensation much misunderstood then. Hands of cold steel suddenly had his wrists. Drops of crimson warmth began raining upon his face and neck as the shadow engulfed him.

The boy had no idea then that it had been all that was left of his father's life.

5:47 a.m.

Michael sighed in the shower as he reached down and turned the hot water off. It was cold without the water. Although Barbara kept the house fairly warm because of the twins, he could still tell that it was only mid-May. Yet, he was more tired than anything else. He yawned and lifted his wet arms and hands high above his head for a good, long stretch. Reaching for his towel, the thought crossed his mind to call in sick and go back to bed. The rule of thumb, however, was to save valuable sick time for days when it was worth it like Monday nights when the Cowboys were playing, or for during the summer when the Cubs were in the state, but never for a day when he *was actually* sick. That would be inexcusable, a perversion of what the founding fathers intended when they first devised of the notion of sick time. Besides, there was the minor matter of finding out what the hell had happened to two of Kingsburg's finest officers.

When Michael opened the shower door and stepped onto the bathroom carpet, his nostrils were met with the fine scent of fresh brewed coffee. It worked to awaken his senses just like soap commercials claimed their products would do. *Fresh coffee.* He could taste it already.

Perhaps today won't be so bad after all.

Michael's heart sank with the first ring of the telephone.

Damn!

His shoulders drooped at the thought of coffee he would never taste. He waited silently, listening for the faintest hint of bad news. Seconds passed and nothing. Another second and still nothing. Slowly and deliberately, still listening, Michael finished drying off.

There was a light knock on the bathroom door, followed by the door opening behind him.

"Sweetheart, it's Mark."

Barbara held out the wireless phone for him to take. She did not avert her eyes at the sight of his naked form, nor did her husband attempt to hide behind the towel. Sex was the furthest thing from either one of their minds.

Michael clumsily wrapped himself in the towel, though still dripping as he stood in the middle of the carpeted bathroom floor. He took the phone and answered as Barbara returned down the hall.

"Yeah, Jacks."

"Mikey, we got another one," Mark answered.

72

"Another what?" he asked, knowing full-well what his partner meant, but finding himself disbelieving.

"Homicide. This time a jogger."

"Where?" he asked, putting his left hand to his forehead and wiping away some moisture.

"Rafer Johnson. East side soccer field off of 14th."

"On my way."

Barbara returned as Michael ended the call and set the phone down on the white tile countertop.

"What is it?" she asked, bracing herself, although she could not have guessed.

"Another homicide," he said calmly, although inside he was anything but.

"Oh, my God!" she whispered. The notion stopped her approach. She stared blankly at his reflection in the mirror, as if she was not really seeing him before her. Finally, her attention returned to the coffee. It was still swirling from when she had stirred the contents of cream and sugar. The motion of the drink seemed to bring her back and so she quickly set it down beside him.

"Here, at least have a sip of this before you go."

6:11 a.m.

As Michael headed north on 14th Avenue, the view before him appeared just as the scene the day before had. There was no reason why it should have been different, just because it wasn't a cop this time; a homicide was still a homicide. To the detective, though, it was just that this was obviously a renaissance year for murder in Kingsburg in just two days, and he wasn't used to it. This made three dead in twenty four hours. He didn't realize then, but one more homicide and it would set a new one year record in just five months for the nearly one-hundred year old city.

He applied his brakes and brought his unmarked vehicle to a stop just behind a cluster of black and whites. As he pulled on the lever to open his car door, his stomach kicked in as if anticipating the worst.

Jesus, he thought, climbing out of the car, attempting to use will power alone to hold back the wave of nausea that was building deep inside of him. *Not again!*

"Mike!" a voice called out to him as he headed for the crime scene. "Over here."

It was Mark. He stood behind the fence, holding a large plastic Zip-Lock bag in gloved hands. Something was inside, but he could not yet see what it was. Mark waved him over. Michael walked quickly over to an access point which got him inside the field. The body lay in the field twenty feet behind the fence that encircled the school. It was covered by a blanket. Caution was staked around the area, and no one was admitted any closer than ten feet in any direction.

"We have the late Mr. William Benton," Jackson began as they walked to the crime scene. "Boys in blue found him almost an hour ago. He had his head caved in."

"What?" Michael asked, grimacing. Fresh waves crashed down upon the existing ones.

"We've got something else, too."

"What's that?" Not entirely sure that he wanted to know more.

"A note written in blood." Jackson handed his partner the bag. The paper was folded inside, revealing the bloody words.

"You're kidding," Michael said, stunned.

"'Hello Nathaniel'," Michael read aloud. More quietly this time he mouthed the words three times before looking back toward his partner. "Any ideas?" he asked him.

"Well," Jackson began, kneeling down and glancing at the note once again. "With the absence of

74

punctuation, I think either our killer is signing his latest work or he is saying hello to someone named Nathaniel. Hello-comma-Nathaniel, or hello from Nathaniel."

Michael glanced back at the note and then over the covered human remains there in the short grass. "What do we know about Mr. Benton here?" he asked.

"Ah, let's see," Jackson mumbled to himself, pulling out his notepad. "William Harry Benton, sixty-two years old. He lived around the corner on Wilson Way. I sent a black and white over there to see if anybody was home."

"Good." Michael sat down in a catcher's position before the blanket covered corpse, preparing himself, most-notably his stomach, to look upon the body.

"How bad is it?" he asked, reaching out and taking a hold of the blanket.

"We've seen worse."

Michael swore.

8:30 a.m.

"I want to thank everyone for getting down here as quickly as you did," the mayor said as she entered the private conference room and not the regular City Council chambers which were visible from the street. All four members of the council were seated and waiting upon her. "I know that it wasn't much notice."

The mayor was the least senior of the group. The two other members that had been elected with her during the last election half a year ago were all serving at least their third term in office. She found herself worrying about every simple detail because of this, especially now. She sat down and mulled around some papers while she ordered her thoughts.

"As you all know there has been yet another murder in our once-quiet town." No one made the least remark at this note. They all knew. "Can anyone tell me the last time there were two murders on consecutive days?"

A couple of the men glanced around, but that had been an easy question. There had never been consecutive murders in Kingsburg, before now. Some wondered what it was exactly they were doing there.

The mayor continued: "Can anyone tell me the last time there has been a murder in Kingsburg, period?" No one moved. "Can anyone tell me...?"

"Katherine," Councilman Roger Price interrupted. The mayor quickly faced him, but allowed him to speak. "Why are we here?"

"We're here because this is getting out of control."

"And you don't think the police can handle it?"

"I don't know whether I am worried about that so much as I just cannot sit around City Hall doing nothing." She glanced over the faces present there in the chambers, her hands palms open as if asking them whether they could either.

"What do you want us to do, Your Honor?" Councilman Johnson asked. He looked petrified. His store was open for business once again, but that full day that he had lost was going to hurt for a while.

It was just this point that the mayor used to pound her point home. "Let me ask you, Bill. Are you going to sit in that empty store all week, waiting for the police? I'm not saying KPD is over its head with this. I'm asking how long you are willing to wait. I've been getting phone calls already. Do you know how many times I have been asked whether we're canceling next week? Many. A great many. The vendors have been calling as well. They're getting nervous. I don't have to tell you how far some are driving to get here. If they don't think they can afford to break even, or worse, they're not coming. It's as simple as that."

Now the members of the council were looking at each other, nervously. They didn't like the faces that were looking back at them. When they looked back in the mayor's direction, she was ready for them. And they were ready to be led.

"That's what I thought," she said simply.

2:36 p.m.

Barbara grabbed the last few pieces of silverware from the counter and dropped them into the soapy-water side of the sink; the other side was filled with warm, clear water for rinsing. She used to hate doing the dishes. At least then she had been able to simply rinse them off and set them in the dishwasher, but not any longer. Barbara hadn't run the dishwasher this late in the afternoon since the day she brought fraternal twins into the house some nearly nine months before. Now, whenever she found herself standing over the kitchen sink with her hands submerged in dishwater, it meant that the twins were taking their late-afternoon nap and that Jerod wasn't home from school yet. It had become her quiet time, a moment to catch up on her thoughts, her dreams. Even though she still didn't care for doing the dishes, beggars couldn't be choosers; a mother had to learn to enjoy all the quiet time she could get. There wasn't much.

Barbara took a quick peek over her left shoulder while she reached into the soapy water for another item to wash. The digital clock in the middle of the gas stove read, 2:38 p.m. That meant that Jerod would be home soon. Her husband, however, would not. Not that he was supposed to, of course. Her thoughts just suddenly went to him. He rarely came home for lunch. Typically, he and Mark spent their entire days together. She had no problem with it because she understood it, spending as much time with Mark's wife, Vanessa as she could. They met a couple of times a week at Barbara's house for coffee and fellowship.

The two families were so close that one might think they were all one family, were it not for the different skin color. Barbara was Caucasian, Michael was Hispanic, and Mark and Vanessa were African-American. However, Vanessa even told her that she was closer to her than she actually was to her own sisters. It was a great regret for Vanessa, but something that she just had not been able to rectify. The years were to blame. She had been two months shy of graduation from junior high school when her mother broke the embarrassing news to her that there had been an accident. Months later it was discovered that the accident had further surprises in store. Vanessa loved her twin sisters, but was a grown woman by the time Elizabeth and Alexandria had begun to flower, themselves. She spoke to them often, but just could not seem to get through the fact that they hardly knew one another. Their mother no longer living, they already had plans for the first week in July where she, Liz and Alex would spend the week with their dad in Sacramento at the family home, and she looked forward to the time with great anticipation.

Barbara wondered what Michael was doing just now, and perhaps more importantly, wondered how he was doing. A murder in Kingsburg was unheard of, she knew, so two dead policemen was extraordinary. What the pressure must be she could hardly fathom. She found herself feeling pressure just thinking about it. He had come home incredibly late the night before. She sighed, wondering when it would be that she would actually get to spend time with him during the day.

Luckily, Barbara didn't need anything from town. The previous day had been so bad that she had spent today steering clear of the news, be it television or radio, so she did not know of the revised murder statistic for Kingsburg. She realized full well, however, what the town would be like. She was grateful that she had had no reason to leave the house. It would be the talk of the town. Her being known for her husband's occupation, if she did happen to venture out to the grocery store or local pharmacy, she would probably find herself attacked from all sides for the latest piece of information. *But I don't know anything*, she would tell them, which would be true. Michael very rarely discussed cases with her. It was for no other reason other than not wanting to bring work home with him.

"It's bad enough that I'm on call at the drop of a hat," he had said one time before the twins had arrived to spice things up. "I don't take you guys to work, and I'm certainly not going to bring work home for you guys."

Although this case was quite different from others, due to its nature, that trend had continued, probably because they had hardly seen each other since it first happened.

As she retrieved a pink baby spoon from the soapy water, the last item that needed washing, a loud noise through the slightly open window above her kitchen sink caught her attention. Stepping to the right of the sink, she was able to catch a glimpse of the next door neighbor's driveway. The Rosen's were leaving for a vacation, apparently. Steve hadn't said anything about going on a trip. They had bumped into each other Saturday afternoon at the mailbox that the entire neighborhood shared, which was situated on the sidewalk between their two houses. They had exchanged the usual pleasantries, but that had been all. In the past, many of the families in the neighborhood had been quick to let them know whenever they might be leaving town for a while, hoping for that extra police protection. And yet, here they were. It didn't take very long being married to a police detective to quickly deduce what it meant when one saw an idling family sized car being loaded with suitcases. Considering both the husband and wife were smiling, happily sharing in the work, it could not mean that someone was making room inside their house for a lover by moving out the current spouse.

Barbara smiled at the thought and shook her head, not wanting to let the sinful notion linger inside her.

She liked the Rosen's, although Michael had never cared much for Mr. Rosen. Steve was always talking excessively about his sales firm in Fresno and trying to get Michael to go golfing with him, a sport that Michael detested. She had never let that bother her friendship with Angie, of course. Her eccentric ways always made her laugh. Before the twins arrived, they had volunteered together down at the local thrift store, a task that in itself was not necessarily odd. Instead, it was during this time together that Barbara began to know the woman within.

She had referred to herself as a lifelong Catholic, but did not attend Mass, not even on Christmas or Easter, and could not tell you the exact date of her last Mass or confession for that matter. She hated sports, she would say, but was frequently seen wearing the colors of the Notre Dame Fighting Irish during football season. One time, as a test to see what she might say, Barbara asked her whether the team had won some big game. Her reply, a typical Angie-ism: "*We* always win! The games are nothing for us," she added. "They're *big* for the other guys!"

Another thing was how she loved to spend time alone, cleaning the house. It wasn't the house-cleaning that she liked so much as it was that she was free to blast her music while she did so. The Doors, the Airplane, Janis, Dylan; all screaming their tunes at ear-splitting volume. She just threw on her old tie-dyed and went about her work. If she was in a particularly melancholy mood she might just lie on her bed and listen to Joni or Baez, but absolutely no Beatles. Barbara had attempted to get her to listen to them once, but Angie just replied, "The Beatles didn't get good until they started taking drugs, but by then I could listen to a band that *everybody* on the planet could agree on!"

80

She watched as Steve Rosen waved at somebody that Barbara couldn't see, then turned and climbed into the driver's seat of the family car, an inferno red 2008 Chrysler PT Cruiser that they'd just picked out at Christmas. It had been a gift to each other. He wanted something luxurious, something that shouted to everyone within earshot how successful he was in sales, but in the end Angie's free-spirited leanings won the day and they went with the cruiser.

As the car began to pull out of the drive, Barbara thought for a moment that maybe Steve was leaving her after all, but soon she came into view as the car turned left and headed past her view. Barbara frowned suddenly. She had counted but two heads in the car. It was then that Tiffany Rosen, the couples' seventeen year old daughter came into view, walking toward the street, waving her parents goodbye.

What! she thought, studying the young woman as she lowered her hand and slowly turned and headed back toward the house. It was incredible to believe that a parent might entrust an empty house to any teenager, either boy or girl. Then again, considering how strange Angie Rosen often behaved, perhaps it wasn't so out of character after all.

She knew that Jerod was growing into a wonderful and trustworthy boy, so far. But she remembered being that young, and knew what could and very often *did* happen. Barbara had been lavished with comments from friends and family alike at how beautiful and blushing a bride she had made during her wedding. However, by the time that she and Michael had finally gotten around to making it legal, there was very little blush left between them.

Had she thought about it any longer, it would have bothered her all day. So, fighting her curiosity, she quickly rinsed that last spoon and set it in the drying rack on the counter to her far right. She drained the sink, rinsing all of the excess soapy bubbles and dried her hands on a clean dishtowel. Then, she made a mental note to check in on Tiffany soon, using some ruse of needing to ask her mother for a favor or something, anything, to discover the whereabouts of her parents. She needed to discover exactly how long she would have to be concerned that a fire might be breaking out next door, or whether the Kingsburg Varsity basketball team might be celebrating some win by helping themselves to the Varsity Cheerleading squad, of which Tiffany was a well-known member.

Poienari Fortress
October 7, 1738

High atop a canyon formed by the Arges River Valley, five kilometers north of the village of Arefu, in a castle that had been fortified by Dracula himself, Vlad Tepes, a young boy awoke and cried out suddenly: "Momma!"

He had been a captive now for over a year, not that time meant much to him anymore. The sound carried no weight and did little to phase the heavy stone walls that surrounded him. Immediately, the boy threw his grubby hands over his mouth in hopes of suffocating anything else that might come rushing out of it, improperly supervised. He did not need to be reminded that his mother was no longer available to him; he only prayed that the one who was wouldn't be as well.

The boy turned and faced the west corner. There, a door had once stood. Why there was nothing now but pieces of exposed stone and metal, he did not know; or why much of the fortress stood in ruins. All that he knew was that he had been warned of unspeakable punishment should he ever decide to venture past the walls of this room, unattended.

He had been napping, but had obviously fallen deeper asleep than he intended. He had been back in his father's house on that fateful night that everything had changed. Fresh feelings of abandonment in his head, the boy covered his mouth tighter still. Yet, deep down, he knew that his parents hadn't abandoned him. They weren't coming to get him because they couldn't, not because they didn't want to.

It wasn't much of a consolation.

"Stop that sobbing!" a voice commanded.

The boy recognized it and obeyed immediately. It could have been no one else. A shudder traveled up the length of his fragile young spine, squeezing off the cries within his throat.

It wasn't the words or the command. It was that voice.

He could have surprised the young boy with "Good morning" and it would not have made any difference. The effect would have been exactly the same, frightening, paralyzing him into silence.

The boy curled up into a ball, bringing his knees as close to his chin as was possible. His hair, much longer now than his father ever would have allowed in another life, fell onto both knees. It gave him a tickling sensation, but he did not seem to notice.

"Enough!" the voice lashed out at him again. "Come here!"

The boy jumped begrudgingly to his feet and approached the direction of the faceless voice. He had been through this routine before. He knew, therefore, that it would be better for him if he obeyed. He didn't want to, he only wanted to cry, but what choice did he have?

Head down, now able to finally see the vampire because he had stepped from the shadows, the boy went immediately to his side. Tears streamed down the young boy's pink cheeks as vivid recollections of his parents, especially those regarding his mother, began to flood his memory again. Beside him, standing in the shadows, was the monster responsible. He wondered whether it was now time for him to join his parents in death. Most days it was the only thing he hoped for. Escape never seemed like a viable option for him.

"I should simply make you my dinner and be done with it," the vampire spoke, almost as if he had read the child's mind. It was an old taunt. He stared down upon the boy. In the dark, he could see him trembling in the awful anticipation. The vampire grinned. "What do you have to say about that, hmm?"

The boy's trembling worsened with the monster's goading and he began to whimper. Tears continued to roll down his face where they spilled quickly off of his chin and onto his musty old clothes.

"Stop that! I'll have no more!"

The sound of the monster's voice, although meant to be soothing, still scared the wits out of the boy. His very pronunciation frightened him, causing a momentary wetness within his trousers. Unfortunately, his clothes had just begun to dry from the time before. The vampire's keen sense of smell noticed it immediately. He started to explode in anger again, but somehow caught himself. The smell of human waste was revolting to his senses. Knowing that he did not intend to kill the boy just yet helped him to bide his raving temper. Snapping at the boy would no doubt just make it worse.

"Come," he beckoned in a tone just above a whisper, having grown weary of the game. "I have brought you new clothes. Are you hungry?" the vampire asked as they walked through the ragged doorway and into the corridor beyond.

"Yes." The boy knew better than to antagonize the monster. Their conversations were few, but they were nearly always the same.

"Yes, *what*?" the vampire asked impatiently.

"I'm hungry."

The vampire turned on his heels, surprising the boy. A whimper escaped his lips. *"No, you little fool!"* he shouted. "I mean, 'yes, *what?*'"

The boy stood frozen. This was new. He did not understand what was being asked of him. The monster quickly moved from calm to storming, often with no provocation or warning. This was one of those times.

The vampire waited, but never very long. Ahead, a sliver of moonlight shone through the partial roof. The boy did not have time to analyze its origin. "Yes, what? What is my name?"

"Vincent," the boy admitted, too intimidated to look at anything other than his own bare feet.

Sudden anger, sweeping like wildfire through an old forest, the vampire sprung. The monster's movement near-invisible, the boy jumped back with a start.

"*Why?*" the vampire shouted at the boy, standing menacingly over him, just inches from his tiny head. "Why must you continue with this pitiful mourning?"

No answer.

"Why must you act in such a way?"

The boy, eyes aimed nervously toward the floor, said nothing.

"Answer me!"

The boy let out another cry as the vampire grabbed his arms and raised him high into the air, his head snapping back in surprise. The absolute cold of the monster's flesh around his arms made his lungs tight, forcing them to work harder to get him the proper amount of oxygen. Although musty and dank, it was still the only kind of air available within the dark old place where he was forced to live.

"Why won't you answer me?" the vampire shouted. Spittle hung from the pearly white teeth of his upper jaw and stretched to the incisors of his lower jaws as his fury grew. Some that had become too heavy to remain attached to his teeth gathered at the corners of his mouth and then dripped past his purple lips.

"Why do you anger me so?" the vampire continued with his verbal assault. "I made a meal of your family: yes! Have I done likewise with you? No! Surely that must mean something!" The vampire gave the boy a mild shake. "Well?"

"Momma!" the boy cried out. Tears streamed down his cheeks as he could hold it no longer.

"You want your mother?" he shouted in the boy's contorted face. "Do you? *Do You?* Because I can give her to you! As far as I am aware she is still lying there in that house! Whatever is left of her-whatever the carrion and the worm have not taken—I can bring to you, if that be your wish! Is it? Is it?" The vampire was enraged. The boy had never seen him this way since becoming his prisoner. "Is it? Damn you!"

The boy was more scared than he had ever been since the night of the attack. Picturing the vampire bringing him back his mother in a spade should have made him inconsolable with grief and horror; however, something caused the boy to stifle his crying. In doing so, the vampire stopped his assault.

"I thought we had settled this," the vampire finally spoke again. Discouraged but no longer angry, he set the young boy down. "Your mother is not coming back." He looked away and sighed. Glancing back to the boy, he said, "You would do well to forget her."

Catching his breath, the boy sniffled and wiped some of the tears from his numb, tear-stained little face. He knew that this was not another one of the monster's games. His mother really was not coming back to him.

The vampire turned away from the boy and began to walk down the corridor toward the promised clothing, which the boy needed now more than ever. His voice was no longer filled with the rage of his heart.

"I have prepared your dinner," he said calmly, walking away. "I will collect your clothes and bring them to you there. Then I must take leave of you momentarily and prepare mine."

The boy could no longer see the vampire, but continued to feel his evil presence. Though both hungry and desperate to be out of his soiled clothes, the boy did not dare move just yet. Finally, the vampire spoke again. As long as Nathaniel lived, he would never forget it, nor forgive.

You must realize that I am your mother now.

*   *   *

Nathaniel suddenly sprung from his rudimentary bed of straw and old musty blankets, sitting up. The words reverberated within his mind as he shook himself free from the memory. It had been so clear, almost as if he were reliving it all over again. He shook his head once again. This was Vincent's fault, he knew. He had thought the past all dead and rotting, nay, even bones, but evidently not. And he knew why. It was because of its father. Not the poor, feeble shell of a man who had fathered him back in Cimpulung, but the one who had "unmade" what he was and turned him into the vile and monstrous thing that he was. He had thought himself free of him many years ago, but now Nathaniel could see otherwise. He knew that he would never be free of him until one of them was free of this world.

8:34 p.m.

It was past 8:30 and Michael was still not home. Barbara frowned as she considered this fact. It was this time of day when she really looked forward to the company of adults. It wasn't as if she never had the opportunity to have coffee with Vanessa or speak on the phone with some of the ladies from church… or even occasionally have one or two of them drop by for some fellowship. But sitting at the end of the evening with her husband, with the kids all put to bed, was, to her, rather like having a fine dessert at the end of a good meal, or perhaps an espresso. In any event, she was alone now.

She found herself wandering through the house for no reason at all. She went back to the master bathroom, but realized that she didn't need to visit. Turning around, she headed back through the house toward the kitchen, but was not hungry, not even a little bit. She realized that she was bored. The television was on and although God knew they had 250 channels of programming, she just did not feel in the mood. She grabbed a plastic cup from the counter and walked it over to the refrigerator to get some water from the dispenser in the door. It was not that she wanted water, but it gave her a moment to consider what it was that she really wanted to do with the remainder of her day.

It was then that she thought of Tiffany Rosen again.

Barbara glanced over her shoulder to peek through her kitchen window into the Rosen's kitchen to see whether there might be any signs of life to be found there. Light was present, but that was currently all. It seemed to be coming from the living room. Perhaps Tiffany was sitting up watching some television before bed. But was she alone? That was the question. Barbara glanced at the red digital clock display on the microwave behind her. It was about a quarter to nine. She had meant to check in on the girl earlier but had not yet done so. Even now, with the kids all tucked in and no Michael as of yet, taking a moment to drop by was not exactly the most optimal of circumstances. It was bad enough with just Jerod to think about, but now there were two babies to abandon, even though only momentarily.

8:45 p.m.

Vincent was unusually hungry tonight.

88

Though the old man's blood still coated his stomach and he could have waited a while before really needing that next meal, he felt famished. It wasn't his stomach that drove it, however. It was the power. Finding Nathaniel after all of these years and now immersing himself in the game made him insatiable. He planned to feed and feed often, to build up his considerable strength even more, and to keep it up until Nathaniel was his possession once again.

Will tonight be the night? he thought as he walked northward along 10th Avenue, brazenly down the middle of the public sidewalk, automobiles going past him in both directions. He paid them no mind. Who could stop him? He was the great vampire. Were there other vampires? Yes, considerably. But just like these humans about him, once they got wind of what they were dealing with they made haste to make way for *him.*

Before him the avenue met another road. It was still quite a ways off but he could easily read the sign from this distance: Roosevelt Street. Long before reaching it, the vampire had decided that he would take it and see where it might lead. Or rather who it might lead him to.

There was that little matter of his hunger that needed appeasing.

8:55 p.m.

Barbara Lopez opened her front door as quietly as she could and, double-checking that she had in fact brought her house keys with her, equally as quietly closed the door behind her. Sometimes using a door quickly was the best course of action, but she went ahead with the silent and meticulous method. Now that she was outside, she acted fast. There was no path between their houses, so, not wanting to accidentally squash one of the many frogs that frequented the

89

neighborhood, she headed down the driveway toward the sidewalk. That wasn't the only thing. In her haste, she failed to think whether she might need warmer clothing. Although summer was nearly here, the light breeze in the air caused her to shiver slightly. For her warm-blooded husband, 78 degrees was ideal; for her, it was downright chilly.

Behind her, heading her direction on the same side of the street, was someone out for a late stroll. Whether man or woman she was unsure because of the distance and the briefest of glances. It was the police detective's wife in her again, doing her job. She ignored the figure and simply continued on her way.

The outside porch light was on, Barbara noted, as she approached the front door. She listened a moment before knocking, but finding nothing out of the ordinary, went ahead and knocked on the door. It took a few moments and one more series of knocks before she heard the footfalls on the other side of the door, followed by the turning of the locks.

"Hello," Barbara announced as the door opened to her. Tiffany was there, dressed in a pair of cute pink shorts and a black My Chemical Romance 2007 concert t-shirt. There was no bra beneath, she also noted.

"Hi, Mrs. Lopez," Tiffany smiled, at least seemingly pleased to have a visitor. "How's it goin'?"

"Pretty good. How about you? I saw your mom and dad taking off this afternoon and thought I'd drop by and make sure that everything was okay."

During the afternoon, Barbara had spent some time considering what it was that she might say to Tiffany, were she able to check in on her after all. She had considered using a ruse, and that had seemed the correct tactic; however, in the end, when suddenly finding herself face to face with her, the truth seemed best of all.

"Yeah, they went to our house in Morro Bay. One of our neighbors there called because something

90

happened with some sidewalk the city is putting in. I was going to skip some days this week and go to the coast with them, but I've got some stupid test to take in French, as well as an extra credit report in English Lit that I really need if I'm going to get rid of that 'C' I've got there."

"Oh, really. What kind of report?" She folded her arms tightly together in order to keep warm. It never really took much to give her a chill.

"It's on *Animal Farm*."

"*Animal Farm*?" Barbara questioned with a puzzled look. "Jerod's reading that this year, too."

"He is?" Tiffany laughed, clapping her hands together. "Oh-my-God! That's too funny. How much does he charge to write a paper?"

"Well, I don't know," Barbara found herself laughing, too, as well as playing along. "Tomorrow morning I'll have to ask him that while he's eating his Lucky Charms. I'd wake him right now and send him over, but I don't think your parents would appreciate you having any boys!"

Tiffany clapped her hands again and threw her head back in further laughter, sending her long blonde hair behind her. When she was still it reached to the middle of her back.

"Did you want to come in?" she asked, still giggling. "You look cold."

She glanced past Barbara briefly and then came back to her, ignoring whatever it was that had momentarily distracted her. Remembering the person out for a walk, Barbara glanced back just in time to catch the person moving past them. It was a man, after all. He was obviously not out for a jog, wearing Levi's and a long leather jacket. He briefly glanced in their direction, but continued on his way. Barbara noted that his hair was longer than Tiffany's.

Barbara turned back to the girl and smiled warmly. Everything was fine here.

"No. Thanks. I've got to get back to the kids before they wake up and find mommy missing."

"Okay," Tiffany said.

"How long will your parents be gone?" she asked before turning to go.

"I don't know. My dad said that they were going to do a few things for the summer since they were going to be there. Maybe a couple of days."

There hadn't been much to say after that. Everything was okay and in order tonight, apparently, but what of tomorrow? She sighed as she headed down the driveway and then turned for home. She had her three to supervise and now a forth one next door. Something caused Barbara to take a look and see whether that late stroller was gone; evidently so because he was nowhere to be seen. What she did see, though, was the fact that Michael's car was still not where it needed to be at this late hour. Once again, she found herself not knowing what to do with herself. Taking her keys from her pants pocket, she let herself inside and locked the door behind her.

She then retraced her steps through the house, this time stopping and checking in on her sleeping children. She dallied a moment at Jerod's door, pausing to consider how little time she had before he would be Tiffany's age. Would she be leaving him alone? Probably not.

Not if he's anything like his father! she thought to herself with a naughty grin.

*   *   *

Brian Zeagler stared incredulously at his girlfriend as she came bounding into the living room of her parents' house to rejoin him, her guest caller dispatched. Although he was a little bothered with her at the moment, his eyes quickly found her breasts as they swayed untethered this way and that. They weren't the

92

most magnificent in the world, he could well imagine. He'd already seen his fair share in Playboy Magazine, so he had a pretty damn good idea how perfect some breasts could be. The difference here, however, was that these particular breasts were *his*, so that made them pretty damn magnificent!

"Are you out of your mind?" he asked her, following her with his eyes as she turned out the main lighting in the room that she had only turned on at the knock on the door. Once again they were left only in the competing light from the oil-fed flame from her mother's antique Green Depression Glass Lamp on the display table on one side of the room and the glow of the muted television on the other.

"What?" Tiffany cried as she jumped onto the couch beside him. She leaned away from him in order to get a better look at his sweet face.

"*'Did you want to come in?'*" he mimicked her. "What the hell was that? You're killing me!"

"She wasn't coming in!" Tiffany laughed. "What's wrong with you? I just had to make it look good, that's all. Come on!"

Brian stared at her silently now. Her smile grew wider. Try as he might, whatever it was that had upset him was quickly replaced by a distant throbbing that he found increasingly difficult to ignore. As of yet there wasn't anything obvious to notice, but she must have been able to read his mind because her hand went right to the spot, making it worse.

"Come on, baby," she purred, leaning into him, her long straight blonde hair spilling off of her shoulders and onto him.

Brian Zeagler never had a chance. Tiffany Rosen was the most beautiful girl at Kingsburg High. That wasn't simply his horny bias, either. All the guys thought that. As a matter of fact, many of them questioned whether she might be the most beautiful woman in the entire town. All of his friends thought so at least, and so did many of the girls, although they would never dare admit it.

Brian glanced up at the ceiling now, giving Tiffany the opportunity she wanted to suck on his neck a bit. She kissed him a while, and then rolled her fine tongue across the base of his sixteen year old neck. He closed his eyes and lost himself in the moment. Before losing himself for good he thought of how this would be continuing for the rest of the week until her parents returned. Tiffany had lied to the next door neighbor when she had told the woman that her parents might be gone for a couple of days when in fact she had known perfectly well that they would not be back for four days.

That meant that they had four marvelous days with which to explore each other's bodies.

"Is there a problem?" Tiffany suddenly broke the moment of silence, and more importantly, the inactivity between them.

"No." He snapped back to life. "Absolutely not!"

With that, Brian sat up and pushed Tiffany back onto the couch. He ripped off his Hard Rock Café Las Vegas t-shirt, tossed it across the room as if this were their first apartment together, and then proceeded to crawl back inside her for the second time tonight.

In the background, the back door could be heard periodically knocking up against the doorframe with the breeze. He had apparently neglected to close the door properly upon taking out the trash left over from their Jack in the Box dinner.

"Is that the back door?" Tiffany moaned as Brian ran his hands down her lower back and pressed her against him.

"What door?" he asked.

"Never mind."

*   *   *

In the hallway, leaning up against a bare wall, just beyond range of the dim romantic light of the living room, the vampire could feel the rising blood pressure on the two lovers and anticipated how the young blood would feel as it rushed down his gullet. He watched, disinterested, as the two lovers began coitus, expressionless, and waited.

9:41 p.m.

The vampire licked his purple lips, ensuring that no precious crimson drop was wasted. The blood, young and vibrant, full of life, flowed within him like a flash-flood raging down a dry river bed. He closed his eyes and felt its power wash through him like a kind of sexual climax. It was invigorating and reeling at the same time. The vampire shuddered as he slowly began to fill out with lovely color: his pale white skin becoming bronze, his slightly withering lips full and luscious, his eyes a perfect green. He moaned as the sensations passed. Tilting his head back, he tried to enjoy every last sweet palpitation.

He reopened his eyes. After a deep breath and a sweep of his now rosy pink tongue over his lips, it was over. Of all those he had devoured over the centuries, it was difficult to find anything better than that of young lovers. It made him feel strong and invincible, as if he could rule the world. The vampire smiled. It was a long, nasty, mischievous smile, proudly and contemptuously displaying fangs.

As he wiped his cold, murderous hands upon a dishtowel that hung from the refrigerator, something caught his attention. A light had come on in the house across the fence. Curious, still feeling the effects of the blood within him, he moved closer. In the darkness of the kitchen where he lurked, he was invisible. The occupants of the home across the pitiful fence between them, however, did not have the same luxury.

The vampire watched as the other woman that he had seen lurking in the neighborhood earlier walked into the kitchen. The vampire's eyes widened as he studied her. She was quite lovely, but that was insignificant. It was what she held within her warm motherly arms which his mad black eyes latched onto. It was a baby. He licked his lips. *Ah! But a baby is by far the best blood!* The blood was fresh and, most importantly, to Vincent, it was the highest thrill of all to snatch them out of the arms of their weak mothers as they begged and pleaded for a mercy which would not come.

The vampire lifted his right hand and inserted a twisted yellow fingernail that was slowly returning to white into his mouth. He almost bit it off when his eyes happened upon the apparent husband who entered the kitchen holding another baby.

"*Twins!*" he whispered, his lips already wet with anticipation.

Within the curvature of his nail, the vampire found a drop of blood which he had previously missed. As he watched the mother and her infant, and the other infant behind, he ran his sandpapery tongue across the nail, licking it clean. The vampire had already forgotten the two bodies sprawled out on the couch in the other room. It was the twin babies that he wanted now, though he was too full to appreciate them.

Tomorrow, he thought, silently making his next day's dinner plans. *I shall have them tomorrow.*

10:15 p.m.

Barbara Lopez leaned against the frame of the twins' bedroom doorway and quietly stole one last look at her sleeping babies before turning out the light. Watching their peaceful slumber gave her a warm

96

feeling. They were not quite nine months old, yet, she couldn't help already feeling proud with the job that she had done raising them. Glowing inside, she turned around and flicked off the light, leaving the door open behind her so she wouldn't rap her knee or face on it in about four hours when one or both of them decided they needed something.

Barbara checked in on Jerod one last time. Since she could not risk turning on his light, even for a moment, for fear of waking him, Barbara had to allow her eyes time to focus in the dark. When she could see, her heart was warmed once again. Jerod had his sheets, bedspread and a thick blanket pulled all the way up to the bottom of his little chin. His cheeks were red with the bed's warmth. It wasn't cold enough for her son to need quite all that coverage, but she had seen him complain of the cold with almost twice the heat so she just left him alone.

All of her children were fast asleep. With a warm smile on her face, she turned and closed the door. Breathing a sigh of relief, the exclamation point on another day gone by, she walked down the hall to join her husband.

Michael was exhausted. It had now been another day of at least fifteen hours of work. When his wife entered the room, she found him with his eyes closed and his feet high on the recliner's foot-rest. She started to speak but immediately stopped herself upon seeing him.

"It's okay, sweetheart," he said just above a whisper, opening his eyes. "I'm not asleep." He yawned. "How are the kids?"

"Fast asleep." Barbara was amused by the obvious show of exhaustion. He was just mere seconds from joining her children in the realm of dreams. Knowing that she was going to have to get right back up, Barbara didn't bother sitting down, but instead, leaned back against the arm of the couch. "You are the only one I have left to put to bed."

He smiled. "And I'm ready, too!"

"I bet!" Barbara stood again. She studied him as he yawned once more and stretched. It was more than just the hours, she could now really see. It was the actual work. "Is the case really that bad?" she finally asked.

He rolled his eyes as he thought the question over for a second. Looking back at her, he frowned.

"If we only had the least little, but we don't have anything."

His frown deepened, Michael begrudgingly pulled himself out of the comfortable recliner and put his arm around her.

"Well, come on!" She hugged him back. "You go on to bed and I'll turn everything off."

"Okay." He lightly kissed her forehead. "Love you."

After turning out all of the lights and double checking all the doors, Barbara joined her husband in the master bedroom. Already dressed in her nightgown, she picked up her side of the covers and gently climbed into bed. Michael, like her three children, was fast asleep. She found herself listening to his light snoring for a moment. After a while, she realized it was because it reminded her so much of her son's. She grinned. When Jerod had been younger, a full day of hard playing always gave him the same snore she now heard in her right ear. Now that Jerod was older, it took much more to completely tire him out. *Like father, like son*, she thought.

"Goodnight, sweetheart." she whispered.

Reaching over to her left, Barbara turned the light out on another day. Twenty minutes later, after she had exhausted herself on thoughts of her children and the good life that she and Michael had built together, and after the bed was good and warm like Jerod's, she too fell asleep.

WEDNESDAY

May 7, 2008
7:26 a.m.

    The driver of the red Ford Mustang convertible saw nothing and no one as she maneuvered expertly through the city streets that made up her normal route to work. Alicia Keys was expertly hitting every one of her notes on the stereo, but she was oblivious to it. She didn't see the other cars, the traffic lights, or the three stop signs that stood between her and her parking space at City Hall. She was slave to her routine while her thoughts were elsewhere. Hands went up as she passed, but no one was smiling. Not many were smiling these days.

    Finally, she safely pulled into the parking spot that was identified on the curbing with the following: **MAYOR**. No previous mayors had ever thought it necessary to label the space that ultimately ended up being left unoccupied each day of the year. However, one morning, without a word, there it stood. The City Clerk was traditionally the first to arrive each morning at 7:00 a.m. sharp to unlock the building and start the coffee. The new paint was nearly dry then. Mayor Peterson never admitted to anyone how in the world she could say with absolute certainty how she knew that, although she was forced to hide her right forefinger for two days until the evidence was gone. Mathew Peters swore that there had been no paint when he had swung his giant street sweeper early that morning. There had been no one to confess that the *honorable* new mayor had either asked or coerced them into doing her dirty work, but there it stood. In the end, no one hated the woman, although very few expressed any kind of love for her. She was liked about as strongly as any other mayor who had graced the town with their service. The day the paint showed up was commonly referred to as Black Monday, however.

When she turned off the ignition, a rather sad little man came into her view and snapped her out of her thoughts.

"Good morning, Your Honor," Councilman Johnson said before she had even fully disembarked her vehicle. He stood in the street beside her driver's side door. "I apologize, but I need to speak with you."

"Good Lord, David," she said, already exasperated with the meek little man, with the morning, and with the cup of coffee she had yet to taste. He said nothing further. He just stood there. She turned to face him finally. "Must you apologize for everything? Is that all you do?" He had no answer. She stared back at him for a moment.

"What?" he asked, meeting her eyes. He suddenly felt like he was back in school and the teacher had just asked him a question in front of the entire class.

"Are you going to let me out or is it your duty to prevent me from doing my job?"

"I'm sorry, Your Honor." He moved out of her way, but not by much. He was standing in the gutter now, blocking out her title there on the curb.

"And that's another thing: Stop calling me that! My name is Katherine!"

She opened the door and stepped out onto the street. She started to slam the door in disgust, but she adored the car that saw her through the divorce, so she caught herself in time. What she really wanted to do was to slam the man. He was calling her at home (four times this week already and it was only Wednesday) and now he was meeting her before she even got into the building.

"When it is just the two of us and we're not doing anything terribly official, call me Katherine."

She was willing herself to become calm now, but he wasn't helping much. Now, if she really wanted access to that sidewalk, she was going to have to go around him.

"I'm sorry."

"What is it you want?" she sighed and began to walk around him. Not that it would take long, the stick figure of a man.

"I tried calling you last night but you weren't home," he said, shuffling his feet in order to stay in front of her.

"The hell I wasn't!" she confessed, before being able to catch herself. *Oh, well. What do I care!* "What did you want? Why are you stalking me?" she said at last. "Does Bea know that you're calling me at all hours of the day and following me around?"

She finally reached the door, Councilman Johnson still shuffling to keep position. She pictured those little Remora fish that secure themselves to the bottom of sharks now when a far more terrible thought occurred to her. Her hand stretching for the door handle, she spun back around to face the man, almost bumping into him.

"Who's dead?"

The councilman retreated a step with the shock of the close contact with the mayor as well as her sudden question. "What?"

"How many dead this time? The only time you call me is when it's bad news. So, what happened? Who's dead now?"

"I think we are," he said. It seemed that it was finally his turn to speak so he was not going to miss the opportunity. He stood a little taller suddenly. "That's why I was calling, I assure you! Do you know that we have lost two vendors already? We lost the lady and her family that always come down from Denver, and we lost someone from San Jose."

She said nothing as she allowed the information to seep in. This was her first Swedish Festival and she was losing it. She was the first female mayor that the town had ever had, but that was not what she would be remembered for. As she stared at the man, the murals behind him on the wall of the old Ostrom's Pharmacy building, which now housed the Kingsburg branch of the Fresno County Library, caught her eye. The five images conveyed not only a wonderful depiction of how well-rounded Kingsburg life was, paying homage to the past while looking to the future, but the images of Olympian Rafer Johnson and Kingsburg Recorder Editor Ed Jacobs. This was a reminder of what became of the town's heroes. *What might become of me if I allow this to continue?*

Now, her tone and basic demeanor changed. Now, both she and the Councilman were standing tall. She nodded once, still looking over the murals, and then turned back to face David Johnson straight into his eyes. If she were to see this through to a quick and logical conclusion, she realized, she would have to do it. If she were going to be scoffed at and vilified by both media and townspeople alike, and characterized as a colossal failure of a mayor, it would be because she failed. It would not be because the Council was weak or slow to react. It would not be because the Chief of Police was immensely under-qualified. If she was going to go down with the ship, then the divers were going to find her skeletal remains firmly attached to the helm.

"Come inside, David," the Mayor said at last, reaching for and opening the door. She held it open for him with an unusual smile. "Let's talk."

8:29 a.m.

Police Chief O'Donnell arrived at the Department a lot later than he ever would have under ordinary circumstances. And these were very far from ordinary, indeed.

The chief had worked in his office until well after hours the night before. Without the presence of any real leads or developments, there had been little to do but monitor the radio traffic and hope against hope for some breakthrough. Pulling himself away from his office by sheer force of will, he headed for home but did very little except monitor traffic from his "other" office on the second story, where Carol would not be disturbed. After another three hours of nothing, he reluctantly turned in for the night.

During the night he awoke several times to use the bathroom. Only once did he actually need to do so; but each time he turned on the radio and monitored the traffic. He did manage to sleep some.

Now he was back at his first office.

O'Donnell parked in his usual spot, facing north on California Street. Rather than head for the main entrance, however, he walked briskly around to the back of the building for the Earl Street entrance. With very little sleep under his belt, he was in no mood for talking. Not until he got some coffee. A lot of coffee. He used his key and snuck inside.

He navigated the route quickly and reached his office without being greeted by anyone. After entering and closing the door behind him, he counted his blessings.

"It's about time you got in!" came a familiar voice from behind his desk.

He froze in place. His left hand was still firmly holding onto the handle of the door. He contemplated the solid oak door, closed his eyes and sighed. His first reaction was to quickly slam it back in place, but even that did not seem *strong* enough. A part of him now wanted to shout the Lord's name in vain at the top of his lungs. It felt right to him; however, the longer he thought about it, the more it felt anticlimactic. Ultimately, he did nothing.

"Katherine," he greeted her simply.

He barely glanced in the mayor's direction. He simply headed for his regular chair for whenever Her Honor was visiting.

"Do you have any idea how long I have been waiting here for you to finally drag yourself in to work?"

Now he wanted to get back to his feet, retrace his steps to the door of his office and slam that sonofabitch for all that he was worth. "No, I don't," the chief said without stopping to think about his words before he threw them out there. "But I plan on asking every single member of this department until I find one of them who does know. You know what I'm going to do then, Your Honor?"

"No." She studied the man with her eyes and said nothing else. Her hands were clasped together on the top of his desk.

"I'm going to fire them!"

"You can't do that."

"You can't keep barging into my frigging office, either, but that doesn't appear to be stopping you! Perhaps if you had an office of your own, you'd understand!"

"Listen," the mayor said, ignoring the comment. Not many knew that the mayor did not actually have an office, but only a mail slot at City Hall. "We can keep fighting like this or we can solve our problems."

"Really?" he asked, extending his hands. "That's fantastic! Now we're finally speaking the same language!"

She sighed with an odd grin on her firm but lovely face. She folded her arms at her chest now and leaned back in the chief's leather chair.

He sat up and rested the palms of his hands upon his knees. "The problem as I see it is this: You can't help me. Oh, you can stay the hell out of my office and out of the way of my men and women while they bust their butts trying to keep the people of this town safe. But that's all!" He jumped to his feet suddenly and forcefully planted his hands upon his desk. He leaned over it. He wanted to really see her now. "Look. I have had a lot of time to think these past three days. I know

108

you're worried about the festival, Katherine. Right now I bet it seems like *your* festival, but it isn't. What's happening to this town was going to screw whoever was mayor whether it was you, your predecessor, or anyone else after you."

The mayor said nothing. She just continued to stare at him.

"But I've got to tell you. Another day or two and we have to cancel the whole damn thing."

The mayor suddenly lost her grip on that grin she had been wearing. She looked like all of the blood had rushed to her head. A bead of sweat bubbled on her forehead and began to descend toward her eyes.

"Absolutely not!" she said in the firmest of whispers. He frowned. "Do you hear me, O'Donnell? Absolutely not! We're not going to lose the festival. We're not going to lose one more damn vendor. Do you understand what I'm telling you?"

She stood and walked around the desk. She did so and did not stop until she was facing the man, their noses almost touching. For his part, he simply stood there and took it. The mayor started to say one more thing but stopped when the sabers behind him on the south wall caught her attention.

"What?" he asked, seeing the mayor lose her focus.

"I want you to look at something," she said, still giving orders.

She's growing too attached to this office, the chief thought. "At what?"

"Your swords."

"They're sabers. I've seen them. In fact, I mounted them there myself, if it's any consolation to you."

She stepped to the side, but did not walk past him. Instead, she seemed to hover there, their shoulders touching neither romantically nor in the least bit friendly. She lowered her voice again, feigning control. "Are they sharp?"

"They might be."

"Good."

"Why?"

The mayor paused a moment then turned so that her lips were mere inches away from the man's right ear. "If I lose this festival, someone will need to fall on a sword. ... Saber," she corrected herself.

She leaned closer. They were almost touching now. He could feel the breath before he could hear the words that were carried there. "And it will be damn apropos that they hang in your office and not mine."

9:09 a.m.

The vampire turned his head to the right in a fitful slumber as two wars were being waged. On the one hand, as the sun worked its way into the sky, the light was trying its level best to locate the vampire as he slept there, buried beneath a thick layer of old blankets in the abandoned barn. Like agents of good, the sun's rays crawled over the fabric, knowing instinctively of his unholy presence there. They pounded against him, somehow knowing that they were individually not strong enough to break through but hoping to weaken the fabric's defenses so that the next ray might get further, deeper. Other rays, like drops of water, ran along the perimeter looking for a hole, but burning off before they could do so.

There was a very distinct part of Nathaniel that wished that the sun's rays would indeed find him there and do their worst. He was tired of everything—living, fighting, hungering.

On the other hand, images filled the back of his eyes.

Images of home...

*   *   *

Why, Lord, have you not answered my prayers? the adolescent boy prayed silently. He knew better than to speak after all of these years. He was alone for the moment, but who could know how long that might be? And he knew what Vincent would say about praying. *How long have I been held captive now? Even I do not remember. How could I? I was but a babe when you allowed that beast to have my family.*

Nathaniel paused here. He could feel the old anger rising up within him. He tried to fight it back, to hold it inside. Perhaps that was his problem after all. He had a suspicion that it was, but he also knew that it should be his right to be angry with the turn of events that had been his life. What had he done to deserve any of this?

What have I done, Lord? Tell me! We were happy and we bothered no one. Father worked the land. He worked terribly hard and for what? Very little. But he never complained. He rarely smiled, but he did smile. He could laugh! I remember that! And Mom? What had she done? I can hear her giggling as I chased her around our tiny home. She would let me catch her but not until she had had her fill of laughter.

Why did you allow this to happen? Why? I want to know. I want you to tell me the reason for any of this. He paused again, the anger having its ferocious way with him now. *Go ahead. I will wait for you.*

Nathaniel found himself pacing around the suite that had recently become his. Why Vincent had moved him to a much larger room he did not know and did not care in the least. He asked no further questions as he moved toward a wall and spun back, his long hair flying behind before resettling upon his shoulder and the middle of his back. It would not do to strike anything here. The rough stone would only bring more pain. There would be no releasing of his anger or his hurt.

Whatever is the matter? he continued. *Have you no answers for me? And why is that? Is it because you do not know what to say? Do you choose these events to take place and not have the least notion of their resolution?* Nathaniel spun again before reaching another wall. Now he was flinging his arms around as if he were arguing a case before a judge.

If that is indeed the case then let me ask you this: What did you decide first? He paused yet again. He still had his torch as well. The light seemed to be brighter than usual tonight. It bothered him the longer that he watched it. He turned away from it, rubbing his eyes a bit. After a few moments he looked back up, straight ahead, but not at anything in particular. Something else. Someplace else. Perhaps the very throne room of heaven. *Did you say to yourself, "My Vincent must feed soon? It is too far for him to do anything but have the lives of the three poor pitiful peasants that I see over here." Is that how it happened? Or did you turn and stumble upon our home and in boredom decide that my mother and father should die?*

If he was angry before now, he had graduated to raging. He was no longer pacing or waving about with his arms, but he gritted his teeth as he held that stare.

"Will He not answer, my son?"

Nathaniel said nothing as Vincent's voice suddenly came from behind. He did not jump. He had grown too accustomed to Vincent's games as well. He simply lowered his head and turned to face him. "Who?"

"Please," the vampire snickered. "It is clear that you were praying. Or perhaps attempting it, anyway. I'm curious. What did He have to say? Hmm? Anything at all?"

Nathaniel walked over to his bed and sat silently.

"Come now, you can tell me." When his question was met with further silence, Vincent continued. "Fine, then. Have it your way. I will guess what was said." He was in the rarest of moods. On most other occasions Nathaniel's silence would have brought instant punishment. For the moment, it appeared that there would be no blows tonight. Perhaps they might yet come.

There was a loud scratching sound as Vincent lit the torch that he had brought into the room. Vincent did not require any light, but seemed to adore the theatrics of it all. He placed the torch in the metal ring behind him, near the heavy door. Its glow provided very little light, but Nathaniel found that he needed to shield his eyes from it, nonetheless. After a few moments he slowly took his right hand away from his eyes and he could see without discomfort. When he did so, Vincent was there standing over him. He was smiling.

It was a terrible smile.

It provided less warmth than even the pathetic torch by the door.

"He said nothing!" The vampire leaned close. Nathaniel had trouble making out his features because Vincent was blocking the light; however, he could well imagine finding a prideful look of disdain there. "He said nothing because there is no one there! There is no god! There is no god to rescue you from me. There was no god that put you in my hands. There is nothing there." He motioned above them. "Do you hear me? There is no god!"

Vincent stepped back. Nathaniel could see a bit. He would have seen more without the light. Unfortunately, his eyes had to readjust every time Vincent stepped in and out of the torch's light. He could see that Vincent was no longer playful and wondered how long it might take before he became angry. It usually did not take very long.

If he thought Vincent was simmering toward an eventual outburst of angry words and worse yet, angry deeds, he was in for a genuine surprise. Instead, he got quite the opposite. Across the room there was a large chair. Nathaniel rarely sat in it because Vincent always did. It wasn't often that he would recline when he paid him one of his visits, but on those rare occasions when he did, that was the chair that he would use. Vincent grabbed the chair and easily slid it close to Nathaniel's bed, sitting down.

"Now, do not misunderstand me. There *is* a God. There are too many cathedrals in the world to discount this; too many priests. I believe that He works one day a week. It used to be on the last day of the week which was Saturday, but He changed it to the first day: Sunday. Do not ask me why. In any event, He apparently listens to the people's complaining and supplications and whatever else. There is a foul smelling incense that the priest walks about with. There is a whole lot of the drinking of wine. It is all ceremonial, of course. No one wishes to drink anything that does such magical things to one's mind. Certainly not!"

Nathaniel continued to say and do nothing. His own anger had subsided, but was not yet put away for another day. He had had many moments over the course of his captivity when he felt like shouting at God or Vincent or even at his own father for not having had the necessary strength to defend the family and kill the beast even when he knew that there might be no force on earth capable of doing so. He was just angry, and anger was very rarely objective or controllable, he had found.

"Have you never seen such things?" Vincent asked him now, but not really.

Nathaniel recognized all of the moods: anger, melancholy, boredom, impatience, gaiety. There was none that he favored more than another, except perhaps ones that did not end in blows for him.

Prone to drone on at length when pleased with himself, as he was currently, Vincent continued. "It is quite the spectacle. Unfortunately, for you and me that God will not be helpful. In fact, I do not believe that He even knows that we exist. Perhaps He does, but simply has allowed us to our own devices."

"What devices are those?" Nathaniel spoke before he could stop himself. It was that anger yet bubbling at the surface. It would have been better had he simply waited for Vincent to grow tired of the speeches and depart. It was always better not to speak. Now it was too late to go back.

"The boy speaks! How wonderful! Please, speak further. What might a boy have asked of the Most High?"

"I wanted to know why He has not answered me."

"Yes?"

"I have prayed, but He does not reply," Nathaniel said, lowering his face.

A moment before he was a young man holding his gaze heavenward, demanding with both word and expression. Now he was a shadow of that man. Still, though he knew in his heart that he should be silent before the vampire, he could not stop himself. It had been too long, and he wanted answers.

"God neither answers prayer, nor does He even acknowledge them. He will not so much as show me His face."

"And why do you think that is so?" Vincent asked.

For a moment Nathaniel said nothing, perhaps measuring his words for the first time today. Nathaniel held his ground as well, sitting on the bed and staring at his feet planted there on the straw covered stone floor. "I do not know."

"Yes, you do!" The vampire suddenly snapped. "And I demand that you look at me when we are speaking! Have you still no manners? No respect? No fear?"

That was how it was with Vincent. His mood could change in a heartbeat. That was if he had a heart.

"Look at me!" Vincent shouted, immediately grabbing Nathaniel by the shoulder-length brown hair and yanking back his head so that he could have his attention. Vincent pressed his nose against Nathaniel's left cheek and stared deeply into his gloomy brown eyes. The pain was immediate and hurt terribly. He grimaced, but forced himself to open his eyes through it all. He knew to expect far worse if he did not look.

"I do not know why!" Nathaniel forced out the words.

Vincent pulled harder, clearly not pleased with the answer.

"*Yes, you do*!" he repeated. "You know because I have made it quite clear. There is no god *here* to answer you. You are wasting your time and mine."

Here, Vincent finally relented, releasing Nathaniel, who started to move away, but quickly thought better of it. He needed to be content with his freedom and nothing more. Greed would only bring more pain and suffering.

Now it was Vincent who was doing the pacing. "Will this never cease? Must we fight endlessly?" He must have realized the irony of the situation because he immediately stopped and turned back toward the boy. "I brought you here to be my companion. Instead, I have brought myself nothing but suffering. Why? Would you have it that I had killed you along with your family that night?"

Yes, Nathaniel thought but, thankfully, did not bring voice to it.

"Yes?" Vincent said with a frown.

It was surprising in its utter sadness. In all the years, Nathaniel had never seen such emotion. Momentarily amazed, he then wondered whether or not it might be just an act. As much as he might wish to, he decided to finally say nothing further for the day.

Vincent once again approached Nathaniel's bed. He set his hands on each side of him, encircling him. He looked into his eyes for the second time, and this time without malice. Nathaniel did not attempt to move away, but stayed his ground.

"Yes, my son. You do wish that I had killed you that night. I can read your mind. You think that had I killed you and fed on your life you would be safe now. However, if there is no god, does it not stand to reason that there would be no heaven as well? If you were dead, perhaps you would just be nothing."

"I am nothing." Nathaniel said.

He was no longer in that large cold room back in Romania, but instead, poking out from beneath musty forgotten blankets in an old shack of a barn that might not make it through one more winter. It was early to be awake, but awake was better than reliving old memories not worth having lived the first time around. Though the sun had not yet gone down for the night, its rays were no longer attacking, searching for a weakness in his defenses. What sun there was, now hit the west side of the barn. He could see something of the ray's nature but they were now no longer strong enough to even blind him were he to venture outside and among them. The vampire would live another night.

Perhaps the sun will find me tomorrow, Nathaniel thought.

10:49 a.m.

Barbara stared at her coffee as she stirred its contents of sugar and Coffee-Mate creamer. She was deep in thought. There had been very little interaction between her husband and her this morning. He was troubled by his work—work that she fought her curiosity very hard not to inquire about. She wondered whether he and Mark needed help, and, if they did, would that help come? Would some other police jurisdiction try and take over? Would that cause KPD not to ask for help?

Finally, she removed the spoon from her cup and set it back down on the spoon rest. She vaguely noticed any of this. She sat down at the dining room table and pulled her Bible closer. She read it most days, missing time only for the occasional crisis at home; with twins, one never knew what might happen. Currently, Jerod was off at school and the twins were on a blanket in the middle of the living room floor. From her position at the dining room table she could watch them well. She was looking at them now, but the thoughts overwhelmed her. She was troubled by the thought of Michael receiving help, but that was not exactly accurate. It was the notion of help that had wormed its way into her mind. Maybe it was the word itself: help.

She glanced away from the twins and looked back at the Bible laid out before her on the table. It was open to no book in particular. Had she opened it? She could not remember doing so, but paid it no mind. There was obviously no other alternative.

Her focus came back to her. She was staring at the book of Romans. Her eyes found Romans 8:28. She allowed the words to play in her mind for a time, but there was no immediate connection or epiphany to be had. It was a popular verse that she had read many times before, and had heard it quoted *ad nauseam*. She frowned. Perhaps that had been too harsh. She allowed her mind to clear a moment and read it again.

"And we know that God causes all things to work together for good to those who love God, to those who are called according to *His* purpose."

Having nothing stop her, no big chill or apparent sign to affect her one way or another, she allowed her eyes to continue to the next verse.

"For whom He foreknew, He also predestined *to become* conformed to the image of His Son, that He might be first-born among many brethren..."

Still nothing.

"and whom He predestined, these He also called; and whom He called, these He also justified; and whom He justified, ..."

Music started playing in her head now. It was Jerod's old Justin Timberlake CD, *Justified.* There were a few songs on it that she had heard that she thought weren't too bad, but that obviously wasn't helping anything right at this moment.

"...and whom He justified, these He also glorified. What then shall we say to these things? If God *is* for us, who *is* against us?"

That stopped her. She read the last verse again. This was another one of these oft-quoted verses; however, this one she never got tired of hearing. It almost sung to her like a beautiful song lyric or line of a poem. She sat back against her chair and took a healthy drink of her coffee. It had cooled slightly so she was now able to do more than merely sip it. Glancing over, she could see that the twins were just fine. She would be feeding them again soon; however, so there was little time left for her to find any comfort or direction or sense of purpose in God's word this morning.

She started to pull away from the moment, to close her Bible and push her chair in and so on and so forth, but took one last look at the pages before her. This time, rather than continuing down the page at what she had been reading to no avail, she changed direction. There, two verses before where she had begun, something stopped her. And the light bulb came on. Finally.

It was one medium-sized word that did it: groanings.

It was a funny sounding word when taken alone. But when one read it in context, especially *this* context, it was extraordinary. Barbara followed this context back a while until she found the apparent beginning of the thought.

"For in hope we have been saved, but hope that is seen is not hope; for why does one also hope for what he sees? But if we hope for what we do not see, with perseverance we wait eagerly for it. And in the same

119

way the Spirit also helps our weakness; for we do not know how to pray as we should, but the Spirit Himself intercedes for us with groanings too deep for words..."

The thought continued over to the next verse, and it was good and important and all of that; however, that word was continuing to haunt her in a pleasing way.

Groanings.

What a thought? she contemplated. *To think that the Holy Spirit helped us, spoke to us, not with words, which we, in our weakness, often have no words to communicate what troubles us, what hurts us, what causes sorrow. Deep within our innermost being, the hurt or sorrow speaks to God, without the flood of our words!*

Just then she began to hear the first whimpering of two babies feeling abandoned. Barbara came out of her fog and smiled as the thought occurred to her that her children could speak with groanings too deep for words as well, and she was quite pleased that *she* could hear them and meet their needs just like the Lord.

Feeling much better about herself and Michael as well, she got up from her chair and pushed it back under the table. Perhaps her husband and she had not had the closest week together thus far. Perhaps they had skipped a few too many church Sundays. Perhaps Michael was spending every waking and even un-waking moment thinking not of God but about some murderer that had been loosed in their once-quaint and little town. However, the Lord God and His Holy Spirit knew well of their weaknesses and could turn around everything that was meant to be hurtful and destroying in their lives and make it beautiful.

The twins were growing restless. By the look of them, they had been doing so for quite a little while, although they were yet to cry. She allowed that last thought to float away like a startled butterfly from a beautiful flower garden as she went to them.

3:21 p.m.

"Hi, Mom!" Jerod announced as he opened the front door after school and rushed down the hallway toward the bathroom.

"Hello, sweetie," she smiled, watching his usual routine with affection.

Kids! He'd rather risk losing it on his way home from school than waste precious time using the restrooms on the campus, she thought.

When her son had completed his business, he retraced his steps down the hall in a completely different state of mind. Quiet and calm now, he casually walked into the space between the kitchen and the dining room.

"Hey, Mom," he began as he joined his baby brother and sister on a blanket on the floor. They looked up at their older brother and, visibly delighted, began to dance about, waving their hands and kicking their feet. "Are we going to Wednesday night Bible classes tonight?" Jerod smiled back at them and began to randomly grab their hands and feet, giving everything a quick little shake.

Barbara frowned. She had not given it any thought. She considered it during that moment between his asking and her answering, while glancing at the twins. After all, at their age, they pretty much dictated every decision, both minor as well as major. She had taken them many times before, and it had been rare that they did so poorly that they became a distraction. However, her thoughts turned to Michael. She wondered what time he would be home tonight. Would he have eaten anything? She wondered whether she ought to dutifully stay home in case he might need something, doubtful as it was.

"No, dear," she finally answered. "I'd better stay home just in case your dad needs me."

"Do you think that I could go, Mom?" he asked. "Neal Jensen's mom can pick me up."

"Have you discussed this with Neal's mom, already?" she asked with a grin as she quickly turned back to her dinner preparations.

She was making a small stew tonight. She had had a craving for potatoes and carrots so badly this afternoon she almost thought she was pregnant again. *Luckily for me, Doctor Bentley's already took care of that possibility. And it wasn't like Michael didn't enjoy his three days off. He couldn't walk, but it hadn't been the end of the world.* She turned because she did not want him to see her amused look. Sometimes it cracked her up how her son operated things whenever he wanted something. It was absolutely true what Mrs. Elms from the school had told her concerning Jerod. He *was* a good boy. He was just good in *other ways* as well, like conniving.

"Yeah. When she was picking up Neal after school she told me that she could come and get me if you couldn't go to church tonight."

"That was nice of her."

"Actually, she asked me to tell you that I could spend the night since it would be late before we got home and she could take us to school in the morning."

Barbara put down the last of the potatoes that she had been peeling and tossed the peels into the trash. She turned back around to face her son. She had already decided that he could go, and spend the night over at his friend's house as well. He had the grades. She never had to fight him over doing his homework. He was always helping out around the house, even volunteering to do jobs that were sometimes unpleasant, like diaper detail, although not that often. However, she couldn't just let him off that easy, could she?

"Gee, Jerod," she began. "I don't think that would be a very good idea...unless I get the biggest hug ever!"

She was sure that Jerod had been preparing himself all along his way home from school today for a "no". Therefore, he simply stared back at her while her words seeped into his head. When they did, he leapt to his feet and ran after her as if he might actually tackle her. Luckily for her, she had the kitchen counter to brace herself against.

"Thanks, Mom," Jerod said, throwing his growing arms around her and giving her the big squeeze that she had been counting on. Barbara laughed heartily and happily hugged her son right back.

What a wonderful boy, she thought. *May the twins be just as good.*

6:00 p.m.

Barbara watched as Leslie Jenson's black Chevy Tahoe quietly drove off. From her position at the end of the walkway near the driveway, she could see their two boys smiling and giggling about something already in the back seat. The Lord knew what silly thing it was, but the sight warmed her heart as she turned around and walked back inside the house. The phone began to ring. She found herself feeling a bit of melancholy at the realization that she wouldn't have Jerod to keep her company tonight. However, he was getting older, she considered as she picked up her pace. The dinners and evenings shared between parents and their children were, after all, a finite number.

Soon he'll be going to proms, graduating, going to college and then getting married. Oh, God! Grandchildren! I'm too young to be a Grandma!

Sighing, Barbara closed the door behind her and quickly turned the lock. She glanced at the twins as she reached for the wireless phone. They were lying quietly in the little used playpen, still doing fine with the few moments alone that they'd had while she had seen their brother off.

"Hello," Barbara said without first glancing at the phone identification display. Her thoughts were still elsewhere.

"Hi, Barbara," the familiar voice on the other end greeted her. It was Jennifer Mitchell. "How are you?"

"I'm good, Jen. Thanks. How 'bout you?" The two of them had met one Sunday morning in church when their families had sat together. Both the Lopez' and the Mitchell's had arrived late just as the worship music had begun, forcing them to quickly jump into the last remaining pew at the back of the sanctuary. It had turned out to be rather fateful. The two women began a friendship that morning that had lasted four years and counting.

"I'm fine. I've just been thinking about you. How's Mike?"

"Well, as you can well imagine, he's hardly been home."

"I bet."

"I couldn't tell you anything about the case, of course, but mostly because I don't know anything."

Barbara moved over to the couch that sat directly before the playpen. She waved at the twins with her free left hand.

"Well," her friend continued. "I certainly didn't call for gossip. I was really just curious whether you might be making it to church tonight."

"No," Barbara quickly replied. "I was thinking about it, but I think I'd better stay home in case Michael needs anything. I don't know what time he might be home, but I plan on being here when he does."

"It sounds quiet over there. Where are the kids?"

"The twins are right here in the playpen..."

"The playpen? You?" Laughter followed. It was an old joke.

124

"Now you sound like Michael," Barbara giggled, too. Michael always complained that he would survive high speed pursuits and fantastic gun play which Kingsburg, thankfully never had, only to be killed by tripping over some infant. The heart of the complaining and endless whining had very little to do, however, with the kids on the floor, but rather the fuchsia playpen that Barbara just had to have back when they first found out that they were pregnant. Michael had fought her on the initial purchase to no avail, and a year or so later when she simply rarely used it, he complained all the more.

"I know. I know." Jennifer laughed heartily. "I remember when Jason and I were there that night for dinner and Jason set Michael off when he asked why you didn't seem to be using it."

The two friends spent twenty minutes on the phone together before the twins began to get hungry and, therefore, fussy. They parted with promises of getting together once the town crisis had been concluded. The mutual hope was that it would be sooner rather than later.

8:10 p.m.

Barbara yawned as she read the last line of the page and then reached up unconsciously to turn to the next one.

"But he was all that she had been able to think about all day. And now, there stood the stranger: tall, dark and laden with muscle. Though the strong breeze whipped her long crepe skirt into a frenzy about her long, milky-white legs, she didn't notice. The young princess was unable to take her eyes off of him. He was a golden god. She could see his heart beating within his strong bare chest even though he was quite a distance from her. Suddenly, he looked up and grabbed her with his eyes. It felt as if he were reaching out with his gentle

hand and caressing her. She quivered, making her drop the basket and the flowers she had picked. His lips moved. Was he speaking? she wondered. Was he blowing her a kiss perhaps? She could only dare hope."

Barbara lowered the book onto her lap with a sigh in spite of the heat of the seduction. *What the hell am I doing reading this drivel?* she thought to herself. She thought of Pat Conroy's *Beach Music*. That's what she really wanted to read, but she'd read it five times, and once this year already. With another sigh, she slammed the romance novel closed and tossed it onto the other side of the couch.

Just then, a sound traveled down the hall.

She turned her head and waited. Looking over her right shoulder, her eyes stared at one spot on the wall which stood between her and the nursery, as if they might penetrate the paint and drywall and insulation and see what might have made the noise. She furrowed her brow. Her ears probed the quiet night for the identity of the disturbance.

Nothing.

Barbara did not want to get up. It was getting late, and she had already logged in a full day. Jerod was away, Michael was still not home and the twins were asleep; why did she need to get up? The only reason to get up now was to turn out lights, double-check locked doors and climb into bed. That was all.

And yet there she was lifting herself off of the couch and heading down the hall for a bed check. She straightened her simple white T-shirt upon standing up. The bottom of her pink pajama bottoms fluttered over the thick beige carpet and her bare feet as she headed for the nursery. When she reached the door which was only half closed, she quietly pushed it back open. The cool breeze hit her with a start, giving her gooseflesh.

The nursery window was standing wide open.
Dear God!

The room was dark except where the street lamp from the next street over shone against the open space and the fluttering curtains. She bolted unthinking for the nearest crib—Robbie's. Barbara clutched the sides of the crib and peered down into it. In the civil twilight she could barely see him, but enough of him to know that he was fine. She touched his tiny pink face. He was warm and still asleep. *Good!* she thought. She quickly turned and went to check on her daughter. She was equally asleep. The only one concerned in the least about the open window was their mother. She put her hands to her breast, trying to force herself to calm back down.

Barbara turned her attention toward the open window, the curtains still dancing there.

The window must have come open, she thought while she walked over to it, as incredulous a possibility as it was. *But how?*

The thin curtains began to beat against her face when Barbara reached out to close the window, as if they could somehow know of her intent and were trying to prevent it. Nimble, delicate fingers stretched outward and took hold of each side of the sliding window. As she did so, she thought of how she had never known a fear like she just felt when she first saw the open window. There were stories in the newspaper all of the time concerning child abductions, and for one very terrible moment she had considered her twins might be the next to grace those headlines. But now it was over.

She just noticed the missing window screen.

Barbara stopped in mid-maneuver and was struck dumbfounded for a brief second. Everything suddenly moved in slow-motion. She almost asked herself the question: "*Why did I stop?*"

Her right wrist suddenly hurt. She followed the discomfort signal back to the nerve ending which had sent it. A hand closed over her wrist, and now on the other one as well. The realization brought her back to her senses. Someone came through her window. She

127

looked up. There was a face now, adorned by long flowing black hair that the wind was playing with. There was a twisted confident grin and piercing, penetrating eyes. It was a terrible face.

She screamed.

The infants awoke with a start and immediately began to cry. Strangely, Barbara did not hear them.

Her hands went numb under the pressure of the vise-grips which held her fast. Interestingly, she somehow noted, they were bitingly cold.

Wave after wave of chills raced along Barbara's spine as the twins' tiny vocal chords sounded louder and louder. But presently the object of her concern was climbing through the open space between outside and in.

She screamed again.

The owner of the hands laughed heartily and continued to hold her as he pulled himself through the window and straightened up. She marveled momentarily at his height.

Barbara's eyes stretched wide at the sight; the long flowing dark hair, the leather coat, the heavy riding boots.

She immediately recognized that this was the same figure that she had seen the night before when she had visited Tiffany.

"Madam," he said to her. "Your children seem to be crying!"

That was when she finally heard them.

Barbara shuffled backwards with the thought of someone hurting her babies, all along trying to free herself from his grip. Her feet tangled as she attempted to jerk herself free and she lost her balance. The man still did not let go of her.

"A pity!"

"Who are you?" She tried to gain some composure by speaking to her attacker as she got back to her feet.

Then, she continued to attempt to shake free of his grip, but could not. "What do you want?"

"So many questions!" He laughed.

As he spoke, Barbara took the opportunity to try once more to free herself with one last violent shake of her arm. "*Let me go!*"

"As you wish."

Barbara suddenly became free and fell down. She let out a cry as the momentum snapped her head back when she hit the floor, biting her lip.

"There!" he laughed, resting his hands at his sides above her. "You are welcome."

Barbara did not care about the intruder's sarcasm, nor did she wait to see if the pain in her throbbing head would subside. Not her, not a policeman's wife. Instead, without as much as a thought otherwise, she pushed herself to her feet and toward her crying children.

"Well!" came that dreaded voice from a heartbeat behind her. "*What precious little throats they have!*"

This time she heard everything loud and clear. Alarms went off inside her head, making the pain a hundred times worse than before. There was no time to escape with her children. Instead, she spun to attack.

The man had her before she could scream. Those cold, claw-like fingers had her arms at the flesh just above her elbows and were pinning them to her body. She tried to let loose a cry but could not. The pain this time made her bite harder into her lower lip. She tasted the copper taste of her blood. He lifted her off of her bare feet with little effort and then brought her close. Suddenly, green eyes which seemed black as pitch to her in the dark, widened and focused immediately upon the trickle of blood upon her lips.

He pulled his face back in a terrible smile, exposing ivory white fangs. The sight made her shiver and she finally was able to let out a cry.

"Careful," he whispered tenderly. "You'll spill it."

He did not seem to notice her revulsion as he pulled her closer still. Instead, he seemed to be mesmerized by that crimson red upon her lips. He brought them down to him and licked them clean with a slow sweep of his rough tongue.

The tongue was cold, too, and it was at that moment when she realized that her attacker was no man. Just what he was, she could not yet fathom.

The last thing Barbara Lopez heard before she blacked out was the terrible sound of her babies' crying. Tears streamed down her cheeks as her throat squeezed tightly shut and her heart bounded within her chest as the walls of the black void burst open and swallowed her. She attempted to fight it briefly, struggling, squirming, stretching, and reaching beyond her frail capabilities to grab onto something, anything, just as long as she wasn't taken away from her babies. Yet, there was nothing to anchor her there in the nursery… in the world.

To her ears, the twins suddenly stopped screaming.

*   *   *

However, the young infants *had not* stopped their crying. In fact, their situation was now much more dire.

Perhaps the tiny girl could sense the terrible evil which stood over her crib, perhaps not. However, as Vincent leaned closer to get a better look, she began to wail and wriggle much stronger than before. Unfortunately for the little girl, Mommy wasn't listening, nor could she do the littlest thing about it.

The vampire reached into the crib and retrieved the frightened young infant. Had she been a fish, he would have lost her as the baby tried to get away from the form that she somehow knew was most definitely not family, and certainly not Mommy. He held the child high above his head. Behind his purple lips, gleaming fangs hungrily protruded from the corner of his mouth. Slowly, confidently, they pierced the air between them on their way toward the baby's warm, vibrating little throat.

The vampire has heightened senses: taste, smell, touch, sight and hearing. All five are far more highly tuned to his world around him than that of his victims. He has better vision than that of a hungry eagle in search of a morsel from high above the forest. He can smell the presence of human beings faster than the deer can smell a mediocre hunter. Not only can the vampire hear a pin drop, but he can recognize the disturbance in the molecules as the pin slices its way through the air toward the ground. In fact, just *one* of these senses makes it impossible for the vampire to be taken by surprise.

Except by another vampire.

Therefore, when Nathaniel suddenly came out of nowhere and swept the baby from his hands, knocking him into the far wall in the same motion; he actually let out a cry of surprise.

Nathaniel replaced the baby in her crib and with but a touch quickly pushed the piece of furniture safely behind him.

"Nicely done, Nathaniel. I wondered when you might show yourself," he added quietly, stepping away from the wall and running both of his hands through his long hair in order to get it out of his face. "Cliché, I know, but I taught you very well, indeed."

"You taught me only to hate. And I hate you very much."

Vincent sighed, and then took a threatening step forward.

"Remain where you are, Vincent!" Nathaniel commanded. "These are under my charge."

"Oh, but Nathaniel, surely you don't think me gluttonous. I will gladly share them with you."

Nathaniel made no effort to respond.

"Ah, but that is right," he quickly interjected. "You don't *feed* on human blood, do you, Nathaniel? Such a pity. Cats and vermin!" he said with a dramatic shudder. "It makes you considerably weaker than I, you realize. In that instance, I guess I will have both!"

"No!" Nathaniel stood his ground.

"I will not be *ordered* around, Nathaniel," Vincent said firmly, taking another step forward.

Nathaniel said nothing and made no effort to withdraw.

Two telephones began to ring in other rooms. No one acknowledged the ringing.

Vincent stopped. "Ah, you mean to challenge me. I adore challenges. It has been a challenge, my finding you. It has been a challenge following a cold trail across the globe." Vincent stepped closer. "And now that I have you…" He stared his adversary down, menacingly. A moment later he reached out delicately with his left hand and lovingly moved a stray hair out of Nathaniel's face. He whispered: "And I do have you, Nathaniel." He lowered his hand back to his side and changed his expression again, this time to a look of intimidation. Then, he shook it off again.

"Just go, Vincent," Nathaniel said, placing his hands on the back of the little baby's crib. In the background, the phones continued to ring. "It is still early. I trust you have more than enough time to acquire for yourself another meal."

Vincent sighed again and smiled, turning his attention back to the nearest baby. They were each still screaming their lungs out, red-faced panic on their tiny faces. Something in that scene coerced a giggle out of him.

"So lovely!"

He reached down into the nearest crib and gently and tenderly caressed the skin of the baby boy's throat with his ugly discolored fingernail. The infant recoiled at the touch and did his best to move away.

"So warm!"

Vincent pulled the hand away from the baby and then, glancing dramatically into Nathaniel's eyes, stuck the caressing finger into his mouth and licked the scent from it. Down the hall in the kitchen, Barbara's voice could be heard as the answering machine engaged.

"No more games, Vincent."

Vincent turned his gaze back upon Nathaniel, his face devoid of expression. He appeared neither pleased nor angered. "It is so good to hear you speak my name again after all of these years."

"It has been much longer than years." There was a pregnant pause where Vincent's name should have followed, but Nathaniel refused to satisfy the monster any further. "And not at all long enough."

Vincent nodded with understanding or perhaps it was acknowledgement that there was nothing more to discuss. No chance at reconciliation. "I'll not be denied so easily the next time, Nathaniel."

Nathaniel gave no response.

Vincent started to walk back towards the open window but stopped short. "I'm almost sorry that this must end, my young Nathaniel: my hunt for you. This chance meeting. Our next meeting." There was the obvious threat in those words, but he showed no hint of it on his face or in his tone. "It is good to find you, finally. I have grown so exhausted with the travelling." Vincent glanced around the tiny nursery as if he could see the Sierra Mountain Range to the near East, the Pacific Coast to the distant West. "I miss the old country. I will be returning home soon." He looked back at Nathaniel. His expression melted slightly. It was almost sweet, he knew, were it not for his black, long-dead heart. "Come back with me, my son. May this not end with the shedding of our blood that mingles inside you."

Nathaniel steadied himself. He wanted to roar back a comment, but held his tongue until he had regained some measure of composure. "I am not your son!"

"No? Are you quite certain? Consider your clothing." Vincent lifted his left hand as if meaning to reach out for the side of Nathaniel's head, but did not. "And your hair... is it not as long as mine?"

"That was your doing. I can do nothing to change it."

Vincent thought to say more, but did not. He just studied Nathaniel as if he had expected as much, but had genuinely hoped for something else. He seemed to sigh, but if so, quickly shook it off. He turned and stepped through the window. Before he departed, he turned to stare deeply at Nathaniel a moment longer. His prodigal son stared back. It had been so long since he had beheld his own reflection in the eyes of the boy. Many years he'd swam in those eyes, never to find comfort there.

Apparently the comfort was to come when those eyes no longer held any reflection.

And then he was gone. The window seemed to slam shut of its own accord.

*   *   *

Nathaniel glanced down upon the faces of the startled infants, first one and then the other. Unlike a parent who might quickly overreact, he was able to stomach the sight and sound of their panic. After a time, he looked deeply into the tiny eyes of each child and whispered: "Be still."

Soon, they both were.

He looked away from the babies' cribs, down upon the woman slumped on the floor. Half of one of her relaxed heartbeats later and he was at her side. Behind them, the phones began to ring once again.

8:28 p.m.

"One-five-four, Kingsburg."

"One-five-four, go ahead." Detective Michael Lopez answered with a yawn.

There was a pause. Michael glanced from the view of his city through his dirty windshield to his radio. "Five-four, go to channel two."

"One-five-four, go ahead," he said on the secondary channel upon obeying the instruction.

"Detective, neighbors report a disturbance at your ten-forty-two. Report the sound of babies crying for long periods of time without end. Phone calls not answered."

Barbara! "She's probably just got her hands full with the twins," he replied. He sounded calmer on the outside than he actually felt within. "Ten-four."

It was late and Michael was already on his way home from another long day of detective work where nothing had been accomplished but the wasting of valuable time in his still young life. The dispatcher's announcement that neighbors were complaining about the sound of infants crying at his house didn't bother him. In fact, he understood it completely.

Maybe the damn neighbors oughta try taking care of twins, he thought to himself. *Maybe then they'd be a little more sensitive to my wife's needs at home when the two little sirens decide to go off at the same time and she doesn't have her husband to help in the damage control.* Michael grinned at the notion but quickly shook it off. *Probably not!*

Completing a right turn, Michael accelerated up to thirty-five miles per hour. It was ten miles faster than was allowed in a residential area.

8:31 p.m.

"Peace to you," Nathaniel softly greeted the woman as she came to.

He leaned only so close to her, using the darkness of the room as a veil, as he did not wish to frighten her further, he being yet another stranger inside her home. He wanted only to comfort her. The ploy seemed to work, under the circumstances.

She recoiled, pushing herself away from him, sliding back along the carpet. Nathaniel made no effort to follow.

"Who are you?" she demanded to know. She was still much too groggy, and not in any shape whatsoever to be making demands. They both knew it. She closed her eyes suddenly and winced. She brought a hand up to her head.

"Oh," she grimaced in agony as a sharp pain seemed to take hold of her.

"I happened to be near when I heard your screaming," he began with a tender voice. "So I..."

"Oh, my God! My babies!" She made a futile attempt to get to her feet.

"Take care!" he said, suddenly out of the darkness and upon her. He took her by the shoulders and pushed her gently back where she lay, careful not to touch her bare skin. "Your children are fine. Nothing at all has happened to them."

"Swear it!" Barbara surprised him by suddenly demanding.

Nathaniel surprised himself by answering.

"I swear it." He uttered the words without thinking about them first.

In the silence that followed, he found himself contemplating how strange it had been to act in such a way. He wondered why he was still present in the woman's house. Why had he not left?

136

"Where are they?" she asked, a bit calmer. Nathaniel could feel the woman's muscles beginning to loosen below his fingers.

"They are safe in their beds, and sleeping."

"Sleeping?" she asked, incredulously. "How could they be sleeping?" She started to tense a bit. "Just how long have I been out?"

"Not very long. I do not know the exact time, however."

"What happened to the...the man who attacked me?" She winced again, but seemed to become more lucid.

"I frightened..." *The beast,* he caught himself about to say. There was no need to go into *that* with the woman. Not after she was beginning to regain her senses. "I frightened him away just after he had gained entry."

The woman attempted once again to sit up. She paid dearly for it.

"Ow," she cried out.

"You are in no condition to stand," Nathaniel told her. "Please, relax."

Nathaniel took his hands away from her now. As he did so, he found himself pleased. She seemed to take no notice of his releasing her, just as she had apparently not realized how long he had been holding her down when she had attempted to stand. Could it be that he'd gained her trust in so short a time without even trying to do so?

He watched her for a moment. He was sure she was unable to see much more than his outline, not that she was even attempting to discern it. Her eyes were closed while she dealt with her circumstance. The woman was quite lovely, he determined. This, of course, was not the most optimal time for judging physical beauty. She was disheveled in appearance, both in hair and dress. Her eyes were red and puffy from crying. He detected a trace of blood upon her lower lip, and menstrual bleeding as well, although very faint. Her last day, he surmised.

Yet, Nathaniel could see the woman that she was, beyond this terrible trial. He found himself strangely pleased that he had been able to stop Vincent from shedding blood (at least in this house). Not that Vincent would go to his vile rest tonight on an empty stomach, but he would acquire no blood here. Whether he had desired to kill them all or to simply destroy the mother's life forever, he was certainly capable of anything. It was a fact that Nathaniel knew all too well, and wished not to think about. He had a great many instances or horrors and degradations safely locked away in the vault that was memory. A vault that recently began to show cracks.

"I must go," he said softly. A part of him wondered whether she had heard at all. *Had she fallen unconscious again?* No, there was movement, however slight. Though her eyes remained closed, he continued. "If you must, I will gladly present your babies to you. I assure you, however, that they are well, so you may wish to reconsider." Barbara could only moan by way of acknowledgement.

"It is settled then."

Slowly, careful not to touch her exposed flesh, Nathaniel leaned close and swept the woman off of the carpeted floor. In no shape to either argue or attempt to fight him off, she could only interrogate him with the meekest of voices. "Where are you taking me?"

"Momentarily, you shall find yourself in your bed."

No sooner spoken and it was so. He softly set her down upon it and turned to go.

"Wait," she whispered after him, as if sensing that she was suddenly alone.

Her eyes fluttered open. He caught her grimace because it seemed even that slight movement hurt.

"I'm Barbara. Who are you?"

"Please, rest," he said from the darkness of the entryway.

He could have said nothing. He should have said nothing. He could have ignored the woman and simply vanished from her life and the lives of her family forever. Before he could contemplate anything, Nathaniel found himself shuffling back to her.

Conflicting feelings began to emerge. It felt like ghosts—things about him that had long since died and were thought forgotten. He could still turn now and be away from here; away from this house, from this meager room, this woman, this…

However, something was delaying him from doing so. Whatever it was, it was very strong. Was this some feeling of servitude? He knew of customs in the world where the individuals rescued from death or crisis who felt indebted to their rescuer spent their entire existence repaying the life gained. Why then did he feel some perverted twist upon the old tradition? Why did the rescuer suddenly feel as if he had to dedicate himself to serve the rescued?

He found his feet and started to leave. For good this time, although even then he knew he would be back.

"Wait," Barbara called out to him. There was returning strength there, but it would not endure. "My husband will want to meet you."

"I cannot," Nathaniel quietly responded.

"He'll want to thank you," she continued as if she hadn't heard his reply. "*I* want to thank you."

"You already have." He cocked one ear. Someone was approaching the front of the house with rushed footfalls. What had taken place tonight had aroused interest, of course. In any event, it was finally time for him to leave.

"I am Nathaniel. I cannot stay. Please, tell no one of what has transpired here tonight."

"What?" Barbara questioned. "How can I keep this a secret? Why would I want to do that?"

"Please," he began, but said nothing else. Too much had been said already; too much had been done.

*   *   *

Though things no longer hurt as they had, everything still ached, so it was that she found herself succumbing to sleep. The comfortable bed and soft pillows began to swallow her whole. Nathaniel's words continued to resonate within her and it was the last thing that she clung to when sleep came to curry her away.

*   *   *

When Michael got inside, he found a dark and quiet house, but everything was in order. His family was already fast asleep, so he knew that it couldn't have been much of a disturbance. Rebekah's crib had been moved from its usual place, but that was all.

Frigging neighbors! I don't have time for this!

However, after he had undressed and walked back to the kitchen for a drink of water, something caused Michael to give the house a good thorough check before he went to bed. He found nothing disturbed; nothing out of the ordinary. All the doors and windows were firmly locked and his wife and children were deeply asleep.

Why couldn't he?

11:33 p.m.

The figure moved slowly and laboriously eastward along West Kern Street, his old shoes doing more shuffling than actual stepping. The man was warmly dressed in several layers of clothing. None of the pieces matched, however, and none were less than ten years old. The brand new Ronald Reagan Elementary School cast a huge shadow over his left shoulder.

"Come here, Beauty," the elderly Hispanic man called out.

The once commanding voice of the former Korean War Veteran bounced weakly off the walls and came crawling back to him, unlike the tiny Chihuahua that had last been seen some seven years before.

"Come here, Beauty."

"Did you lose something?" a voice behind him asked suddenly.

There had been a time when nothing and no one would have been able to catch the Master Sergeant off guard, but everything comes to an end one day. Or night.

The man stopped, which was not the easiest thing for him to accomplish, nor very wise. Once he got stopped, it was often difficult for him to get started again. He turned, which was equally difficult.

"My Beauty," he said simply.

"I am very sorry to hear that, sir. May I offer a hand?"

"I don't know," the man tried to explain, finding himself staring at the strange looking man with long flowing hair. He hated to see such hair on males. Back in the day he might have immediately grabbed the man and shaved him himself. "I woke up and found her missing. I love that damn dog, but you can see how she treats me. It's the middle of the night, practically, and here I am traipsing all over town to collect her."

He was trying very hard to keep everything together, but ultimately losing the battle. He continued to stare away, trying to decide what manner of man this was before him, but said nothing further.

"Well, sir," the other man began. "I do not know whether you have heard or not, but the town is not

141

exactly safe these days to be wandering about. I understand that you miss your Beauty, but we really should get you home."

The old man saw the logic in this, although he wasn't entirely sure what he was being told about the safety of the town. He glanced to the West and then toward the East, uncertain how to get home.

"You *do* remember the way?"

He paused, prideful, his chin high. "I sometimes get confused, I'm afraid."

He looked down at his feet and absently scratched his head with his right hand.

"Do not trouble yourself about that, sir. The strong will not help you remember."

The stranger put his hand upon his shoulder, turning him back the way that he had come. He reluctantly allowed himself to be led.

"I appreciate your help," he said to the strange fellow.

"Not at all."

"My name is Benjamin Molina. My friends call me Benji."

"I am very happy to be making your acquaintance."

"Who are you?" the elderly man asked.

The stranger laughed, lightly patting his old and tired back. "Would you believe, a friend?"

11:51 p.m.

The man his friends called "Big John Lancaster" knocked back the remaining quarter of his Budweiser tall boy in two large gulps and then hastily set the empty can on the TV tray to his left. With a low grunt, he pushed himself out of the dingy brown Lazy-Boy leather recliner. He stomped into the kitchen without turning on any lights. The lighting was being provided by his absolute favorite DVD in the entire world: *Apocalypse Now Redux.*

It was difficult to tell whether Vittorio Storaro's famous cinematography was creating shadows or merely chasing others away along the bare walls and uncovered sliding glass door. The haunting first few notes of the Doors song, "The End", were now filling the house, causing mental shadows as well. He yanked open the refrigerator and grabbed another tall can of Bud. It would be his fourth of the night. Thanks to the newer and longer version of the film, Big John had time for another beer.

As he closed the once white refrigerator door with his left foot and headed back for his chair, crossing in front of the slider, he heard the unmistakable sound of his aluminum trash can as it was being knocked over.

"Damn coyotes!" he cursed, as the sound of the can being dragged along the makeshift gravel driveway grated on his last nerve. He angrily shoved a two day old empty pizza box from the cluttered dining room table so that he could clear a spot to set down his beer. The box was empty. It flew off of the table easily and fell onto the short carpeted floor below, sprinkling pizza crumbs about. He made a mental note to borrow the old lady Johnson's vacuum again when he noticed the mess he'd just made. All he really cared about right now was to find a safe place to set down his beer so that he could go hunting for the animal responsible for interrupting his movie. If Francis Ford Coppola and his editor, Walter Murch, were going to endeavor to perfect perfection, then by God, no one was going to bother him until the credits were rolling. Perhaps not even then. Marty Sheen had even suffered a heart attack, for Pete's sake!

Big John did not stop to see whether he could glean anything about how many of the hungry devils he might be about to surprise. The city might be directly across the street now with the near completion of the new elementary school, but there was nothing behind him. He had seen coyotes many times and could hear their yelping nearly every day. Instead, Big John just unlocked the slider with a quick flick of his meaty fingers and yanked open the door, stomping his way like the tank that he was to the back of the driveway where he kept his three cans: recycling, green waste and trash.

While walking through his dining room, Big John had the Doors in the left speaker and coyotes at his trash in the right speaker. Now, half way through the yard, there was little or no sound at all.

"Damn!" he muttered under his large breaths as he slowed his assault and ultimately stopped.

Isn't that always the way?

He had pictured himself so vividly sneaking up on the animal before it knew what hit him that he had already scared it away. Even now he could hear the sound of his boot making contact with the can, and the coyote's yelp of surprise as he launched the both of them into the night. It would almost have made missing his favorite all-time movie somehow worth it, not that he could actually kick anything that far anymore or even sneak up on anything, as big as he had become.

In any event there would be no action here tonight; he was missing the end of the movie and the beer was getting warm. Whatever mess there might be would still be there in the afternoon, Big John surmised, so he turned and headed for home.

While he waited, the can started moving again.

Big John spun. *What luck? Maybe there was some action to be had after all.*

"Here I come, boy!" Big John whispered quietly under his breath as he resumed his attack.

As silently and as quickly as he could, he crossed the remainder of the yard to the spot where he parked his cans. It seemed to take longer than usual in the dim moonless light, but eventually he came to the spot where the animal would be feasting on his garbage.

Nothing.

The can in question was there, to be sure, knocked on its side with half its contents spilled out for him to clean. However, the perpetrator of the crime had vanished.

"Damn!"

Big John took one last desperate look around, his only thrill of the day gone, and headed back for that Budweiser. *A good thing, too,* he thought. *That little buzz is almost gone!*

Behind him there was an audible pop as the electricity went out.

Big John started at the sound of it. He stared in quiet disbelief while the realization seeped in. *Damn!*

He suddenly thought about the old widow Johnson, knowing how worried the least bit of nothing always made her feel. He glanced her way. Her house was east of his which was just a little further than a stone's throw to his right now as he faced the back of his house. Her motion detector light at the rear of her house caught his attention immediately. Its light seemed to shine only for him, almost winking just like the girls in his life used to about a hundred twenty pounds ago.

While his inebriated mind attempted to get the realization out to him, he glanced back toward his house and beyond. Across what—until a couple of years before—had been Magnolia Avenue and now West Kern Street; what had been orchards years before that and now busy neighborhood houses and the new Reagan Elementary School... they were now winking at him, too. Lights were everywhere about him, twinkling, winking, making fun of him since his was the only power that had gone out.

Damn!

Carefully, he made his way across the yard toward the house. There was no way that he was going to be able to do anything now without a flashlight to see where he was going. He knew how poorly he kept the property cleaned up. All he needed to do was trip over something, full of beer as he was, and break his neck in the dark. *What a pretty picture that would make!*

His eyes unable to muster the necessary skill of helping him to see in the dark, he was forced to do relatively without. Moving slower than usual, his hands outstretched in case he did fall or bump into something, he finally found the open sliding glass door. Carefully, he stepped inside, his throat heavily anticipating that next swallow that would have to wait a bit longer.

He stood between his kitchen and dining area, now wondering where he might locate that flashlight. He knew that he owned three. In fact. They were all black Mag-lite flashlights, the best in the industry. The problem, however, was trying to remember where in the hell one of them might be right now.

Big John made his way across the kitchen floor safely enough. There was nothing left there to give him trouble, but that was the easy part. It was the living room and subsequent hallway where the trouble awaited with its abandoned clothes baskets, alternatively piled high with both clean and dirty clothes. Then there was the occasional box of this and stack of that: Fresno Bee newspapers; vinyl albums that he no longer had the technology to play them on; Field and Stream; Guns and Ammo; and Playboy Magazines to name a few. All of the subscriptions had long since expired. Even the Playboys were ten years old or more.

Before attempting to navigate further, he reached out for the nearest wall. This wall would lead him to the hall and the closet there that would likely reward him with a flashlight should he make it there without killing himself. Although he could not yet see, he began to picture the possible obstacles in his way. He was delighted to recall that once he got to the hallway, he would be relatively safe. Indeed, once he moved beyond the living room and could feel both walls of the hallway he found the closet very quickly. He opened it and his right hand immediately stretched out and knocked over a Mag-lite. He grabbed it, found the button and it sprung to life.

He closed the closet door and headed back the way he had come. Relieved that he could now see, it dawned on him that whatever buzz he had had was now long gone. He would have to start again. Considering that he was on vacation from his forklift this week and had no obligations other than to his stomach and his bowels, he quickly set off to fix the problem so that he could quickly get that good buzz that he had anticipated when he popped that first can. He shined the light ahead of him and started moving. He didn't stop until he got into the living room and noticed a tall shape standing before him.

The realization threw him.

He directed the light at the intruder. Standing before him was a very tall, well-defined figure of a man who appeared to be even more frightened than he was. The man was shivering as if he had just stepped outside with wet clothes on. However, the man was dressed very warmly indeed. His face and head couldn't be cold, he noted, on account of all of the hair. In his right hand he had a firm grip upon something, but Big John hadn't seen it yet.

"What the hell are you doing in my house?" Big John asked, regaining his composure. There was not much that could scare a man of John's size, but it wasn't every day that one found an intruder in one's home.

"Please...please help me!" the intruder said, his left hand extended before him, quivering. "I need your help! I can't seem to fight it any longer!"

"Fight what any longer?" Big John asked. "How'd you get in my house?"

Big John wasn't afraid of too many men, nor had he ever backed down from a confrontation; however, something about this one, this particular night, made him uneasy. In the poor light, he could see that the front of the intruder's clothes was wet. He appeared as if he had just run through some sprinklers on his way over.

"Look, I don't want any trouble!"

The intruder stepped toward him. It was a very loud sound, but Big John was still oblivious.

"I can't do it any longer. Rats and dogs and cats. I need..."

"What?" Big John stepped back with each one of the intruder's steps forward. "What do you need?"

"I need blood. Human blood. *Your blood!*" The man lunged for Big John and caught him by his flannel shirt. Big John dropped his light. In doing so, the body of Mr. Benjamin Molina was highlighted in its brilliance. The eyes held open in frozen terror; the mouth in a perpetual grimace; the throat torn open, revealing the mechanisms for both breathing and the swallowing of food and drink. The sight of the wound was surreal due to the lack of blood. To Big John it almost appeared as if it was normal; as if the poor man had been born with a second mouth.

Big John stepped clumsily backwards, desperately attempting to shake free of the intruder's grip.

"You don't understand," the intruder cried, finally releasing the body at his feet. And then, using both hands, he forced Big John easily against the east living room wall.

"Help!" Big John screamed out like he never had screamed before. "You... you're the one they're looking for. The one who was leaving bodies piled up all over Kingsburg.

"Help!"

The vampire gripped the large man, spun and threw him against the south living room wall, sending a bunch of cans and kitchen items rattling on the other side of the wall. He let out a cry of agony as all of the air seemed to go out of him and something snapped within his chest. It was bone; one of his ribs. Big John had broken a rib once before in an automobile accident, so he knew what it felt like. It was excruciating.

However, as he looked up from the floor where he landed, and saw his attacker coming back for more - and quite possibly far worse that just another broken rib, by the look in its eye - he was forced to ignore the pain and fight for his life.

Big John climbed to his feet, gritting his teeth hard to swallow the pain and put his hands out just in time to stop the vampire from grabbing him again. Tears welled up in his eyes as he tried to speak. "Please, don't hurt me." He could barely get the words out. "I can help you!"

The vampire let go of the man and backed off. Turning away, he whispered, "How can you help me? I am beyond help. I can only do what must be done to survive. It is not my fault. I am forced to do this because of Vincent!"

"Vincent?" the big man said, repeating the name.

"Yes. It is he who has forced my hand." The vampire looked back to the man before him. "I apologize, but there is nothing that you can do for me." He started for him again.

"Wait!" Big John threw up his hands and took a step back. "Whatever you're thinking, don't!"

"Oh, but I must," he said, and then he was upon him. "Nathaniel must drink!"

"Who's Nathaniel?"

Big john tried to avoid capture. He stepped back one last time and was pushed into the wall again.

"I am!" And then the vampire bared his teeth; the ones that gripped the flesh as well as the two that drove deeply for the rich red nutrients beneath.

Big John screamed.

THURSDAY

May 8, 2008
7:08 a.m.

"Good morning, sunshine!" Michael said with a wide grin as Barbara opened her eyes. "Sleep well?"

"Yeah," she answered softly, getting her bearings. "I slept hard."

An image suddenly leapt across her mind just behind her eyes. It was the face of an intruder, and cold vise-like hands. She could hear the babies screaming. She sat up too quickly. The room started to spin.

"It's okay," he said, catching her and pushing her back to the covers. "They're already awake." The hands at her bare arms were Michael's, but the face she pictured now was another's. And then it was gone. Or was it ever there at all?

"They are?" Barbara said incredulously, holding up one hand, signaling that she was going to sit up again, but not nearly as rapidly as before. "I can't believe I didn't hear them cry." Her eyes went damp.

"That's 'cause they never did," her husband answered. "I walked into the nursery when I got dressed and the both of them were just lying there, watching me." He giggled, stood and removed some change from the end table beside them. "It was almost as if they were expecting me. I took them into the living room and set them down inside the 'pen'."

"You're kidding," she said, glancing toward the master bedroom door, heavily in thought. Never had the twins done anything quietly, much less wake up and patiently wait upon their breakfast. Barbara wrestled with the thought for a moment longer and then looked over toward the alarm clock. "Wow! Is it that late already?"

"Yes, ma'am, it is!" he laughed. "You only slept eleven hours. For a while there I thought you'd sleep forever."

"It kind of looks like I did!" she said, stretching her arms out above her head. "Are you leaving?"

"No," he said, getting off the bed and standing to give her room. "I've got time."

Barbara got out of bed slowly, recalling some notion that she might be injured. She reached over and gave her husband a hug. Why she thought she might be hurt, she could not fathom. She felt good. In fact, she felt better than good, and something else, too. Holding her husband there on the edge of the bed, a thought occurred to her. She slipped her hands underneath his sport-coat and ran her fingernails down the length of his back and the white dress shirt beneath.

"About how much time would you say we have, Detective?" Barbara purred, lightly kissing the man's neck.

"Not *that* much time!" he sighed, blowing the exhale out of his mouth as if he were in need of catching a quick breath. He stirred within his jeans as she rubbed against him one last time and reluctantly pulled herself away.

"Too bad," she sighed dramatically.

"Wait. I thought you were on your five-day vacation?"

"I *was*."

"You really know how to hurt a guy, you know that!"

"Reconsider and I'll make it up to you," she grinned, gliding softly into the master bathroom.

*   *   *

He watched her go and then glanced immediately at his watch.

It's 7:13 now, he thought, *and by the time we...ah,...let's see, it'll be around...um, nine...oh, forget it!*

Michael tore at his coat and quickly tossed it aside. A second later and his shoulder-holster and forty-five were on top of his coat in a small pile on the bedroom floor. He threw his shirt and pants on top of them.

"Sweetheart," he said loudly as he pushed open the bathroom door and stepped through. The shower had just come to life. He forced his way between the door and his wife and turned it back off. He grabbed her hand and led her back to the bed.

"But what about Robbie and Rebekah?"

"Who?" he said seriously as he pulled off his briefs and tossed them on the floor behind him.

"A quickie it is!" Barbara announced, pulling her husband into the shower with her and wrapping her arms around his neck.

*   *   *

Inside the living room, sitting in the rarely used play-pen, the twins played happily and contently with their stuffed animals and other miscellaneous toys. Both had been fed earlier by Daddy and had absolutely no thought whatsoever of needing anything more. They never even noticed that Mommy and Daddy had left them alone for the half hour that they were left unattended. When Daddy returned, on his way out, as Mommy finished drying off, Robbie and Rebekah looked up at him, smiled and then went back to the play at hand.

7:19 a.m.

Big John Lancaster awoke with a shiver. As large as he was, it had to be fairly cold for him to even notice.

During the fall while others were beginning to reach for sweaters he was still sporting one of his T-shirts. This morning, however, he noticed. Although it was 55 degrees outside, that was not the cold that he was feeling. Instead, it was the fever that had set in during the night because of the extent of his injuries.

His shaking uncontrollable, something else began to make itself known to him: foreign smells. They were familiar smells but strangely out of place. One was urine. The odor was strong in his nostrils and must have been what ultimately brought him back to consciousness. His eyes stung as they attempted to focus. He knew that it was his own because upon identifying the affect, he felt the causing wetness inside his jeans. The other odor was blood. He knew that that was his own as well, but whether the wound causing the escape of his blood was minor or major was unknown.

He found himself on the floor, staring up at the ceiling. What room he was in, he was not yet sure. He turned his head to the left and found his living room staring back at him; he turned to the right and found the dead old man and that horrible face staring back at him.

Big John rolled away from the body and immediately whimpered in excruciating pain. He froze for a moment, hoping the pain that was seemingly shooting throughout his entire body would subside. Eventually, it did just enough for him to attempt to crawl across the living room toward the entrance to the kitchen. Each movement brought with it an agonizing breath. His chest and arms screamed a furious protest. His head reeled.

Large, frankfurter fingers stretched across the space between him and the wood-paneled wall that loomed before him, desperately out of reach. It almost appeared to take a step away from him with each of his pathetic centimeter advances. He closed his eyes as another contraction of pain suddenly swept over him like an ocean wave of cold foamy water. It was as figurative a swell as it was literal. A trickle of crimson blood rolled up and over his quivering lower lip. He pictured himself touching the wall in some psychic attempt to block out the pain and the growing desire he felt within him to simply roll over and give up his ghost.

However, there was a reason that he refused to die: he *knew* what had attacked him. The thing that had plagued the city for days, keeping it at bay in fear, had tried to kill him. By all rights, he knew he should be dead. He was tore up pretty good inside. Each push forward, each attempt to claw his way along the floor, tore him further, but he couldn't stop. He *refused* to stop; to die. He had to help the cops nail the sorry bastard before he hurt anyone else. He even knew the bastard's name. Big John Lancaster had a story to tell.

Swallowing another wave of pain, although considerably smaller from others he had felt since waking, he gritted his teeth and forced himself to push off with his legs to close the distance between him and the wall.

"AH!" he screamed, tears streaming down his fingernail-scratched face as his fingers finally made contact.

Waiting for the pain to subside, he allowed his head to fall onto the dingy floor, his body to rest on its side. After a moment, he raised his head and looked up the length of the wall. His fingers gripped it as tightly as they could; the muscles inside his partly mauled right arm, weak from the attack, screamed bloody murder through their various nerve-endings in contempt of his work.

Pull! he screamed inside his brain as the work began. He let out a long whimper as he dragged himself painfully along the floor and into the other room. The telephone was five more feet away.

He coughed painfully, spitting up blood. The thick, warm trickle poured out of his mouth and onto his cheek.

157

If I can just make it to the damn phone!

His eyes transfixed, he held the phone in sight as if he might look away from it and lose forever. He reached out for the carpet before him and pulled himself further along. 911 was all that he needed to live.

911! 911!

Big John winced in agony as another wave of pain swept over him, sending more blood flowing out of his mouth. He coughed it up, spitting it out before him where the carpet and dingy linoleum met. He ignored it, dragging himself over it, smearing it all over his front as he pulled himself along.

Just a few more pulls! Big John Lancaster thought to himself as the phone slowly approached.

8:05 a.m.

The squad room of the police department, which had been a gym in a previous life—although it did have a few large pieces of exercise equipment still left in the north-west corner—was Standing Room Only and quite the amazing sight. Red, tired eyes and yawns abounded with dispatchers and sergeants, lieutenants and cadets, community service officers and patrol officers. Various colors and badges were present as well: Reedley, Hanford, Fresno, Tulare, Visalia and Selma.

"Hello there, stranger," Detective Jackson sarcastically announced as his partner finally walked through the door. "Nice of you to join us this morning."

"Come on, Jacks," he said over his shoulder. "I'm not that late."

"Almost! Where the hell have you been?"

The faintest grin crept across Michael's face as he did his best to ignore his partner and prepare himself for the meeting that was about to take place.

Mark Jackson picked up on it immediately, as well as its meaning. "Why you dirty dog!"

Michael gave no acknowledgement of his partner's alleged discovery. He just continued to maintain his professionalism and await his chief. He was at the front of the room, conferring with members of the Fresno and Tulare County Sheriff's Department. There was a delegation of the California Highway Patrol. He recognized three of them. They were taking seats now at the front of the room, preparing to begin.

"You know I had the same offer at my house this morning, but I chose to uphold the community's trust!" Jackson leaned over and whispered.

"Alright, already!" Michael complained with an embarrassed frown. "Do you want to stand up at the podium and announce it to the group?"

"Yes, I do!"

"Alright," the chief suddenly spoke without introduction.

The room quieted down immediately. The chief didn't wait for it. There was no time for propriety with so many having been murdered in as many days.

"I don't need to tell you sitting here this morning that we have come together to tackle perhaps the most challenging case some of us may ever face. Were this San Francisco or Los Angeles, we might not even be having this conversation. This little town is under siege. We've lost three, two of which were our own."

No one interrupted while the man spoke. There were no notes passed back and forth between the men and women; there was no whispering, no leaning over in some secret communication. This was big, and there was no time for games.

"We're being joined in this by many jurisdictions. All three of the counties are being represented here today: Fresno, Tulare, and Kings. And we have members of the California Highway Patrol as well. Beginning this morning, the citizens of this town will begin to see and

159

feel such a police presence as has never been seen before. Yesterday, we had four to seven cars on the street at any one time. This afternoon, before the start of Farmers' Market at four o'clock, we'll have fourteen. Tonight, we're hoping to have twenty, and that will be around the clock."

Michael and his partner both caught sight of the Graveyard Dispatcher in the small window in the squad room door to the left. She had been filling in while the regular dispatcher, Lainie Bishop, was on leave. Rochelle Serpa peeked through the glass, wondering whether to interrupt. At forty-four, and the eldest of the dispatching group, she did not act anything but professionally while on duty. Off, she was the life of the party, holding her own with the liquor, the dirty joke, the dart or the pool cue. She knew the politics of both the police department and City Hall. She did not seem to be awed by the display of force assembled within the room before her.

Serpa held information that needed to be passed on to the chief and she meant to deliver it. So, with a look of determination and a demeanor that told all of those assembled that *I know what I'm doing and what I have is just as important as what you can do*, she quickly entered the room and walked over to her chief. She handed him the note and took a step back, awaiting possible further instructions.

The chief took the note without a word and quickly tossed it upon the podium before him. The dispatcher, wearing a wireless unit on her belt connected to a microphone at her ear, briskly walked out of the room.

"Lopez, Jackson." The chief was speaking only to them now. "This morning we answered a 911 on West Kern. A man was attacked last night. He's en route to Selma. Guerra and Alaniz need you." He sighed. "There's another body."

10:11 a.m.

Barbara laughed, making silly faces and odd noises in between doing so, as she sat on the floor of the living room with the twins. The twins found the entire scene endlessly amusing, holding frozen smiles as they studied only her, awaiting further entertainment. There were toys scattered here and there along and beyond the baby blanket where they laid, but at the moment at least they didn't seem to notice or care. The game had been ongoing since she had finished feeding the babies and set them down, fully intending to step away from them to do her Bible study for the morning. Robbie and Rebekah, however, would not allow her to leave them.

It wasn't as if they had begun throwing tantrums, sensing her desire to walk away. Rather, something about them was so intriguing this morning that she felt herself unable to pull away. She paused with the nonsense for a little while and waited, leaned back into a sitting position, and simply watched them. Neither did anything but watch her and continue to smile.

"What in the world has gotten into you guys today?" she asked them. She waited on them as if she fully expected a response. "You haven't cried today, haven't been fussy. Momma took her time with your breakfast this morning and you acted as if you were two of the most patient babies ever to walk across God's green earth. What's up with that?"

The babies smiled and just stared away, always at her, never taking their eyes off of their mother.

Barbara played with them a bit more, but as incredible as they were behaving, she ultimately needed that last cup of coffee. And if she was going to continue to hold fast to the routine of spending a few moments with the Lord every day, then she figured she had better get to it while the getting was good. *This can't last forever*, she told herself, taking one last look at the babies as she climbed to her feet. Their smiles had wilted somewhat but immediately sprang back to life as she once again gave them her full attention.

"What?" she said as she walked away, continuing to look their way. "Momma needs some coffee, angels. You had your milk, now I'm going to have mine. Okay?"

They just giggled.

Barbara took her favorite tan mug from the counter and dropped two non-dairy creams and two sugars into it. She had bought the cup from church. It read: Kingsburg Community Church in bright red letters. She poured herself another cup, mixed the contents well with a spoon she had left in a spoon rest and turned off the coffee pot. She carried the coffee to her seat at the dining room table next to her Bible and sat down.

She turned to where she had left off the day before—Romans, chapter 8. Finding the place where she thought that she needed to resume her reading, she closed her eyes and offered up a prayer.

"Lord, I thank you for everything that you have provided to me and my family. You are so gracious; so kind. You bless me so much beyond what I deserve, since what I deserve is death." Something stopped her there. What was it? As fast and as clearly as it had come it was gone again. Was it something that she had said? She couldn't pinpoint what it might have been. There was some recollection there at the tip of her memory.

She continued. "Thank you for my children, Jerod, Robbie and Rebekah. Thank you for their health and well-being. Thank you for protecting us in all that we do, and wherever we go. Thank you for my husband, especially now, as he struggles under these present circumstances. Help him and Mark to be protected, while they work to keep this community safe. I pray that you will give them insight and wisdom to discover what it is that has been hidden from them. Help them to decipher clues and evidence. Reveal the evil that has begun to afflict this town to the authorities, to Michael and Mark. I know that Michael doesn't even give a thought to being a hero to this town, but would rather see the criminal or criminals brought to justice. Praise you, Father, for being Lord over this town and this family, and for loving us the way you do, in Jesus' name. Amen."

Prayer closed, Barbara took a peek at the twins who she found continuing to stare her way. *At least they're not fussy*, she thought, and set her mind to her study. She began by skimming over what she had read Wednesday morning. Silently, she read until she got to Romans 8: 31. It was yet another bit of scripture that she was well familiar with, but it stopped her just the same. It read: "What then shall we say to these things? If God is for us, who is against us?"

Barbara glanced away from the words on the page and found herself staring at a picture across from her on the mocha painted wall. It was a picture of the Plaza de Porlier, taken by Alan Blaustein that she had picked up one day, but couldn't remember where just now. It was a large expanse of brickwork between buildings which had an arrangement of benches between some trees, back to back. The picture appeared to have had been taken in the early morning because there were no people about. Beautiful street lamps provided a warm glow to the scene, but she stared only at the nondescript tree at the center of the picture, its leaves long gone. She brought a solitary finger to her lips as if she was waiting for some thought to occur to her. God's word continued to play somewhere between her ears. It made her feel empowered suddenly, protected. As if nothing could harm her or her babies, no matter how hard they tried to break down her door or climb through her window.

Climb through my window?

She heard a distant voice. It wasn't coming from the street or from a neighbor, but from a recollection of something that had occurred very recently

163

It was a mean voice. Not loud or vulgar, but lacking of love or decency.

And it was addressing her.

"*Madam*," he was saying to her playfully. "*Your children seem to be crying!*"

"Oh, my God!" Barbara panicked, as the memory came flooding back to her for the first time since the attack. Her hand fell onto the table with a thud, causing her coffee to rock within her mug like the ocean in rough seas, nearly spilling some.

The beast was coming through her babies' nursery window once again as vividly now this morning as he had the night before when it had been real. She began to shake in her seat. He was speaking to her again, mocking her because they both knew that she was utterly powerless to prevent him from doing anything at all should he please to steal her babies, rape her or murder any one or all of them. She felt herself being thrown to the floor as if she were nothing of consequence, and now she felt the dull ache of the bruise on the back of her right leg and buttock. She wondered how Michael hadn't noticed what must be terribly ugly today when he was making love to her.

The thought of their quick lovemaking didn't stay in her head long as the voice was speaking again. "*Oh, but surely you don't think me gluttonous. I will gladly share them with you.*"

Share what? Barbara screamed in thought, her mouth tight, her heart racing, her hands clawing slowly at the ruby colored dining tablecloth. *Share what? My babies? Share with whom? Who else has been in my house?* Before the answer could find her, however, there was movement to her right, on the floor. *Who's there?* She started to pull herself from the tree on the wall and the memory seemingly contained only there. Her babies came into view finally. Though she realized that it was important that she remember what had taken place the night before, after apparently suppressing nearly everything, the sight of her children shocked her free. And by the looks on their tiny faces that was currently more important than her memories

The babies appeared as if they had seen not only her, but the horrific visions in her head as well, because they sat transfixed, as if frozen with fright.

"Oh, my babies!" she said, leaving the table and quickly going to them. "Did Mommy scare you?"

She went to her knees before Robbie and kissed him on the side of his little face, then hugged him. Reluctantly, she let him go, but she had two to think about. She repeated the gesture with her daughter. It seemed to do the trick for their expressions started to change back to nearly what they were prior to her beginning her Bible study. It occurred to her now, however, that there would be no going back today, nor did she want to. It wasn't a protest to the Lord or any such thing. She wasn't going back for coffee either. For whatever reason—and she knew it wasn't some unknown, mysterious aligning of the planets, but God— she and her babies had been rescued, saved. With that in mind, she didn't plan to do much of anything else this morning, and perhaps the entire day, but baby her babies.

There was one thing that she did not entirely let go of. And that was the question of who exactly had it been that had done the rescuing. Who had the Lord of heaven and earth used to do the work? The answer to this question was the one thing that had not come back to her. Who was it that the beast was speaking with when he wasn't speaking to her? And why did she continue to characterize her attacker as a beast? Where had that come from?

As she wondered this, Rebekah turned her head. This was not the end, however. She then began to move about as if attempting to turn her entire little body as well. Barbara followed her progress. Both of the twins had begun to show much maturity of late, especially today, but this was new. At first, she shuffled only her little feet, kept warm by yellow socks not nearly as tiny as they had once been. Now hands had joined in providing balance. Barbara would have thought her incapable of getting very far with this endeavor, whatever it was, but now that her hands were in play, she seemed to be picking up steam. And not only her, but suddenly Robbie was doing his level best to turn himself around as well. Incredibly, both were turning the same direction. Rebekah must have finally found the place that she liked, seemingly facing the kitchen table, because she stopped and just sat there. Barbara might have wondered whether she was looking for something, or perhaps at something, had she had her wits about her, but she didn't and she did not ask herself or them.

Behind the table in the background, Barbara could also see the front door from her vantage point. As if on some cue, there came a knock upon it.

Barbara only glanced at the door and did nothing. She felt frozen.

Another knock. It sounded like Vanessa Jackson's friendly knock. Barbara should know it, considering her best friend visited a couple of times a week between substitute teaching in town. As if in a fog, Barbara stood and slowly walked over to the door.

"Good morning, my dear," Vanessa announced cheerfully, immediately stepping over the threshold and giving her girlfriend a quick hug. "How are you? Wow, you look terrible! Are you alright? You look like you've seen a ghost!"

She walked into the dining room and set down her purse upon the table. Smiling, she stepped out into the open area between the dining room and the kitchen upon spotting the twins on the floor of the living room and waved at them dramatically with both hands; her short straight black hair did not move, but her long gold hoop earrings did.

"Well, I don't know exactly what I've just seen, to tell you the truth," Barbara said after a momentary pause.

Vanessa turned back to her friend and looked her over. "You look beautiful, as always." Barbara was dressed in a Liz Claiborne v-necked tan blouse with a bit of lacing around the "v" and brown capri pants. Her feet were bare. The outfit was nothing at all to write home about. It was comfortable and nice enough to simply throw on some sandals and go to town should the need arise. "You just look troubled."

Immediately, Barbara had two sets of "troubling" things, to borrow Vanessa's word, that she could have mentioned. It's not every day that one finds oneself attacked and lives to tell about it. The policeman's wife inside her knew that it did, in fact, happen all the time, at every hour and minute of the day somewhere in the world; however, it didn't happen to her, and that was the key. Not as exciting, but certainly as intriguing was the notion of her babies suddenly becoming psychic or paranormal or whatever they were now, other than just a few days older than the last time Vanessa had seen them. They could have sat down and discussed both topics at great length. Barbara could have put on another pot of coffee and used her friend's surprise arrival as the excuse necessary to get more coffee into her. However, in the end, she blinked instead.

"No, everything's fine."

"Are you sure?" Vanessa asked, giving her a chance to reconsider.

"Yep."

"Good." Vanessa flashed a wry smile. "Now step aside. I didn't come to see you! I just came from the doctor. I need all of the positive reinforcement I can get."

She quickly moved away from her best friend and plopped herself onto the floor with the babies, leaving Barbara to close the door behind her, a sad expression crawling onto her face as she began to understand her meaning. The twins grinned wide with the attention and showed no sign of any unpleasantness that they may have previously concerned themselves with.

Barbara sat herself down beside her dear friend, throwing her right arm around Vanessa Jackson and giving her a squeeze.

"Are you okay, sweetie?"

The woman closed her eyes briefly and quickly shook her head before devoting herself to the babies before her.

11:30 a.m.

The detectives stood outside the Recovery Ward of Selma District Hospital like two impatient expectant fathers from the 1950's waiting outside the Maternity Ward. They had arrived at the hospital twenty minutes prior. Before that, they had spent a couple of hours at the Lancaster residence, yet they still did not even know what John Lancaster looked like. He had gone through a successful surgery and was now into his recovery. His doctor had explained to them that his patient would be coming out of the anesthesia soon. He was unsure, however, as to what kind of condition he might be in when he did or whether he could field any questions at all.

The doctor had just gone in to see the patient again at their urging. A few moments later, he reemerged.

"Can we speak to him, Doc?" Jackson jumped from the chair and asked the man in the white coat.

"Detectives," he began. "I understand your position, so I'm going to let you in. However, don't stay long. Please don't force him to talk if he isn't coherent or finds it difficult to remain conscious. He's a strong man, but he's got a lot of healing to do, and he's just now coming out of the anesthesia."

Inside the private room, behind light green curtains, Big John Lancaster lay silently. Only the sound of his even breathing could be heard within the room as his tightly bandaged chest rose and fell. His eyes blinked as he stared at the ceiling above him, as if his thoughts were lost in the recollection of the attack which had put him there. When the detectives came into the room and approached the bed, he closed his eyes and swallowed.

"How are you feeling, Mr. Lancaster?" Michael asked him with a smile. He was surprised that the man had survived, considering the condition the medics said they found him in when the ambulance finally got to his home.

"Ca' me, Bi' John." The man turned the few inches he could without hurting himself and whispered. "E'ry'body does."

"Okay, Big John, this is Detective Jackson. I'm Lopez."

Big John blinked. It was the only way he had of acknowledging them.

"And are we glad to meet you, Big John!" Jackson smiled. "This case has been a regular S.O.B.! Frankly, we wondered whether we'd ever get a break in it!"

"'ell." He turned his head back to the ceiling and closed his eyes to focus his spinning thoughts. "'irst thing's 'irst. W'at the papers say is 'ot 'ullshit! 'ee's a 'ampire..." Big John coughed. He took a second and cleared his dry, hoarse throat.

The detectives looked at each other, not certain that they were following the victim well. Big John wasn't speaking very clearly, and although there wasn't much he could do about that, he knew he had to try harder.

"He is a vampire!"

"What do you mean?" Michael glanced first to his partner. Jackson furrowed his brow in surprise. "You mean he wears a cloak and turns into a bat or something?"

Big John opened his eyes wide and shot an angry look toward Michael. "You 'ink I did 'is to m'self?"

"I'm sorry." Michael held out his hands, signifying that he had meant no offence.

The man closed his eyes again, swallowing some pain swells and, it seemed, an urge to sleep. "ees six 'eet tall wit' long da'k 'air. Rea' long." He coughed again. When he was ready to continue, he glanced back to the detectives. "'ees stronger 'an a' two a' you!"

"PCP?" Jackson said, looking at his partner. He was referring to the drug commonly called "acid" on the street. It was known to give some extraordinary strength under como circumstances such as extreme duress or during moments of adrenaline.

Big John laughed. It made him cough and wince. He shook his head as he cleared it, holding his eyes closed, concentrating on speaking. "No, man. The guy 'ain't no dope 'iend. ' ee 'ain't no psycho! ee's real!"

"C'mon, John!" Michael said. "What are we supposed to do with...?"

"Look, man!" Big John interrupted him the best that he could. He gingerly opened his eyes and gave him another look, but yet another cough rose up to prevent him from saying anything further.

"Look, John." Michael leaned over him to get his attention through the coughing fit. "That's more than enough. We'll get the doc!"

Big John nodded. He knew that however important it was to tell his story to the detectives, all of the activity was making things worse. He was becoming weaker by the moment. He closed his eyes and turned his head in the other direction to try and get some much needed rest. In doing so, he clearly displayed the deep marks on his throat.

Jackson turned and silently stared at his partner, but he could see that he, too, saw the same distinct lacerations.

As the detectives turned to leave the man to start what looked like a long recuperating process, Big John cautiously turned his head back toward them and seemed to nod for him to return to his side. Michael saw it and stopped his partner.

"Yeah, Big John?" he said, reaching his bedside and leaning out over his face.

"'ee said 'is 'ame was Na'aniel."

"What?" Michael stepped back from the man with a start as if he had just been told that the killer was his own brother. "He told you his name?"

Big John closed his eyes and nodded once, then turned away.

Michael turned around as well. He joined his partner at the door and said, incredulously, "The bastard's name is Nathaniel! Sound familiar?"

As he grabbed the door handle on his way out of the room, Michael stopped and turned around. "As our only witness, John, we'll be putting an officer at your door for twenty-four hour protection."

Big John didn't bother turning around this time. He didn't have the strength. Instead, with the fingers of his wounded right arm, he waved the police detectives off. Michael studied the man for a few moments and finally understood why.

It was as if he were saying, "U'less you 'an have him sit on my win'ow-ledge, don't 'aste your time. Find the 'astard's coffin!"

12:23 p.m.

"I'm sorry, 'Nessa," Mark Jackson said into his personal cell phone as he heard nothing but silence on the other end of the line.

"It's not your fault," came an eventual reply from his wife.

171

"Well, actually it kind of is, isn't it?" he sighed, running the fingers of his left hand over his beard that was beginning to feel in need of a trim once again. He stared out the window absently as the conversation continued to erode negatively. It had never been a very uplifting discussion in the first place. Vanessa had just called because she was feeling blue with the latest setback in their attempt to become pregnant.

"We don't know that. Don't blame yourself," his wife told him, but her voice was cracking and he could tell that she would not be able to talk for much longer without tears. "Listen, we'll just keep trying. Okay?"

Mark nodded silently

"I need to go, baby," she said.

"You gonna' be alright?" Mark asked.

"Yeah. You be careful out there."

"I will," he said, sitting up, preparing to end the conversation.

"Bye."

"You know, Jacks, sometimes I feel like a complete ass!"

"Why?" Mark put his phone inside his slacks pocket and turned to his partner.

"I sit beside you and tell you about my kids, sometimes proud as hell, and other times taking them for granted. Here you two are, trying to have one, just one, and not yet able to. I'm just sorry."

"It's fine, Mikey," Jackson told him, slapping his right leg. "I love your family. You know that. Hearing about them just makes me want one of my own more and more. In fact, since we're apologizing..."

"Yeah?"

"That bit about me upholding the community trust this morning..."

"Yes?"

A pause.

"Yes?" Michael was beginning to grow a little exasperated by the delay.

172

"I think I had the same breakfast you had!"

"No!" Michael threw up his hands dramatically, feigning disgust. "After the hard time you gave me!"

Jackson smiled, not at his partner but in the reliving of the experience. "Sorry."

They saw the familiar Ford Taurus making its way toward them. It made a left turn and drove down the lane of the Selma District Hospital, eventually snaking its way back around and joining them there beside them. Bold white letters read: **CHIEF OF POLICE**, contrasted against the black paint of the car. Michael watched as he approached, measuring his words, wondering whether what he had to tell the man would sound any more tangible aloud than it did swimming around inside his head. He was sure Jacks did the same, and that he also didn't think very highly of his chances.

"Alright, boys," the chief said through the open driver's side door as he parked beside them. "You got me out here. What's so damned important?" His eyes immediately found Jackson's beard that Department Regulations dictated he was not supposed to be wearing. The chief had been reminding him of this fact since it had first appeared after Thanksgiving, to no avail. He blinked and looked off of it.

Michael sighed, still not yet fully prepared to speak.

"We spoke to John Lancaster," Jackson began. "It took a while. We had to wait for him to get out of surgery. He's got broken ribs. He's going to be here a while."

"Was he able to give a description of his assailant?"

"Yes, he was."

"Well?"

"You're not going to like it," Jackson added. He and Michael exchanged glances.

"Chief," Michael was speaking now. "When I spoke to the coroner he told me that the bodies had no blood in them; with the damage done to Mancuso, that wasn't difficult to believe. However, Browning, who had very little damage done to him, appeared to the coroner like he had been siphoned."

The chief just stared at him.

"He found bite marks."

"The man back there in room 31 told us that he was attacked by a man, claiming to be after his blood," Jackson said, leaving one piece of the story behind. "He claims he saw the teeth and they are real."

The chief sat there motionless for a moment, visibly contemplating the implication of the facts. His face twisted in a grimace. "Let me guess. We've got a freak in town who thinks he's a vampire, right?"

The chief looked away from his detectives and shook his head in disgust or exhaustion or perhaps a combination of both. "A serial vampire killer in Kingsburg!" he said softly to no one at all. "We're in over our damn heads!"

3:18 p.m.

"Hi, baby," Barbara said with a wide smile as she got down on her hands and knees and crawled up to her son's little face. He grinned back at her as they touched noses, and then he reached out and tried to grab her cheeks. "Boy! You and your sister have been quiet today, huh? Yes, you have," she said softly, smiling. "How come, sweetie?"

Then she moved to the left and kissed her daughter's cheek. She was lying quietly on her back on the same blanket with her brother. At the sight of her mother, though, she began to smile and speak her baby-talk, mildly kicking her arms and legs about her. "What's my name?" she smiled down at her and then kissed both of her cheeks again and again. "Say, 'Mommy!'" Then she sat back against the couch to watch them. *Robbie and Rebekah are usually pretty good together,* she thought. *But not like this.*

Barbara let her mind trail off as she looked over her children. Today they seemed so...content. They hadn't cried when it was time for them to be fed, but had simply waited patiently like a good boy and girl until Mommy came to feed them. When it had been time for another diaper change, once again they hadn't made a fuss. All day neither baby had cried once. They were the babies that every expectant parent hoped for but never got. Barbara shook her head at the difference in her children, pleasantly thankful. She glanced heavenward in thanks, enjoying it while it lasted, fully expecting that normalcy would return soon.

"Hi, Mom!" Jerod said as he quickly opened and then closed the front door behind him, turned and ran for the bathroom. He dropped his books outside the door in the hallway just seconds before the dam broke.

"Some things never change!" she giggled. "Huh, babies?"

5:19 p.m.

"Sleep as long as you want, Mom," Jerod had smiled when she asked him if she could go take a nap. "The twins are fun today."

"Thank you, honey," she had told him. "Watch what you want on TV, but please keep it low, okay, and make sure you keep an eye on your brother and sister."

"No problem, Mom."

That was nineteen minutes ago. Now she was completely asleep. Lying on top of her bed underneath a light blanket, Barbara turned quietly and readjusted her position. The movement didn't wake her. Inside her head, she did not dream of the previous night's events, but of something new. She was sitting at the dining room table, just as she did every morning; a mug of coffee placed on her right. However, today there were no children present, nor was there a Bible on the table

175

before her. She sat with her hands clasped together, back straight, head held at attention.

Beside her there was a man. Though he was as close to her as any man had ever been, excluding Michael, who had been the only man to have gotten any closer, she could not really decipher his facial features. His hair was dark brown, she thought, and a bit long, curling around the edges. He seemed a strong presence though not necessarily muscular, and nothing in these first moments gave the impression of him being possibly threatening. He was speaking to her with the slightest smile. His words were like light music. He was speaking scripture, and later would come to realize that it was from the Book of Romans. The same book that she was currently studying, although *ahead* of her, not something that she had yet read.

"It is not as though the word of God has failed. For they are not all Israel who are descended from Israel." He wasn't reading the scripture to her, but rather *teaching* her the scripture, *relating* it to her so that she might better understand it. She understood this implicitly, though she still could not recognize her teacher. All that she knew was that it was right and good that he was there in her home.

"Neither are they all children because they are all Abraham's descendants. It says, 'Through Isaac your descendants will be named'. It is not the children of the flesh who are children of God, but the children of the promise. Shall we say," he said with a warm grin, "there is injustice with God?" Barbara waited. He pointed at her in the direction of her heart. "May it never be! He told Moses that He would have mercy on whom He would have mercy. Is this right? And compassion on whom He would have compassion. So then it does not depend on the man who wills or the man who runs, does it? But on the God who has mercy."

"But what of those who have terrible things happen to them?" she found herself asking suddenly, surprising herself.

The teacher sat back in his chair with this, ever smiling. "The scripture said to Pharaoh, 'For this very purpose I raised you up, to demonstrate my power in you, and that my name might be proclaimed before the whole earth'. So He has mercy on who He desires, and He hardens who He desires."

At this point Barbara had no more questions. At least none that she felt brave enough to ask.

Perhaps sensing this very fact, the teacher continued: "You will ask now, 'why does he still find fault? For who can resist His will? But on the contrary, who are you who answers back to God? The thing molded will not say to the molder, 'Why did you make me like this,' will it? Doesn't the potter have a right over the clay, to make from the same lump one vessel for honorable use, and another for common use?" He addressed her now. "Barbara, what if God, although willing to demonstrate His wrath and to make His power known, endured with much patience vessels of wrath prepared for destruction? And He did so in order that He might make known the riches of His glory upon vessels of mercy, which He prepared beforehand for glory."

The teacher leaned forward, taking her hands in his own. His smile never seemed to fade. She leaned forward some, too. There was no threat, no impropriety here. This was just fellowship and God's Word. This was unfolding the Lord Jesus Christ out on the table to reveal his heart and his life for us to follow after. There was only peace to be found here.

"Barbara," the faceless man before her said. "What do you think of my Nathaniel now?"

"Who?" she asked, and the sound of her own voice startled her.

She flung open her eyes. She was no longer in the dining room, but alone, in her bedroom. How long had she slept? She turned toward the clock on the nightstand. The numbers didn't register for a moment. She did the quick math. The nap had not lasted long at all by the look of it. Why had she awakened? Had something disturbed her? Typically, Barbara had never been one to take much stock in her dreams. But this time she remembered all of it and the first one as well; the one where she had been standing in a sea of flowers.

She sat up on her bed, throwing her feet over the side. She slid down until her bare feet touched the carpet and then sat there a moment, reliving all that she had seen and heard in the dream. It was impossible to picture the teacher that had sat at her table, but she could still hear his words like music. As she clasped her hands together again, this time in her warm lap, she could almost still feel the teacher's hand there atop her own.

5:20 p.m.
Poienari Fortress
February 12th, 1747

There was a knock on the large metal door. It was not closed. That was not allowed.

"Good day, Nathaniel," the vampire announced, stepping from the shadows of the dark corridor and into the torch-lit room. There had once been a time when Nathaniel was forced to make his home in a tiny pitch-black stone room with a pauper's bed. Now he had a large suite with a torch for light, rugs on the floors, and a real bed. Warm blankets were stacked in an ante chamber, along with an abundance of fine clothes.

Reluctantly, Nathaniel turned around. "Hello," he said rather coldly, and only glancing up at his host.

Vincent sighed. "What is it now?"

"What?" Nathaniel asked, oblivious to the question.

"Your lack of warmth," the vampire said. He stepped closer and folded his arms. "I could understand it coming from me," he said in a hush, as if trying to control his vicious temper. "My blood not being nearly as exquisite as yours, though I do not let that stop me. But you...? Are you not glad to see me?"

Nathaniel did not answer.

"Hello?" Vincent smiled sarcastically, and then quickly straightened up. He gritted his teeth together, clearly attempting to swallow the rising anger. It was one of the few, if not the only, battles that he ever lost.

"You already said that," Nathaniel said, disinterested.

Suddenly the vampire grabbed Nathaniel and easily lifted him off of his feet. Had he blinked, he would have missed the action completely.

"What?" Nathaniel yelped like a dog, suddenly yanked by his choke chain, his feet dangling around the vampire's knees.

"Be short with me once again, my son, and...!"

"I'm not your son!" Nathaniel screamed defiantly into the vampire's face, spittle misting its eyes and cheeks. It was that utter defiance which had pushed Vincent's anger and frustration over the edge, sealing his fate.

The vampire acted instantly. He did not wait to think. He growled loudly and then tossed the young man across the room as if he were still the boy that he had kidnapped a decade before. Nathaniel's arms waived spastically as the hewn stone wall and floor came rushing up to greet him. Upon impact, his body went limp and his defiance went silent; his long hair scattered about him, hiding him from view. Still blind with fury, the vampire followed and was quickly on him again. He reached through the mane of hair and grabbed him by the ruffled collar, shaking him.

179

"Where is that sharp tongue now, Nathaniel? Hmm? Where?" He did not stop shaking him until his eyelids had begun to flutter open. "It is due time you awoke, Nathaniel," he shrieked. Spittle broke free of his vile lips and splattered Nathaniel's face this time. "Since you detest the reference so badly, I've come to the decision that it's high time I gave you a real reason to hate being called my son!"

Nathaniel's eyes bounded open. He was not yet fully conscious; however, the beast's words struck a chord of fear within him so deeply, like a prophecy long foretold, finally coming true. His reaction was pure instinct. This was not simply more of the vampire's goading. This was different. There was some secret meaning here. Ever since his first day held captive, Nathaniel had wondered what fate could be worse than watching his parents being butchered before him, and then being taken as a prisoner, learning to hate each and every horrible second of your life. Now much older than that boy, he had decided that there could be nothing worse. Death certainly wasn't to be feared after so dreary a life; it was to be tearfully longed for, prayed for. Therefore, as the vampire lunged for him, he almost smiled.

Death, finally!

But then he knew.

Vincent wasn't into mercy, was he?

The realization struck him in that last second and his eyes widened in complete and utter horror.

"No!" he screamed.

The vampire's fangs pierced his throat.

Nathaniel tried to muster the strength to scream again but could not, and there was no one to hear him anyway. Not high above the Arges River in this terrible place that had heard so much death and torture. A great many nobles from Targoviste had been impaled by Vlad on account of its lime mortar, brick and stone.

Horrible teeth bit deep into young jugular.

180

Nathaniel tried to work his way free but was suddenly so weak.

Vincent did not draw blood slowly. It wasn't his style. Like a young virgin, unpracticed, he took it as fast as it would come.

And it came.

It gushed from the wound at an excited pace almost too quickly for even he to swallow.

What followed was the worst of all as Nathaniel suddenly found himself drinking something that was being offered directly to his lips. It was thick and wet and salty, and he found himself thirsty for it. In fact he was insatiable. Vincent's arm had been cut, but by whom he did not know. All that he knew was it was being applied to his lips and his tongue swept the small but gaping wound for everything that it could give him.

*   *   *

Nathaniel pictured the memory as if it had just happened, not like the two-hundred and sixty-one year old recollection that it was. He awoke from the nightmare, but did not open his eyes. It was still light out. He could feel it against his skin through the old musty blankets that kept it out of sight and out of danger. Instead, attempting to shake free from the horror of the past, he thought of the woman. Suddenly, no longer sleeping, but not exactly awake, he really began to dream. He could see himself walking amongst the light. First, there was a beach and his feet sank in the warm sand, and then in the bubbling tide as it crawled up the beach and against him. It hit him again as it rolled back from where it had come. It felt marvelous.

He felt what it might have been like to be a boy on the beach for the first time, considering that he had already become a vampire by the time that he had seen his first beach; his first view of the ocean. He had touched the water, but felt nothing in particular. Now, it was spectacular. He had tasted the salty air long before the water had even come into view that first time. Yet, this was completely new. The salty air was choking him now, and he wanted more!

He stood there and spun around like a boy, taking it all in in one giant gulp—the perfect blue water, the sand that seemed to stretch for miles on either side, the dunes of sand rising up to meet the rocky cliffs, the woman watching him spin with a look of pure delight on her lightly tanned face, the other side of the beach.... He stopped and looked back. Barbara was there. He had never seen such a beautiful smile. And it was all for him. Wait! She was crying. Had he missed something? What could there possibly be here that might make someone cry? This was paradise. Must they leave this splendid place? Is that the explanation for the tears? He reached out to her with a well-manicured hand to touch one tear, and it only later he realized that his hands were claw-free. They were simply strong and fine, nothing more. They were hands for holding the woman of your heart, or the tiny hands of children. They touched no blood or dead thing.

Nathaniel wiped the tears from Barbara's eyes, but more followed. Why? He meant to ask, but before he could do so he watched as she brought her hands together and clapped. She was clapping her hands as if watching a spectacle and that was when he realized that the spectacle was him. She was celebrating everything that he was and it was bringing her tears of joy!

7:15 p.m.

"Mom?"

Jerod's voice pulled Barbara out of deep thoughts. She was looking at one of the many tabloid news shows, but wasn't really watching it.

"Yeah, honey?" she smiled warmly at her son as he got up off of the floor and stood before her.

"Can I play PlayStation 2?" he asked. "You don't look like you're watching TV anyway."

How perceptive he's getting, she thought with a smile. Then her smile faded. *Or am I just that bad at hiding what's eating me*? "Sure, honey. Go ahead."

"Thanks, Mom!" the boy grinned happily and then quickly turned around and headed for the shelf where the equipment sat.

Barbara swung her feet over the side of the couch where she had been lying and got up. Jerod had asked her how come it had been that she had moved to the couch after her nap only to doze some more. She had just made a joke of it and laughed with him, revealing nothing else. In fact, she did very little dozing. She didn't do much resting of the eyes, either, but rather scoured the mental picture in her head for clues to what was suddenly going on with her.

She suddenly felt thirsty, which was odd considering the medium size Diet Pepsi that she had had with their fast-food dinner of Carl's Jr. She had not felt like cooking; actually she hadn't felt like much of anything since her aborted nap. In any event, she headed for the kitchen and the refrigerator to grab another one. A bottle of water would have been the better choice, but she hoped the jolt of the soft drink would be just the ticket to get her off of the couch. She took the drink, opened it and took a healthy swig until she felt the burn and could stand it no longer. It was then that she noticed that the garbage that had been generated from dinner was overflowing the trashcan. Unable to find any room in the can, Jerod had taken the easy way out and simply piled the trash on top of the lid rather than taking it out like he should have. About to raise her voice to get Jerod's attention—not enough to wake the twins, of course, but loud enough—another suppressed recollection turned in the currents of her mind and floated to the surface. It was one of her, not Jerod, absently setting the trash there on the lid.

"Oh, good Lord!" she sighed. "What's wrong with me?"

"Sweetie?" she finally did call out, but not as loud as she had originally intended, and not before turning the corner so that she could see her son. "Listen for your brother and sister. I need to take out the trash."

"Do you want me to do that, Mom?"

Oh, my angel! She smiled inside as well as out. "No, sweetie. I'll take it out. You go ahead and play."

"Thanks, Mom!" he grinned back, happily.

Barbara stopped as she closed the door behind her. She shuffled the two bags of garbage in her arms, walked past the side of the house and then headed through the backyard for the alley trashcans. As she walked across the tall grass that Michael would have already cut had he ever been home, a route she had walked perhaps several hundred times, she looked to the heavens and star-gazed. The sky was so clear, it was almost unreal. Every star in the sky was there to be touched or spoken to. *It's so clear, it's almost wrong*, she thought. It was as if two different pictures were superimposed in some Hollywood special effect. She wasn't an astronomer by any stretch of the imagination; instead, she was simply one who had an eye for beauty. And this scene above her was exactly that: beautiful. She sighed.

When she had reached the back of the yard, she set down the bags and opened the special gate that Michael had built, enabling him, and one day the children, to access the area behind the trash cans. Being in law enforcement, if it were after dark, Michael did not want any member of his family walking in the alley in order to dump the trash. The gate had a latch with an extra ring attached to it. She hooked this ring through the nail that could be found protruding from the fence just behind the opened gate thus holding it open for her. Barbara reached for the lid of the nearest trashcans when something caused her to pause.

*   *   *

The vampire watched as the woman stood her ground, wondering what had stopped her. He had been following her since she first stepped from the door to the garage and then all the way out to the alley. He had studied the gentle grace of each cursory step: the hypnotizing effect of her hips as she walked, lost in thought; the gradual curve of her fine back and hips, the innocent sweep of her neck. With his superior vision, he continued to watch her from the concealing shadows of her own back yard.

"Who's there?" Barbara asked aloud without a moment's hesitation.

She seemed to think that she needed to do so, as though she knew someone was directly behind her. So there she was, ignoring the open gate and the trash at her feet, she methodically turned around and faced the exact spot in the shadows where Nathaniel was standing.

"Barbara?" The vampire was completely taken aback by this turn of events. *What was...? Did I say that?*

Nathaniel stepped back in surprise at the sound of his own voice breaking the silence in the dark. In doing so, he inadvertently kicked an abandoned skate board, sending it slamming into the West fence with a loud crash. Perhaps Barbara could have very easily dismissed hearing her name whispered in the quiet of the dark, believing that she was probably only hearing things because she was tired, but surely not this racket.

"Hello, Barbara," Nathaniel said, quickly emerging from the shadows. "I apologize. I never intended to startle you." He stepped close enough for her to see him, but that was all.

"Who are you?"

"It is I."

"And who is that?" she interrupted, although her voice faltered, as though she found him familiar.

"Nathaniel."

Realization spread across her face.

"We met yesterday," he said simply, though the notion that she could have forgotten the events of the previous night sounded quite ludicrous to him.

Barbara didn't respond.

"Barbara," he offered, "I know what you are thinking. How could I not know? I am a voice in the dark. You would be quite wise to fear what you cannot see, and often what you can."

"Exactly," she replied quickly.

"Test my motives."

"Excuse me?"

"Test me. Test me that I might gain your trust."

"That won't be necessary," she said.

"No. Are you certain? Does that mean that you remember me, and trust me?" Nathaniel asked. "You do remember, don't you?"

"I didn't at first. Now I do." Her voice trailed.

"I asked you not to speak of our meeting, Barbara," the vampire clarified. "I did not, however, ask you to forget. You and the children are well, I trust?"

"Yes."

"My lone regret was that I had not come sooner."

"The person who tried to hurt me, my babies..." She paused. "You know this person?"

Nathaniel did not answer immediately.

"You do, don't you?"

"Barbara," he warned, seeming to ignore her question. "I am going to walk before you and then behind, and complete your task. I mean you no harm."

Barbara said nothing further and simply watched as Nathaniel did exactly as he had described. The bags of trash were dispatched and the gate was locked. She watched intently as this was accomplished; however, it seemed to be completed too quickly.

Nathaniel felt Barbara recoiling again, more anxious than trusting.

"Please," he said with a great sigh, choosing his words carefully and measuring his movements. He clasped his hands before him. "I will not attempt to touch you or even move closer. I can move very quickly, as you have no doubt noticed. However, I promise you that I will not."

"Okay," she whispered, trying to sound brave.

"It is true that I am acquainted with this one who attempted to harm your family," he told her. "But it is no person. How I wish that neither you nor I were so acquainted." He paused with a mournful sigh, briefly looking away from her. He drifted away, as if his spirit had flown off or perhaps momentarily lost its bearings. But as quickly as it left, it returned and he was looking her way again. "It is for this reason that I thought to call upon you. I worried for your safety."

There was a silence between them for a time. It was obvious that she not only heard his words but felt them out at the same time. He already sensed a bond forming between the two of them. *Strange*, he thought as she stared at him. Perhaps it had always been there. It felt right to him. Even though there was danger with him; there was nothing to fear, nothing to distrust, nothing to be wary of. With her, it seemed like some life-long friend had returned, and the only thing to do now was to recall the days gone by and begin new ones.

For Nathaniel, a melancholy was beginning to settle in, burrowing itself deep within him. It was a sensation that he had never felt before. He had felt it the night before during the brief time that they had spent together. Was it a feeling of wanting to care for her? Or maybe it felt like he owed her because the menace known as Vincent was here, in this town, because of him. Did he just feel like he must not allow any further people to become destroyed or brought to ruin because of the beast?

"In fact, I should leave," he abruptly broke the silence.

"What?" Barbara half-cried.

"I know the beast. Too well, indeed. Should he return, it may very well be because he wished to hurt me by hurting those..." Now he was looking away again. It happened so quickly that neither of them caught it until it had already occurred.

"By hurting those, what?" she asked softly, stepping forward ever so slightly.

"By hurting those that I might care for."

"Do you?" she asked, moving closer still. There was now not much distance between them.

"Before yesterday I did not care for anyone but myself. I could not. Now, strangely, that all feels wrong to me. It feels like so much wasted effort. So much a wasted life."

"It seems to me that the opposite is true," Barbara said, her comfort with him seemingly cemented. "You have become our protector. Instead of leaving us, maybe you should do your job."

This took Nathaniel by surprise. "What?"

"I assume you can do this."

"Do what? I don't understand."

"Don't you?"

Nathaniel smiled faintly. He didn't realize that he was doing it.

"Yes, Barbara," he said at last, standing suddenly rather proudly as if the melancholy had left him. "I can do this."

There was a silence again. Each just gazed upon the other, there in the darkening yard. Finally, Barbara broke the spell. "Do you *want* to do this?"

"I..."

"I mean," she interrupted. "This is not more than you bargained for when you answered the screams of a lady in distress?"

"Absolutely not."

He found himself appreciating the sound of this woman's voice, much as one might melt at the sound of beautiful music, something that he could still appreciate. There was another voice, too. It was the voice that had attempted to stop him in the beginning from speaking to her at all; the one that tried to stop him from returning to this neighborhood in the first place, now that he had thought about it.

She was just so breathtaking.

He heard a second voice now, battling with the first. It was an old voice; one that he had not heard in some time. He almost did not recognize it. It reminded him of his mother's voice from long ago. Not her actual voice, mind you, but her direction for him; for his character, his maturation. To become the man that she had hoped for before the world for him was suddenly and irreparably changed forever. Could it be that even he had a heart after all?

"I trust the children behaved well today," Nathaniel suddenly changed the subject.

"Yes..."

Her eyes widened then, as if a thought smacked her in the head. "What's wrong with my children?" she asked calmly, although terror sneaked in her tone.

It was just a simple question. He hadn't taken any time to think about it, or to think what it might mean for her. There was nothing wrong with them, nothing to be worried about. Nathaniel stepped toward her at the implication. There was now very little space between them.

"Nothing!" he answered, insulted. "I have not harmed them!"

"But something's wrong with them! They haven't cried all day!"

They were no longer whispering to one another. Both raised their voices in alarm, but they were not shouting.

"Is that such a bad thing?" he asked, though not expecting an answer. "They are the same children they have always been. I merely promised them last night that no harm would ever come to them."

"Promised them," she said aloud now. "How could you possibly do that?"

"Easily. I have done the same for you."

Her look was now one of amazement. She opened her mouth as though to ask him something, but didn't. She was probably wondering what it all meant; how he could do what he did. In any case, though, what Nathaniel had told her was the truth. There was nothing wrong with her, and other than not throwing any fits today, there was also nothing at all wrong with her babies. In fact, one might argue that they were better for it. She looked away from Nathaniel, embarrassed.

"I'm sorry," she whispered.

Nathaniel watched her reaction with a fondness that he had never known since...

"Please, there is no need to apologize."

Then, without thinking, he reached out and softly, tenderly, cupped his right hand beneath her lowered chin and raised it. He realized his actions too late as he laid his cold flesh against hers. At first, Barbara flinched; however, possibly feeling the same warmth Nathaniel was feeling, she took notice of it no more. It was as if he had reached down into her very heart and removed all of the weight of her insecurities and inadequacies. As he stared deeply into her eyes, he moved to speak, but could not find the words. Barbara had no words either.

"Now I really must go," he said, removing his hand from her. Her face fell at its withdraw.

Barbara closed her eyes at the sensation. When she felt it part from her, she opened her eyes.

Nathaniel was gone. She never heard him leave. Her head feeling light, dizzied, she turned silently and made her way back to the house. When she walked back into the living room and sat down on the couch, Jerod glanced briefly up from his Madden NFL 2007 and smiled warmly.

"That was fast, Mom!"

7:49 p.m.

Oh, so...pathetic! Vincent thought. From the Rosen's yard next door, Vincent watched and heard nearly all of the conversation Nathaniel had just completed with the woman that he had allowed him to *save* the night before. Nathaniel should have detected Vincent's presence there, he realized instantly upon emerging from his new lair to find the two of them together there in the back of the yard. Yesterday he would have, but not now, Vincent knew. He also noticed how obviously difficult it was for him to tear himself away, and how badly the woman really wanted him to stay. Nathaniel had been the last to leave. He had remained, loitering within the shadows, ogling the woman until she had left even his eyesight. Vincent waited for both parties to leave earshot completely before he laughed loudly.

Patience! he reminded himself. *There will be plenty of time to make my son regret the day he crossed me because of that woman. And the day he abandoned me all those years ago!*

9:50 p.m.

When Barbara next saw Nathaniel, she was standing again among a sea of flowers and he was against that tree in the shade. She felt that warm sun shining on her back and shoulders as she gathered up her sundress to quickly navigate through the thick meadow toward him. She stopped for a moment to catch her breath. The shade caused by the overhanging trees gave Nathaniel a sinister look as he stood there half-in, half-out of the dark and stared in her direction, unmoving. However, she wasn't afraid.

What reason did she have to be?

She waved at him and then started toward him again. Finally, Nathaniel made a move. At the sight of her approach, he stepped clear of the shadows and waved back. The smile on his face as he recognized her warmed Barbara's heart.

"Barbara," he whispered as she fell in his arms, slightly winded from the trip. He gave her a moment to catch her breath and then pulled her face out of his chest. "I've missed you. I never thought I could ever miss anyone like that again, but you make it so. Please do not leave me again, I beg you!"

Barbara closed her eyes with the man's words. His voice was so warm; it moved her in ways others had not been able to accomplish with a touch. His eloquent words, that European accent, that soft strength, all worked together to make her melt in his arms. It was the one place where she was at her safest. No one and nothing could ever reach her there. Any strength she had ever known was lost forever as long as she could live within his arms. Barbara closed her eyes and allowed the moment to work. A silver tear broke through her eyelid and raced down one milky cheek. Nathaniel brushed them away with a gentle sweep of his fingers and another came.

"I love you," she heard him say as she drifted deeper into bliss.

"I love you back!" She felt her own lips move and then tasted the tears there. "I've always loved you!"

"Then why are you crying?" His voice flowed over her, bathing her. It covered her and then penetrated her, warming her thoroughly.

"Am I?" she smiled, her eyes unable to open because of the pleasure; almost afraid that the moment would die if she dared look upon it.

"Yes, honey, you are!" Michael spoke again, wiping the salty water from her face.

Michael?

She opened her eyes. It was Michael, her husband.

Oh, dear God! she thought. *What was I doing?* She went to sit up. Her pillow was wet. She stared at it, dumbfounded. *How long have I been crying?* She glanced down. Her chest was heaving within her light nightgown, her nipples hard and showing through. "Oh, Nath..."

"What?" Michael asked, yawning. He leaned close. "I'm sorry, honey. What did you say?"

"Nothing," she whispered and forced a grin. *God!* she thought. *What the hell is happening to me?*

"Sweetie," Michael whispered. "It's late. I just got home a little while ago and I'm exhausted. I've already checked on the kids so go back to sleep and I'll see you tomorrow." He leaned over before getting off of her side of the bed and kissed her tear-stained cheek. "Love you."

"I love you, too," she whispered. Her mind found truth in the words. She loved her husband very much; there was no questioning her sincerity about that!

But why am I so uncertain all of a sudden?

Nathaniel, she thought. It was because of Nathaniel.

Nathaniel...Nathaniel...Nathaniel...

And then she fell back asleep.

11:21 p.m.

The patrol car crept along Madsen Avenue like a snail. It headed south bound. Before it, two headlamps lit the way while one solitary spotlight prowled everywhere else. The police officer glanced west down Sophia Lane as he drove by, but continued on his way. On the left was a small ditch. It was full and the water was flowing quickly.

In the distance, several blocks down, another car turned onto Madsen, heading his direction. It was another patrol car, but of whose city he was not yet able to identify. Recognizing one another for who they were and for the job that they were doing, the other police officer flashed his high beams once before making a left turn onto Winter Street.

Just before the patrol car reached the intersection of Madsen and California State Route 201, the officer raised the volume on his car stereo a hair. Slash was playing his guitar solo on *Sweet Child O' Mine* by Guns N' Roses on Jack FM. It was at the end of the first part of the solo, just before he kicks it in to another gear and the tempo jumps. He turned it up only slightly because although he loved the classic song, it was far more important that he be listening tonight for other things. He needed to be able to hear anything and everything that might be taking place around him. As he did so, he grinned to himself, thinking that *Welcome to the Jungle* might have been a slightly more apropos choice considering the state of things in Kingsburg.

"Where do we go now?" Officer Stevens sang along as he made a left turn on 20th Avenue. He continued to sweep the streets and neighborhoods for anything out of the ordinary. Careful not to shine his powerful spotlight into windows and cause more of a panic than had already begun, he instead checked for insecure doors and gates. He aimed his light over shrubs, bushes and trees, checking for anyone who might be out and about at this late hour. And anyone he discovered in that light had better have a damn good reason for not sitting in front of the eleven o'clock news, or better yet—be in bed.

Richard Stevens was a Hanford Police Officer. He was a veteran of eleven years of service. The last nine of those years he had spent with the much larger city to Kingsburg's south west, and about twelve minutes away. It was considerably longer for anyone not driving a car with an official seal or a light rack across the top of one's vehicle. He was on loan, along with three other Hanford officers. He had relieved Officer Carlos Perez who'd covered the midnight to noon shift. Somewhere out there in the darkness was another partner of his, Janice Jennings. He and JJ had another half an hour on their twelve hour shift, and then they were headed for home.

Headlights appeared before him as another patrol unit emerged off of Lindquist Street, his spotlight crawling across the neighborhood about him much like his own. Officer Stevens quickly reached for his lights and flashed his high beams. The markings on the car read: Selma Police. The other officer repeated the gesture. He did not know the officer or even whether they were male or female. He simply offered his due respect.

The song ended and it was followed by Van Halen's, *Top of the World*. Stevens liked Diamond David Lee Roth, but he adored Sammy Hagar, so he snuck a bit more volume and lip-synched along. Ahead of him the road came to a "T" as 20th Avenue met Mariposa Street. The front of a school suddenly came into view. He didn't know the name of the school, of course, having never lived in Kingsburg. The only time he ever spent in this town was for the Swedish Festival, but that had been when he was a kid and his mother brought him for the Swedish Pancakes. He hadn't really been back between then and now. The Bullpups of Hanford and Kingsburg's Vikings never met in any games, either football or baseball, so the only thing he ever saw of it in his adult years was driving by it on his way to Fresno for whatever reason.

He brought his vehicle to a halt in the middle of the street, and shined his spotlight onto the sign that displayed the school's name: Lincoln School. He spotted a bare flagpole and what appeared to be a cafeteria or multipurpose room. There was a long corridor as well that cut through the separate wings of classrooms. His light swept over everything, but found nothing.

"*Standing on top of the world for a little while,*" he mouthed as he drove into the bus garage parking lot.

He came to an alley that appeared to continue along so he followed it. A row of portable classrooms to his right and a chain-link fence to his left that housed God knew what. He slowed down while he attempted to discover what it was. He flicked on the spotlight that was mounted to the driver's side door and shined it through the fence. Just as he began to realize that it was a baseball field, a banner greeted him: Cal Ripken Field. Creeping along, he shined his light through the fence across the bricked left field dugout; across the metal bleachers; over the area behind home plate where the snack bar was apparently located; across the back of the tall man with long hair, looking through the fence. The man suddenly turned and stared with hateful eyes directly into the beam.

"Shit!" Officer Stevens cried out, hitting his brakes.

He had been driving less than five miles per hour, but he jerked forward as if he had been doing fifty. He had only taken his eyes off of the man at the fence for a moment, but it was apparently too long. When he glanced back the man was at his door, reaching through the window as if he were attempting to climb in with him. *Shit! Shit! Shit!* his brain screamed. *I think we've found Nathaniel!*

Police Officer Stevens uncontrollably urinated himself as the cold vice-like left hand went to his neck and held him as if he were nothing. Luckily for him, his bladder had been relatively empty. The vampire sneered, pressing his nose into the flesh just below the officer's left eye.

"It is I, Nathaniel! Are you ready to die?" he asked him, his long dark hair spilling everywhere, draping everything.

Stevens could not answer; he could barely breathe.

"You are going to die, you know. I just want to know whether you're ready."

The man changed his expression suddenly as the scent of Stevens' wet pants reached his nostrils. He glanced down toward the area where one might expect the smell to be coming from. Taking his right hand from the side of the patrol car, the vampire poked Stevens' crotch irritably. He gave the man's testicles a mild slap in anger.

"Do you know what that will do to the bouquet of your blood? You have ruined everything!"

Stevens was in a panic. The air was about gone from his lungs and there did not appear to be much hope in obtaining more. He could feel his eyes bulging out of their sockets like a fish brought to the surface from deep waters too quickly. Two camps were at odds with one another—the police instinct in him that was trying to find some way of turning the tables on his attacker, to free himself and apprehend the killer; and the man who was simply trying to escape. Neither camp was having much success.

"Were I not in a great hurry, I might leave you to soil yourself further. Unfortunately, I am in no shape to be particular."

Stevens felt himself losing consciousness just as the man… no, the *thing* barred its fangs and twisted his head around to reveal his neck.

His eyes fell upon the orange pointer that cut through the letter "D" on his dashboard, signifying what he had forgotten: the patrol car was still very much in gear. He would only need to remove his foot from the brake and depress the accelerator to get him the hell out of there.

When he felt hot breath and the prick of the fangs as they began to descend into his flesh, he summoned the remaining strength that he had and yanked his foot from the brake. Unsure of what might happen, he simply threw his foot and weight forward in the general direction of the accelerator pedal, flooring the car.

Something screamed, but he could not swear whether it was his attacker or his tires or himself. In any event, he neither questioned it nor slowed down to find out. He simply gripped the steering wheel with both hands and held on for dear life as the air rushed into his lungs and the cool air outside the car whipped around him. The car jumped into a street suddenly. He knew the city was ahead of him on the right, so he yanked the car that direction. The car protested, but he paid it no attention. He just kept that peddle floored until he saw the lights of town ahead of him. He knew he needed to alert the cavalry and that the area needed to be cordoned off. He was an eyewitness. He probably could have his neck swabbed for possible DNA evidence, for heaven's sake. If he could just find the courage to stop his car he might possibly become a hero to not only a community, but perhaps the entire valley. Not only that, in very simple terms it would mean the end of twelve hour shifts in a town not his own, for him and many others who serve all over the valley. His name could be spoken in police departments from Hanford and Visalia on the south, Reedley to the east, and Selma, Fowler and Sanger to the north. They might hear of the ruined front of his pants, and perhaps even how he got felt up by the killer himself, but he doubted that anyone would treat him as a pariah.

Yet, that was all moot because Officer Stevens just could not get his foot off of the gas. He glanced around nervously. He couldn't even see the school anymore. Finally, he began fumbling for his radio, but his fingers either no longer functioned properly or something was wrong with the microphone.

Suddenly there were headlights. He could see the emblem of the CHP, and even the panic on the face of the patrolman as he realized that he was a millisecond from a traffic accident that he would not have to personally write the report on since he was going to be in it. Still, Stevens couldn't stop. He slammed into the driver's side of the car at fifty-five miles an hour just a hair after California Highway Patrolman Kenneth Alan Simmons, divorced father of three, dove across the seat. He never made it.

It sounded as if a bomb had gone off in town. Windows shattered, sending glass fragments in all directions. Metal groaned and twisted and broke loose. Stevens drove the other car eighty feet before everything in their worlds came to a stop. His right foot still tried to push the pedal through the carpeted metal floor, but the motor no longer responded to him. Whatever urine had remained within him during the attack no longer was.

In moments, first interior then exterior lights began to come on. Faces peaked cautiously through curtains. It was nearly ten minutes before the first brave soul reached what remained of both cars. Stevens' car was crushed in front; Patrolman Simmon's was headed for the scrap heap, but not before three children, an ex-wife, a father and mother buried a loved one, surrounded by fellow peace officers in full dress uniforms, wearing the badges of every department in the Central Valley.

Officer Richard Stevens would not be a hero, and by the time that anyone figured out what in the world had caused a police officer to speed through town in the middle of the night, his attacker would be long gone. His detail in Kingsburg would come to an end, however.

FRIDAY

May 9, 2008
6:08 a.m.

When Barbara Lopez' eyelids fluttered open at a little after six that Friday morning, she couldn't believe how great she felt. Immediately, she stopped and listened for the twins. Luckily, they were still asleep. In the distance, she could hear that Jerod was already awake, getting ready for school.

Barbara turned to her husband. He was lightly snoring and looked very comfortable lying there to her left. She watched his chest rise and fall and thought about how terribly hard he had been working lately on the recent wave of murders that had swept over Kingsburg. She didn't know much more about it other than the fact that they didn't have much in the way of leads. Since he had been getting home rather late each night, she hadn't had much of an opportunity to discuss things with him. And she wouldn't press him too much about it unless he brought it up, since he had probably been eating, sleeping and thinking about it ceaselessly for the last four days.

Quietly, Barbara pulled the covers back and got out of bed. She tip-toed out of the bedroom and looked in on the twins. They were fine. She watched them for a while and then headed back for the master bedroom.

"Good morning, sweetie," Michael greeted her upon entering the room. He was still in bed but wide awake.

"I'm sorry, did I wake you?"

"No!" He quickly leaned up onto one elbow. "No, Barb, I was just snoozing anyway."

She offered him a knowing smile as she went to the bed and sat down beside him. "How are you and Jacks doing?"

"The same." He shook his head, dismissing the questions. "But let's not talk about that."

"Okay," she said.

"Let's talk about you," he smiled warmly. "I mean, I haven't spoken to you much these last few days. What's goin' on? What have the kids been up to? What's new?"

"Well..." she began.

The telephone rang.

"Ah, hell," Michael sighed and immediately reached over and picked up the phone.

Barbara sighed at the interruption and listened for the twins. She had looked forward to spending some quiet quality time with her husband, but now with the phone ringing, she knew she could almost kiss that dream goodbye.

"Lopez." *Poor, Michael! He can't even answer the phone normally at home with a common, "hello?"*

"Mike, it's me," Barbara could hear Mark answer

"I hope you're calling me to inform me that a Cub's pitcher threw a no-hitter last night!"

"I want you to go to your front door and pick up the paper."

"Jackson," he sighed. "We don't get the paper."

"You do today. I had the boys in blue swing by and leave one on your doorstep."

"Alright," he said. "What page?"

"We're all over the front page today. And then you'd better get in here."

"Yeah."

"Yeah," he said. "There was an accident last night. Something scared the shit out of one of Hanford's finest. He slammed into a CHP, killing him."

"Holy shit!" Michael muttered to himself, dropping his head into his left hand.

"Chief's called everybody in. Now he's got more mayors than one ripping into his ass! He wants us at the station ASAP. Before ASAP, even!"

"Damn! Where are you?"

"Still at home, but I'm on my way."

"Alright!" And then he hung up the phone.

Michael moved past his wife as if she weren't even there. "What is it?" she asked as he disappeared into the bathroom. He didn't answer. "Dear?" she asked after him, following him to the door just as he closed it in front of her, nearly hitting her.

"They left me a paper by the door," he said finally. "Can you get it for me?"

Without a word, she walked out of the room and headed down the hall for the front door. She peeked through the peephole. The newspaper was there alright. It lay flat and perfectly on her doormat, the top of the front page was upside down to her so she couldn't read anything from her vantage point. Cautiously, since she was still dressed in only her pajamas, she opened the door enough to peek. When she was sure that there was nobody watching her, she kneeled down, reached out and quickly grabbed the paper.

She nearly forgot to close the door behind her. The large bold headline jumped out at her, causing her to forget everything else.

VAMPIRE KILLER ON THE LOOSE
Beth Milligan

Kingsburg--A series of unexplained homicides has suddenly plagued this small suburban town leaving the police department dumbfounded. Yesterday, Kingsburg detectives spoke to a man who claims to have been attacked by a vampire. John Lancaster, reported to be in his late forties, was attacked early Thursday morning inside his residence. Mr. Lancaster spoke with his attacker during the struggle. He was rushed to Selma District Hospital where he is expected to make a complete recovery. Early indications are that this would be the first victim to have survived an attack. A source with the city reports that the chief of police himself admits that the incident is tied in with all of the others, and is the work of a serial murderer. Police have currently no clues as to the identity of the "vampire killer" and have no leads.

The killing spree began early Monday morning when two members of the Kingsburg Police Department were found...

Oh, God! Barbara gasped.

She suddenly pictured the events of two nights before with clarity she hadn't yet known. She brought her hand to her mouth. She could almost feel the cold steel fingers reaching once again into the nursery and wrenching her wrists together. She rubbed the places where sharp claw-like fingernails had nearly torn into her. And then she felt Nathaniel's cold hand touching her face. A shudder went through her as she recalled what Nathaniel had said to her.

"It is true that I am acquainted with this one who attempted to harm your family, but it is no person. How I wish that neither you nor I were so acquainted. It is for this reason that I thought to call upon you. I worried for your safety."

"Did you find it?" Michael's voice came down the hall, making her jump. He did not attempt to hide his voice. There was no time for worrying about waking the kids. She immediately headed his direction as she continued to study the paper.

I can't keep this from Michael!

"Please, tell him nothing of this."

But Nathaniel, she thought to herself as if he was in the room and she needed to convince him of her side of the argument. She began to pace in the kitchen as her thoughts bombarded her. *I've got to tell him! I really can't keep this from him now!*

"Please," the voice kept repeating the same old line. *"Tell him nothing."*

Michael was suddenly standing before her. She jumped again.

"Whoa!" Michael said, apologizing. "Sorry."

Michael said nothing more to her. He simply took the paper and headed back down the hall. A few moments after he disappeared she heard him curse.

Barbara frowned at the sound of what this case had done to her husband. She knew she couldn't blame Michael for reacting in such a way, but she didn't have to like it. *Maybe I'll wait just a little while longer*, she suddenly thought. *He doesn't need any more bad news like this.*

Fifteen minutes later and Michael was kissing her goodbye just as plainly as before and was out the door. As she watched him go, her thoughts went to Nathaniel and of their last meeting. *Why can't I get you off my mind, Nathaniel?*

Barbara continued to analyze her relationship with the mysterious Nathaniel as she glanced at the clock in the kitchen to see how much time she had to shower before Jerod left to go to Judge Harris' house. It wasn't much. *I'll have to hurry,* she realized and headed down the hallway. Before knocking on her son's door to tell him to watch his brother and sister while she took a quick shower, something stopped her and made her look in on them first. She quietly pushed open the door to the nursery and peeked inside.

The babies were already awake. At the sight of their mother, Robbie and Rebekah began to kick their feet and wave their arms. They made happy little squeals. Barbara stood in the doorway, awestruck. Both smiled at her as she looked them over, and they continued to wriggle about in their cribs.

"What's up with you two?"

Barbara ran her fingers through her bed-head of shoulder-length light-brown hair and then sighed as the name came back across her lips. She didn't say it, but it was there nonetheless, as always these days.

Nathaniel.

7:53 p.m.

Barbara watched as the twins studied the objects before them. They were lying on a blanket in the tall grass of their backyard beside a floodlight. It was several days past its mowing date, but Michael had become too preoccupied of late to even realize that there was a yard to maintain. She held two stuffed animals, one a bunny and the other a bear, and made them dance and fly in front of their faces to hold their attention. She used them to both entertain as well as to pass the time while she waited for the guest she was not entirely sure would come.

All she knew was that she had spent the better part of the day thinking about the stranger who had saved her and her children from certain peril only days ago. The man seemed to captivate her, to fill her curiosities and perhaps to liberate her somewhat from the doldrums of her daily life. He was exotic and gentle and friendly, and held no expectations of her. It was better than a sordid affair because it was far more exciting, filling her time with adventure, yet, hurting no one because there was no unfaithfulness of any kind involved. She shook her head to rid herself of the thought. A light wind played with her hair as she did so.

Barbara put the animals down for a second and readjusted the twins' clothing. Anticipating that the evening would grow chilly, she had put light blankets around them and covered their heads and ears with warm caps. It was past their bedtime, but she had hoped to see Nathaniel. However, with the darkness swooping down around them, it was with a hint of disappointment that she stood to take her children back into the house.

She had put on a pretty long blue dress for nothing.

She had fixed up her hair and expertly applied her makeup for nothing.

"I fear the children are cold, Barbara."

208

"Nathaniel?" she said, spinning around to find the face.

She turned her head from side to side but it was nowhere to be seen. She stood up on the tips of her blue pumps, trying to peer over the fence, but she still couldn't see anyone. Had she wanted to see him so badly that she was now hearing things as well?

"Nathaniel?"

"I am here."

"Where?" she said, still looking for him. She stepped away from her babies. "I can't see you."

"My apologies, Barbara," he said. "You happen to be standing next to a bright light and I happen to have...sensitive eyes."

"Oh!" she said, turning toward the light. It didn't appear particularly bright to her, but she started to head toward the house where she could turn the light out. "I'll just turn it off."

"Not at all," he said, suddenly standing behind her.

Barbara spun at the proximity of the sound. Nathaniel was already standing behind her and near the babies.

"I will be fine." Barbara noticed that he seemed to be standing beyond the outer reaches of the light's reach and power. "Thank you."

"How did you do that?" she asked.

"Do what?" he asked, innocently.

"Get in here so fast."

"I apologize if you were frightened by my entrance," he said softly. "But I was already climbing inside when you turned around."

"Climbing?"

"Yes," he answered. He turned and motioned toward the back gate. "You see, the door is locked, and I certainly could not climb over your refuse container and come through the secret gate."

"Oh!" she put her hand to her mouth and giggled. "That's right! I'm sorry!"

"Please, there is nothing for you to be sorry about." Nathaniel stepped before her and touched her shoulder gently, careful to only touch the material of her dress. "I do not mind."

Barbara grinned as she listened to Nathaniel speaking to her. Although there wasn't any reason for her to feel anything but a frigid touch, she actually felt warmth upon the tops of her arms at her shoulders through her dress and swam in its comfort. Suddenly, she found herself drowning. She lowered her head.

"Please."

He knew that he should not touch her flesh directly. He had already crossed that line the night before. Perhaps it was the fact that she had not recoiled at his touch that gave him the courage to attempt it now, as if he *needed* to touch her again. Nathaniel put his hand delicately beneath her chin and raised her head back up so that he could gaze into her eyes. Once there, he quickly removed his hand. She felt his longing, but he knew that he could not touch her. He pulled his eyes off of her and surveyed the children.

"Perhaps we should move inside."

The thought of her children brought Barbara back from the daze. She turned and quickly went to the twins. They were cool, but neither made a fuss about it. As in the last few days, whether it was their feeding time or time to change a diaper, they were laying quietly, patiently awaiting her arrival. They smiled as she picked each of them up and placed them into the stroller that she had used to bring them out. When she was finished with picking up everything, she turned their stroller around and began to push them to the house. She went to ask Nathaniel if he would like to come inside, but she felt him next to her the entire way and somehow knew that he had already been invited.

When they reached the back door, Nathaniel walked passed her and opened it for her.

"There you are," he said, and then followed her inside.

He opened one last door for her and eventually they were through the kitchen and dining area and into the living room.

Barbara turned to see whether she could offer her guest anything, but stopped with the words cued on her lips.

Nathaniel was gone.

"Nathaniel?"

"Barbara, could you please turn down the lights in here?" The voice came from around the corner inside the dark kitchen area.

"Sure," she said.

She didn't have the living room lighting on any kind of dimmer, however, so she simply turned two of the three lamps out. There *was* a fourth lamp: a large floor model that had three heads on it that stretched out toward the middle of the living room like the heads on the spaceships from the original *War of the Worlds*. It was hideous, but a gift from Barbara's father, which was the reason why it was still haunting the corner of the living room and not decorating some less fortunate family's house today. They referred to it as the H.G.Wells lamp and never ever turned it on. In the end she left the lamp sitting beside her recliner on, but turned out the two lamps on either side of the couch. Then she turned around to call him out of the kitchen.

"Nath...!"

She jumped.

Nathaniel was already in the living room, sitting before her on the edge of the fireplace.

"I apologize," he said softly. "I keep frightening you." He started to get up.

"No." She put out her hands. "Sit down. It's alright."

Nathaniel sat down. Barbara reached out with her left hand and brought the stroller to her. The babies smiled and waved at her as she pulled some of their

211

heavier clothing off since they were inside. She removed the clothes and neatly folded and set them at her feet. She took Robbie and Rebekah out of their stroller and set them down on the blanket that they had played and napped on all day. When she was finished, she sat down in her recliner and looked up to see Nathaniel watching her. The vampire had the slightest grin.

"What?" she smiled back.

Nathaniel looked away from her toward the children. "I apologize once again," he said. "I was thinking about my mother. I wonder whether or not she had done much the same for me."

"I'm sure she did." Barbara held her smile. She had often thought the same thing herself on occasion. "Is she still alive?" she asked. Her mom wasn't.

"No."

"I'm sorry. Were you very young?"

"When?" he asked, straightening up.

"When she passed away."

"Yes, I was."

Barbara noticed how very suddenly Nathaniel became stoic with the conversation, so she quickly changed the subject. "Can I get you anything to drink?"

"Thank you, no."

"Something to eat, maybe?"

"No." He shook his head and continued to watch the playful infants on the floor before him. "Thank you." She noticed what color his pale cheeks wore seemed to drain suddenly as he looked toward the front of the house. He stood. Barbara jumped out of her chair and joined him there in order to see the front door. The children seemed to stop what they were doing as well.

A key turned inside the door and Michael stepped inside. All eyes met. Michael said nothing at first, as if measuring his words. Eventually he closed the door behind him and quietly walked into the room. Barbara watched his expression as he seemed to ignore her at first and study the strange long-haired man standing beside her. She saw him as he turned to her, at first taking in the sight of the blue dress. Only then did his eyes rise up to meet hers. In that moment she suddenly felt guilty of a great many things.

"Hello, *dear*," he greeted her softly, but firmly. "Who's your friend?"

"Michael," she began, glancing up at Nathaniel. "This is a new friend of mine." She motioned back to her husband. "Nathaniel, this is my husband Michael."

Michael methodically turned back toward the man before him.

"How very nice to meet you, Michael," Nathaniel said without extending his hand.

"And you," Michael returned the greeting. "Nathaniel, is it?" he said, turning to his wife and then back to the man.

"Yes."

"How interesting," he shrugged. "That's the second time I've heard that name today."

"Oh?" Barbara said, looking back at her husband. "Where did you hear it?"

Michael looked toward Barbara and then back toward the stranger before him. "I'm a police detective, Nathaniel. Last night a man was attacked in his living room and barely survived to tell the tale." Michael stepped deeper into the room, careful not to step on his children at his feet. "You know what he told me his attacker's name was? It was Nathaniel. Just like yours. He had long hair, too."

Barbara frowned. She knew what Michael was doing and did not like it one bit. *Nathaniel's a good man, Michael. He saved me and our children from the killer, not the other way around. How could you make such an insinuation!*

Nathaniel gave no outward response as to what was taking place. Barbara glanced back at him. It appeared to her that Nathaniel also knew what her

213

husband was doing, but he simply stood there and did not utter one word in his defense.

"That's one hell of a coincidence, wouldn't you say?" Michael asked.

The silence was powerful between the two.

"Why is it so dark in here?"

"Nathaniel has sensitive eyes!" Barbara snapped, unable to mask the anger with her husband. "I turned the lights off so he'd be more comfortable."

She looked at Nathaniel and gave him a friendly smile. He nodded in return to her smile, but wisely did not acknowledge it with one of his own.

"I am afraid it is true," Nathaniel agreed, returning Michael's stare with one of his own.

"How do you manage to function during the day with a problem like that?"

"I am quite unable to do much of anything during the day. Now I just use the daylight hours for sleep and do much of my work at night."

"Like a vampire!" Michael said, matter-of-factly.

Barbara spun, showing shock at such a remark, and gave her husband a dirty look; Nathaniel's eyes grew wide, never anticipating such a response.

Nathaniel quickly swallowed whatever surprise he felt initially and nodded. "I imagine so."

"What kind of work do you do?" Michael changed the subject.

"Actually, I do not work any longer. I have the good fortune of being rather wealthy..."

"I see." Michael cut him off, as if not really listening anyway.

Barbara was uneasy. Now she knew why it wasn't a good idea to tell Michael about the attack on her and the kids, and why Nathaniel was in so much of a hurry to leave that night. She started to speak, but Nathaniel beat her to it.

"I have worn out my welcome." Nathaniel made a move to take his leave. "I should be going." He glanced briefly at Barbara. "Goodnight."

"I'm sorry to chase you away, Nathaniel," Michael said.

"Nonsense," he replied. Stepping around the children on the floor, who watched him the entire time, he paused in front of Michael before leaving. "Have a pleasant night," he said. "Perhaps we shall meet again."

Michael smiled. "I'm certain of it."

Nathaniel paused momentarily at the remark, but continued to take his leave. He did not wait for anyone to escort him out; he just opened the front door, quickly closed it behind him and then disappeared into the night. Michael followed, locked the door behind him and glanced into the peephole to ensure that he was gone.

"I cannot believe you, Michael," Barbara began, not waiting for him to return into the room before berating him for his conduct. Michael said nothing. Instead, he raised his right hand and held his open palm out as if to silence her. This infuriated her further than she already was. "What?" she said, her hands on her hips. "Don't you silence me, Detective! I'm not one of your suspects!"

He pulled himself away from the peephole and approached her, stopping short near the hallway. He looked her over once before he spoke. "Oh? Are you sure?"

"What the hell does that mean?" she demanded to know.

"Nice dress!"

"So?"

"So," he said, slow and calculating. "Have you been wearing that all day, taking care of the kids, or did you slip into that just in time for your guest?"

"Just what is it that you are insinuating, Detective?"

Michael appeared as if he wanted to say more, but seemed to stop himself. He held his hand out to her once again, but shook his head as he did so. "Nothing."

"It isn't 'nothing'," she responded. "I want to know. What exactly is it that you think you stumbled into here tonight?" Michael visibly sighed, turned and slowly walked into the kitchen. She was hot on his heels. "Don't walk away, Michael! Tell me, what?"

"Stop it, dear," he said, lightly slapping the counter with his open hands and turning back to face her. "Just stop it. I'm sorry! It's just…"

"It's just, what?" she asked. She felt herself calming slightly. They had not been in a fight in quite some time, thankfully. She was unsure if that was what *this* was.

"Who is this guy?" he asked her.

"A friend."

"A friend? When did you meet him? *How* did you meet him? And how come I don't know anything about this guy before tonight?" He approached her, but stopped short. "I need to know everything."

Barbara paused. If she said anything about what had happened that first night, there would be some kind of fight for sure. "I just met him." It was all that she could think to say.

"That's it!" Michael asked, incredulous. "That's all you've got?" He went to her and set his hands on her bare shoulders. "Listen, dear. I was jealous. I'll admit that. My beautiful wife, sitting in the dark with another man! But I don't have time for that right now. We've got bodies suddenly piled high around here. There have been three missing persons reports filed in the past two days. Maybe there are more bodies we don't even know about yet. Lying in a bed in Selma was very nearly another one! I can't remember the last time I heard the name, Nathaniel, and suddenly there's one with you in my house."

"It's not *him*, Michael!"

"How in the world do you know that, Barbara?" He held her steadfast by the shoulders, but leaned back a bit to look her in the eyes. She tried to look away but couldn't avoid his gaze. "How, honey? How? Who is this guy? What do you know of him?"

Barbara stared at Michael. She realized that there was not much known about her Nathaniel. And what she did know, she would have to soon reveal. Whether she wanted to or not.

It was going to be a long night, she thought.

9:03 p.m.

High alert.

That was the last thing that was said to every incoming shift. *We are on high alert.* The week wasn't yet over and there were five dead, three of which were Peace Officers. Three missing person reports had been filed. A fourth had been reported, but having not been twenty-four hours, it would not become official until the morning. Normally it wouldn't, but every officer, detective and patrolman thought of it as such. They just did not have the means to do much about it other than pray the person would return home after too much drink, or with an armful of flowers and a mouthful of apologies. This was a war-zone and they just did not have time for a lot of anything else but keeping the peace. This was particularly true once the sun went down.

Which it was doing now.

On the north side of town, Selma Police Officer Daniel Perez kept an eye on a small group of high school kids playing basketball at the end of a cul-de-sac. There wasn't much light, but they were not letting that stop them. There were two that should be playing in the gym, leading their school to a league title. They either were doing just exactly that or they would have agreed with the officer's assessment because the other players kept getting out of their way while they basically played one on one. Teenager number one dribbled three times and then suddenly crossed over and took the ball to the basket. Teenager number two stuck onto teenager number one like glue for most of the way, but fell off in the middle of the key, side-stepped and swatted across the head of the other player as he rose for the lay-up. Just as the ball left his hand another hand came into view, reversing its direction and sending it into one of the neighboring yards. Laughter ensued as the other players began to tease the one that had been rejected. Inside the patrol unit, a half block away, Officer Perez clapped his hands together lightly, saluting the play.

East of his position a retired couple walked their white poodle. Reedley Police Officer Meredith Cooper absently played with her red hair as she watched from her parked car while the man nervously glanced behind them. Officer "Coop" to her friends nodded her head and said under her breath that he could escort his wife and the dog back home and then he wouldn't have to worry about the dark or any possible doom at all. She wondered whether the wife was forcing him to reluctantly make this trip. Perhaps he usually kissed her off and then welcomed her back, but was being forced into the chaperone's role because of the state of things in town. In any event, since "Coop" wasn't doing anything else, she waited for them to leave her line of sight, drove until she caught up to them again, stopped, and then repeated the process until she watched them enter their home. Only then did she drive away.

In Memorial Park, just west and across the street from Kingsburg High School, a young boy and girl sat on the large fountain that sits facing both Conejo Avenue and the mouth of Draper Street. Their body language clearly gave the impression that these two were more than friends. They did not touch one another, though it appeared rather obvious that had they the necessary courage to do so, they would. Neither said much of any real significance. They spoke of shared music, mostly. They were freshmen this school year, soon to be sophomores since summer vacation was right around the corner.

The lanky stick-figure of a boy nowhere near becoming a man any time soon would have been thought to have a cute face by the equally skinny young girl, not yet a woman. Each had pretty good skin for teenagers, and long hair. Hers was dark and straight; his was blonde and curly.

Suddenly, a motorcycle came roaring up to them, stopping near. The two turned to watch as the rider shut off the ignition. The bike was lime green and looked fast. The man getting off of it removed his helmet, also lime green. He wore a dark blue t-shirt that read: Fresno Police in large bold white lettering across the front of it. The man approached.

"Hey, guys," he began. "You planning on going home anytime soon?"

"I don't know," said the girl, glancing at her new boyfriend, although neither Pam nor Billy had confirmed the nature of their budding relationship aloud.

"Maybe," Billy said. Neither one gave the man attitude; they simply spoke the truth. They hadn't considered going home yet.

"Well, look. I'm not trying to be bossy or anything, but I highly recommend that you two pick a house." He pointed to each of them. "I don't care if it's your house or his house. I do hope *someone* will be home to supervise."

"Are you a Fresno cop?" Pam asked.

"Yes, I am," the policeman nodded his head. "But I live here. I'm doing some volunteering until this thing is over. And I don't want to read anymore headlines unless it reads: Suspect apprehended. Do you know what I'm saying?"

There was a small chorus of yes's.

"Good," he said, moving his helmet to the other hand. "But I was young once, too, so I understand you two trying to find some time to be alone." He smiled. "I just want to make sure that you have many years' worth of opportunities to do so. Do you understand?"

He was greeted by another chorus of yes's.

"So you guys pick a house before it gets any later." He started to walk back to the bike and looked back at them over his right shoulder. "If I come back and you two are still hanging out here, I'm going to call separate patrol cars and have you driven home. Okay?"

Officer Brian Hamlin smiled wide beneath his motorcycle helmet but neither kid could see it now. He started the bike up and quickly drove off without looking back. A few moments later he came back from the north to check up on their progress, but they had indeed left for home. Of course, he couldn't know which house they had chosen, hers or his. *Perhaps one day they will call one house theirs*, he thought as he headed off to see whether any other kids were still out and about that he could save.

Kingsburg Police Officer Henry Rodriguez turned south onto Simpson Street, heading for Police Headquarters. He stopped only to use the restroom. They had all been advised to stay on the streets. They were not to hang out with one another, not to stop for meals, not to do anything other than remain present on the streets. However, all of that driving, for him, meant a lot of soda, so here he was.

As he slowed his patrol car, preparing to make the left turn onto Earl Street, something caught his attention down the street. It looked like a woman was walking in the middle of the road. He needed to use that restroom, but just knew that he would hate himself later if he didn't at least drive by and make sure everything was alright.

He aborted the maneuver and continued south.

220

As he approached, he could tell that what he had seen was indeed a woman, but actually a young woman to be more specific. Her back was to him so he could not see much but long straight blonde hair, tight, low-rise jeans and a long white button down shirt. It looked to him as if some daughter was wearing her father's dress shirt. She walked quite haphazardly down the exact center of the street, seemingly ignorant of his approach. He got as near as his high beams lighting her bare feet before he stopped.

She stopped, too.

The young woman turned and faced him. She wore a stupid grin that gave the indication that she might be stoned, so he studied her for a moment. The shirt was oversized on her and untucked, preventing him from seeing anything higher than mid-thigh. However, the shirt was only half buttoned. She made an attempt to approach but stumbled a bit, leaving very little to his adult male imagination. There apparently was no bra to be found on her.

Officer Rodriguez put his car in park. Just then the young woman turned on her bare heels and started back the way that she had been headed. Where that could be, who could know? Union Pacific Railroad tracks bordered on the east while small businesses bordered the west; ahead, the Aslan Cold Storage property. There appeared to be no automobiles and certainly no homes anywhere near here.

"Miss?" he called after her. She wasn't walking all that quickly, but she continued on her way, oblivious to him and his authority. *Stoned!*

"Kingsburg, one-six-zero." Officer Rodriguez said, keying the microphone clipped to his shirt just below his left ear. He could hear the girl giggling ahead of him.

"Kingsburg. Go ahead, one-six-zero."

"I'm on Simpson and Earl. I've got an unknown female. Teen. Looks intoxicated. I'm going to make contact and issue field sobriety."

221

"Copy that, one-six-zero. Will send back-up."

"Ten-four."

By this time, the girl had in fact gotten much farther than he would have hoped, so he went back to his car, quickly jumped back in and drove to her new position. He slowed and circled in front of her, cutting her off. She was still giggling; he could see as he jumped out of the car to make contact. In his left ear, he heard the traffic as the dispatcher requested that back up.

"Alright, dear," he said to her. "I want you to come over here and lean against my car for a minute. Do you understand these instructions?"

"Yes." And she approached him as if she were planning to do exactly as he had instructed. When she got to his car, however, instead of leaning against it, she missed the target and ended up leaning against him, causing the both of them to lean onto the car.

"One of us has had too much of something tonight, Miss," he said, sarcastically.

She had fallen into his arms, still giggling, and did not seem the least interested in getting out of them. Officer Rodriguez did not hug her back. He held her by the shoulders as he tried to bring the both of them to balance. She brushed strongly against him, but he tried not to think about that too heavily. He did take one quick peek down the front of her shirt, but just one.

"What's your name, Miss?" he asked her, carefully leading her to the side of his car. He let go of her when she appeared like she was not going to fall over.

"Tiffany," she said, staring into his eyes. She had ceased giggling, finally.

"Hello, Tiffany," he began. "I'm Officer Rodriguez. I'm going to ask you some questions. Is that okay?"

"Sure," she smiled. It was more of a grin actually. She crossed her arms at her chest and gave her head a quick jerk, sending some of her hair back behind her where it belonged. He noticed that she seemed to be sobering up already, and it had only been a moment since she had appeared as stoned as one could be. "But I kind of doubt it."

"I'm sorry," he heard himself asking as there were suddenly hands at his face, coming from behind him. They were strong hands. It felt like he was suddenly in a vise. The world lurched to the left. He saw lights spin past and thought he heard an awful cracking noise like wood splitting. Now he was looking into cruel, hate-filled eyes. There was no smile, no victory, no laughter, and certainly no remorse.

"Come, my daughter. Drink quickly."

It was the last thing that he would hear on this earth.

9:25 p.m.

Quietly, Barbara sat in her favorite chair and listened to her thoughts prattle around as she waited for her husband to come out of the bathroom. He had told her how he had to go back in tonight after a small break because of some massive effort to find the perpetrator in the city's worst killing spree ever. It had been right after Nathaniel had left, so she decided not to needle him about his attitude and detective insinuations concerning her new friend until after she had calmed down.

So there she sat, still upset, but not thinking of what she wanted to say to her husband at all. Instead, she thought of that new friend of hers, and wondered how that wedge had been driven between her and Michael. At first, she had been angry.

Michael was incredibly rude to Nathaniel! Why? Because he happened to share the same first name as someone the police were looking for? Probably the same man who tried to kill her and the twins? It's a crazy coincidence, but it certainly isn't the same man! It can't be! Damnit! Nathaniel, why didn't you let me tell

*Michael how you saved us? Certainly then he'd know
that it couldn't possibly be you!*

"Please, tell him nothing of this!"

*Damnit! Nathaniel, why not? What could it hurt?
You and I are friends! You saved us! You're a hero, for
God's sake! What's with all the secrecy?*

"Please, tell..."

*Yeah, yeah, I know... don't say a word! Well, I'm
tired of it! The secrecy! The feeling I get like I'm
cheating on Michael and the kids! Letting Jerod stay the
night at his friend's house tonight because it'll give me
time to spend alone with you and not have to worry
about him catching us! Damnit! It's killing me just as
much as Jack the Ripper out there in the city's killing
innocent people! And that's another thing—what I know,
or what the inside of the nursery knows, somehow
might be able to tell Michael who this murderer is or
where he might be found. Certainly that's reason
enough to tell Michael!*

"Tell him nothing of this!"

Barbara sighed. "Why do I obey?" she whispered,
barely moving her lips. "Why?"

"Excuse me, Barbara. I didn't quite catch that." It
was Michael. He was back in the room.

Barbara wasn't ready for him to be standing there;
however, in the end, she merely turned her head in his
direction and smiled. And by this time, her anger over
the way he had treated Nathaniel was also gone.

And oddly enough, Michael never said another
word about the strange man he had found in the
darkness of the living room with his beautifully dressed
wife.

"Nothing," she smiled, getting up out of her chair.

"Wait," he said softly, pushing her gently back down
into the recliner. "You don't have to get up. It's late and
you're probably tired. Why don't you just sit back and
relax until you feel like going to bed? I'll take the twins to
the nursery before I leave."

The twins! Barbara hadn't given them much thought in a long while. She looked but they were fast asleep. She gave a silent sigh of relief as she looked over their still bodies, their tiny chests rising and falling.

"No," she insisted, shaking her head, "I'll take them. You're right, though," she lied. "I am tired! But you go on. I know what kind of a case you've got going on down there. You go ahead. I'll be fine!"

"You sure?"

"Yeah," she smiled warmly. "Go on."

"Okay, sweetie." He leaned over and quickly gave her a kiss on the cheek. "But when this is all over, we're taking a vacation!"

"Sounds wonderful."

"Great!" he stepped away. "I'll see you later, okay. Love you!"

Michael turned around and disappeared around the corner on his way toward the door. She heard it squeak as he quietly pulled it open and then a click as he closed it behind him.

"I love you, too!" she whispered as his footfalls slowly faded down the walk until he stepped onto the grass on his way to the car. She almost didn't realize she had said it.

Eventually, Barbara got out of her chair, picked up the twins, one by one, and put them to bed. When she was done, she quietly turned out the light and went to bed.

9:39 p.m.

The first police car to respond for back-up was Reedley P.D. Meredith Cooper. She had been west of Henry Rodriguez' position, checking Roosevelt Elementary School for young stragglers. She caught some basketball players on their way home, but no one else. She would have thought that she had been

225

extremely quick to respond to the call that had gone out, but had a bad feeling when she turned south on the old highway. From several blocks away, she just knew something had gone terribly wrong.

The police car sat in the middle of the road. Parked would not have been the right word. Left or perhaps abandoned looked more fitting. The driver's side door stood open and the headlights were off. There appeared to be a large shape on the hood of the car.

She gunned the accelerator and made a screeching halt beside the car.

"Coop" jumped out of her cruiser and quickly surveyed her surroundings for danger. As she reached for the microphone at her shoulder, she could hear the sound of additional back up. A single headlight approached from the west from Frontage Street which bordered Freeway 99. Glancing back, she could see three sets of headlights coming her way in quite a hurry. One officer and two cadets came running since the Police Department was only a couple of blocks away. She ignored them and continued to move toward the Kingsburg police car. She knew before she saw it that it was another dead police officer. He was on his back, his boots facing her. She went around to the other side of the car to find the face of the dead man. It was looking in an unnatural direction. She ignored the face and went to his neck, and saw the blood stains there. There was no pulse.

"Damnit!" she shouted, following that with a string of other colorful profanities as the other police joined her.

The sound of screeching tires drowned most of it out.

9:40 p.m.

Nathaniel sighed as he watched the woman slumber. She looked so peaceful curled up beneath her bedspread and blankets, *and warm*. It had been a long time since he had considered what it was like to be warm. He glanced down at his hands, raised them and brought them close to his eyes. They suddenly looked so gray to him, so sickly. It had been centuries since he had been warm, whether wrapped in blankets, his mother's arms, or simply standing out in the hot summer sun. He dropped his hands and quickly looked away. Too many haunting memories rushed toward his mind's eye from long hidden quarters of his past, colliding into one another, making it hard to see any of them with any real clarity. Not that he would want to, which is why he now turned away.

His eyes found the place where the bedcovers rose and fell, which helped to distract him from memory. Unfortunately, it stirred him in another way, bringing up other haunting thoughts. He listened to her breaths go quietly in, then out. His breathing began to rise, too. The two rhythms mingled together somewhere in the dark like dancers. They held each other not like teenagers who know nothing and understand even less, clutching onto one another, stumbling lustily about. This was a waltz. There was lust, to be sure, but it was so far below that it could only be tasted like an herb, not as the flavor of the main dish. And he wondered why he was there. Wasn't it obvious? He had only danced with his mother. And as for the other things a male could have with a woman, he would take his place in Hell one day, undead and damned as he was, having experienced none of it.

I shouldn't be here, he reminded himself. *Not so soon. I was here a short time ago.*

Yet, he could not seem to get enough.

Why? What is it with this Barbara? Why does she plague my thoughts so? The woman's breathing changed, but the vampire missed it. The music had stopped but he was still dancing.

"Can't sleep either?"

Nathaniel almost jumped.

Father would be proud! he thought and then hated himself for thinking it. It was Vincent he had been thinking of, not his own father.

He waited a moment before speaking, as if he had not really heard what he thought he had heard, even though he knew that he had. It was just that he *shouldn't* have heard anything. Barbara should have never been able to detect his presence there in the darkness of her master bedroom. No way, indeed.

"Nathaniel," Barbara whispered, sitting up a little. "It's okay." She paused. "I guess I just had a feeling you'd come."

"My apologies," Nathaniel whispered. "I should go."

"Why?" she asked, sitting up fully and sweeping the hair from her face.

He could not answer her.

"It's okay, Nathaniel," she added. "I've been rehearsing some things I wanted to ask you anyway." There were a great many things for Barbara to be concerned about here; many questions to be answered. He could just imagine...

Was this a mere man? Someone who wanted love from her, to pursue an affair? Was this a monster? Someone who intended to steal, vandalize or rape?

Yet, all she said was simply: "Please, stay."

Nathaniel glanced at the doorway to his right as he decided what he should do; looking for the courage to do what was right, or in the best interests of the two of them.

Barbara called out his name once more and he was done for. If there had been any doubt at all of what course of action he might take, there was none now. She was patting the side of her bed with her hand, beckoning Nathaniel.

"Come sit by me."

Standing there in the dark, he closed his eyes and thought about what it would be like to sit next to Barbara. When he reopened them, he was.

"Nathaniel, why do I feel like you're some big brother of mine or something?" she asked in a whisper. "I mean, here you are, practically a stranger, standing in my bedroom in the middle of the night, and yet I feel completely safe. I feel almost...like I need you here."

Nathaniel glanced away from Barbara's questioning eyes. He knew that he felt the same as she, wanting to spend time alone with her, knowing how wrong it was.

The answers to her questions were easy enough to explain, but what of his questions?

"Nathaniel?" she asked, reaching out and setting her hand upon his clothed shoulder. "Can you answer me?"

He closed his eyes at her touch. He could not feel much of it other than the light pressure because of his thick coat. It was warm and delicate. Her soft young skin and fingertips gently caressed the tension and apprehension away forever so easily. And although he had never felt the touch of a lover and should know nothing at all about it, he could somehow well imagine it. He swallowed hard.

What am I thinking? All I can give her are endless questions and nothing more! I'm dead to her! Damn Vincent to hell! I'm dead to her!

He opened his eyes and turned to face her.

"What do you want to know?" he asked in a whisper of his own.

Barbara waited a moment before answering, while he agonized over her questions.

"Let's start simply," she began with a deep breath. Nathaniel saw it and felt it now—that she could *see* him in the dark, that she understood his feelings more than he wanted...

He was trying to listen to what she was saying only, but found he was powerless to stop himself from thinking other thoughts.

"Who are you?"

"I do not know how to answer that."

Barbara stared at Nathaniel and allowed the words, such as they were, to soak in.

For a moment, Nathaniel glanced away. He had prepared himself in the few seconds for the many questions she would ask; however, he had not expected this. His black eyes rose up the length of the wall before him as he pondered his answer. Of course, he was not really looking at the wall.

"Nathaniel?"

"Does it matter who I am?" Nathaniel finally spoke, his eyes once again falling upon the soft, gentle features of Barbara's young face. "What I am?"

There, I said it. Nathaniel looked away. He could not bear to see her reaction. *Then why did I say it? After everything, all we have been through, I ruin it now with but a single phrase. Why?*

Nathaniel's body suddenly ached. His flesh, long dead, should have been immune to the powerful feelings that could plague humans, yet, he felt something.

Barbara thought a moment and then spoke, "What do you mean, 'what you are'?" She spoke in a whisper, almost only mouthing the words. Something was choking them.

Nathaniel looked back at Barbara, curiously. *She is not afraid?* He probed the surface of her eyes. Those captivating eyes! *She will be,* he thought.

Then he reluctantly spoke. "Barbara, I am no man."

There was a short pause between them.

Barbara lowered her head. "I…I don't understand."

For a few moments neither uttered a word. Barbara looked at him in confusion, clearly unable to guess what it was that Nathaniel attempted not very hard to explain. For his part, he felt trepidation.

"I'm sorry?" Barbara whispered at last.

Nathaniel opened his mouth and looked up toward the ceiling, silently laughing at the thought.

"You apologize to me!" he said, shaking his head. "It's no more your fault than my fate is my own. The creature you met that night is the vile thing responsible for everything! No, sweet Barbara, it's not your fault."

Nathaniel paused one last time to enjoy what he determined to be the last peaceful moment that he would ever have with this woman who had so captivated him.

"The simple truth is, however, that beast and I are the same."

"What?" Barbara asked, but did not recoil in terror.

He paused, allowing himself, for a brief moment, the unfathomable notion that she might accept him no matter what form he might be. She even leaned forward rather than back away. When she spoke next, he realized that it was not meant to be.

"You are nothing like him. How dare you place yourself in the same category, much less the same breath as that... that... I don't even know what that *was!* I just know it could never be you."

Nathaniel's head sunk, yet Barbara continued. "You're the man who saved me. I don't even want to think about where I might be had it not been for you rescuing my babies from God knows what!"

"God?" Nathaniel repeated the name, interrupting her.

"Yes, God!" She didn't miss a beat. "I've been having dreams about you."

"Dreams?"

"Yes, dreams. Two different ones in fact."

"It has been too long now," Nathaniel said, and incredibly he felt detached from himself... drifting away just like that night in the yard. "I can no longer remember ever having had any." The sound of the words even felt transparent.

"Please," she attempted to continue. "An angel told me about you. He asked me what I thought of you."

"And what did he say? Did he tell you to flee? To escape with your babies before it was too late? Did he tell you to have me destroyed? To hide while he did it? To run without looking back while he destroyed me like Sodom? I wish that he would hurry and do it!"

"What?" Barbara leaned back as if slapped hard across the face suddenly and without provocation. "Nathaniel, what is all of this?"

His voice trailed, seeing her reaction. He glanced away from her. "My life ended so long ago."

Nathaniel closed his eyes and fought the anger that he felt now. He was being hunted by Vincent the devil on the left and God himself on the right. He felt backed into a corner, awaiting the first blow and wondering from which direction it might come. And like a martyr, resigned to his fate, he allowed his guard and his anger to fall. Would it be the one which brought his demise, figuratively speaking, of course? It was always easier after the first one, right?

Barbara listened while Nathaniel vented his long held frustration. Now she would have many more questions and understand nothing. She curled up into a ball.

Nathaniel looked at her panic and then away. "You see, it is I who should apologize to you."

Nathaniel stood. He felt her fear, though he knew that she still did not understand the truth of it, and was ashamed. He was afraid now, too. Afraid her reaction to him would get worse than simply needing a moment to get her wits about her.

What if she never gets over her fear? What will I do then?

Nathaniel knew. He walked over to the doorway and waited while his invitation into any part of this beautiful woman's life was about to expire.

"What is it that you are not telling me, Nathaniel?" she asked. He could hear it in her voice that she was preparing herself.

"My life was ended by the beast that attacked you, almost too many years ago to recall. He killed my mother and father and spared me. It turns out that they were the ones to get the better of it."

"How could you say that? How can you just...?"

"My dear," he began, cueing the words at the tip of his cold tongue, interrupting her. "I am a vampire. I live off of the blood of others to survive. Vincent did this to me. Unlike Vincent, however, I have never taken a human life to get it. No, I am far more pathetic, trolling about for stray animals that no one would miss." He started to pause and then thought better of it. Far better to say what he could now while still having the chance. "You never need fear me, Barbara. It appears that I have great feelings for you which I had thought myself incapable of having. I shall cherish the time that I had in your presence."

Barbara never said a word; she simply sat there in the dark, quivering. Nathaniel turned and faced the darkened hallway, speaking to her over his shoulder. He simply could not bear to remember her any other way than the way that she had used to greet him with the most wonderful smile.

"I have to destroy Vincent. You and I will never know peace until this is accomplished. There are rules against this, but I have no choice." Nathaniel prepared himself to go. He was almost inaudible now. "Please do not hate me, Barbara."

And then he was gone.

*　　*　　*

233

Barbara watched as he disappeared into the darkness of the open doorway. She could not see Nathaniel anymore and somehow knew that he had left the house. She stared in the direction of the hallway for ten minutes before the tears came. It was not until nearly an hour later that she was able to release herself from the ball that she had rolled herself up into and give herself back over to sleep. When she did, she began to dream. Yet, these were not dreams, as dreams go. These were memories. The first one was not hers…

February 12th, 1747

"*You bastard!*" Nathaniel screamed at the top of his lungs. "You horrible, evil bastard! How could you? All these years I have stayed here, faithful as the sunrise. I have done all that you have wished. I have even learned not to detest your very presence even though you butchered my family, and look what you have done! Why? Damn you, why?"

"My son," Vincent calmly spoke. He knew full well his effect on Nathaniel. "I am really quite surprised at your tone."

"Foul creature of Hell!" he howled back at him, stepping closer. Long strands of spittle stretched with his fury from the top of his mouth to the bottom, and poured out of the corner of his light purple lips. Yesterday, his lips had been pink.

"Nathaniel, please!" Vincent grinned. He displayed his healthy, gleaming incisors, fangs which had now, after all of these years, finally tasted the young man's blood. The sight of the beast's smile sent Nathaniel into a fury that he had never known. It sprung him like a trap.

"*AHHHH!*" Nathaniel lost control and pounced.

The attack was as clumsy as it was unsuccessful. To Nathaniel's eyes, it was like passing through a ghost.

He tried to stop himself but his momentum had carried him too far already. He did not stop until he struck the wall and slumped groggily to the floor, his long blonde hair cascading about him.

"Really, Nathaniel! Don't you see why you need me now more than ever?" He was standing over him now. "You would be absolutely lost without me. In fact, you would probably perish."

"Get away from me, Vincent!" Nathaniel shouted, sitting up with his back against the wall that he had struck. "I have never needed you! Never!"

The vampire put his hands upon his hips and laughed. "Of course you have, dear boy! Of course you have!" His laughter rose. It grew crueler. "That is precisely why I have made you in my own perfect image, so you could finally see that!"

"Go to Hell, damn you!" Nathaniel screamed.

The vampire smiled.

"Oh, but my dear Nathaniel, for one to go there, one must be able to die!" His smile grew into a hearty laugh. "Don't you finally see? You and I can never die!"

Barbara stirred. The scene was over, only to be followed by another...

There was someone coming through the twins' nursery window. She looked up. There was a terrible face adorned by long flowing hair. Piercing, penetrating eyes were staring back at her and into her, looking into everything that made her who she was on this earth. There was nothing that she could hide from those eyes.

She found herself screaming. The twins were screaming, too, but she had to take great pains to hear it.

Her hands were numb as bitingly cold, vise-like hands gripped her.

The owner of the hands laughed heartily at her while she continued to scream.

"Madam," he said to her. "Your children seem to be crying!"

Barbara shuffled backwards, trying to free herself from his grip. Her feet tangled as she attempted to jerk herself free and she lost her balance. The vampire still did not let go of her.

"A pity!"

"Who are you?" She attempted to shake free of his grip, but could not. "What do you want?"

"So many questions!" He laughed.

As he spoke, Barbara took the opportunity to try once more to free herself with one last violent shake of her arm. "Let me go!"

"As you wish."

Barbara suddenly became free and fell down. She let out a cry as the momentum snapped her head back when she hit the floor, biting her lip.

"What precious little throats they have!" she heard and suddenly alarms were going off inside her head. Her babies were in horrible danger. She attacked.

The beast had her before she could scream. Those cold, claw-like fingers had her arms above her elbows, pinning them to herself. She tried to let loose a cry but could not. The pain made her bite again into her lower lip. The vampire lifted her off of her bare feet with little effort and then brought her close. Suddenly, eyes that seemed black as pitch to her in the dark widened and focused immediately upon a trickle of blood upon her lips.

The vampire pulled his face back in another terrible smile, exposing ivory white fangs. The sight made her shiver and she finally was able to let out a cry.

"Careful," he whispered tenderly. "You'll spill it."

The vampire did not notice her revulsion as he pulled her closer. Ignoring her, seeing only the crimson upon her lips, he brought them down to him and licked them clean with a slow sweep of his rough tongue.

The tongue was cold, too, for her attacker was no man.

Barbara was blacking out now. She could see it coming as if she were hovering above the room in some out of body experience. She heard the babies screaming at the top of their little lungs as she watched herself collapse there onto the floor.

Barbara removed her gaze from herself and followed what incredibly seemed to be a vampire that was inside her house. She watched, powerless to stop him as he moved over to her daughter's crib. Rebekah wailed and wriggled as if she anticipated what was to come. The vampire reached into the crib and picked up the baby. He held the child high above his head. Behind his purple lips, gleaming fangs hungrily protruded out from the corner of his mouth. Slowly, confidently, they pierced the air on their way toward the baby's warm, vibrating little throat.

Instead of watching in utter transfixed horror as her daughter was about to be consumed alive by the vampire, or in the very least turning away from the scene in order to spare herself the horrible and graphic sight that would haunt her dreams and paralyze her waking hours forever, she turned her gaze toward the open window. As if she knew what was to happen next, she waited for the precise moment when her beloved Nathaniel would come flying through. In one glorious ballet of movement, Nathaniel swept the unharmed baby from the vampire's hands and knocked the vampire into the far wall.

"Nicely done, Nathaniel. I wondered when you might show yourself," the vampire said as he attempted to regain his composure. "I taught you very well, indeed."

"You taught me only to hate. And I hate you very much."

Vincent sighed dramatically, and then took a threatening step forward.

"Remain where you are, Vincent!" Nathaniel commanded. "These are under my charge."

"Oh, but Nathaniel, surely you don't think me gluttonous. I will gladly share them with you."

Nathaniel made no effort to respond.

"Ah, but that is right," he quickly interjected. "You don't *feed* on human blood, do you, Nathaniel? Such the pity. Cats and vermin!" he said with a dramatic shudder. "It makes you considerably weaker than I, you realize. In that instance, I guess I will have both!"

"No!" Nathaniel stood his ground.

"I will not be ordered around, Nathaniel," the vampire said firmly, taking another step forward.

Nathaniel said nothing and made no effort to withdraw. Barbara felt herself bracing for an attack, as if she might be able to assist in the defense of her children.

The vampire stopped. "Ah, you mean to challenge me. I adore challenges. It has been a challenge, my finding you. It has been a challenge following a cold trail across the globe." Vincent took one step closer. "And now that I have you..."

He stared his adversary down, menacingly, for a moment, then reached out delicately with his left hand and lovingly moved a stray hair out of Nathaniel's face. He whispered: "And I do have you, Nathaniel." Now he lowered his hand back to his side and changed his expression, this time to a look of intimidation. Then, he seemed to shake it off again.

"Just go, Vincent," Nathaniel said, placing his hands on the back of the little baby's crib. "It is still early. I trust you have more than enough time to acquire for yourself another meal."

Vincent sighed again and smiled, turning his attention back to the nearest baby. They were each still screaming their lungs out, red-faced panic on their tiny faces. Something made him giggle.

"So lovely!"

The vampire reached down into the nearest crib.

No! The beast was touching her baby.

"So warm!" Vincent pulled the hand away from the baby and then, glancing dramatically into Nathaniel's eyes, stuck the caressing finger into his mouth and licked the scent from it.

"No more games, Vincent."

Vincent turned his gaze back upon Nathaniel, his face devoid of expression. He appeared neither pleased nor angered. "It is so good to hear you speak my name again after all of these years."

"It has been much longer than years." There was a pregnant pause where Vincent's name should have followed, but Nathaniel refused to satisfy the beast any further. "And not at all long enough."

Vincent nodded with understanding or perhaps it was acknowledgement that there was nothing more to discuss. No chance at reconciliation. "I'll not be denied so easily the next time, Nathaniel."

Nathaniel gave no response.

"I'm almost sorry that this must end, my young Nathaniel: my hunt for you. This chance meeting. Our next meeting." There was the obvious threat in those words, but he showed no hint of it on his face. "It is good to find you, finally. I have grown so exhausted with the travelling. I miss the old country. I will be returning home soon."

Barbara could see herself stirring in the corner of her eyes, but paid herself little attention. She held her gaze to the interaction before her there in the middle of the nursery.

"Come back with me, my son. May this not end with the shedding of our blood that mingles inside you."

Barbara felt for Nathaniel and marveled as her children's protector stood ground and said in the most composed of voices: "I am not your son!"

Barbara stirred yet again and more pronounced. So much so that she awoke. Barbara sat up in her bed. She was alone. Michael had not yet come home. Behind her eyes the images continued to loop. Everything that she had dreamed and more was there to be relived and examined, but she needed no more of it. Though she was alone, she could hear Nathaniel's words as if the confessed vampire were still lurking about her bedroom.

"My dear, I am a vampire. I live off of the blood of others to survive. Vincent did this to me. Unlike Vincent, however, I have never taken a human life to get it. No, I am far more pathetic, trolling about for stray animals that no one would miss. You never need fear me, Barbara."

It was clear who the villain was in this drama that had slammed into the town just days ago. That was plainly evident. It was just so terribly sad that there was nothing to be done for poor Nathaniel. *Indeed, how could such a one be redeemed?* Barbara seemed to ask herself, but quickly realized that they were not her words, or if they were, it was certainly not her own voice that she was hearing. The words continued: *There could be no saving grace. What amount of the Lord's blood could cover the stain of this walking death when the living corruption was itself covered in the blood of so many others, be it animal or otherwise?*

Barbara thought to argue with the words that filled her head and not her ears. She did not know what or how she might argue; she simply felt compelled that someone should be arguing *something* on Nathaniel's behalf! It had been God, the Father, in heaven who had spared her babies from certain death, and it had been the Lord Jesus Christ who had done the work; but Nathaniel was the tool for that dispensation of grace! Before she could utter a single word, she felt her heart drop into the pit of her stomach.

How could such a one be redeemed?

One could see the hopelessness of the circumstance.

"I have to destroy Vincent," Nathaniel had said; apparently oblivious to the battle taking place about it that the vampire was destined to lose. And lose decisively. *"You and I will never know peace until this is accomplished. There are rules against this, but I have no choice. Please do not hate me, Barbara."*

Barbara had been staring at the ceiling of her bedroom but not really seeing anything as the words played and played—Nathaniel's voice, as well as the other voice that was not her own. At last she lowered her eyes and simply looked at her hands that were clasped together over her bedspread-covered lap.

"What do you think of my Nathaniel, now?"

Barbara looked up. If anything that she had heard tonight seemed to be coming from directly beside her, it was those eight words, yet she was still alone. Or was she? It was the same voice as the one in the dream that she'd had the day before during her early evening nap: the teacher. If it had been his voice all along that condemned Nathaniel, why was it now defending the vampire? It was a deepening mystery.

What was not a mystery, however, was how she felt about Nathaniel. She was not *in* love, but she did love Nathaniel. Any confusion that she had felt before, though she understood far from everything, was now replaced by direction; by a call to arms.

And she was not afraid.

She felt strangely empowered suddenly, and as she flipped away her bedspread and sheet, Barbara meant to use every ounce of that power.

11:30 p.m.

The sky over downtown Kingsburg was lit up like South-Central Los Angeles. Patrol cars of every persuasion were adorned with circling blue and red, blue and white. There was flashing yellow, too—so much artificial light that it nearly felt as if it were day and the sun was doing the lighting.

Detective Michael Lopez studied the scene before him with a bit of glaze over his eyes. It was late, nearly midnight. If asked, he might have not been able to reveal just how many hours he had already put in with seemingly no end in sight. He was exhausted. Whatever adrenaline he possessed had been burned up long ago due to the fact that he'd been borrowing the stuff heavily for days now. Lastly, with yet another body lying before him, and yet another police officer, he could not help but feel like giving up.

The hell with it! If the chief wants me replaced, replace me! They can have the God—

"Why don't you go home, Mikey?" Jackson said in a concerned tone, ignoring the mass of peace officers, the encircling lights, and the covered body upon the police car in the middle of another cordoned off street in their beloved town.

"What?"

"You heard me. Get out of here while you can. Go home and kiss the wife, watch your kids sleep for a while, and then get some yourself."

"No way," Michael said, momentarily snapping out of his daze. "This is where I belong. This is the job I chose." Heavy words; his voice betrayed them, however.

"Bullshit!" Jackson loudly exclaimed, catching his partner off guard.

"What did you say?"

"Bull! Shit!" He did not step closer. He did not attempt to cover his voice. He didn't give a rip who heard and what they might think about it. "Of course what you say is true. That goes the same for me, too. But this case is kicking our asses, man. And there's no Calvary to call in. Oh, this is the Alamo alright, but we cannot lose. And the only frigging way we're going to be able to figure this thing out and stop this sonofabitch is if we're smart."

Michael started to interrupt, but Jackson waved him off. "No. I don't want to hear it. I can see it in your eyes. You're about ready to shut it down, and not just for tonight, but maybe for good. Now, I want you to go home right now and get some sleep. I'll give you five hours. After that, you get your ass back here so I can get mine." He glanced around. A few were watching them, listening to everything that they could hear. Finally, he lowered his voice and approached. "We'll probably still be out here."

Michael laughed. It was gallows humor—brief and not overly obvious to anyone but Jackson. "Alright," he said. "I give up."

"That's why you're going." Michael stopped and gave his partner a hard look. Michael waved that off, too. "Hey, maybe tomorrow morning when you come back I'll be the one who needs the kick in the ass." He reached out and put his right hand on Michael's shoulder, patting him a few times. Michael answered it by sliding his left below his and patting the small of the man's back.

The two men separated and Michael quickly walked through the throng of cars and police to get to his vehicle. Luckily, it was not blocked in. Had it been, he would have simply continued on by foot the necessary fifteen to twenty blocks to get to his pillow.

SATURDAY

May 10, 2008
12:08 a.m.

Michael drove up Kern Street per his routine in order to come around the west end of Roosevelt and park his car in front of the house on the street. It would have been easier to come up Roosevelt and simply park in the driveway, but he was through with trusting city vehicles not to leak oil. *If they're going to leak, better it ends up on the asphalt.*

As he came around the corner, his headlights picked up the figure in the front yard. His heart skipped a beat until he realized that it was just Barbara. His head full of multiple homicides and unfortunately, very little evidence or hope of solving them to go along with, he now had to think about the doings of his wife. And this was most definitely not the time to have to also worry whether or not she was cheating on him. Perhaps even more important than that thought was the surreal possibility that this new man might in fact be the killer that the entire Central Valley of California was hunting.

More detective than husband now, Michael slowly got out of his car and headed toward the house and his wife, who was now seated upon the patio bench there in front.

"Hi, dear," he said simply, ignoring the absurdity of the moment. It was after midnight and here he found the mother of his children sitting alone, but most likely waiting for someone other than him. At least she was dressed in more than just a nightgown.

"Hello, Michael," she said. "Funny meeting you here in the middle of the night."

And then she laughed. She was wearing a pair of pajamas with one of his heavy jackets on top. It was an odd pairing for 64 degrees and the witching hour, but at least she was warm.

Michael smiled. How could he not? It was precisely what he would have wanted to ask her. Grinning, he took a seat beside her. "I would have rather met you in the bed, but this could be nice, too."

A few moments of silence passed between them before Barbara broke it up. "I suppose that you would like to know what I'm doing out here?"

"Only if you're interested in telling me," he answered her.

"First, let me get this out of the way. You do need to know what I have been up to, but it certainly isn't what you may have thought. I won't lie to you. For a while even I wasn't exactly sure what my relationship with Nathaniel was. I do care for him very much, but it isn't like that. Anything other than friendship is impossible for him and me for a couple of reasons."

"I hope some of those reasons are your wedding vows," Michael said, and immediately regretted it.

He knew that he was probably allowed the outburst given everything that he was beginning to discover of his wife's secret life of late. He just wished now that he hadn't done it. It smelled like just the cheapest of shots.

"I'm sorry," he said quickly. "I'm just tired."

"No, it's fine," she said. "I'd probably do the same. But I hope you'll let it go now. We don't have time for that. I know *you* don't."

"Barbara," Michael began, but was cut off.

"Please, honey," she said quickly. "I have much to say. I know who the killer is. A couple of nights ago, he broke into the house." She raised her hand to stop him, knowing full well that he would explode in either rage or with a barrage of questions upon hearing the news. "Nothing happened. It was Nathaniel who saved you from having to organize three funerals. Somehow, he heard the screams. In any event, I praise God for his intervention. The papers have it wrong, Michael. He's not the vampire killer. As ridiculous as it sounds, your killer *is* a vampire. And so is Nathaniel."

248

Michael was already cueing up the first "what?" when another leapt in front. "What?" he said, vaulting to his feet. How he managed to stand, though, in wake of all of the shocks of the past few minutes was incredible.

"I know this because he came back to see me tonight after you had gone. He told me. And then he left. I don't know where he is. I believe that he will be very near until Vincent is dead."

"Vincent?" Michael asked, his voice loud and uncertain.

"That's your killer. Nathaniel is the reason why he is here. He's been searching for him."

"Why?"

"Because in some misguided way he thinks of him as his son."

"Why is that? Did he make him a vampire?"

"Yes. Exactly."

"This is ridiculous!"

"Yes, it is," Barbara answered simply. "But it is what it is. And we have to stop him."

"We?"

"That's right! We! I probably know about as much as you do concerning all of this. We can work together, we can work separately. It doesn't really matter to me."

12:49 a.m.

Jackson glanced alternatively from Michael to Barbara and then back to Michael. Eight minutes ago he'd been summoned here by the partner that he had instructed to go home and go to bed. Two minutes ago he greeted his friend and sat down. One minute ago he was told the most fantastic tale he'd heard since he had been a child. Now he did not know what to say.

There was a knock on the door.

Everyone in the room just stared at one another. It was Michael that got up.

249

His gun was still holstered below his left arm. He unbuckled it and pulled it free as he went to the door. He peeked through the peep hole before opening it. As he turned the knob, he held the weapon behind him, but did not put it away.

"Hello, Mr. Lopez," came a young female voice on the other side of the doorway.

Barbara wore an expression of recognition and raised her hands to her forehead as if she'd just remembered something she'd forgotten about. She got up to join Michael at the doorway.

"I'm sorry. I don't remember you."

"It's Tiffany."

"Hi, Tiffany," Barbara greeted her. "C'mon, Michael. Don't you remember your own neighbors? Tiffany used to baby-sit, remember?"

Michael sighed. "I'm sorry, Tiffany. He turned and quietly returned the Glock to its holster, hiding it from the girl's view.

"That's alright. I'm sorry, too. I know it's late."

"Doesn't anyone sleep anymore?" Jackson asked as Barbara motioned Tiffany inside the house.

Tiffany turned toward the man with a shy grin. "Some still do."

"Is everything alright, Tiffany," Barbara asked guiltily.

It was extremely late and barely 60 degrees outside and here the girl was dressed only in a pair of low rise jeans and a Matchbox Twenty concert T-shirt.

"Well, I feel a little embarrassed to ask this, but..."

"Don't be silly," Barbara said. "As you can see we're all still up. What is it?"

"Well, I was staying up, watching some movies with my boyfriend..."

The two detectives exchanged quick skeptical glances that read: *That's not what you were doing.* When Michael glanced away from his partner and scratched his head with another look, this time that seemed to read: *I don't have time for this!* Tiffany appeared oblivious to everything other than her mission of acquiring assistance from the neighbors; however, Barbara did notice it and shot one back herself which read: *We'll be talking about this later!*

"...when we heard some noises coming from the back of the house," the girl continued, undaunted.

"What did it sound like?" Barbara asked her.

"Where's your boyfriend?" The detectives asked in unison.

Tiffany looked to Barbara first and then to the two detectives as if unsure of who to answer first; perhaps cobwebs were forming due to the lateness of the hour. Finally, looking back to Barbara, Tiffany said: "My boyfriend just stares at the television, ignoring everything. I finally ran over here when I noticed the lights on."

With that, Tiffany glanced down nervously at the linoleum covered floor and said nothing. For their part the two men kept Tiffany in their collective sights while they decided the best course of action or perhaps the next set of questions. In either event, neither made an effort to move. Finally, with a sigh, as if she had been waiting patiently for someone to decide to act, Barbara went to the girl and rubbed a comforting hand across Tiffany's back. The poor thing seemed too frightened and was most definitely cold; Barbara could feel through the girl's flimsy T-shirt. She looked up in the direction of her husband and good friend and sighed at their apparent lack of interest.

"Can I get you two *detectives* to walk Tiffany back to her house and check everything out for her, *please*?

1:15 a.m.

"I don't know what's wrong with these kids today," Jackson said sarcastically as he and his partner walked

251

across the Lopez driveway on their way next door. "You wouldn't catch me staying up this late *just* watching movies with the old ladies' parents out of town. Not unless I needed a fifteen minute break."

They continued on their way until they got to the Rosen's front door. Tiffany had told them that she'd left it locked for her boyfriend. According to her he had told her not to worry about it and stay with him on the couch, but she had locked him in anyway and had gone for help.

Jackson knocked lightly upon the front door, wanting only the boy to hear them. Neither of them actually thought that their mission would discover anything out of the ordinary. These days, even nervous imagination was the norm. They knocked a few more times, louder the last time, but no one seemed to be answering.

"Damn!" Michael sighed, shaking his head.

"Do you think we'll ever get to bed?" Jackson asked in a tone that said he already knew the answer.

Next, although what Michael really wanted to do was to break down the door, the two men decided to check around the back. The unspoken thought between them was that the kid had decided to get up after all and check that everything was indeed alright. They went around the Rosen's driveway and headed for the side gate entrance to the back yard. Upon arriving at their destination, each man quickly pulled both their guns and their Mag-lite police-issue flashlights. Then they separated: Jackson leaning up against the side of the house and Michael moving over on the other side of the gate and against his own back fence.

"Ready?" Jackson mouthed. Michael nodded in return.

Jackson aimed his Mag-lite toward the spot where the gate latch string should be. The gate was closed shut, but only partially. He glanced toward his partner. Their faces were visible thanks to the street lamp that stood directly across the street from them. Michael nodded in agreement. Holding his Mag-lite in his left hand, and parallel to his chest, Jackson laid his gun hand atop his arm in the shape of a cross. Quickly, he kicked open the gate. It flew open, slamming back against the body of the fence with a crash that would not only betray their position but would announce it to the entire neighborhood. Ignoring it, he swept both his light and his weapon back and forth across his entire viewpoint, revealing the west side of the yard to be unoccupied. Fescue grass grew from the cement slab by the pedestrian door all the way to the back of the yard. Alongside the grass appeared to be bark, decorated here and there with small flowering plants. Some of the coloring could be discerned with the dim moonlight. Sweeping the light back and forth, he looked for anything else that might be of importance.

"Clear!" he said in a firm whisper.

At that point Michael moved across his partner's line of sight momentarily, holding his Mag-lite and gun in like manner and moving in. After a few steps Jackson joined him and the both entered deeply into the yard. Michael cast his light ahead, while Jackson double-checked where they had come.

There was suddenly a hand on Michael's back. "Mikey," Jackson said. He turned around, casting his light upon the ground before him as he did so. "Take a look at this."

Laying atop of the medium sized walk-on bark along the base of the fence was the missing gate hardware with the Master lock still attached to it. It looked relatively new. They could now see why the wooden door had opened to them. Someone very strong had simply yanked the hardware from the fence thus negating the necessity of a key.

"Shit!" Jackson said under his breath, but mostly not.

The men continued more carefully now. Half way down was the kitchen window. Both men glanced at it, shining their lights across its area. The window appeared closed at first glance, but appearances were deceiving.

Jackson stopped, glancing back. Michael continued a few steps, but also stopped when Jackson fell back and watched as he stepped close to the window. In the meantime, Michael took a couple of quick steps forward, took a quick peek around the corner, and swept his light in all directions to make certain that there was nothing awaiting them while they discerned what type of pie his partner just found in the kitchen. At first glance the rest of the yard was just as safe and quiet as the side had been.

"What did you find, Jacks?" Michael asked upon reteaming with his partner. "Cherry pie?"

"Not likely," Jackson answered. "I'm hoping it's just some chicken that your neighbor absently tossed in the trash a few days ago." He paused. "Otherwise, it might *be* your neighbor."

1:26 a.m.

"So," Tiffany began, absently fingering some cookies that Barbara had set before her.

There might have been a time when Tiffany would have devoured those cookies, but apparently not tonight. Perhaps it was just too late for that. Perhaps it was because she was too worried about what the detectives might be finding next door.

"How have you guys been?"

"Good," Barbara said. "Just busy."

"How are the babies?"

"They're fine. I can't believe that they're still sleeping after all of the noise around here."

"I'm sorry," Tiffany said.

"No, dear. It isn't you." She reached out toward Tiffany's hand for consolation. She didn't quite reach it, but it was the thought that mattered. "Everything has been turned upside down in this house, this town, this everything."

Tiffany smiled absently. This was followed by a strange silence. Tiffany turned to the left and toward the front door as if expecting someone. Barbara followed Tiffany's gaze, but could hear nothing. She was reminded now how the twins had done nearly the same exact thing the day Vanessa had visited unexpectedly.

Things seemed to flow in slow motion suddenly as Tiffany got up from the chair without a word or even the slightest glance her direction. There was no thank you for the cookies. There was no acknowledgement of the time that Barbara had spent visiting when she could have just as easily gone to bed. Tiffany simply stood up and went, gliding easily to the front door, taking the knob in one casual move and, without a thought to any possible danger, walking out the door.

Barbara started to get up herself, but a pair of cold hands at her shoulders and a much colder voice above her right ear stopped her. Then there was that face. She would never forget it for the duration of her days. It was Vincent. This had been a charade, Tiffany's coming over, and Barbara knew it at once.

She also knew that it might be too late not only to warn Michael and Mark, but to save their lives as well.

A name came to her mind, but she wondered if it might be too late for that, too.

Vincent reached to his right and took the chair that he found there. He moved it close to where Barbara sat and took a position beside her.

"So." The vampire grinned, inquisitively. "How is Nathaniel?"

1:31 a.m.

The two detectives moved away from the window and went back to the job at hand which was to secure the perimeter. There might indeed be something quite nasty inside the residence; however, before they took that on they needed to make quite certain that there was not something also nasty hiding in wait on the outside. While Jackson hovered around the sliding glass door which no doubt led into the living room or kitchen/dining area, Michael continued on his way through the rest of the well-groomed back yard and patio area.

The cement pad at the slider was dyed and stamped concrete. It was very nice and also very expensive. Had it stopped there it might not have been that rough on the Rosen's budget, but it did not. Rather, it continued down the side of the house, extending into the middle of the yard and nearly all of the way to the fence on the east side. Michael followed where it led, taking pains to shine his light southward where he found fruitless pistachio and cherry trees. The bark continued all throughout the border of either grass or cement. A large toad hopped twice, causing him to flinch. He caught the second hop in his beam.

Along the east side of the house were some old metal stakes and some firewood that had been hidden away or forgotten. There was nothing for anyone to be hidden behind, so Michael quickly retraced his steps back to his partner. He found Jackson waiting impatiently for him.

"Clear?" Jackson asked. He was alternating using his flashlight to peek in the house and turning it off and using only the naked eye. Neither worked all that well. Whatever movie was left playing when the girl had gone for help was still rolling, sending mad shadows across the room. "I think the boyfriend's asleep. Does that look like him, laying there wrapped up on the couch as if it were winter."

"God, I hope that wasn't him we smelled at the kitchen window?"

"Let's find out, shall we?" Jackson reached for the handle on the slider. He stopped and pulled back. "Wait!"

"What is it?" Michael asked.

"Tiffany just walked in. I thought you told her to stay with Barbara?"

"I did," he said, turning to see for himself. He had to wait a while for the scene to change in the movie. Once it did, he was able to see her advancing into the room. She walked over to the couch, either ignoring them there at the window or perhaps not able to see much in the dark just like them. Again the room went dark. When he could see again, Michael saw Tiffany kneeling at the couch in front of her sleeping boyfriend.

"We'd better get in there before she moves to another part of the couch and decides to wake him up the old fashioned way," Jackson whispered.

He went for the handle on the slider and pulled. Originally, he thought that it, too, was locked, but upon giving it one good pull, it came open. It hit them both as they stepped over the threshold. It was not any attacker. It was the smell of death.

"Shit!" Jackson cursed a moment before Michael got far enough in the room to catch the brunt of the odor of rotting human flesh in the living room. Michael grabbed his shirt and yanked it quickly over his nose and mouth. He gagged twice before he shielded himself enough from the assault.

Slowly, casually, Tiffany Rosen turned around to greet the two detectives in the dark, but both men were oblivious to it. The movie continued its march; the scenes now occurring during the night. As far as they knew, nothing had changed.

*　*　*

Jackson took a few steps toward the couch, but then stopped in his tracks. Although he could not yet see the girl staring at him, there were now too many conflicting thoughts within him suddenly. His arm raised on instinct, bringing the beam of the light up toward the body on the couch. At the same time, he fought against the rising bile within his throat which grew worse by the second. He shined the light into the face of the boy, the only part of him that was exposed. The heavy blankets covered the rest. The eyes that he found staring back at him had a look of horror frozen upon them. In the lifeless eyes, Jackson could see the reflection of the television. The detective followed that gaze and looked toward the movie playing on the screen. Below the 42 inch Sony was a DVD player. That was where the movie was coming from. It was a Tom Cruise film. It took him a moment to identify what it was.

Interview with a Vampire.

Jackson cursed under his breath.

When he glanced back toward the couch, he cursed again. The room lit up as the movie switched to another bright scene. The body was still there below the blankets on the couch, but Tiffany was nowhere to be seen.

"Where did Tiffany go?" Michael asked. He was standing beside him now, appearing to be doing a much better job holding down what little dinner they had had many hours before.

The scene went dark again, sending the detectives once again into shadows.

"Buddy," Jackson whispered.

"Yeah."

"I don't like this at all."

That was when they heard Tiffany giggling.

And then she was behind them. They turned, but even with the television sending mad shadows everywhere, they could see that she was gone again. There was something else, however. Jackson felt lighter somehow.

His gun was no longer in its holster.

1:45 a.m.

Nathaniel sat and watched, rather uninterested, at the events taking place from his vantage point upon the housetop across the alley from the Rosen House. He had heard every word that had passed between Barbara and her husband earlier, having sat above them in the dark. He replayed her words when she had said that she had grown to care for him very much. Afterwards he moved to this new location. It gave him the ability to catch any and all activity coming from their back yard or southern position, as well as any movement from their eastern front. In that regard he had caught both the approach of the detective's partner by automobile, as well as the young next door neighbor girl as she made her way from her house to theirs sometime after that. Everything seemingly quiet; he had spent the past few minutes watching while the men combed the Rosen house for whatever reason.

A few moments ago, he noticed that the Rosen girl left Barbara's house and headed back for hers. He paid her no mind. He simply went back to the theater taking place before him: Barbara's husband leaving his partner to check the rest of the premises; his partner holding his ground, staring into the house, looking for what, he did not know or care to; the room in shadows thanks to the television which had been left on; both men gaining access.

Nathaniel began to think of food again. He had done his level best to try and put it out of his mind while he stayed vigil over his charge and her babies, whether she still wanted it or not.

The young girl was inside the darkened house now, he could see. It was dark for the two men, but not so dark for him. He could see her as she approached the couch in the center of the living room and knelt.

Suddenly, something changed, and Nathaniel began to question everything that was going on. The girl was on her feet now and behind the men, her back to the sliding door. He refocused his vision, wondering whether he had that right. Had he looked away? Had he missed something? He did not feel tired. So just how was it that this girl could have moved so quickly?

Nathaniel found himself rising to his feet without thinking about it. It was then, as he continued to question everything, that he finally noticed the scent of death in the air. *Barbara!* At first the thought occurred to him that it might be coming from Barbara's house. Quickly, however, he realized the truth.

It was just as the girl was stealing the weapon from the other man.

In a flash, he was off of the roof where he had camped out and vaulted two fences. But he was too late. Just a heartbeat before the first bullet was fired, ripping a gaping hole in the right side of Detective Mark Jackson's abdomen, sending him backwards through the open sliding glass door and into Nathaniel's arms; the vampire had thought that he had closed the distance in time.

He was wrong.

The impact knocked them both to the ground. Nathaniel rolled and was upon the detective immediately. They stared into each other's eyes and suddenly Nathaniel had a clarity that he had not known in nearly a week.

This police detective was about to die.

The young girl somewhere behind him was a vampire.

Vincent had not only been near, but was to blame for her creation; had been next door at Barbara's for quite a long time for the stench was suddenly thick in Nathaniel's nostrils; and lastly, he had played Nathaniel for a fool.

Nathaniel shook off the realization – not because he didn't believe it, but because he was through being played. He studied the detective beneath him momentarily. He was in great pain, but also seemed to be filled with understanding as to who Nathaniel was. Either that or he had more pressing things to be concerned about. He watched the man pull his hands away from the wound and bring them to his face. Nathaniel could see all too well, but apparently so could the detective. In the dark of the patio the fresh blood on his hands glistened. The man's eyes unfocused and Nathaniel knew that he was close to breathing his last. He turned his bloodied hands and presented them before Nathaniel.

Nathaniel snatched his hands by the wrists with lightning speed, placed them back down over the wound and held them there. The man's eyes widened in surprise.

"Do not move!" Nathaniel commanded. "Unless you wish to die."

Nathaniel leapt from him and rushed into the house.

The smell of human decay was terrible in the house as Nathaniel came rushing inside, and he wondered how in the world—even Vincent—was able to tolerate it. Somewhere in the darkness ahead of him lay Barbara's husband. He could not see him yet, but he heard the man moaning somewhere in the shadows. He had heard but the one weapon discharge and little else, so he hoped that Michael was well enough. For the moment, hope was all that he had, however. With two men down, and himself just reviving as if from a long slumber, there was time for little else. First, he had to consider his own well-being.

He heard a muted giggle.

Then he smelled the oil.

261

Nathaniel spun, but he was too late. He caught a glimpse of Michael Lopez coming at him, but that wasn't quite right. He had a blank look upon his face as he was neither attacking nor capable of doing so.

Nathaniel crashed into the television, knocking it over as Michael slammed into him. It somersaulted once and slammed into the nearest wall, sending a shower of blue and white sparks and ending the mad shadows forever. The detective was on top of him, pinning him there. Nathaniel shoved the man off of him and it was then that he knew for certain that Michael was unconscious. He had been thrown at him.

Nathaniel rose to his feet quickly, but was again too late.

There was another crash as something small was thrown against his feet. He knew instinctively that he was in trouble before he could see the blue flame go red or even feel the heat. The Green Depression lamp struck his boots and the carpeted floor and exploded into a million glass pieces. The fire raged immediately as if it were hungry for his undead flesh. Before his own welfare, however, his first thought was for the woman that he had grown to care for in so short a time. Almost ignorant of the fire upon him, he saw the flames crawl across the floor toward her husband.

New shadows danced about because of the rising flames as he rushed for the unconscious detective. Ignoring his own peril as the flames quickly engulfed his own legs as well as the location of his attacker, he caught him by the front of his clothing and pulled him away from harm. He rolled the man ahead of him into the kitchen and threw himself upon his legs. Michael moaned as Nathaniel quickly patted out the flames. Nathaniel turned and surveyed the room behind him. He could see no immediate threat save the fire in the living room. It was growing wider and taller by the moment, gaining strength.

He had just turned away when he heard the giggling again. It was soon drowned out by smoke detectors that began to sound, one after another.

He thought to turn back but the female vampire had him by the collar of his trench coat, yanking him backward with incredible strength. He tried to fight against her but she was strong and she had the element of surprise. And it wasn't very far for her to drag Nathaniel into the fire. Nathaniel felt himself released and fell backward onto the flames which suddenly engulfed him and began to consume his jeans, coat and his once beautiful hands.

He spun and turned, gritting his teeth together, grinding the tips of his long incisors, fighting back the screams that rose within him as the flames got higher and started to do their intended work to devour him. He began to lose his sense of direction now as the fire became a virtual box that he could not find his way out of. Nathaniel threw the burning coat off of him and flung it about with his hands, desperately attempting to put out the flames. It was hopeless. The coat was nearly consumed already as were his shirt and pants. He found himself losing the fight.

Yet, his thoughts turned to Barbara. His heart went out to her, knowing the danger that she was in, knowing how incapable he was now of fulfilling his self-appointed charge to care for her. He was dying and she would soon be following, along with her beautiful children and her husband, who he wondered whether he might already be dead. The only question remaining was: who would precede who in that black parade?

Nathaniel began to flail about like a baby in a crib, throwing a tantrum. That, too, proved useless. It was unclear whether he himself was attempting to put out the flames or whether the flames were driving him to it. Still, he thought of Barbara. He could picture her now. He tried as hard as he could to picture her, lovely, soft and smiling in his direction, but all he could see was her pain. Then tears came. He could feel them well up in his eyes and pour down his burning cheeks. The flames were doing their work, but they seemed unable to turn the salty water into vapor.

Somehow he found the strength to stand, but was unsure whether he truly was doing so. Ceiling felt like floor and left felt like right. Still, his body flailed about, jumping, twitching, and dancing on fire; his skin rolled back in places like a scroll and floated off toward points unknown.

And then he was down again.

Pain had knocked his legs out from beneath him and the crackling fire beat him down, pinning him there to meet his final moment. There was some peace to be had in that realization, though he wished with all of his black heart that he could rise up and go to Barbara. Death would bring the end to his hunger; a hunger that caused him revulsion and shame. And maybe he might see his mother and father again. Perhaps that was too much to hope for.

From somewhere he heard a voice. The female vampire, no doubt, he thought, but he could not make out what she might be saying. *Just more giggling, perhaps.* Apparently she was hitting Nathaniel as well, not content to simply allow the fire to finish him off. He felt as if Tiffany was striking him again and again and again from all sides.

Soon, he began to see a shape hovering over him. Before, he had been unable to see anything but the box of fire. Now, the flames seemed to lose their strength. He could hear the steady din of the many smoke detectors again, but ignored it. The shape was now clear in his eyes. *Could it be?* His attacker was no female. It was not Vincent. In fact, it was no vampire at all. As he studied the face of the man, trying as he might to beat back the flames, he beheld a savior.

It was Barbara's husband.

Nathaniel quit thrashing about, but did not realize that he had done so. He watched in amazement as Michael climbed off of him, took him by the legs and pulled him away from the charred carpet and the flames that climbed up the walls around them. He was coughing from the smoke, as well as from the exhaustion. Yet, he managed to find the strength to pull Nathaniel to safety.

"Why?" Nathaniel asked simply.

Michael looked away from him and took a moment while he surveyed the burning house. He was nearly out of breath.

"You could have left me to die. Why did you save me?"

"My wife seems to think the world of you, though it beats the shit out of me!" he finally said, through more fits of coughing. "But we don't have time to debate the subject now. We've got to get the hell out of here! Can you walk?"

"Yes," Nathaniel said, doing his level best to ignore the pain and the unsightliness of his physical condition.

Slowly, he arose. Michael reached for him and helped him the rest of the way to his feet. He released him once he had regained his balance, studying him to make certain that he would not go down again.

"We'll have to go out the back way," Michael shouted over the fire alarm, motioning behind them at the door that led from the kitchen to the garage. He started in that direction when Nathaniel reached out feebly with his right arm and stopped him.

"Wait!" he said.

Michael first glanced down at the hand that held him, then to Nathaniel's face. "What is it?"

Nathaniel did not really have the strength to hold him, but instead used him mostly for balance.

He pointed with his free left hand toward the wall of spreading flames at the south end of the house where

265

the sliding glass door once stood clearly. "Your friend is there! He was shot, but alive when I last saw him!"

"Oh, God!" Michael cried.

He started past Nathaniel, then doubled back and pulled him along.

Nathaniel held his ground as best as he could. The action slowed Michael; that was all. "You said it yourself that the way is this way! We will have to go around!"

Realizing the truth in this, Michael quickly turned, wrenched himself free of Nathaniel and made his way into the garage. Nathaniel had to reach for the nearest wall in order to maintain his balance.

"Wait!" Nathaniel called in vain after the detective.

It was too late, Michael was gone and he was alone. As quickly as possible, using the walls to propel him and to hold himself up, he followed after him.

2:11 a.m.

The phone rang again beside Dispatcher Lainie Bishop as she attempted to juggle what seemed like ten things at once. On a typical graveyard shift she had the responsibility to track and support two, maybe three, patrol cars. This morning, her first shift back since the terrible deaths of Police Officers Nick Mancuso and Larry Browning during her shift on Monday, she had twelve.

"Kingsburg Police Department," Lainie answered calmly. "How can I help you?"

The voice on the other end of the line practically blew her eardrum out. "Lainie, it's Detective Lopez! I've got an officer down! I repeat, officer down! I need an ambulance and fire crews to respond to 994 Roosevelt Street. Detective Jackson has been shot!"

"Copy that, Detective," The dispatcher answered without much thought.

A year of training and on the job experience took over and she no longer thought about stress or fear, she just reacted. She quickly sent the alarm to the firehouse just two blocks north-east of her position in the old building that had since been remodeled since the two departments had shared it. "Ambulance and rescue on the way."

The line went dead as the detective hung up. A moment later it began ringing again. She let it ring.

"Kingsburg Rescue, we have an officer down at house fire at 994 Roosevelt Street. Be advised detective on scene."

"Ten-four, Kingsburg," the dispatcher at the firehouse said as she sprang into action. "Kingsburg rescue has a copy."

Next, the dispatcher dutifully jumped back on the microphone. "One-five-zero, Kingsburg. One-five-zero, Kingsburg. Do you have a copy?"

"One-five-zero, Kingsburg," the Chief of Police quickly responded. "Go ahead."

"One-five-zero, be advised fire and rescue teams are en route to Detective Lopez' ten-forty-two. There is a fire next door and he has reported an officer down."

The chief was still down on Simpson and Mission Street at the scene of the previous officer down. "Ten-four!" he gruffly replied, along with a string of profanities.

Beside the Dispatcher the phone finally stopped ringing. She took a second to catch her breath just in time for it to start ringing once again. She cursed under her breath and quickly picked it up.

"Kingsburg Police Department, May I help you?"

"Where in the hell have you been?" demanded the strong female voice on the other end of the line. Lainie pulled the receiver away from her right ear and gave it a funny look as if the caller could notice such a thing as her displeasure from over the communication line. She could hear the woman still reading her the riot act, although Lainie could not accurately detail what that was exactly. She started to pull the receiver back to her ear, at which time she was forming her words carefully. She wanted to explain to this lady, who had neither the right nor the comprehension of what she was going through during her first shift back since that terrible first morning, just exactly what she could do with all of her complaints. It was at that moment that she saw the LED display on the phone, detailing the phone number of the caller. The heading above the phone number read: Mayor.

"Mayor Peterson, I am so sorry to have kept you waiting," she quickly apologized.

"I haven't been waiting!" came the reply. "I have been sitting here all night, fully expecting to find out what in the world is going on. I've been trying to get a hold of this department, as well as Chief O'Donnell all damn night and I can't get anyone!"

"Ma'am." Lainie tried to calmly settle down the mayor with as much information as she could. "Another police officer was killed tonight and the chief has been at the scene since nearly the beginning."

"Yes, I know that!" Mayor Peterson interrupted.

"I'm sorry, Ma'am."

"Quit apologizing!"

"Ma'am, we just received a call of a second officer down in the 900 block of Roosevelt Street. Fire and rescue crews are responding. I just spoke to the chief, and I believe that he is heading that way."

There was silence on the other end of the line now. Lainie listened and waited for a few moments.

"Ma'am?"

"Alright," the Mayor said at last. "Have the chief contact me when he's free there. I don't care how late the hour. Do you understand?"

"Yes, Ma'am."

The line went dead.

2:19 a.m.

Slowly, by the time Nathaniel navigated through the kitchen door and the garage for the most part without handholds, down the grass walkway and back to the patio, he had regained some ability. It was not much, however, since he still had not fed since the previous day. He was able to walk some without having to use the walls around him to hold him up. The pain, for the most part, had subsided. Perhaps he was riding the storm out, or simply comfortably numb. In any event, he found Michael leaning over his friend in the middle of the back yard. He had evidently pulled him from the sliding glass door and into relative safety. Yet, the fire raged ever higher and out of control.

"Behind you, Mikey," Detective Jackson fought to say to alert his partner at Nathaniel's approach.

Michael turned to look, and then turned back. "It's alright."

Jackson seemed not to hear his friend and partner. He tried to say more, but could not find the words or perhaps the ability.

"Never mind him," Michael said as Nathaniel suddenly sat down beside them on the grass.

The maneuver was more akin to falling down than sitting, but it achieved the intended purpose. Jackson stared at him with unblinking eyes as Michael opened the cell phone that he held in his hand. He dialed a number.

"Where the hell is that ambulance? I've got an officer down and I need it right now!" he yelled

Nathaniel said nothing as he watched Michael toss the phone in disgust. Instead, he leaned forward and looked deeply into the eyes of the man dying before him. Jackson continued to stare back. Though heavily scarred and now disfigured with second and third degree burns covering most of his face, peels of skin curling up but still relatively attached, he was sure that the detective could still recognize the face of the figure that had caught him upon becoming shot. He saw the fangs, too.

Michael noticed the exchange. "Jacks, this is our mysterious Nathaniel. I believe that he is a real flesh and blood vampire, but he won't hurt you." He looked at Nathaniel and added: "Will you?"

"No," he said with a frown directed towards Michael. He looked back at Jackson and nodded. "I am as he says, but I will not harm you. I have neither the will nor the strength."

"Will I die?" Jackson suddenly managed to form the words and ask.

"Yes," Nathaniel said simply.

"No!" Michael snapped. "No!" He gave Nathaniel an ugly look that he either registered or did not care to. "You fight! I need you! Vanessa needs you! You fight, you hear me?"

Jackson looked into his partner's eyes, but turned his head back to the living vampire before him and asked again. This time he did not have the power to say the words, but Nathaniel read the question exactly.

"Yes," he answered. "You will die. You have lost too much blood to survive now. Trust me. I know these things."

Michael began to raise his voice in dispute of this fact just as the blaring sirens from the ambulance broke through the steady scream of the fire alarm inside the Rosen residence. Four fire engines had joined it, but Michael was too agitated to acknowledge them. He leapt to his feet.

"Don't listen to him, Jacks!" he commanded. "You fight! I'm bringing help!" Michael continued to urge his partner on even as he ran from him and went for help. "You hear me? You fight!"

Above them water began to fall upon the house as if it had begun to rain just upon it. It was the water cannon. Soon, another jet of water could be seen. The fire would gut the home, but it would not spread.

The vampire within Nathaniel found himself staring at the dark area of clothing upon the dying detective beside him and began to remind him suddenly of the fact that he had yet to feed. Repulsed and ashamed as it made him feel, he could still not tear his eyes away. The blood was speaking to him. As desperate as he was becoming, even the dried congealing blood was asking to be lapped up by his parched tongue. He gritted his teeth and pulled himself away, staring skyward.

"I don't want to die," the dying man said to him.

Nathaniel looked back to earth and studied the man's face. Already there wasn't much left there.

"Everyone dies," he whispered back. It never dawned on him that he should think to console the man in his final moments. There were too many conflicting emotions stirring up within him at this present hour.

"Even you?" the dying man asked.

"One day," he answered quickly, without first thinking about it. Perhaps it was more from longing than from knowing. "Yes, even I shall die."

"Why?" Jackson's words were coming out in gurgles now, a trickle of blood now appearing by his lips as well. "Can vampires die?"

"I think one will die very soon," Nathaniel said. He was not looking at the man anymore, although his face was pointed his way. His eyes were suddenly somewhere far away.

He could see home.

His mother was young again and in the act of mending some clothes for him. He could even see himself now. He sat in the cool early morning dirt, stacking some rocks that he had gathered. There had always been rocks everywhere at his home. One could not walk three feet without kicking a rock or tripping on one. He was still talking, but he scarcely heard himself doing it.

"I wish that it were I. I have grown so tired. If I could just go home and see the land again. It is cold and dreary, but it was home. I wish to visit the land of my birth and lay my head upon the mountain top of my childhood and await the dawn. My father and I used to do this. We would do many of the chores and then take a break to watch the sun climb into the sky from its slumber. It is such a glorious sun." These thoughts had been long banished to the depths and yet here they were, rising back toward the light. Nathaniel paused. Reality was beginning to pull him back. "I would like to come to that dawn one last time without the strength to flee. I imagine those first rays of the sun would hurt a great deal while they begin to undo what Vincent has left me with." He paused once again. "There is nothing for me here. No one."

"Who's Vincent?" Nathaniel barely heard the man ask him as his life trickled out of him and more sirens had begun to arrive.

"The monster responsible for what kneels before you. And for all of this," he answered, motioning behind them toward the burning house and toward the house next door.

Nathaniel's eyes fell on the other house. His thoughts turned to Barbara. Sweet Barbara. He stared at the house, saying nothing.

"When you...and I...are gone," Jackson whispered nearly inaudibly. He was beginning to lose multiple functions at once. "'Nessa wanted...a child...so bad. And...Barbara?"

Nathaniel scanned the property for signs of life, finding none. Soon, help would come for the detective, he knew, but there would be nothing to do for him but cover him from the prying eyes of all those gathering, both city servants and onlookers alike.

"I don't know."

Detective Jackson mustered all of his remaining strength which was nearly nil. All it afforded him was the raising of one solitary small finger on his right hand. With it he managed to reach the vampire reclining beside him and pull him back for one final word.

2:27 a.m.

Michael ran across the Rosen driveway as the volunteer firemen began to leap from a fire engine that had pulled up ahead of the ambulance. Some of them still rubbed the sleep from their eyes. He nearly bumped into two on his way to the Emergency Medical Technicians.

"Over here!" he shouted over the sound of the sirens. A second fire engine was pulling up, closely followed by a second ambulance, and by even more police cars. "They're in the back."

He waited but a moment, but once he registered their receiving of his message, he quickly turned on his heels and ran back the way that he had come. His partner had little time, if he wasn't gone already. The EMT's were hot on his heels. He could hear the sound of the gurney's wheels on the cool driveway cement.

The gate still hanging open, Michael jumped through it. The sound of glass breaking and the flash of red flames stopped him there, however, as a beam gave way and pierced the Rosen kitchen window.

"Get back!" a commanding voice shouted as two firemen burst between them with their fire hose. They did not wait for an argument, but went quickly to their work, sending gallons of water to the site.

"We don't have time to wait!" Michael yelled at no one in particular.

"We need another way back there," one of the EMT's shouted over the din. More sirens had joined the fray.

"Yes!" Michael answered, fishing for his house keys in his pocket. He turned back around and jumped over the hose that stretched down the driveway. "Follow me!"

In a flash, Michael had one gate unlocked and was running up the walkway toward the back gate. The patio light lit the way that he knew all too well, but he took little notice of it. The men behind kept up with him as fast as they could. They ran through heavy mist as the breeze blew water from the Rosen house to the immediate east into their collective faces. When the men with the gurney arrived at the Lopez back gate, he was already on his way to the Rosen back gate. He tried not to think of what he might find upon his arrival.

The EMT's followed him with confused faces, but he had no time to explain. After he led them from one house to another and back, he stopped and pirouetted, dumbfounded.

EMT Steven Howell took a place beside him and glanced over the grounds a moment, catching his breath. The young man was in fantastic shape so it did not take long.

"Fire's too hot," the older EMT said, joining them in the center of the yard.

They stared at Michael, as if sensing there was another, bigger problem at hand.

"Detective?" Howell began quietly, almost as if he did not want his partner to hear. "Where *were* we going?"

Michael turned toward the man reluctantly. He pursed his lips as if to speak, but caught himself and started to look away nervously.

"Where's the officer down?"

"I don't know," he said through clenched jaws, the shock overwhelming him. His eyes darted around, looking for a clue.

"What?" Howell turned fully to the detective, but got no response.

The elder EMT grabbed the detective by the arms and pulled him out of his daze. "Where is the officer down?"

Glancing back over the grounds of the Rosen home one last time, or rather what was left of it, the patio light in his yard to his left beckoned his attention as if speaking some secret.

"Detective Lopez?"

"In the house," he said finally.

"In the house? He was caught in the house?" Howell dropped his hands and stared at the scene unfolding before him, the undoing of the Rosen House. Sections of the roof, specifically over the kitchen and living room areas, had given way, revealing huge maws that looked like some terrible house monster drinking deeply the water from the firemen's hoses. Fire engine water cannon had obviously joined in the fray as well, for whatever good it might do. If anyone had been alive when caught in that they were no longer, to be sure.

Yet, Michael was not looking into the Rosen house for survivors. He was looking squarely at his own.

2:39 a.m.

When Michael Lopez approached the patio light standing above his sliding glass door there were many things on his mind. First and foremost was the fate of his partner and friend. Somewhere a close second was the uneasy feeling that he had concerning how long it had been since he last saw his wife or kids. There were red and blue and white lights that continued to light up the neighborhood although no longer accompanied by blaring sirens. The firemen were well on their way to winning the fight against the fire that had previously threatened his home. Of course, there was the reality of the fact that he had been awake for longer than he would have liked to admit and working on nothing but adrenaline.

As Michael reached for the sliding glass door, the thought occurred to him that it should be dutifully locked; however, he knew instinctively that this would not be the case. He pulled the handle and the door opened easily. He was not surprised.

The curtains appeared dark, but he knew that they were in fact beige. Barbara had bought them one weekend on a shopping visit with her sister in San Francisco. He stepped through them and into the living room, but the room was dark as well. Typically, whenever he had to work late she would leave the kitchen light on for him or at least a table lamp in the living room. In the living room, there were four lamps to choose from: three table lamps from Pier 1 and the H.G. Wells lamp that was plugged in, but that was all. This morning there was nothing but the glow from the kitchen window from the dying fire next door.

"You may turn on a light if you wish?" came a voice.

He had hoped that it might be Nathaniel, so that he might discern the fate of his partner, but it did not sound like anyone he had ever met before, which made matters far worse.

Michael walked over to the northeast corner of the room for the table lamp beside his chair, across from the television set. He chose it because it was the farthest point in the room from the voice that had spoken to him. It occurred to him that fifteen feet was not the safest position in the world when it came to vampires, but it was all that he had at the moment.

He flicked the three-way light into the first position and turned toward the direction of the voice. The other side of the room was empty. He stood up slowly and took a longer look. The hall seemed empty. The entrance to the kitchen seemed empty. He was alone.

Great! He thought. *Now I'm hearing voices.*

"Looking for me?"

Death from behind.

Michael spun but was grabbed by the throat. He had no time to think or react. The world seemed to rush by him suddenly and then came a blow as the opposite wall of the room jumped out to meet him, knocking the breath from him. Everything hurt. He held his eyes tightly shut as his sense of balance and direction returned. It took quite a while for his head to stop spinning. It finally did but did not stop hurting. There was a hole in the wall where his head rested, eight feet off of the ground.

He felt a little better after a full minute, finally able to open his eyes again. Staring up at him was another vampire; a mean one. No one had to tell him who he was for he knew instinctively. This was the monster responsible for everything that he was aware of, and probably more that he was yet to be aware of. He was holding him against the wall and high off the carpeted floor.

"Better?" the vampire sneered. "The breath has returned to you, yes?"

Michael tried to nod, but the vampire held him so tight he couldn't move.

"I'll take that as a 'yes'," the vampire smiled. Then he began to squeeze. "And now?"

Michael found his hands finally and threw them against Vincent's one hand which was beginning to crush him like a vise, but to no avail. His head began to hurt worse and his chest tightened. The room began to darken once again, but this time it had nothing at all to do with electricity or the closing of his eyes. It was his life going out. In the far distance, he could hear soft voices and wondered if they were angels calling him to their sweet by and by.

*   *   *

"Stop it!" Barbara yelled, breaking free of her captive down at the back of the hall.

Tiffany hissed and tried her best to corral her, but somehow she managed to break free and get down to the living room. She allowed herself one momentary glance at her husband as she jumped against Vincent. She knew that she did not have the power to free her husband with muscle, and that no weapon that she had could harm him.

All that she could do was use coercion and rely on the power of the Holy Spirit.

"Please, Vincent," she pleaded, clutching his leather coat with her right hand and his vise arm with her left. She did not dig her nails into him or attempt to pull his arm away from Michael's throat. She just held onto the vampire and looked into his eyes, praying somewhere within for the Lord to bring some manner of help. "Don't do this!"

Tiffany quickly slipped her right arm around Barbara and held her across the breast. She pulled her away some but was unable to free her from Vincent without doing harm to either her or the master, so she simply held on, awaiting instructions.

Vincent continued to squeeze Michael's life away, but paused ever so slightly as he turned and gazed into Barbara's eyes.

"This isn't necessary. You have the power. There is nothing to stop you. Even Nathaniel has been powerless to stop you. Please, give me my husband's life. Be merciful."

Vincent loosened his grip, but only a little. A wicked smile crept across his countenance.

"Well done, you," he said, and at once released her husband completely.

Michael fell like a sack of potatoes onto the end table, knocking it over loudly and sending picture frames and knick-knacks across the hallway like shrapnel. The second Pier 1 table lamp briefly shot sparks as Michael's one hundred and ninety pounds crushed it against the wall. Barbara heard the violence and caught a whiff of the electrical discharge, but fought the urge to look at what was left of her husband. *At least he was released!* was all that she could think of now.

"Now I see," the vampire continued, ignoring Tiffany at Barbara's back as well as Michael crumpled on the floor at his feet.

"What?" she answered carefully.

"Now I see what it was that so fascinated the boy."

"What boy?" She had lowered her hands now, but had as of yet to try and back away from the vampire. She tried to take things very deliberately. The vampire's hands were lowered as well. Yet something warned her that it would not be very long before he had his hands upon her next.

"Do not toy with me, my dear." Vincent set his hands upon his hips and flashed a toothy grin. "You know precisely who I mean. I have spent much time this week watching, studying the two of you together. It was so sweet and so very moving. You make a very beautiful couple together, if one could just get past the dead cold flesh and the odd hours that he would keep." At last, he raised his right hand and caressed her left cheek with the back of it. His fingers trailed from cheekbone to chin and then over to the other side. "Tell me," he asked. "Did he ever touch you? I mean, inappropriately."

"No."

"Now, now." Vincent seemed to stifle a grin. "You answered much too quickly. I am certain that he collected you from the floor that night and carried you oh so tenderly to your bed. Just how gentlemanly was he while you were passed out? He took no liberties?"

"No." Barbara held her tongue. She knew exactly what it was that he was attempting to do.

His touch was cold like a cold can of soda placed against the small of one's back on a warm day; a piece of ice dropped into one's blouse in the fall. She dared not move for fear of angering him. While his hand continued to crawl over her, she held her place, waiting for guidance. Even when those fingers went from her face down the length of her neck, dallying there for a time and then continuing on their way, slowly, seductively, down the front of her blouse. With a quick twist of his thumbnail, the first button flew across the room, followed by a second. She winced as those nails traipsed between her breasts.

"No? Are you quite certain of this?"

He waited while she did nothing but increasingly lost the fight within her to control her revulsion. She gritted her teeth. Vincent ran a solitary finger along each breast, sliding within one cup then the other. Barbara fully expected the worst, but it did not come.

"Very lovely, my dear," he said, finally removing his hands from her. He collected the fabric at the base of her neck, making her respectable once again. "Very lovely, indeed. If he did not, in fact, touch you, I would surmise that he very much wanted to. Perhaps those feelings did not manifest themselves until much later. I do not know. Perhaps I, too, would care to spend a great deal of time with your body. Perhaps not. Perhaps I would simply spend much time on your neck until I was unable to stop myself any longer from drinking your life."

Vincent sighed loudly with the thought and then turned away, looking upon the ruins of Barbara's husband.

"Attend to your husband. He lives, but not for much longer if he does not inform me of the death of your one time paramour."

Quickly, Barbara went down to her knees and began checking on Michael. He was breathing, but seemed unconscious.

"Vincent," Tiffany finally spoke. "We must leave this place."

"Yes," he answered her, turning his full attention toward her. "That seems to be the forgone conclusion. Before we do, however, I must know what happened to Nathaniel."

"He's dead," she added, matter-of-factly.

"Is he?"

"Of course."

"And how do you know this?" He was growing impatient now. Barbara noted this but did not act as if she was even listening to the conversation.

"I saw him die!" Tiffany raised her voice.

"So you say," Vincent said. "As I recall, when you returned, you told me that everyone was dead." He motioned past Barbara to the crumpled heap before her. "Yet here one lies before me. Quite alive, I would say."

"Do you need me to go out there and drag what's left back here for your approval?" Tiffany said, growing more aggravated.

"Yes, I do!" Vincent snapped, causing both Barbara and Tiffany to flinch. "I want you to sneak out there amongst all of the fire fighters and police and the onlookers and retrieve my son from the smoldering embers without being seen. I want you to do this! Even I could not do this!" Tiffany took several steps back from the verbal assault. "Go and do it now! If you are captured, gouge a chunk out of your neck! Should you be seen and are followed back here, I will do worse!"

Surprisingly, there came a rapid, impatient knocking on the front door.

"Get the door," Vincent said, reaching out and nudging Barbara with his booted foot. "Whoever it is, get rid of them!"

Barbara looked up at the vampire as she stood, hardly taking her eyes off of him. Without a word she marched to the door. In her mind, she was scrambling for the words to say to whoever it might be. She did not expect to find the chief of police to be standing there in the middle of the morning.

"Chief," she said.

Quickly, she began to act as if she had just woken up from a deep sleep. How she would be able to explain how she had been sleeping in her clothes, she did not contemplate.

"Mrs. Lopez," the chief began. "How is everybody?"

"Fine."

"Really?" he answered. "My wife would have been out of her mind with worry with a fire next door, and you're fine! The house is almost gone, by the way. Have you seen what's left?"

"No," she answered. "Michael was there for a while, but I didn't go out. Too busy watching the children."

"Right, right. Speaking of Michael, where is he? I've been trying to get hold of him for a while. He hasn't been answering." He paused momentarily. "You haven't been answering either. Your phone is off the hook."

Barbara just stood there. Vincent had yanked the phone from the wall after the second call while he had awaited word from Tiffany as to the events next door. She had not cared about the phone at the time. She'd silently followed the vampire's every move and heard his every utterance. Inside, however, she had been busy praying for her husband and friend in the house next door once she'd realized that Tiffany's tale about a noise had been a ruse.

Now she was the one who must lie. It had never come easily for her even before she had become a committed Christian. Yet, she most certainly could not invite the man inside to show him just why it was that her husband was not answering. Pressure came at her from all sides now. Chief O'Donnell stared at her and she could almost feel the laser beams coming from his eyes as he waited for her to respond; from behind, the vampire awaited her, equally impatiently. His disdain was much worse than the chief's. The worst thing that the chief could do was to fire her husband.

It was so difficult to think of what was right and what was wrong—what was logical. So she froze.

"Mrs. Lopez? Barbara," he asked again. "Where's Michael? He was downtown at a crime scene. He was then at the fire next door. That's the last that he has been seen. Now, I have a report that he called in an officer down and we don't know where that officer is, or even if there is one."

Still Barbara did not move or attempt to say anything. It was as if she were frozen in place.

The chief's eyes searched hers. "What is it you're hiding?"

"Perhaps I might be able to answer that," came a new voice.

Vincent was at the door suddenly, bringing Barbara out of her trance. She made an effort to satisfy the chief's questions but Vincent silenced her with a look that spoke volumes. There was much that he could do to not only the man standing in the doorway, but to her family as well. A thought occurred to her now which she tried to shake out of her mind. It had to do with reasonable collateral losses. What was the chief of police to her when she had her children and husband to think about?

"And who are you?" the chief asked as Barbara pushed the thought away with a sense of shame.

"Won't you come in and I shall explain it to you," Vincent invited.

"No." Barbara found her voice. "It's late. Michael's here, but he's asleep. He was so exhausted by not just tonight, but by everything! They've been working too hard to try and end this madness!" She turned to Vincent and gave him a look. She knew it did not escape the chief's notice.

"I can understand that," the chief said. "However, there is only so much rest that we can have when people are dying all around this city. Now I've got Vanessa Jackson calling me, asking me where her husband is because she can't find him. Your husband is on tape as having phoned desperately for an ambulance because there was an officer down. I've got EMT's next door that report that Michael was leading them around only to find nothing."

"Come in, sir," Vincent interrupted. "I shall take you to him."

"And just who in the hell are you exactly?" the chief demanded to know. His eyes seemed to be burning holes in Vincent's forehead now as firmly as the vampire was studying him. His right hand moved to his waist near his holstered weapon and stayed there.

"I'm about to answer that!" Vincent sneered. "And when I do, you will need more than that weapon to stop me."

"Vincent, no!" Barbara said, quickly moving between them, though neither had made any effort to advance toward their adversary. The chief popped the snap on the holster, freeing the weapon should he so choose to remove it.

"I'm here, Chief!" Michael said, catching everyone by surprise. He squeezed past the two in the doorway and out next to his boss. "I'm sorry for all of this."

He reached out and took the man by the arm, moving him away from the doorway and down the walkway.

"Michael, what's going on here? What happened to Jackson? And who the hell is that? Barbara heard O'Donnell ask.

"I'll explain it all," Michael said, glancing back toward the door and at Barbara as they continued to move into the yard.

The chief stood his ground and pointed his finger at Vincent who was still standing in the door by Barbara, watching everything. He shrugged Michael off of him. "And I want to know who that sonofabitch is right there!"

"Yes, sir," Michael said.

"Tiffany," Vincent said suddenly, not yet taking his eyes off the two men in the front yard, but specifically the much older man. Then he closed the door.

"Yes?" she answered.

"Prepare the children. We are leaving now."

*   *   *

Michael was still speaking when he heard the door slam. He turned and swore under his breath. He needed to get the chief out of here, quickly, and needed more help if there was to be any escape from the vampire in his house and his city.

But the chief was not the kind of help he needed.

"Lopez, I want to know who that is and I want to know it now!" He gripped his weapon and began to remove it before Michael stopped him.

"Don't do that, sir." Michael had his hands upon his boss once again, attempting to get him out of harm's way.

"Why not? And take your hands off of me!"

"Chief," he began. "This is a family matter. I will take care of it."

"Why don't I believe you?"

"I don't know," Michael said flatly. His thoughts were crashing into each other now as the pain from getting up continued to pound against the inside of his skull. He was in no shape to be standing up right now, much less try and convince his chief to leave him and his family alone. With each passing moment, he was afraid of what more might happen to him and his family. So, he braced himself and got tough. "And right now I don't really give a shit!"

"What?"

"You heard me!" he said, taking the man by the arm again. This time, however, he did not allow the man to get free. He pulled him along the rest of his walkway

285

amid protestations and led him down the length of the driveway. He did not let him go until he had him by the sidewalk. Many of those in uniform and robe alike turned and watched this new spectacle while the fire was nearly put out.

"Lopez?" the chief protested further as he turned on his heels after being shoved into the street by his employee. "What's gotten into you?"

Michael did not answer. He simply turned and jogged back to the house.

"Lopez?"

Michael had half thought that he might find his way to the house barred, but the door came easily open and his access was not impeded. Vincent was waiting for him in the dining room, however. He did not appear to be pleased.

"Did you get rid of him?" Vincent growled.

"Yes."

"Good. Your family is still alive, but we leave immediately. I am putting my faith in you and your wife's trustworthiness. Should I decide that I can no longer count on that, I will shred the entire clan and leave the pieces behind. As head of your household," the vampire said, raising a solitary finger and pointing it at him. "I will kill you last!"

"May I ask you a question?" Michael leaned against the dining room furniture now because had he very little strength.

"What is it?"

As if taking note of Michael's vulnerability and wanting to taunt him, Vincent turned and walked into the living room, forcing him to follow and exert further energy that he did not have.

"Why are you doing this?" Michael asked as he entered the room.

Using his peripheral vision, he could see diaper bags stacked in the hallway. Barbara came in, holding Rebekah. Behind her, Jerod held Robbie. The babies

286

were awake and appeared perfectly fine with being up at this early and ungodly hour. Tiffany followed at the rear.

"I am here because I have been searching for Nathaniel. At last I have found him in your fair city and, since he refuses to come home, I mean to have my revenge for an abandonment done to me so long ago."

"That's not true!" Barbara said suddenly. "You killed his parents and turned him into a vampire, just like you! He may have escaped you, but there was no abandonment!"

"All true," Vincent sighed.

"Besides," Michael added. "He's dead!"

"Is he?" Vincent said absently.

The vampire looked in the direction of the sliding glass door. It was obscured by the slightly billowing curtains. Now he turned and looked toward Michael. He appeared displeased by some new occurrence.

"Is this your doing?" he asked.

"What?"

The vampire flashed a grin but it was neither from pleasure nor from sarcasm. It was from someplace ugly and vile and rotten. He moved forward suddenly and took hold of the table that Michael had knocked over earlier, snapping one of the legs off with very little effort. Michael flinched. Faster than they could follow, Vincent was standing before the curtains. With his left hand, he reached through them and took hold of something, pulling it forward. It was the chief. Vincent had him by his thinning salt and pepper-colored hair. With his right hand, he ran him through with the wooden leg, burying it deep inside his belly.

Oh my God! No! Barbara turned and put herself between the horror and the eyes of her eldest son.

"What happened, Mom?" Jerod asked, his voice elevating with each subsequent word. "What happened?"

287

"Ssh!" She attempted to console her son while her eyes filled with anguish. Michael swallowed; there was nothing he wanted more than to spare his family this horror.

"I won't lie to you, baby," she told him, looking deeply into his young eyes as tears sat there, cued at the precipice and preparing to crest. "Please don't look. It's too terrible."

Michael stood immobile. What had taken place was exactly what he had feared would happen. He buried his face in his hands and shuddered. A scream rose in his throat, but it was not out of fear. It was from anger. Yet he knew that he was quite powerless to do anything at the moment but obey, and wait.

Chief O'Donnell stared at the vampire at first, and then glanced down at the object that had pierced him as if in unbelief.

"I had already invited you inside, remember?" Vincent said through clenched teeth, still holding the man by the graying hair. "So come in!" With that, the vampire let go of the dying man, allowing him to fall inside. Chief O'Donnell landed face first into the carpet, driving the table leg deeper into him and forcing it further out on the other side. The sound of it was awful—all wet and tearing flesh. Vincent turned and left him there.

"Come. We leave now."

Michael moved past the vampire toward his chief. Vincent eyed him as he did so, but seemed unconcerned. It took him some time to get to the man.

"Chief," he whispered, losing his voice now at the sight of the leg and the blood and the pasty face of the man who had done much for him and his career. The man looked up at him. "I'm so sorry. I tried to get you to safety, damnit! Why didn't you just leave us alone?" Tears were coming now.

"Hoping to help," was all that Michael could hear though the chief's lips seemed to be saying much more.

"I know it," Michael grimaced, fighting to hold on to his voice. "I know it." And then he took note of the exact moment when the life left the chief. Though the man had not the power to close his own eyes, from behind them it was as if a television had just been silenced for the night.

"Come or I leave you with him to share the same fate."

Vincent was at the kitchen door which led to the garage. Tiffany was holding it for everyone as the family was being led away. Where they were headed was unknown to all except perhaps Vincent. He seemed to be operating slightly off plan, but all that Michael could surmise was that they were about to be herded into Barbara's Saturn Outlook Sport Utility Vehicle.

Michael took one last look at his chief as he stood very slowly. He did not trust his balance. He said a quick prayer under his breath, something that he had not done in a very long while. Even from his living room, Michael could see patrol cars from the different parts of the valley. With the street light across the street and the glow of the fire yet to be completely put out, it looked like the dawn. When he hesitated to follow, Vincent moved through the doorway and allowed the door to slam before Michael.

*   *   *

The sound of breaking glass echoed within the space of the two car garage as Vincent quickly shattered both the single 80 watt garage light bulb as well as the electronic garage door light through the plastic shield. Tiffany and Vincent then hung back in the darkness of the space while Barbara surveyed the crowded street.

"It won't be easy trying to get people to move for us," Barbara said, still holding onto Rebekah. She just sat silently within her mother's arms, casually eyeing the pretty lights and watching the water works next door.

"Think of something!" came her reply from behind.

"And just what would you have me do exactly?" she chided.

"I do not know. Shall I ask your children what they would have their mother do? It would only take a moment."

"Mom," said Jerod suddenly as the sound of screeching tires could be heard in the distance. "Is that Aunt Vanessa?"

"What?" she asked, turning to face her son. He pointed behind her toward the street. Following his finger, she caught her best friend leap out of her car, leaving the lights on and heading their way.

Oh, God no! she thought, but said nothing as she watched the woman run toward them. She looked hysterical, and Barbara could only imagine what had been going through her mind all night while she attempted to locate Mark. What she would find upon reaching the driveway would be worse in so many ways.

"Who is it?" Vincent demanded to know from just behind her in the darkness.

"Vanessa Jackson. Her husband may have died in the fire."

"Oh, splendid," the vampire said hoarsely. It was probably meant to be a whisper but came out sounding one thousand times worse. "This just gets better and better. Good of her to leave her car on for us, though!"

3:25 a.m.

"What will you do with us when it is time for you to lay down to rest?" Barbara said into the darkness.

She was sitting on one side of Vanessa Jackson's loveseat. Casually, as if they were family or perhaps old

290

friends, the vampire reclined beside her. Prior to her speaking, they had sat mostly in silence. They were alone in the room. In stark contrast with the houses surrounding them, the shades were open wide, revealing the neighborhood outside. The only light came from the street lamp directly across the street.

"I have not yet decided. There are a few options."

Barbara turned away from it. "Which of those will I like?"

The vampire grinned. She could not see it, of course, but could feel its presence. "None."

"Why does it have to be this way?" she asked, looking absently at the reflection of the light that came through the open window and landing on Vanessa's hardwood floor. "Why do more people have to die? Nathaniel is dead. Go in peace."

"Yes," Vincent said. "Everyone keeps telling me this. Yet I believe none of you, including young Tiffany. Trusting her was a mistake, I see this now. When I locate a pile of foul ash tonight that smells precisely like him, only then will I depart."

"And what will happen to Tiffany?"

"Unlike Nathaniel, I find that I do not make close acquaintances with females," he said almost mournfully. "Perhaps you may be the first."

Barbara ignored that comment as best as she could. "You will tire of her, and then what? Kill her?"

"Certainly not!" Vincent turned to face her better, resting his left arm across the back of the loveseat, his right on the arm rest. He appeared rather dumbfounded at her question. "There are rules even I must follow. Nathaniel never told you this?"

"He told me *some* things."

"There have always been vampires. The world is full of them."

He raised his hands palm up for effect. Barbara could see his hands outstretched, but only that. Vincent was still mostly a voice in the dark.

"Perhaps we could not fill New York or London or Rio de Janero, but our members are there and there and there," he said, pointing at imaginary locations before them as if they were reclining in some general's map room. He motioned to himself. "And here."

"So what will become of her, then?" she asked, still concerning herself with the girl.

"I will probably simply give her her freedom at some point."

"Freedom to what? Roam some strange locale? Some strange country?"

"Freedom to live."

"*Freedom to live!*" Barbara turned in the voice's direction beside her. The vampire sank back in the chair and feigned surprise at the woman's tone. "Her life is over! Her house has been practically burned to the ground. Her parents will have to presume that their daughter is dead, too. What freedom?" An ironic thought occurred to her. It gave her voice a confidence. "And what if, without any life for her here, she instead decides to hunt *you* down as you did Nathaniel?"

"Please! The girl adores me." Vincent laughed. "Worships me, in fact."

"But you constantly bark orders at her and berate her!"

"Never," the vampire said, feigning surprise with the accusation.

"Yes, you do."

"I assure you that I have never barked."

*   *   *

In the back of the house, in the master bedroom, behind the closed door, Jerod could hear the laughter and wondered whether his mother was still alright. He had seen and heard much not only this morning, but during the entire week as well. He had heard talk of police officers dying or being found dead all over town.

Other people had been attacked as well, according to his best friend Steven Harris. Steven had heard the judge talking about some of the terrible things over the phone when she had thought him not listening. He had heard kids on the playground talking about vampires, which had sounded completely ridiculous, at the time. However, most had seemed so convinced of this. Now, he, too, was convinced.

Jerod glanced up toward the darkened outline that was Tiffany Rosen. She was standing, hovering over them. His eyes had adjusted well to the dark. He had known her his whole life, though they'd never spent all that much time together. She babysat a few times that he could recall when he was younger. However, though this girl looked like Tiffany, she was most definitely not the same girl.

The longer that he looked up at her, the worse he felt. Whether she could see him studying her, he was unsure; however, he could almost feel the heat of those terrible eyes upon him. Therefore, he stole his look and then quickly looked away.

He was sitting on a rug that appeared as black as pitch in the dark atop the hardwood floor between the bed and the wall. Beside him, the twins were there as well, and Aunt Vanessa, who was not really his aunt. She sobbed quietly to herself, sniffling every so often. He was not sure why, but was worried that it might be something to do with Uncle Mark. She had also been beaten up pretty severely by the mean man that had his mother. He wished that he had never seen it happen, but he did. The right side of her face was a bright tomato red. Her knees were scarred from being dragged across the house from the front doorway to the master bedroom at the very back of the house.

Jerod was tired, but his brother and sister seemed not to be. He was also a little bit hungry, but he tried not to think about it for fear of awakening that desire in them as well. If his little brother and sister wanted something to eat, he knew, they would not be taking no for an answer and that could be disastrous for them all.

*   *   *

Tiffany heard laughter coming from down the hallway and felt a pang of jealousy. It was not as if the two of them were lovers, although she could feel *something* that seemed to exist between the two of them. Was it Stockholm Syndrome? Some rapidly forming bond between captor and captive? Whatever it was, she simply did not appreciate getting pushed to the back of the house to do the babysitting. She glanced first at the police detective passed out on the bed, then back at the children on the floor.

There was also the little matter of her not having fed as of yet. She was terribly hungry.

Kill the children and then take my place in the front of the house, she thought. *Their father won't find out until he wakes up and who knows how soon that might be?*

*   *   *

Back in the living room Vincent had stopped laughing, but was still amusing itself with Barbara on the love seat.

"Are you hungry?" he asked.

"No," she said, curtly. Then she quickly added: "Thank you."

She thought it an odd exchange that he would care anything at all about her comfort, considering the fact that he very well might be debating whether to end their lives before the dawn. She thanked him not because she appreciated the concern, but out of fear. She needed to keep him friendly until she could think of something. She had seen what he had been capable of with her own eyes. With Mark and Nathaniel possibly dead, and Michael passed out in the back of the house, she might be all that her children had to rely on.

"Me, neither," Vincent added.

The thought of Vincent feeding or needing to feed sent shivers down her spine. She could vividly picture just how he might do that should it become necessary.

"Did you eat?" she asked, but was afraid of what his response might be.

"Yes."

"When?"

"Before paying you the visit tonight," he answered. "You are welcome, by the way."

For what? She started to say before the thought occurred to her that he could have waited and then fed at her house. "Thank you."

"Young Tiffany has not fed, however. She is young and stupid, and not nearly as patient as I am."

Oh, God! Barbara thought, leaping to her feet. Tiffany had been at the back of the house for a long time, supposedly watching over the children. Barbara had never thought to be concerned that Tiffany would harm them. She was a vampire just like Vincent. Maybe she just thought that the girl would remember something of her former humanity and do nothing to harm the children that she had known since their birth.

She headed for the hallway but never made it. Vincent got in front of her and she slammed into him, knocking herself backwards and hitting her head. It snapped back hard, but not enough to knock her out.

She never saw the vampire, nor could she see him now. She only saw stars. He did not make a move to come to her aid or even appear the least bit sympathetic. He just stood there, hovering above her. She wanted desperately to get to her feet and get past him, but there was no way that he was going to allow her to do so.

"Please, Vincent. I beg you. Please don't let anything happen to my children."

Vincent continued to stare at her.

"Vincent?" she said, lowering her voice. If he were angered, there was no telling what he might do. She could not tell the nature of his disposition, so she treaded carefully. "Please, Vincent."

The vampire sighed. "Did I lead you to believe that something was going to happen to them?" he asked finally.

"No," she answered. "You said that Tiffany had not fed."

"Did you believe that I would allow her to feed on your babies?"

Barbara said nothing.

"If anyone feeds from those precious little throats," he said, his eyes boring down upon her. "It will be me."

Barbara felt as the vampire quickly moved over her and into the middle of the living room.

"Do not move!" he commanded.

Vincent moved closer to the front windows. He took his time looking through them, and she deduced he found nothing at all, but was not in any hurry to rush to judgment. Barbara obeyed Vincent's command not to move; however, she did turn her head a bit and looked toward the open windows. Vincent was a large shape, blocking most of the view. He started to leave the windows, she saw, but turned back. She did not know why.

"Vincent," she began carefully. "May I get up?"

The vampire said nothing. She could only see his shape there so she had no idea of his expression or mood. He continued to stare, study or wait, for what, she did not know.

"Vincent?"

"You may stand," he said at last. "Do not attempt to leave this room again. A car is approaching. It has no lights on, but I can see it. Do not think for an instant that I cannot kill all of you well before the vehicle arrives." He made not the slightest move while saying it.

Barbara stood and slowly approached Vincent from behind. She stepped beside him, careful to remain a step to his left. She was also careful not to antagonize him further, not that she thought that she had, but with her children in the balance she could not be too careful.

"It looks like a police car," she offered, hoping that he would be at ease, realizing that she was not simply biding her time for the right moment to plant a stake through his heart.

Vincent took his eyes off of the car for a moment and eyed her somewhat surprisingly. "Does it?"

"Yes," she added. "Across the top of the car you can see the light bar. The car has a square look to it. You'll see."

"Oh, I can see it," Vincent replied. "I am simply intrigued why you would assist me with the identification."

The car continued to crawl towards them with no lights. Eventually they could see but one lone passenger. When it had reached them, the Jackson house sitting on a corner lot, the car turned without using its turn signal.

Then it stopped.

Right there in the road just through the intersection.

Vincent studied the car. Although Barbara knew there was no man alive capable of taking him by surprise, she could see him brace himself.

The sudden beam of white light burst through the open window, knocking Vincent back. It was clearly not at all what he had been expecting. Barbara shielded her eyes from the beam, but the light was not aimed at her. She peeked at the vampire beside her carefully as he backtracked, holding both of his hands across his face. They glowed luminescent in the darkness of the Jackson living room. Vincent moved to his right but the beam followed him as if he were an actor on some elaborate stage. He moved further right, but so did the light. He attempted to backtrack further. In the middle of the room, the beam was still too strong.

Barbara followed its progress with the knowledge that whoever was behind this particular stunt would not hold the vampire at bay for long. She also knew that when it had run its course, there might be no getting along with him after that. She took her eyes off the spectacle for a moment, wondering who was behind it. Perhaps no one. Perhaps it was just a poor cop, doing his part to locate the missing detective.

Suddenly, Vincent was behind her, growling. She let out a cry as the vampire lifted her easily off the ground and held her up as a human shield. His icy touch and the jagged finger nails gouging into her soft flesh stifled any further cries from her throat. However, the police car's spotlight was immediately extinguished.

Vincent held Barbara there, peeking out from behind her. She glanced up upon feeling the presence of the ceiling just a mere inches from the top of her head. Thankfully, in all of the tension, the vampire had not blindly shoved her head through it.

Barbara watched as the car began to slowly back up. It moved twenty feet back and then stopped once again. Nothing happened for a moment. She winced as Vincent's nails dug deeper into her during this time. Even Barbara could detect movement from within the car, so it was clear to both of them that something was about to happen. The only question was what.

Still clutching Barbara tightly, Vincent began to slowly back up.

Tires screeched suddenly as the driver of the car seemed to shove his foot through the accelerator pedal, driving what was left into the floor of the vehicle. The Ford Crown Victoria took a hard left turn. It hit the curb with such brute force that dancing sparks were sent in all directions. The front end lifted up momentarily as if it were about to take flight, then slammed back to earth. It did not slow. Rather, it picked up speed as the tires, like some great predator's claws, dug deep into the earth for traction. Vincent turned and moved both of them to the safety of the hallway.

"Tiffany!" he yelled.

The car raced onto the front grass, snapping a nineteen foot Chinese maple in half and crushing a number of bushes and various flowers. Barbara anticipated the sound of glass breaking and the force of shrapnel slamming against them as the walls caved in while they retreated, but none of that occurred. Instead, the car stopped just feet before doing just that. The explosion that they heard now was not the front wall but the vehicle's horn as something heavy seemed to hold it down.

"What's happened?" Tiffany yelled over the horn. She nearly ran into Vincent as she came rushing his direction.

"Get back to the room!" Vincent roared, though Tiffany was a mere foot away from him. Still, his command could barely be heard over the blaring horn. It sounded as though it were coming from inside the middle of the house. "This is but the diversion!"

Barbara's heart sank with Vincent's remark and she was suddenly overcome with doubt. She had spent a great deal of time praying for a miracle. Even the smallest of ones. Yet, at no time did there seem to be even the slightest chance for escape or for some turn of hand. It was clear that everything that she did with her conversations, with her actions, or the actions of others, was simply delaying the inevitable. She and her family would never see the sunrise. Even if Nathaniel was still alive, and there did not seem any hint of this, what chance would he have against the stronger vampire?

Vincent suddenly spun her around and set her on her feet. He did not wait for her to gain her bearings, but simply dropped her. She slumped against the nearest wall and was forced to right herself. He then grabbed her by the right hand and pulled her forward as he carefully studied the scene unfolding before him.

The horn continued to blare as something leaned against it in the front seat of the police car. She could make out a shape, but that was all.

"Make it stop!" Barbara shouted, cupping her hands over her ears, feigning pain.

Vincent eyed her suspiciously as if reading her intent. "*We* will!" he said, dragging her cautiously toward the front door. He never took his eye from the scene before the window until the last possible moment. In a flash, Vincent yanked open the door, allowing it to slam against the opposite wall, and pulled Barbara through. Everything between three feet from the front door and her being thrown against the grill of the police car was a blur.

"Check the driver!" Vincent commanded as he launched himself onto the hood of the vehicle. "The driver is either dead or pretending to be!"

By the time that she glanced up at him, he had moved to the roof of the car. She quickly ran around from the front of the car, stumbling over the carcasses of bushes, doing her level best to ignore the bruise from the car's grill. Vincent seemed to be in a sort of wild frenzy, posing as if ready for any upcoming attack, auditing his perimeter.

*　　*　　*

At the first blast of the horn, Michael Lopez awoke.

Wait! A voice sounded not in his ears but from somewhere within his head. *Not yet!*

He did not open his eyes. He felt so groggy, and now the pain was coming back to him. There had been a question at his lips, but he had forgotten it. He waited.

*　　*　　*

300

Tiffany reluctantly maintained her watch over the occupants of the room but spent much of her depleting energies listening for whatever was taking place at the front of the house. The twins, who had oddly enough been sitting quietly in the dark, suddenly turned in unison and focused on the window opposite them. Then incredibly, they threw themselves onto their little faces as if throwing some silent tantrum. It all happened in a moment.

Tiffany turned, and was immediately taken aback as Nathaniel came crashing through the window like a missile. She did not have time to scream or yelp in surprise as glass and pieces of wood and sheet rock and other building materials exploded about the room. The force of the attack drove her across the foot of the king size bed and into the opposite wall...

*　　*　　*

Michael rolled off the bed and landed as carefully atop his children as he could, hoping to shield their heads and faces from the materials raining down all around them. The pain from just rolling off the bed was excruciating enough, but he had to ignore it. There would be time to hurt later, he knew. Right now was all that they could hope for. Vanessa had material rain down upon her, too, before she finally dove for cover...

*　　*　　*

Tiffany's head was in an awful position against the wall. Bones had been broken and flesh had been torn from her, but she would not die this easily, Nathaniel knew. Seeing her in this condition, he felt pity for her. What must have been a lovely young woman in life was gone, irretrievably. She might heal, and heal well, but she would never be the same. A part of him felt bad about the girl who had been, but he knew that it was

301

already too late for her now. Perhaps there would be time for mourning later. Right now, they only had time to do this once.

"Is everyone well?" He shouted the question as he quickly crossed the short distance to the place where Michael was covering his children. Vanessa was shaking there in a ball on the floor, but did not move otherwise.

"Yes," Michael said.

A quick glance across their three faces showed some shock in the oldest child, but only peace in the other two. Michael began to gather them up in his unsteady arms and climbed to his feet.

"We must leave at once!" Nathaniel said. "Take your son and the woman."

Michael looked at his empty hands in disbelief as he discovered that Nathaniel had removed the toddlers from them without him realizing it. He was holding them now and they, to their credit, seemed perfectly fine with it.

"Now, Michael! There is no time!"

*   *   *

Barbara was torn as she reached the open driver side door. She knew that she should take great care with whoever was slumped against the horn in case the person was terribly injured. On the other hand, she knew that she needed to put more emphasis on what Vincent had commanded her to do, in spite of who may or may not be hurt…or worse. She said a silent prayer for the victim while she worked, quickly shoving her left hand through the open window and pushing the person back in the seat. The horn immediately ceased.

"Who is it?" Vincent snarled from above.

Even in the dim light Barbara could immediately recognize her best friend's husband. She and Michael had known the two of them for years. They had a fantastic past together and had always dreamed of sharing their futures together as well.

This was the end of that dream.

She reached for his neck to check his pulse, but there was dried blood all over his clothes and in his beard. It appeared that he had been dead for quite some time. How he had managed to pilot a car in such a condition, she did not know.

"It's Mark Jackson," she said through the growing lump in her throat. "Vanessa's husband. He's dead."

"How convenient!" came his reply, and then she heard the loud crash of something heavy land atop the roof of the house above her. Barbara stepped back and looked up but Vincent was gone.

* * *

In the alley behind the Jackson house, Vanessa Jackson's large Saturn Outlook SUV was parked. She had loved Barbara's so much that she had talked Mark into letting her buy one of her own. Their only anguish had been that she and Mark had yet to fill it with children.

While Barbara's model was gray or *Quicksilver*, hers was a shade of dark red called *Red Jewel Tintcoat*. This morning, and considering all that had transpired during this week, one might say that it appeared to be *blood red*. The car came with ONSTAR and was equipped with XM satellite radio as well as a hand's free cell phone and special cell phone number. The car seated eight comfortably with plenty of room for luggage or merchandise or diaper bags and whatever else a set of twins might require. All of the doors were conveniently open, interior lighting on, as if it were an escape vehicle for a large family or group. The ignition key was engaged and the motor running.

So it was when Vincent leaped from the roof of the house, landed in the back yard and quickly shot through the gate that had been left open, a trashcan braced against it to hold it there. The vampire had arrived just in time it appeared because the vehicle was still empty. He grinned to himself as he retreated to the shadows of the alley, preparing to spring the trap.

*　　*　　*

"Get in!" Mark Jackson commanded suddenly as this waking nightmare continued in a shocking new direction. Barbara let out a cry of surprise. The dead man's eyes were open and his face contorted as if in panic. These were all things that he should have been incapable of doing. Now he was leaning across the seat to his right and throwing open the passenger door.

"Mom!" a voice that sounded a lot like Jerod's now filled the air.

She looked left through the windshield of the police car just in time to see her son leading Michael through the front door. *My God!* Barbara thought, but was actually whispering it at the same time. *Jerod! Michael!*

"Get in!"

It was a virtual chorus of yelling voices. Impossibly, Mark was one of them, suddenly animated and throwing the transmission in reverse, his left foot pinning the brake against the floor while his right prepared to do the same to the accelerator pedal. Michael was another as he followed closely behind their eldest son into the passenger seat. Then there was Nathaniel, carrying the twins under each arm as if they were two footballs and the end zone was in sight. Lastly, there was Vanessa, half running before Nathaniel, half being shoved from behind.

Barbara had prayed and hoped against hope for the tiniest of miracles. It had become increasingly difficult with each passing moment not to lose all hope and heart as doubt had begun to choke everything. Yet, what she received—what all of them had received—was a parting of the Red Sea kind of miracle.

The left side backseat door flung open, followed by another course of yelling. Finding her wits just in the proverbial nick of time, Barbara jumped into the car. It was still unclear to her just how a dead body could be mastering such a feat, but Jackson released the brake and slammed the accelerator pedal into the engine, well before Barbara had gotten completely inside.

Grass and dirt and plant-life sprayed against the front of the house as the car leapt backwards. The adult occupants all struck their heads against the ceiling of the car as it flew over the curb. They bounced about as the car's brakes engaged, throwing them against the seats as well as into each other. There wasn't time to be careful, even though small children were in the car. The adult passengers simply shielded them as best as they could under the circumstances. Lastly, four tires screamed and large pieces of the Chinese Maple scraped the asphalt as the friction ground them to nothing as the real getaway car got away.

4:05 a.m.

Tires squealed as the battle-tested police car swung onto Draper Street from Church Street and headed northeast at a high rate of speed. What it had lost in making the turn it quickly gained back and more. It drove in the middle of the street and only took its proper lane as the driver ignored the fast approaching red traffic light and crossed Simpson Street without as much as a passing glance in either direction. The car slowed marginally just before hitting the railroad tracks, launching it several feet and causing it to land hard on the other side. It turned right on California Street and quickly accelerated once again, passing the dilapidated

Historic Train Depot, and did not begin to slow until just before turning into the parking lot of the Kingsburg Police Department.

Tires screeched and screamed in protest yet again and the smell of burnt rubber was noticed by all as the police car braked and then skidded to a halt near the main entrance. The driver did not attempt to park anywhere but simply skidded to a halt near the entrance.

"Take the children!" Nathaniel commanded, leaning over and handing one to its mother and the other to its aunt. The twins made no qualms about it, happily receiving a big hug from each woman. "Michael," he continued as Jackson killed the motor. "Get the women and children into the building. I will assist Mark."

"I can help my partner!"

"Just do as I say!" Nathaniel snapped. "There is no time! Vincent will find us shortly. This was no escape. This was simply an exchange of blows." Quickly, everyone filed out of the vehicle as ordered. "Turn out all light inside!" he said, lifting Jackson out of the car and holding him up as they made their way to the double-doors. Jerod held one of them open. Everyone filed in, led by Michael, trailed by Nathaniel and Jackson.

"Detective Lopez," a frail sounding young voice greeted them as they entered the lobby. There was a large green tiled lobby. Behind her, the telephone was ringing. "Am I glad to see you! The phones have been ringing off the hook! Where is everyone? The Mayor has called five times, looking for the chief! I can't get a hold of him! No one can!"

"Lainie," Michael interrupted. "Buzz us in!"

A loud buzz and a heavy metallic click sounded as the door was unlocked for them. Dispatcher Lainie Bishop moved quickly to the door as she took notice of the large man following the group into the building, holding up and half carrying a very much wounded Detective Mark Jackson.

"Oh, my God!" the dispatcher cried, covering her mouth with both hands in shock. His head was hanging limp against his chest. Blood was everywhere. "What happened?" she cried out.

"The lights!" the vampire shouted.

"Lainie, turn out the lights!" Michael ignored her and commanded. When she did not move fast enough, he pointed at the far wall. "Jerod, get those switches off." Jerod quickly obeyed.

Surely, he had seen and experienced enough in just a few short hours to teach him all that he would ever need to know about circumstances dictating obedience and quick reaction. The artificial lights went out, casting the room in shadows other than the steady glow of red and blinking yellow and green lights along the Dispatching Board.

"Lainie," Michael addressed the young woman again. "Is anyone else here?"

The young woman seemed frozen in place. From what little Michael knew of her she seemed like a bright individual. If anything, she was a bit young. This morning, it was painfully obvious that she was not equipped to handle sudden and extreme pressure. As the group lined up in the dispatching area, Michael quickly went to her and set his hands upon her shoulders to calm her.

"Lainie," he began. "I need you to focus for me." She turned her eyes from the eclectic group surrounding her and gave her full attention. "That's good. Perfect." He took a long breath, not only to help her calm down, but for his own well-being. The pain was incredible. He was afraid that were he to think too much about standing, he might actually go down. "Are there any other people in the building?"

"No," she said. "There were a while ago..."

"That's okay," he interrupted. "I don't care about that." He switched gears. "I need you to do some things now. First, I need you to go through the entire station and turn out the lights." The woman's expression went blank suddenly and it was at that moment that he realized that she was in no shape to do him and the others any good. She was also young, with her entire life ahead of her, and too many had died already; therefore, he changed his mind. "You know what? Never mind. I want you to get your things and go home."

"What?" Her face went pale.

"Jerod." He turned from her bewilderment and addressed his son. "Go with your aunt and turn off every switch in the place. You will find small lamps throughout most of the offices. Turn one on in each room first. When you are done, come back here."

Vanessa stood next to her wounded husband and studied him in the dark. Michael was sure she did not yet realize the full extent of his injuries. She didn't realize that she was being asked to go with Jerod, either, until the boy had taken her hand.

"'Nessa," Michael said. "I know you need to be with Mark right now, but I need this done first. Please." The woman was clearly torn. Michael did not need to see her face to know this, but she reluctantly went.

"I need to sit your friend down," Nathaniel said.

"Barbara, take everybody to my office. You know where it is."

"Wait!" Lainie Bishop was finding her voice at last. "What's going on here? Why are you sending me away? I can't leave my post!"

"You can and you will!"

"The mayor needs the chief!" she continued, undaunted. "We've got about sixteen uniforms out there, not to mention the crew putting out the fire next door to your house, I believe. Someone's got to be here!"

"We're going to be here, damnit!" he snapped. "The chief is dead!"

"What?" Lainie cried, stepping back in shock.

"Many have died, Lainie. Many more might die, but not out there, in here. I'm trying to prevent you from joining that number." At this, he threw his weight forward and went to her, taking her by the arm. "Now, get your keys and go home. I'll call you when it is safe to come back."

Typically, whenever a child is sent to do a job as Jerod had just been instructed to do, an adult must come back through and complete the job correctly. In this instance, however, it was unnecessary. The boy did exactly as he had been instructed.

*   *   *

Jerod soon returned after completing the task, with Vanessa rushing back to her husband's side. They met back up just as Barbara, a toddler in each arm, was leading them all into the detective's office.

Nathaniel carefully placed the wounded detective in the chair at his desk and then retreated casually toward the front of the room where he might be able to hear anything should Michael call out. His senses offered no hint of any forthcoming danger. At least not yet.

He surveyed the room. The detective's wife took a chair next to her husband and began to give him whatever care that she could. There was not much that she could do for him but to remain beside him. Barbara's oldest child, Jerod, took his place beside his mother. He stood like a dutiful child that was being forced to grow up too soon, and he reminded Nathaniel of himself in that regard. Though Michael was on the premises, the young man did his best man of the house impression by standing sentinel near Barbara, but above his little brother and sister should he be needed by them, as well.

Nathaniel listened to Michael as he sent the young woman away up front. Soon he would need to change places with him, allowing him to be with his family, which all of the occupants of this tiny square room seemed to be. *Too many have died already*, he thought to himself. *No more shall join them if I have anything to do about it. If more are to die I shall be next.*

Glancing back to the room for a moment, he noticed that Barbara was studying him. He offered the slightest nodding of his head, feeling self-conscious for a moment. His body had been set to healing since the last terrible lick of fire had done its work on him, but he knew that he was far from completely whole just yet. He glanced at his clothing; his long-sleeved shirt was little more than rags upon his back; his pants were blackened now and missing large swatches here and there. He was uncertain as to the damage that remained. It felt odd that he should be concerned with vanity now, yet he was.

He recalled the last time that the two of them had been together. He turned away. That same heartache was coming back now. He tried to shake the mounting emotion. There wasn't time for that type of nonsense now, not with Vincent out there on the loose, no doubt hunting them in earnest.

"Nathaniel," Barbara said.

He saw her stand up and walk over, so that was reassuring. He had even noticed her muscles tense as intent became action and she headed his direction. Previously, as if in some love-blinded state, he had missed this sort of thing. The great beast that had both created as well as pursued him across the globe had taken up residence in the very house next door to Barbara, had been living there for a while, in fact, and Nathaniel had noticed nothing.

"How are you?" she asked.

"Better," he said, which he realized could have referred to a great many things.

He had healed since the fire earlier this morning. However, it could also have referred to the dull pain in his heart from having had to leave her the day before when it appeared that he would no longer be a welcome vIsitor to either her home or her heart. He did his level best not to allow the latter thought to make itself obvious.

"I am unaware how badly I appear. If I am horrible to behold, I apologize."

"Now, why should you have to apologize for anything?" she chided him. "I owe you so much. We are all standing here because of what you have done..."

"You are also in grave danger!" he snapped, cutting her off. Everyone in the room turned to watch the exchange, including Jerod and the twins. "Because of me, people are dead!" Pent up frustration spent, he lowered his voice. "Because of my presence here, this town has become haunted."

"You have to quit blaming yourself for everything," she interrupted him back, placing a hesitant hand upon his charred and disfigured clothing. Now it was her voice that was elevating. "He did this to you! He took you from your family and changed the course of your life. You have done the best that you could to do the right things. You and he are nothing alike. Nothing!"

Her words seemed to strike a nerve. He met them with a sigh. "I want to believe this, Barbara," Nathaniel said, first glancing down at the delicate hand upon him, then to the lovely face that looked up deeply and powerfully into his. "With all my..." He paused as if suddenly slapped. "With all my being I want to believe that I am different, but there is no escaping the fact that we are the same, he and I. The same."

"How can you say that?" She put her other hand upon him and shook it as if he were her child needing a stern rebuke. "You are not the same, damnit! And I'm sick of this! You have got to listen to someone other than that voice in your head. You do not know

311

everything. There is no way that you can be the same. There isn't!" She paused again and drew a steadying breath. "A moment ago you were about to mention your heart, but you stopped. I know that. Why? You do have a heart. I've seen it! Too many times! Stop acting like you don't have one.

"Was it coincidence that you happened to be near my house the night Vincent attacked or was it a miracle of God?" At the mention of God, he began to squirm with discomfort. "Was it good fortune that enabled you to rescue not only my entire family, but my two friends as well?"

Somewhere in the far reaches of his awareness, Nathaniel wanted to believe that he could be used for good in the world, at least in this small part of it. Yet, there was simply too much to overcome. He lived on the blood, on the lives of others! Perhaps those others were not human, but something had to die every night in order for him to survive for one more twenty-four hour period. And for all of Barbara's talk of the scriptures, Nathaniel was not unaware of them. There was a time when he had attempted to search out some way to be in God's good graces; some technicality that might bring him even the slightest measure of the salvation that only mortal men seemed to be able to take hold of.

He knew the verses. 2 Corinthians 6:14 read, "Do not be bound together with unbelievers; for what partnership have righteousness and lawlessness, or what fellowship has light with darkness". 1 John 1: 5 read, "And this is the message we have heard from Him and announce to you, that God is light, and in Him there is no darkness at all".

Just what more did he need to read or know? Light assured destruction for the vampire. He could not live in it. Instead, he was forced to spend his miserable existence hiding in the shadows, cowering in fear of the light.

"The Bible..." Barbara began.

"Barbara!" Nathaniel seized her wrists and pulled her off of him, allowing for his cold flesh to interrupt her thoughts. It did its intended work. "The Bible is love and life! I have read it! It is concerned with little else. I am a vampire. Undead! The Bible and its scriptures condemn me and others like me. I need not read them further. I can hear their very judgment from the rocks and the trees!" He paused. "And from you."

"No!" Barbara said, enduring the cold vises at her arms.

She shivered and her discomfort showed through, but she did not attempt to free herself. Instead, she took those hands and reached up to Nathaniel's scarred and singed face. She looked at him—*through* him, to his very soul, to that budding heart he kept refusing to acknowledge. "I was trying to tell you before about dreams that I had been having. Please let me finish." Nathaniel sighed once again, but made no effort to stop her. "An angel was sitting with me at my dining room table. His words played to me like the most fantastic melody. He was teaching me the scriptures."

Nathaniel started to squirm again, but Barbara kept going.

"He was not simply telling me the word of God, he was teaching me. Really teaching me! He said to me, 'What if God, although willing to demonstrate His wrath and to make His power known, endured with much patience vessels of wrath prepared for destruction? And He did so in order that He might make known the riches of His glory upon vessels of mercy, which He prepared beforehand for glory'. Then he leaned forward and asked me one more question. He asked me, 'What do you think of my Nathaniel now?'"

The vampire studied her, dumbfounded at this revelation.

"And there was another. I never understood it until now. I was standing in a large meadow of beautiful flowers and you were there. You were standing beneath

313

some trees in shadow, in darkness, and I was coming to you. God's voice was calling out to you, but you didn't hear Him. He called you many times. 'Nathaniel, Nathaniel!' It was just like with Moses on the mount and with Paul before his conversion on that road to Damascus: 'Saul, Saul?'. I was coming to you, but it was you who were supposed to come out. Not to me, but into the Light. Not sunlight, Nathaniel. The Light of God!"

He was almost powerless to move. He had once declared the scriptures off-limits, without intrinsic value to be discovered or gained. And worse, he had found the Bible to be condemning. In a sudden reversal, he could nearly envision the first ray of uncondemning Light begin to shine over the mountaintops.

4:06 a.m.

Methodically, Vincent crossed the distance between the alley and the back of the house with a cool confidence which surprised even him considering the fierce anger that had taken hold of him. Everything had been going along well, according to plan, even in light of things that spiraled out of his control, such as the fire that had engulfed the Rosen house, bringing too many witnesses with it. The meddlesome chief of police that he had dispatched with very little effort had been another.

Up until now, Vincent had weathered every storm, and certainly all of Nathaniel's best shots, and yet, had stood the triumphant victor. As the putrid stench of burnt tires wafted over to this side of the Jackson house, clueing him to a fact that he did not need to be informed of—that all had escaped. Doubt crept into his black heart.

Doing his level best to push back that doubt, to squelch it with screams, blows, bloodshed or simply his own strength of will, he took hold of the locked back door. Paying no regard for the locked doorknob or the deadbolt above that, or even for the three metal hinges and nine bolts that held everything in place, he pulled the door through the frame, making it scream. Wood creaked, cracked, splintered and ultimately gave way in less than the time it took a human being to blink. As if he were simply walking though a doorless pedestrian walkway, he dropped the door behind him as he went.

The action did little to salve the wounds, however. What Vincent needed now, other than to quickly regain the upper hand—which obviously was not something that would be happening any time soon by the sound of things—was to shed some blood.

And a lot of it.

Unfortunately for him, even though he was hungry and could feed and feed well, the thought of bloodshed did not seem to be doing the trick, either. As he walked past the kitchen, the stainless steel coffee maker seemed to tease him with its sheen, laughing at his failure to anticipate more than one diversion. He sent it flying through the air with a flick of his left hand, its cord following after it like some dragon's snake-like tail. It became entangled with a chandelier and yanked it out of the ceiling. The combined crash was deafening for someone such as he, with quite possibly the world's most sensitive hearing. But he ignored both the sound that it made and the amazing holes that were caused in the ceiling over the dining room table, as well as the wall on the opposite side.

Vincent walked on.

Next, as outside light played off of the glass on two picture frames that hung in the short hallway just before he turned to the larger one, Vincent smashed them as well. Two shots in quick succession. The glass disintegrated instantly and what was left of the frames flew like exploded shrapnel in every direction. The glass that became embedded in his powerful hands fell to the

315

carpet as if fearful of touching the vampire for any length of time.

Still, his fury was unabated. A third picture took the brunt of it, followed by another two as he made his way to the bedroom where he knew that he would find young Tiffany. Smiling faces beamed and then exploded into millions of tiny pieces.

He smelled the girl before he could actually see her. She was crumpled in a heap between the bed and the wall. Pieces of building debris littered the entire room, but Tiffany seemed to be buried under much of it. Vincent glanced across the room toward the shattered window. It looked as though a guided Intercontinental Ballistic Missile had decided to enter the house through it rather than a door. Lights outside the gaping maw seemed to wink at him, trying his thin patience further; however, the things he could destroy out there were too far for him to reach and eradicate just this moment, so he turned away.

Tiffany moaned steadily beneath the rubble so it was clear that she would survive the experience. Part of him wished that she had already expired while another part (the part that was violently destroying the Jackson house piece by piece) wished to help her along in that regard. And very slowly.

He leaned over and quickly threw off the glass, wood and insulation that blanketed Tiffany. Vincent towered high above her, disdain filling him while he was yet unsure of her fate. Thumbs up or thumbs down? Death for the vanquished or mercy? Vincent gritted its considerable teeth momentarily while he reached his verdict. When Tiffany came to, he forced a look of sympathy upon his taut face and knelt beside her.

"Tiffany, my dear, can you hear me?" Tiffany only moaned all the more, and there was something else, too. Vincent cocked an ear. "Tiffany?"

"I'm sorry, my master," came a feeble voice, muted by the carpet that her head and face were pressed into. "I failed you."

"No. No. No," came the feigned response. He reached tenderly under Tiffany and moved her onto her back. "The fault was mine, my dear," he lied. "It is I who has failed you."

"You?" Tiffany asked incredulously as Vincent helped her like a father would his daughter—or a man, his lover—into a seated position. "How did you...?"

"Never mind all of that," Vincent said, softening his voice further as he lifted her to her feet, all the while holding her gaze with his eyes and forgiving lips. "Suffice it to say that I have treated you poorly. You who have stood by my side while my son has abandoned me. You, my precious one, who I left to be overwhelmed while I amused myself with the woman."

Vincent pulled her closer to him and embraced her. Gently, he slid his fingers up and down her back. Once she had fed again, she would begin to heal, although some of the wounds appeared to be permanent.

"Barbara never cared for you. None of them did. And what is worse, I, the one who should have loved you with everything that I am, cared little for you as well. I am so ashamed, my daughter, my love."

Tiffany seemed to grow weaker rather than stronger, suddenly becoming limp in his arms. Vincent did not allow himself a smile, though he was quite pleased with his act. His were a great many skills, indeed.

"Please forgive me," Vincent pleaded, moving ever closer still, his eyes appearing to water, though no water had touched his dry eyes in just over three hundred long years.

"Of course, my Lord." Tiffany shuddered once and seemed to stifle a cry. She had only been a vampire for mere hours compared to Vincent; however, she could not have produced a single tear, either.

"Not Lord," Vincent proclaimed. "Love."

And as softly and as delicately as if she were a rare flower to be seen and not held, Vincent moved his hands from the small of Tiffany's back past folds of torn flesh up to her scared and bruised face. Ignoring wounds, and there were many (a single nail jutted out from her head directly behind her left ear), he cupped her cheeks and brought her lips up to his own and kissed them. He tugged on those lips gently and then released them. Vincent swept the dry but full lips with a quick dart of his tongue like a snake feeling the air before it while in search of a meal. Before pulling away, he kissed them once again.

*   *   *

Tiffany was stunned. The young vampire felt such stirring now as she had never felt before; such passion. She recalled making love to that boy that she had known in what seemed now to have been some other life many years before and wondered how the fumblings of a naive boy could possibly compete with the power and strength of a lover who controlled lives and had obviously seen the world. Tiffany could not now even recall the boy's name. Not only that, but when images crept back of their past lovemaking, it was no longer his face but Vincent's. It was Vincent who was suddenly holding her down on the couch or bed or floor. It was Vincent's rough tongue doing wonderful things to her.

She felt so many wonderful sensations; among them was what it must feel to be a child's balloon as it is accidentally released into the air to float away to parts unknown. But it was her beloved Vincent who reached up and caught her before she could be lost forever.

"Tiffany, my love."

"Yes?"

"Though I would dally further *and farther*, we must not. Not yet."

318

"Yes."

"Do you understand me?"

"Yes."

"Good. There is much to do."

"I would do anything."

"Would you?"

"Yes."

"That is good, my dear, because I have need of you."

"Tell me."

4:20 a.m.

Lainie Bishop had had an extremely rough week. It had begun with two police officers, that she had known well, dying horrible deaths during her shift. She remembered speaking to them, and a short while later, they were gone. It had taken her a couple of days to get her legs back beneath her. She missed work and didn't speak to anyone, not even Jeremy. She had only been seeing him for a few weeks, and although she could definitely feel the love beginning to swell between them, she needed some time to heal from the pain of losing those officers that she had been responsible for. Both he and her dad phoned her several times a day during the entire time that she had been off. It bugged her, but she could never be mad at either one of them so she endured it. Her dad phoned a couple of times last evening as well, so she finally drove over and had dinner with him before she went off to work.

It was not something that she had spent any real time deliberating about, just a back of her mind kind of hope that she could simply get re-acclimated with one quiet and by-the-numbers kind of night. She knew that the city was being supported by members of other police departments, and that was going to be more work

319

for her, having all of these patrol cars crawling all over town. Still she hoped for the best.

Unfortunately, on her first real night back behind the desk, she was hit not only with chaos, but well more than that. Now, she found herself being sent home.

She pulled her 2000 Volkswagen Beetle slowly out of the parking lot and her eyes followed the front entrance of the police department as she slowly crawled forward toward the street. Just then, she noticed a tall shape on the sidewalk. Anywhere else she may have ignored him and continued on her way; however, although she was being ordered off the premises by Detective Lopez, that did not make her any less an officer of this city, and she would continue to do her part. No matter what.

"May I help you?" she asked, opening the driver side window.

"I sincerely hope so, my dear," the odd-looking man said.

He leaned forward and rested his hands upon her door. Long fingernails curled over the side of the door, and Lainie wondered whether or not the stranger in the dark might be a musician. She had always adored Spanish guitar playing, ever since she'd been a girl and her father had taken her to Spain one summer to visit her dead mother's family. It had been a promise kept on her mother's—a too-young cancer victim—deathbed to take her to the place of her ancestors.

"I am looking for four adults, one child and two babies."

4:26 a.m.

In the Dispatching center at the front of the police station, Detective Michael Lopez saw his dispatcher to the door and then quickly locked it behind her. He took one last peek in the parking lot, seeing only Lainie

320

Bishop as she began to drive away. Then he moved back across the lobby and cleared the door that he had propped open so that it would not lock behind him. Now he allowed it to do just that. It closed with a bang, followed by an extremely audible click as the automatic locking mechanism activated. In the dark and silence of the early hour, it sounded like a distant solitary cannon shot.

Nathaniel appeared in the entrance of the hallway when Michael glanced toward that direction.

"Everyone is well," he said, as if reading his mind.

Michael stopped and surveyed the figure before him. He had grown comfortable with the vampire, but he was just that—a vampire. Just like the one that was out there behind some very weak locks, sheet rock and windows.

"Good," he remarked.

"How about you?" Nathaniel asked.

Michael thought the question over for a moment before answering. "If I were at full strength would I be any help to you against that thing out there?"

"Perhaps not," Nathaniel replied.

4:31 a.m.

Barbara and Jerod tended to the twins who did not seem to need anything, or even notice that they had been awake for a very long while. They acted as if they were neither famished nor exhausted. Barbara had changed both of their diapers. Both had needed it, but neither had complained.

Mark continued to simply recline in the chair while Vanessa sat beside him, quietly, allowing him to rest. Barbara knew he was still awake, although he held his eyes closed as if he were not. She knew this because he would shuffle in is seat periodically, reach up to scratch an ear or his beard and because his breathing was never the same and appeared labored. Barbara looked upon Vanessa's countenance. She could see a great many questions there. Why she held back from asking them, she did not know, but was grateful. She didn't have many answers.

"Mom?" Jerod broke the silence.

"Yes, honey?"

"What's going to happen?"

Barbara reached out and touched her son's left shoulder, smiling warmly, at least the best that she could under the terrible circumstances. After all, there they all were huddled together in the darkened police station, tired and wounded from all that they had been forced to endure.

"Are you scared?" she asked. Jerod looked down at the floor and said nothing. Barbara moved from her son's shoulder to his chin, lifting it gently so she might be able to look into his eyes. "It's okay to be scared. Everyone feels a little bit scared."

She noticed her friend Vanessa looking their way and gave her the briefest of smiles. "Aunt Vanessa's scared. Your dad is scared." She thought of Nathaniel and paused. "We're all scared. But no one is going to let anything happen to you or your brother or your sister. I promise."

"Is Mr. Nathaniel scared?" Jerod asked, noting the omission.

It was the first time that he had ever questioned about the mysterious stranger that had become a big part of his mother's life, she realized. Most of the interaction had occurred when he had been either away or sleeping, so he had not really been introduced. The twins knew the vampire, of course, but they were too little to know anything, and would, no doubt, forget after a few days once he had departed from their lives. That was just how it went with small children. It was the folks who were in their lives daily that they became comfortable with.

"I'm sure that he is a bit worried as well, yes."

"Mom," Jerod continued. "Just who is he anyway?"

Barbara sighed as she thought about what it was that she might be able to report about her new friend. Once again, she noticed that Vanessa was looking extremely interested in that same question as well. And eager to hear the answer.

"A friend." She offered no other explanation.

"What kind of friend?"

It was Vanessa who asked the question now. As she watched Barbara struggle with her response, she did not notice as Mark's eyes finally opened. It was not in the direction of the conversation that they turned.

It was toward something else.

4:45 a.m.

Michael Lopez surveyed the blinking lights and listened along for radio traffic. There wasn't much. He had lowered the volume so that it would not distract them from any local noises. He was surprised that not one of the multiple patrol units or even members of the fire crew had attempted to make any form of contact with the dispatcher. Since the current dispatcher was no doubt making plans to curl up in bed for the approaching day, and the fact that he was too exhausted to fill in for her, he was glad that no one seemed interested in following them.

"Michael," Nathaniel spoke up. There was a directness to the tone.

"Yes."

"It is time."

Michael spun. The vampire had found them. He was staring at them through the thick glass at the front entrance, his nose pressed firmly against the glass. He stood there like some statue that high school kids had removed from a rival's park and placed there to scare

323

the graveyard dispatcher. He wasn't some young college age woman attending to the police matters in the lonely hours of the day, but a seasoned police detective. And yet, it carried the same intended result.

"Shit!" Michael whispered.

"My sentiments exactly."

4:45 a.m.

With hardly much effort at all, Mark Jackson jumped up from the chair that had just moments before seemed to be keeping him from falling onto the floor. Now, he cast it aside as if it were nothing at all.

"Mark? Where are you going?" Vanessa asked, stunned, as he moved to leave the room.

"Barbara." He turned toward the group, ignoring Vanessa's question and addressed her instead. "Take Vanessa and the kids and lock yourselves down the hall in the soft room."

The soft room was an elongated but tiny room for the interviewing of children or female victims and furnished by the Junior Women's Club of Kingsburg. It contained a couch, chairs and a table or two. Perhaps more importantly, there was a plethora of stuffed animals for the kids to play with.

"Mark!" Vanessa protested as she watched him turn to leave. "Where are you going? You're in no shape to go anywhere but the hospital!"

"I'm far better than anyone suspects."

He finally glanced her direction. He could see that she was dumbfounded by this admonition. Her face twisted at his tone and he knew she was hurt, but there was nothing he could do about it now.

"Mark?" Vanessa said, rising to her feet as if to follow. Barbara jumped up as well, reaching out for her friend's arm as she did so.

"Vanessa." Barbara tried to sound soothing as she attempted to stop her from following after her husband.

"No," she said, pulling the arm away.

"We need to do as he said. We need to lock ourselves up in the back of the building!"

"You go on ahead and do that!" she yelled. "My husband is out of his mind with shock or something and I need to take care of him." Mark stopped at the doorway and turned back before crossing the threshold, waiting.

"I don't know what it is, but whatever it is, Michael and Nathaniel will take care of him."

"Michael needs help himself!" Vanessa continued to shout. "The last time I saw him, he could barely stand. Aren't you worried about him in the least?"

Now it was Barbara who raised her voice. "Of course I'm worried about my husband! Don't think for a minute that I'm not! But I have more to think about than just him. Plus I have you and Mark! Right now, I have got to get you and these kids behind a secure door. And I'm talking right now!"

Vanessa stared at Barbara—usually calm, gentle Barbara—in surprise. Then she half glanced over at him, hoping for some support. He gave her none.

"'Nessa," Mark said, pointing down the hallway in the intended direction. "Take the children and go with Barbara. We don't have time to argue. This place is going to become a war zone in about two minutes."

"Now how do you know that?" she replied, putting her hands to her hips as if to take her stand against everyone in the room. Her cracking voice betrayed her, however, as if on some level she knew that her husband was correct in the assessment.

A voice at the front of the building confirmed it. It was Nathaniel. "Barbara, take them now! Vincent is here!"

Mark did not wait any longer, but he turned and headed toward the sound of Nathaniel's voice.

* * *

Barbara immediately went over and scooped up the nearest of her toddlers.

"Jerod, Honey," she said as she moved. "Grab your sister!"

He quickly obeyed.

Vanessa just stood and watched.

"Come on, damn it!" Barbara yelled as she reached her friend. Using her free shoulder, Barbara shoved the woman forward through the doorway and pointed her down the hallway. Finally, she seemed to get the message and reluctantly let them lead the way.

4:48 a.m.

Vincent continued to stand unmoving against the glass front door, staring at the occupants of the room like that statue. Nathaniel studied him. The sunrise was about an hour away, but he did not seem to be concerned about the time. Perhaps he simply knew that he had more than enough time to accomplish whatever it was that he intended, which was no doubt as black as his shriveled heart.

He glanced briefly away as the phone rang, catching Michael as it made him jump. Michael took a peek at it but was either too far away to be able to read the display to see who was calling or didn't care. Nathaniel could read the LED display of the phone number, but would obviously not know who was calling.

"Go back with the others!" Nathaniel ordered over the ringing telephone.

"No!" Michael replied and finally broke himself free from the figure at the door. He rushed to the phone, picked it up and then immediately slammed it back down. He just turned the handset upside down and

326

flipped it over onto the counter so that it would not ring again. "I'm not going anywhere!"

"Not you."

Nathaniel did not turn around, but could see as Michael did so to catch his partner who was now standing against the door frame at the mouth of the hall for support. It was Mark that Nathaniel had been addressing. He had sensed him join them.

"You are not yet ready," Nathaniel said.

"Would you like me to come back tomorrow when I am, or the next day?" Mark replied.

Nathaniel heard him take a few more steps into the room, no doubt to get a better look at Vincent. He did not answer his sarcasm. It was true that it might take every one of them to subdue Vincent in order to destroy him once and for all.

As if on cue, Nathaniel saw Vincent begin to move. He was retrieving something from his right pants pocket. It took him no time to remove the set of objects and to begin to try each one until he had found the magic one which would do the trick.

Nathaniel saw Michael creep closer to the large front window which separated the Dispatching Center from the Lobby and strain his eyes to see what Vincent might be doing. The glass was five feet high from counter to ceiling and twelve feet across from north wall to the pedestrian door on the south. Michael stopped when he reached the counter. "What's he doing?" he asked.

"He has keys," the other two in the room answered in unison.

4:53 a.m.

In the heart of the police department was the soft room. Vanessa pushed the door open while Jerod and Barbara carried the toddlers in. The only light came

327

from the two small table lamps in the room. It was enough. Barbara surveyed the room momentarily. It was a simple room. She wondered whether it would be strong enough to slow the vampire that would attempt to get through, but the answer to that question was clear. As she set her youngest son down at the back of the room, she did her best to visualize Vincent not even making it this far. And as she watched Jerod set his sister down beside her twin brother, she realized that the consolation was that, should they fail to make a stand, she and her husband would be dead long before the children

"Vanessa," she called her friend over as she closed the gap between them. Vanessa closed the door behind them and approached. Barbara took her by the hand. "I need you to stay with the kids," she whispered.

"What?" Vanessa said, incredulously.

"I have seen what this monster can do. Him knocking you to the ground and dragging you across the house is nothing compared to what he can do when really motivated, and right now it's pretty frigging motivated!"

Vanessa stared back at her life-long friend and studied the eyes that looked back at her. Barbara gave her a gaze that was purposeful and unflinching—hiding nothing. She saw eyes there that had seen something profound as well. They were eyes that had once beheld beauty and seen tenderness and peace, but had been driven to unyielding purpose by something terrible.

"I don't understand any of this," Vanessa confessed, dropping her hands like dead appendages at her side in tantrum. "What is this?" Tears quickly formed and poured down her cheeks as everything was just suddenly out of her control or manageability.

"Sweetheart." Barbara took the woman in her arms and held her tightly. "Didn't you read the papers? What has turned our world upside down is no serial killer and certainly no man!" Vanessa made a move as if to separate herself from her, but Barbara was not willing to let her go just yet. "It's a vampire! Nathaniel is one, too, and I have seen them in action. Three nights ago the bad one came through the twins' nursery window, intending on making my babies his dinner. Nathaniel stopped him. He's been hunting us ever since."

Barbara released her friend.

"What?" The tears were still coming.

"You have to stay here with the children."

"But what about you?"

"I can't wait a second longer and hope that Michael and Mark and Nathaniel have enough within them to kill it! I just can't!"

Barbara never let go of Vanessa completely. She turned the woman, goading her in the direction that she must go. Then she turned her eyes to her three children. The great loves of her life. Jerod stood with a torn expression on his face—half standing guard over his brother and sister and half wanting to rejoin his mother, especially after what he had just heard her say. There were tears welling up in his eyes as well, but he seemed to be holding them back at the moment. Behind him on the carpeted floor, the twins continued to appear composed. It was Nathaniel's doing, she knew. Somehow, that one tiny intervention had secured their comfort, their confidence, their everything. They would never be the same. They were still Robbie and Rebekah, would still grow up and laugh and play, and eventually become splendid adults. And it was in that last visualization that Barbara convinced herself that the task ahead of her could be accomplished.

"I love you guys," she told them.

She quickly blew them a kiss and moved to the door. "Momma's gonna be right back." She paused one last time half in, half out of the door.

"Vanessa," she said, addressing her with firm eye contact once again. "Lock the door…and pray."

4:58 a.m.

At long last, Vincent had located the correct key, turned it in the lock and gained access. Before entering fully; however, he leaned toward the ground with his left hand and retrieved something. Michael could not make out just what it was. While Nathaniel held his ground beside him, Michael glanced nervously from door to door, deliberating and calculating in his head whether or not he believed that the last door between them and the vampire might hold. It seemed too much to hope for.

When Michael tore his mind away from the what if's and what might happen, Vincent had reached the other side of the large lobby window.

"What'd he just drag in here?" Michael whispered the question. He waited for the reply, but none came. "Nathaniel?"

"You may wish to turn away."

With still surprising little effort, Vincent reached up and slammed an object against the glass. Michael cursed in horror as the lifeless body of Lainie Bishop struck the glass with her back and head. The blow did nothing to the thick bulletproof glass, but it collapsed several of the plates that had once made up her beautiful skull. There was a sickening squashing sound as some of the contents inside were loosed. Yet, there was very little blood.

For good measure, Vincent pulled her down and slammed her three more times in some sick, twisted rhythm as if she were simply the door knocker of an even larger castle.

"She did not seem pleased that she was being sent away," Vincent broke the silence between them. "So I decided to invite her back inside."

"My God!" Barbara cried as she entered the room just in time to witness the carnage. "What kind of monster are you?" she screamed, unable to hold back

her outrage at the sight of the dead woman's hanging limbs. Whatever blood she had remaining stained the glass in dark splattered rivulets.

All three in the room turned to look at her as she did so. Michael wondered just the same thing. Though he and Mark had already seen and tasted some of what the vampire had been capable of, only Nathaniel really knew what the monster was like.

Michael swallowed hard.

For it was all there—the proof of the monster Nathaniel considered Vincent to be—written so clearly in the stark horror on Nathaniel's face.

Poienari Fortress

It was his last night.

Nathaniel had realized that fact since just before falling asleep the morning before; the first time he had actually felt the allure to sleep during the day. The last conversation that he hoped he would ever have with Vincent replayed in his mind as he, a brand new vampire, pulled open a large metal door to make good his escape.

He had never been this far before, at least not that he could remember. Perhaps in the time of his youth, he might have been let down this particular corridor and through this door, but he could not recall. Ancient petrified torches were mounted every twenty-five feet but sat dormant. Nathaniel would no longer need to rely upon them, unfortunately. Movement just to his right caught his attention. He turned with a start to see a giant four inch spider crawling along, webbing in a corner eight feet above the stone floor. The sight caused him to hurry along the length of the corridor to the next door. It was not out of arachnophobia, however, but self-preservation. Nathaniel had found himself beginning to wonder just how succulent the spider might taste.

He felt a growing apprehension with each step. Behind him was the world he'd known for a long time, and he was abandoning it without a thought as to the future.

He remembered Vincent's visit the day before...

"Go away!" Nathaniel commanded Vincent before he even saw him. His newly found senses sharpened, he had felt him get close. It was also surprising that someone who was so unaccustomed to being ordered around had taken it so well.

"I plan to feed long and heavily tonight," Vincent declared.

It had been an open invitation. One which Nathaniel had found to be in as bad taste as the reason his mother's God had created the infernal monster to begin with.

"And what? You would give me time to attempt an escape?"

"Escape? Where would you go, my son? You are a vampire now. There is no place you can go. Your place is here...with me."

Nathaniel did not respond. He could feel his anger boiling once again, but what good would it do. He had already attempted to attack Vincent before to no avail.

"I will bring you a meal..."

"Don't bother!" Nathaniel snapped angrily.

"But you have not fed, my son."

This had been the case and still held true. The only blood that had touched his lips had been Vincent's. Vincent had warned that a temporary illness would follow while the metamorphosis had its terrible way. Reliving that fateful moment had caused Nathaniel to vomit miserably well past the designated period. The beast had not realized that it had continued not due to the changes taking place, but because Nathaniel abhorred the thought of what Vincent had done. Since the attack, vermin scurrying about the fortress that he had once been afraid of now represented food, and easy pickings as well for even one as clumsy as himself. Those meals would be humiliating and disgusting, but he would not be able to hold back the terrible hunger for much longer.

Even now, he felt himself weaken already.

Nathaniel came to another large metal door. Thick spider webs covered nearly all its frame except the door itself. He took the handle within his right hand and quickly swung it open. It creaked, but he did not concern himself with that, nor did he close it back behind him. Vincent would undoubtedly know of the escape instantly upon his return.

Nathaniel stepped through the doorway and into a great hall that had once hosted large gatherings. He felt cold now, but could not yet detect the reason for it. The room contained tables and chairs, tapestries and rugs; however, everything appeared unkempt or perhaps forgotten, even to an escaped prisoner such as Nathaniel with little experience of such things.

As he neared the next door, the chill grew worse. Nathaniel wrapped his arms about his chest, fighting the cold back as it attempted to chill him into lethargy. The door appeared the same as all of the other doors, but this one proved difficult to open. Perhaps it had to do with his increasing hunger? When he finally managed to pull it open, the cold hit him at once, knocking Nathaniel back a step, unprepared as he was for its stark reality.

The next room was not a room at all but yet another corridor. This one was longer than any he had seen until now. More importantly, at least one section of wall was missing.

Nathaniel found this to be quite unexpected and approached cautiously. Upon close inspection, not only was there a gaping hole on the right side of the corridor, but the top of the corridor had at least two sections missing. Light shone through the missing stones. It was the moon, and it was the most beautiful thing that he had seen in what seemed like a hundred years. Nathaniel went to it quickly, not wishing to waste a single moment building up his courage. He stood directly in the spot and gazed up into its face, allowing the muted light to bathe him.

Soon, Nathaniel realized that by standing at the mouth of the missing wall section, he could see the moon in all of its glory. Moments passed, after which he resolved to continue moving for fear of never seeing the moon again, but it was extremely difficult to move his foot. The moon was full and high in the overhead sky, as if it had been set there only for Nathaniel's delight. Yet, when he began to finally pull himself away from the light to see what else there might be to see, his concern began to grow anew.

Wherever Nathaniel was standing he was higher than anything else on the horizon. He took his time as his new eyes struggled to fathom just what it was that existed beyond the dark. Then he realized it was the mountains that he saw before him, and they were shorter than his field of vision. And far below there appeared to be movement. He waited and listened. It was water.

Vincent had spirited him away to some remote location.

Now, perhaps, getting out of the fortress was not the end of his problems, but merely the beginning.

Where would you go, my son? Your place is here…with me.

Nathaniel quickly grabbed the sides of the open maw in the wall and stuck his head out as far as he thought he safely could. The wall seemed to be on the precipice of a sheer cliff. Though he needed to escape right this moment, this hole would not do.

He ran through the corridor to the other side. It was the first time that he felt his legs take flight in as long as he could remember. Memories began to creep back into his head, but he fought them off. This was not the time.

He came upon a doorway, but there was no door to be found. Nathaniel paid it little mind and simply continued on his way. There came a high balcony, overlooking a much larger gathering place than the room before. To the right stood a staircase. He followed it down. Nathaniel had a sense that the fortress had become warm once again, but did not stop to analyze whether it simply had to do with the work of running and being under anxiety to run faster still.

At the bottom of the stairs, Nathaniel ignored the contents of the room and headed for the nearest corridor before him which seemed to beckon to him. He could not remember anything about having ever visited the parts of the fortress that he was seeing now, but he stayed confidently along the current path as though he'd been here countless times. He came to three corridors, each with a closed door at its end. He headed down one and quickly threw open the door there only to find a room with no roof and two missing walls. Once again, he was struck by the cold. He could see the moon and the mountains again, so he turned back without closing the door.

He headed down corridor two, but was frustrated yet again. The room that he found there was intact, but there was no further advancement to be had.

Nathaniel heard ragged breath and spun around before realizing that the breath had been his own. He ran to the final door and flung it open, revealing the outside world. There were more walls but they were far below. Another stairway led the way to them. Above them stood a tree line.

The cold hit him harder this time as he descended the steps, and no matter how hard he fought off its icy fingers, the cold began to slow him. Nathaniel nearly lost his balance three times. Try as he might to concentrate upon each individual stone step, all that he wanted to do was take in these first few steps of freedom. Below, he could already see not stone or even brick floor, but dirt.

Unfortunately, there was something else now as well.

A terrible stench, growing far worse with each subsequent step.

Nathaniel jumped the last five steps, his incredibly long hair trailing behind him like the tails of a cloak, and landed smartly upon the ground. He nearly fell again. The ground was slick. Had he remembered the days of his youth, he might have guessed that it had been muddy because of recent rain. There was grass as well, but mostly a disturbing wet earth. *Was it the vampire?* No. It could not be. Vincent had never smelled anything like this. He kneeled low. No, the grounds seemed to be the source of the odor, though not entirely. There seemed to be other underlying scents here, too.

Nathaniel heard mad laughter. It was nothing *like* laughing, actually. It sounded horrible and ghastly and took his breath.

And it filled his head with a sudden memory, which sent an awful chill down his spine.

Is this the end? So close to freedom only to be thwarted at the last? No. Vincent's beady, hateful eyes were not about to come climbing out of the darkness; it wasn't the vampire's sarcastic giggling which was about to come upon him there in the courtyard.

The madness continued, though Nathaniel could not yet locate its source. He wished that he could so that he might make an end to it. It was far worse than any cold that might chill him.

And then, just as suddenly as it had appeared, the laughter was gone.

Nathaniel froze. *Am I hearing things?*

With the full moon seemingly directly above his head and so close that he could almost reach out and grab it, there was very little that could be hidden.

Nathaniel stood in what seemed to be the middle of a large courtyard. High outer walls surrounded him on all sides. No other doors were present, nor were there any other stairs save the ones behind.

Laughter erupted and then it was gone again.

Nathaniel simply stood there as he decided upon his next move.

Am I being watched? Am I being played with?

Was this yet another one of Vincent's games? First, his *modus operandi* had been to frighten and keep him in place; *was it now simply to remind him of who the master was?*

Yet, still, something gnawed at Nathaniel; something from the deep recesses of memory. It slithered slowly over the mountaintops of his consciousness like the dawn, first appearing only as a lighter darkness and then a light haze before revealing itself—from somewhere deep in his subconscious mind. Although he did not realize that he was doing so, Nathaniel did his best to keep whatever it was at bay.

Ahead, almost as if it had been there all along, a phantom of some manner moved on the ground. He held it in his gaze, afraid to blink for fear of losing it. Whatever it was, it did not seem to realize that he was there with it.

Nathaniel began to inch forward. If it was not Vincent then nothing should be permitted to stand in the way of his escape. The figure became clearer now, as well as its activity. He could hear wet sounds, the tearing and ripping associated with wild dogs as they pulled apart the flesh of their quarry. Something was having dinner.

He just hoped that it wasn't Vincent.

Slowly, still seemingly undetected, Nathaniel crept forward. If Vincent was there, then this was simply a game or trap. If he wasn't, then the creature before him was simply mad. Another poor creature such as himself that had been caught up in some terrible drama.

The closer he got, the worse the stench. Nathaniel knew then that this had been the source of the additional odors. Another step or two and the figure turned out to be female. She was making herself a meal out of whatever it was that she had either caught herself or perhaps what Vincent had left for her. She was giggling, clueless to his presence. She was also unclean. Her body smelled as though covered in dry defecation and urine. This creature apparently slept in her own waste and thought nothing of it.

It was here that Nathaniel decided that he could not involve himself in everything. Right now, he simply needed to escape.

Escape this place. Escape Vincent's clutches. Escape.

With that in mind, he began not to concern himself so much with what was huddled there on the ground, but simply with sidestepping it.

As he slunk past her, the woman turned and faced him, dropping a large section of raw, freshly harvested meat. Glancing down, he could fully see what the animal had been, and wished that he had not. His heart kicked into overdrive as the realization washed over and through him. His breathing became short and quick.

The woman before him was familiar.

Nathaniel screamed.

The woman was his mother.

The high full moon spun suddenly and the courtyard walls loomed, threatening to collapse upon Nathaniel, pinning him there so close to freedom until Vincent could return and escort his beloved son back to his suite. The woman reached out and took him by the arm, pulling him close. It was here, finally, that he finally fell. His arms, shoulders and head slammed hard onto the cold slick ground.

Rough hands were upon his now, clawing, digging their way into his flesh, drawing blood in places, ripping and tearing at the clothing as she threw herself upon him, apparently preparing herself to devour him, too.

"Please, Mother. Stop!" he pleaded with her, raising his hands between them.

The plea was answered with more mad laughter. Nathaniel lost himself in the eyes of the face that stared back, but did not see his reflection there. It wasn't as if he no longer had one, but rather the person looking back at him saw nothing familiar there.

Nathaniel was transported back to his childhood home in that moment. He could hear his mother praying now. It was a recollection of that last night at his real home; not the suite in the fortress above, or the tiny cell of a room before that, but the modest cottage of his birth. Nathaniel remembered thinking at the time of that fateful attack that his mother had lost her mind then. As it turned out, that was merely the beginning. Now it appeared as if she finally had.

For many years, he had thought his mother dead. He had known his father was dead for he'd stumbled upon his dead body. What had come of his mother he had never really seen with his own eyes. Incredibly, like some great uncaring beast, Vincent had not even allowed his mother that dignity.

Closing his eyes tightly, Nathaniel mustered all of his strength and shoved the mad woman back. She giggled louder as she flew back and then fell over, striking her head hard upon the cold ground. As if it had been the most hilarious thing in her world, the woman began to laugh even more as if the entire performance was just some game to be shared between mother and son; some perverted facsimile of the play they had used to share.

Nathaniel rolled over and climbed to his feet, preparing himself for the next attack. This time, at least, he could see it coming. He stepped to the right and allowed the woman who had once been his mother to fly past and fall harmlessly to the ground. He turned to watch her regain her feet. She giggled more and reversed her attack.

Nathaniel winced and readied himself for what he knew he must do. As the shell of his mother ran to him, he sidestepped her and reached around, catching her in the crook of his right arm. He slowed her and took a position behind her. Her momentum threatened to take her past, but he would not allow it. Being the stronger, it was a simple thing for him to stand her up and hold her there.

"How could you?" Nathaniel whispered, staring directly above. He was not speaking to the full moon which simply bathed him in light. He looked past it. "How could you?"

Grimacing one last time, the woman's former son squeezed her neck as tightly as he could, bracing the left side of her head with his other hand, and gave it a quick twist, snapping it.

This was no vampire, just a shadow of the most wonderful person that Nathaniel had ever known in the entire world. He had spent a great deal of those early days in Poienari Fortress crying out for her, hoping that she could save him. He'd known she was no match for the strength of a vampire, but it was all that a young child could do—plead for his mother.

As he stood in the sudden silence of the courtyard, surrounded by walls nine feet thick and made of brick and lime mortar, and filled with rubble, it was to that woman that his thoughts turned to. Not the one who was currently sliding limply out of his arms, but the one who would never have been able to advance on the fortress and save her little boy—nonetheless, the woman who would have tried to anyway.

Nathaniel held the shell of his mother for a while before allowing her to fall. When he finally did, the pain was overwhelming. He quickly ran for the nearest wall and threw himself upon it, mounting it with ease. Part of the new vampire wished as he ran along the width of the brick and rubble that he would find that sheer cliff once again on the other side, where he could simply throw himself to his death. Yet, at the same instant, he knew that it would never be as easy as that. No, this escape was no end, but merely a beginning. On the other side of that wall was nothing but the world; Romanian earth. Beyond that, he would have to see for himself. It appeared as if he would have plenty of time.

4:59 a.m.

"He is the great beast," Nathaniel said. "There is nothing that he is incapable of."

Vincent appeared to survey the young dead woman within his grasp as if admiring his handiwork. With a sigh, he tossed her aside and began to slap his hands together as if intending to clean them. Nathaniel knew that no amount of cleaning could remove the stains that had become encrusted there. Between them in the center of the glass was a thin area which allowed the visitor the ability to converse with the person on the other side.

"Name calling," Vincent said. "Just call me father and let us be done with it, once and for all."

"Father?" Michael asked.

"Certainly," Vincent answered, never taking his eyes off of his alleged son. "Did he not tell you? I am his father. I have raised him since he was a boy!"

Nathaniel's knew that his face seemed emotionless to those assembled. Vincent had hoped to enrage him, but it was not working. For the past few days, Nathaniel had gone about as if in a daze. He had thought only of Barbara and, in doing so, allowed a great many things to take place essentially under his very nose. His was a nose, a pair of eyes, and a fantastic sense of hearing which should have interacted flawlessly with one another to ensure that he never got caught by surprise.

However, that proved not to be the case. Thankfully, now, his senses had returned, and he was not going to allow anything to distract him again.

So it was that he did not allow himself to become riled.

"I am not your son," he said calmly.

"Oh, no?" Vincent said. He seemed a little bit surprised that Nathaniel was still holding his temper. He moved toward the last door that stood between them. "Who are you then?"

"I am the son of a mother and father that you murdered. You are nothing to me."

"Wait," Vincent said, as if shocked by the statement. "I thought that you were the one who killed your mother. Broke her neck, I recall."

Barbara, Michael and Mark all glanced Nathaniel's direction, waiting to see what he might do. He could feel their eyes on him, too.

"Vincent," Nathaniel began, measuring the words carefully. He approached the large glass window, choosing a spot directly before his long-time adversary, stopping just short of pressing his nose against the glass. "I am ready for you now. You shall not rile me as easily as you did in those early days in Poienari Fortress. These past days I have been equally blinded by the woman that you have been terrorizing, along with her family. You will not find me so blinded again." The voice grew more booming with each word uttered in the darkened building. "And they are all here, securely under my charge. Husband, children, all."

By the look of him, Vincent was beginning to lose control himself, not Nathaniel as he had initially intended. "You are weak, my son!" he sneered. "I have fed." He glanced toward everyone in the room beyond. "I have fed very well." Vincent glanced back toward Nathaniel. "Have you?"

Nathaniel stared at Vincent and smiled suddenly, completely out of character.

"The hour is getting late, *father!* Are you coming in here to get me or are you not?"

With that, Vincent roared. The vampire took a step back and began to attack the door that separated them. Again and again, he kicked at the door. It was strong, but soon the metal door and doorframe began to squeal and groan with the assault, slowly giving way.

5:10 a.m.

Jerod sat on the couch in the soft room next to Vanessa. They did not speak while attempting to hear something, anything, of what might be happening on the other side of the building. The only thing to be heard, however, was their own breathing. His eyes moved toward the bookcase to his left. There did not appear to be anything of interest to him upon close inspection. He wasn't a big reader, although he could do it very well. Even had he spotted some treasure there amongst the donated stuff, he no doubt would have found it impossible to maintain any decent concentration. The twins seemed to be doing alright, however. Vanessa and he had moved the coffee table over to one side of the room in order to give them lots of space to sit on the floor with a small assortment from an overflowing box of stuffed animals.

"They don't seem to mind being cooped up in here, do they?" Vanessa broke the silence. She did not turn toward Jerod when she asked the question. She just stared at Robbie and Rebekah as if envying their naiveté.

"I guess not," Jerod answered.

"How about you?"

He was now watching his brother and sister as well. "I guess not," he answered, although his response did not sound very convincing.

She looked as though she wanted to say something more, but didn't. All she did was wring her hands and sneak looks at the door to the hallway, as if worried over what might happen any minute now.

"What about you?" Jerod asked to break the tension.

"What?"

"Never mind." He looked down at his hands and got quiet.

Vanessa caught his reaction.

"What?" she asked. "Do you mean do I like being cooped up here with you guys? Of course. I just wish everything was different, you know. I want to play with you guys and sing and laugh."

"But you got stuck having to baby sit?" Jerod asked, still not looking up from his hands upon his lap. He played nervously with his fingernails.

"Well, maybe," Vanessa answered. "But I love you guys, and I would do anything for you."

She reached out for Jerod's chin and gently raised it using her bruised forefinger with the broken nail. Their eyes met, and she reassured him with her gaze, even though she looked all beaten up and tired.

"Do you hear me?" she asked as his eyes swept the room and moved in her direction. "I love you..."

His eyes were wet but he was not crying.

"I love your brother..."

His eyes widened when something caught his eye.

"And I love your... What is it?" She turned.

Oh, my God!

The twins were holding onto the coffee table.

They were standing and holding onto the coffee table. And they were looking right at them. Or were they? They actually seemed to be staring past them at the wall, almost as though they could see through it.

"I didn't know they were standing already!" Vanessa exclaimed.

"Neither did I!"

5:15 a.m.

Mayor Katherine Peterson raced in her red Ford Mustang convertible, west down Draper Street through empty twilit streets. The car slowed and rolled through the intersection of Draper and Marion. She was in one hell of a hurry and counting on the police being too busy elsewhere to be concerned with some mild Hollywood stopping. She continued west, slowing when she got to California Street where she made a hard left. Tires squealed as the driver gunned the accelerator half-way through the maneuver. It picked up a high rate of speed and slowed one last time as it prepared to turn left again into the Kingsburg Police Department parking lot.

"Jesus!" she exclaimed as she was forced to go around a Volkswagen beetle that appeared to have been abandoned at the mouth of the parking lot. She took the turn slowly, peeking around the car to make sure that in fact no one was kneeling beside the car, changing a tire or something. When she was convinced that the car was without an owner, she continued on her way. The driver did not waste time looking for a parking spot, but simply pulled up behind a patrol unit that had been parked at the sidewalk near the front entrance.

Something loud gave her a start as she jumped out of the vehicle.

Crash.

It sounded as if some heavy construction was taking place, but she knew that that could not be the case. A week before the Swedish Festival, all of the projects, both large and small, had already been completed.

However, there it was once again as she hurriedly made her way to the door. Crash. Crash. Crash.

The sound was coming from inside the darkened police station. She quickly grabbed the front door by the handle and swung it open. Crash.

"What the hell is going on in here?" the mayor yelled as she stepped over the threshold and into exactly that: Hell.

*   *   *

"Oh, shit!" Michael cursed.

Mark got off of the wall that he had been leaning against and moved toward the glass. "Run, mayor! Run!"

Vincent stepped back after his last kick, not really noticing the woman enter until she had shouted. He quickly spun and made a move toward her. The mayor did not move. She was frozen in place. She was too busy attempting to determine the nature of what she had stumbled upon and understanding nothing.

"*Vincent?*" Nathaniel shouted, but did not wait to see whether the vampire would stop and turn back before killing yet another human being, no matter how innocent. He simply glanced left, and quickly slammed his left hand across the bank of light switches, closing his eyes tight as he did so.

Vincent screamed and Mark ducked down the hallway as the florescent lights leapt to life, momentarily blinding vampire and man alike. The light was not true light, but it would give Nathaniel just the opening that he needed to strike. Squinting, Nathaniel threw everything that he had into the wounded door. It gave with a yelp, breaking the last of the lock and collapsing forward, catching Vincent square in the middle of the back, knocking him off balance and onto the tiled floor.

As if overwhelmed by extreme panic, Michael quickly ran out of the room and headed for the chief's office, leaving Barbara behind.

346

Mayor Peterson did not retreat when the voice in the dark had told her to make a run for it. Nobody told her to do anything; she was the one who gave the orders, and this morning she was good and pissed off. However, as the lights suddenly came on, her eyes went immediately to the crushed body at her feet. It had lifeless eyes and a mass of something terrible and gray leaking out of the side of her head. A thought leapt into her mind as she recoiled in terror that this was the poor girl that she had yelled at on the phone. She tried to dismiss it, but found herself unable to do so in that lonely moment right before the door exploded to her right and an image came rushing behind it to do God knew what. It was only then that she attempted to turn and flee for her life.

*   *   *

Vincent was on the ground, crushed by the metal door. As he attempted to regain his footing, Nathaniel was upon him, and a succession of blows began to rain down upon his face. With a quick clockwise turn, Vincent spun and heaved his considerable weight and strength into the door, throwing both it and Nathaniel off and across the lobby. Both struck the woman as she attempted to flee, knocking her feet out from beneath her. Pictures rained to the floor and glass shattered, scattering everywhere.

Vincent repeatedly blinked his eyes as he regained his feet, and stood before the open doorway. The light was no longer having the harsh effect. The vampire could see very clearly now. He saw Barbara there in the other room. Without delay, Vincent rushed her, fingernails barred.

*   *   *

Nathaniel threw the door off of himself, sending it back across the room. It knocked more picture frames free of their hooks and brought them crashing to the floor. He heard the woman beside him moan in pain, but there was another woman that was currently more important—Barbara. Nathaniel hoped that he was not already too late.

"Look out!" Michael yelled as he leapt back in the room, carrying something in his hand.

Barbara barely had a chance to look when Vincent was nearly upon her. She jumped to her right, and that took her further from the hallway which might have made her a better escape. Nathaniel knew what she thought—that at least it was also farther from her children.

The object Michael carried was now clearly visible. Even Vincent saw the saber as Michael attempted to bring it down upon him. But, it took no effort for him to grab the arm wielding the vintage Civil War weapon before it could be used against him. Vincent used Michael's own momentum to toss him across the room, sending him sprawling into the wall below the Dispatcher's counter. The detective ceased all movement. The saber rolled harmlessly out of his hand.

Barbara followed her husband with her eyes as he was discarded, and tried to make a move toward the saber. Vincent had her in his viselike grip and slammed her against the nearest wall. The force of the blow dented the thin metal door of the cabinet. She tried to scream as the air within her was suddenly trapped by the vampire's grip around her throat. Nothing was getting in and nothing was getting out.

Vincent turned as another took aim upon him. As Nathaniel came rushing back into the room, Mark came flying into Vincent, knocking Barbara free and Vincent into the dispatcher's microphones and console. Vincent attempted to throw Mark away, but found it not nearly as easy as it should have been. His eyes widened in surprise as the man bared his teeth.

Barbara fell to the ground and rolled away as the sound of violence continued to her right. She cried out when Nathaniel suddenly grabbed her by the arms and helped her up rather forcefully, pushing her back into the hallway.

Nathaniel quickly rejoined the fray.

"What's this?" Vincent strained to say as he continued to fight to free himself while Nathaniel rushed in to help subdue him. "What have you done?"

"Anything that I need to do to destroy you!" Nathaniel roared just inches from his face.

"You blame me for so much, but we are the same! We are the same, do you hear me?"

Mustering his strength, Vincent rallied against the two, sending them off of him just enough to regroup. Mark was the nearest when Vincent regained his balance. Vincent had a hold of him and threw him against the large glass window. He fell onto the counter and then rolled off of it, coming to rest atop his partner's legs just as Michael was beginning to climb back to his feet.

Nathaniel rushed back, but having not fed much during the night, he really was no match for the much stronger vampire. Vincent caught him easily, picked him off of the ground and drove him backward into the small wall near where the lobby door had once stood. Nathaniel cried out as the blow did damage. Vincent smiled, gritting his teeth with delight as the long awaited moment had finally arrived. Years, decades and centuries of waiting were upon him. The vampire slammed Nathaniel into the wall five more times. With each blow, it took Nathaniel more energy to hold his head up; his arms dangled aimlessly at his side. Soon, holding open his eyes became difficult as well.

It was only as Michael approached Vincent from behind, his saber pointed purposefully before him, did

Nathaniel spring to life with whatever reserves he had left. He grabbed each of Vincent's arms and held them as tightly as he could.

Vincent grinned. "So much the better! It would be a pity if you put up so little a fight!"

Nathaniel grinned back as Michael drove the saber through Vincent's back, driving it through the brown leather coat and into Nathaniel a few inches as well. It hurt a great deal, but the pleasure of seeing the smile fade from the great beast was well worth it.

Michael let go of the blade and retreated as Vincent dropped Nathaniel and spun around to face him. The end of the blade was black with the mingled blood of countless others as well as Vincent's. The vampire looked at it dumbfounded for a time, and then looked back up at Michael as he began to approach him.

"You missed my heart," Vincent hissed. "I am going to leave it there until I rip off your head. Then I will use it to draw and quarter your children, as well as your wife!"

"I'm right here, you sonofabitch!"

Vincent spun just in time to take the second saber. Barbara had a wild look on her face at Vincent's mention of how he was planning on murdering her children. There was no squeamishness in her actions as she focused her aim and pierced Vincent's heart. She did not stop driving until the hilt of the saber rested evenly against his chest.

"No!" Vincent screamed as all of his power began to drain down his front and down his back in dark rivulets. Soon, the blood began to stream out, splashing and puddling upon the thin carpeting. He quickly fell onto his knees.

"Barbara." Nathaniel called for her assistance, stretching out his hand for her to take. She took it immediately and helped him to his feet. It was not easy but she managed to help him up.

Michael appeared uneasy as he watched Vincent dying. Much could be attributed to his wounds. They would need to get him to a hospital soon. Nathaniel also wondered whether Michael feared that Vincent he might somehow pull off some miraculous resurrection, just like in horror movies. Meanwhile, Mark began to stir there on the floor.

"Nathaniel," he called out, but did not make a move to get up. "The light."

Nathaniel limped across the room as quickly as he could manage, dragging one leg as he moved behind Vincent. Nathaniel then took hold of the saber that Michael had driven into Vincent's back. The mortally wounded vampire almost took no notice of it as he fell onto his hands now. His once strong hands shook as they attempted to hold up his weight.

"Barbara, can you turn out the lights, please?" Nathaniel asked, glancing her way.

Barbara appeared as if she was not yet through with punishing the dying vampire; the look she wore seemed to indicate that she wanted very much to knock him over and kick him repeatedly in the face. She held her composure, however, although it took most of her remaining strength to do so. As she turned to do what had been asked of her, she noticed the mayor standing against the Lobby glass. It gave her pause.

"Please, do it now, Barbara."

*   *   *

The mayor saw Barbara walk out of her field of vision as she held her eyes on the figure in the middle of the room. It was the last clear thing she saw as the lights went out.

"Are you alright?" Barbara asked as she carefully made her way through the dark and through the destruction and approached the mayor.

Fragments of the police station crumbled beneath her feet as she reached the woman close enough to lay her hands upon her. "Mayor Peterson, are you alright?"

351

"What is that thing?" the mayor whispered, her voice laced with pain, shock and bewilderment. It was not due to fear, but rather due to her injuries. She was leaning against the glass because it had taken all of her efforts just to get her that far.

"That is the end of all of your troubles. As well as ours."

5:36 a.m.

"That wasn't the light I was referring to," Mark said as Michael helped him up.

He did not need the help, but it was welcome nonetheless. He looked past his partner and reached out for Nathaniel. Michael watched the interaction and was perplexed by it. Nathaniel could see it very clearly because the room was no longer as dark without lighting as it had been seemingly just a few moments before. He glanced back over his shoulder and out the front door. The sky was a medium blue as the sun's initial rays had begun to peek out over the Sierra Nevada Mountain Range to the east.

"Time is almost past for all of us," Vincent whispered.

At the sound of the vampire's words, Nathaniel gripped tightly the handle of the saber in his hands by his left, and gave Vincent a spin until the handle of the other saber came into view. He grabbed that one with his right and began to pull the vampire across the room as if he were the main course, hanging upon the rotisserie.

"Michael, we are leaving," Nathaniel announced.

"Where are you going?"

"I need to finish this."

"Finish what?" Michael said.

Nathaniel lifted Vincent off of the floor, using both blades to do so. The vampire screamed a pathetic spit-riddled whisper of a scream. The look on his face confirmed the pain that he was under, though the sound could no longer convey it. "The beast is not yet finished." Nathaniel pulled the vampire around and brought his face close to his, nose against nose. "But it will be."

"I'll come with you," Michael said, heading for the door.

"No."

"What do you mean, no?" he said, surprised. "Whatever it is, you can't possibly handle it by yourself. Not in your shape!"

"Mark is going to help me."

"Mark?" Michael turned and faced his partner. "Why, Mark?"

"Tell him." Vincent splattered blood upon Nathaniel in a fit of laughter, spitting out the words.

"Where's the girl?" Nathaniel demanded to know, ignoring the instruction.

"What girl?" Vincent asked, but not convincingly.

"Tiffany?"

"Why do you want to know?" The words were coming out slurred now, and only Nathaniel could understand them. "She is dead! She has failed me for the last time!"

One more dead! Nathaniel thought. Having had quite enough, Nathaniel roared one last time and lifted Vincent into the air only to bring him back down, and slam his head into his knee. Vincent went limp immediately.

"Tell me, *what?*" Michael asked as Nathaniel dropped the vampire onto the carpet.

"We do not have time for this!" Nathaniel shouted, still full of adrenaline.

Mark stepped before his partner and addressed him fully. "Surely you knew all along, Mikey. I wasn't coming back from injuries like that."

"Jacks?"

"Don't worry about it, Mikey. Everything worked out."

"Mark, we leave now or we are all three dead!" Nathaniel warned. "Michael, attend to your family."

5:45 a.m.

Michael smiled as the soft room door opened, revealing Vanessa Jackson and three out of four of the most beautiful faces in the world to him. All three smiled back at their father.

Everybody was standing.

Including the twins. They were still holding onto that coffee table, but now they were facing the open door.

"Is it over?" Vanessa asked. Michael acted as if he had not heard her. *"Is it over?"*

"It's over."

Michael knelt to see the amazing sight up close. "Barbara, honey?" he called out, never taking his eyes from them. They were smiling as if they, too, recognized the achievement that they had now realized.

"What is it?" Barbara asked, stepping into the doorway. "My God!" she murmured suddenly, bringing her hands to her face in shock. She knelt as well. "But they never even crawled!"

"Where's Mark?" Vanessa waited as long as she could under the circumstances, but finally asked.

"Vanessa, he's not here. He left with Nathaniel."

"Why?" she asked and appeared extremely hurt that he did not wait to see her.

Michael stood and walked over to her. He leaned close to her, his mouth just inches from her right ear and whispered. "The vampire was not dead yet. Wounded, but not dead. They are taking care of that once and for all."

"My babies!" Barbara cried as she quickly made her way to them.

354

Pent up emotions began to tear at the mental wall that they'd all erected in the last few days and mostly-- hours. Tears welled up in her eyes but she did not cry... yet. But it was over, and there was no denying that she, like so many others, would need to let it all out and mourn for those that fell during the ordeal.

"Mom!" Jerod exclaimed. "We were just talking on the couch and suddenly there they were. Standing! All by themselves!"

Barbara looked up and motioned for her son to join her and his brother and sister in a giant hug. She kneeled between them all and swallowed them up in her arms.

To Michael, it was the most beautiful sight in the world.

Squeals of delight sounded out from all four of them as the pressure and tensions of the previous several hours let off like so much steam. Mayor Peterson entered the room just in time to witness the event. She was banged up, but she would be fine.

"Are you okay?" Michael asked her. He had met her before but could not say that he knew her very well. He almost wasn't sure that she remembered his name.

"I'm glad you seem to understand all of this because I don't."

"Many have died, Your Honor," he said gently. "The creature that you saw was responsible for all of it. Thanks to the efforts of all of those here, no more shall be added to that list."

Slowly and delicately, Michael put his left arm through her right and patted hers a couple of times with his right hand. She glanced at the children before her and their mother, and then back at Michael. She wanted to smile, he could see, but he was unsure as to what exactly stopped her from doing so. If nothing else, he planned right then to smile a hell of a lot more from now on.

Just as soon as he got some sleep.

"Come on, Your Honor. *Katherine*," Michael said, leading her gently to a nearby chair so that she might sit down. "Come sit with us and I'll explain what we have just witnessed this past week. And then we'll start making Swedish Festival plans."

EPILOGUE

5:55 a.m.

Methodically, the sun crawled up over the Sierra's and climbed into the sky over the Central Valley of California. It found Orange Cove, Dinuba, Reedley, Fowler, Selma and, ultimately, Kingsburg. At first, light shot across the sky like tiny microscopic lasers, coloring it, revealing the few lingering clouds overhead to the joggers and commuters who might happen to glance overhead. For those it was as if there had been some sort of race to see with which the darkened sky was lit. Each individual fragment of light darted across the sky toward a finish line somewhere on the other end of the world. As the stragglers filled in the cracks and thus chased night away for another thirteen hours, they found an unsuspecting, most unlikely audience.

Watching first as the sky began to lighten, becoming more blue than black, Vincent was foggy as to what was taking place. The vampire had a pain in his head that he had not known in a long while, and he had not the brainpower to attribute it to Nathaniel's delivered blow. All that he knew presently was that something nameless and faceless hovered overhead and began to completely encircle him.

As the vampire's cold skin began to warm, Vincent slowly came out of his daze. The sun became recognizable for what it was. Its rays were a peculiar sensation. It was odd, both because it was unfamiliar, and then ultimately because being undead, the vampire did not believe it possible for him to be feeling much of anything at all concerning the elements of this world. Inside, however, somewhere behind his eyes, there was a buzzing about him.

Suddenly, just as the sensation began to become bothersome, he began to remember why it was that he usually had nothing at all to do with the sun. The sun was death to vampires.

Initially, it was nothing more than a slight irritation. Now, it caused him genuine pain.

Vincent looked himself over as pain raced up his body. He was only wearing his blood-stained shirt and jeans. His leather coat was in a heap at his feet. He still had the two US Calvary sabers impaled in his chest; however, this time, he could see both leather spiraled handles, not just the one. The fullered blades had Vincent fastened tightly against the side of an old barn, somewhere out in the country and away from the city.

Vincent smelled something burning suddenly.

It was him.

His skin began to sizzle. Tiny fires erupted, setting his clothing on fire and burning it off of him. In various places, sections of his flesh danced, rose and ultimately popped, sending milky fluid into the air on a microscopic plane. Before his very eyes, it then flaked off, rolling back like so much paper on fire and float away in the gentle summer morning breeze.

The vampire attempted to get free, but none of his efforts were successful. What he did not know was the blades had been driven through the vampire first, the weathered pine wood and lastly the blades pounded flat against the boards, making sure that the only way Vincent could escape was to bring down the entire barn. He wondered whether they were waiting for him inside—waiting for him to die.

The matter below his skin now being revealed in droves, the pain was excruciating. Soon, unendurable.

The vampire shrieked as he regained complete consciousness only to realize that he was being cooked alive.

"Nathaniel!" he managed to scream. "Nathaniel!"

The vampire hissed, squirming and flinging his arms and legs about, doing his evil best to pull himself free, but was far too weak.

"Nathaniel!" he screamed.

"Nathaniel!"

The vampire's vision was the first to go, leaving him thankfully blind to the horror which was about to befall him.

The last ounce of moisture within him dripped from shriveling lips as he fought to scream. "*aahannnnuulll!*"

The vampire's last sensation was the feeling of his weight as it dripped like melting wax from his bones. The final act of decomposition was the great beast's skull as it fell in and all of its bones turned to dust. What did not blow away with the light breeze fell like dirty snow upon what remained of his jeans and riding boots.

*   *   *

Inside the old abandoned barn, Nathaniel was falling asleep beside Detective Mark Jackson. They were both buried heavily beneath layers of old quilts on the second story. On some level, Nathaniel did not let go completely of his consciousness until all of Vincent's death throes had been completed. Only afterward did the vampire lose himself in blessed sleep.

11:15 p.m.

The smell of eggs and bacon, cooking oil and coffee filled the house as Michael and Barbara Lopez went back to living their lives after the terrible ordeal that had disrupted and threatened to end that life over the past week. Husband and wife sat mostly in silence; not because anyone was upset or uncomfortable, but for the simple reason that they were all dog-tired. Even after over ten hours of sleep, everyone was still

361

exhausted. At least the adults were. In the living room, Jerod was back at the video games, his baby brother and sister standing on either side of him, holding onto him unsteadily, but sure enough. They were watching his progress, dazzled by the sights and sounds of the action.

There was a dark cloud hanging over everything that would take some time to dissipate; however, for the most part, life was coming back to normal.

"Is Vanessa still asleep?" Michael asked after taking a large drink of his coffee and pulling his eyes from the still amazing sight of the twins standing

Barbara nodded, but continued to be captivated by the sight as well. In fact, she had been quietly thinking about her friend, wondering how the Lopez family could have been so untouched while the Jackson family was laid to waste. Vanessa and Mark had spent the last two years attempting to have a baby. Now, she had no baby and no husband. Mark was still around, they assumed, though they had yet to see their friend since the events of the morning. Unfortunately, the unspoken thing between Barbara, Michael and Vanessa was *what* her husband was.

As the two became lost in thought once again, Barbara noticed as the toddlers began to slowly turn around and face her. Neither lost their balance. Incredibly, Jerod was not distracted in the least. She smiled at them, but as someone on the other side of the front door began to knock, she realized that they had not turned to look for their mother.

It was Nathaniel.

I'll never get used to that! She thought.

Michael did not pick up on the trick. He was still oblivious. *Some detective!* Barbara thought.

Michael checked his watch. She knew it was late, but with all that had gone on, there was bound to be some oddities, such as all of them waking up to start a day when most of the state was heading off to bed. He flipped on the outside light and then took a peek through the peephole to see who it might be. She watched him flinch, pull back from the sight and immediately flip the light back off. He glanced toward Barbara who nodded with a grin.

She jumped up from her chair and turned off the main kitchen light, leaving on only the small light over the sink. Michael lowered the dimmer to the dining room chandelier and then opened the door.

"Hi," Michael said, greeting Nathaniel.

"May we come in?" the vampire asked. He looked odd without his long coat, but that needed replacing. He held a towel in his hands. Two spiral leather grips protruded from one end of it. The chief's Calvary Sabers were being returned. It had been nearly one-hundred and fifty years, but they had been put to good use once again. They were scarred now just like all of the occupants of the house.

"Of course."

"Thank you," he said, handing over the bundle.

A few feet behind the spot that Nathaniel had just vacated stood Mark Jackson. He held his ground and said nothing.

"Hey, Jacks." Michael stood his ground as well.

"Michael."

"Whoa," Michael said, stepping out into the darkness of his front porch. "What's this 'Michael' crap? It's 'Mikey', remember?" Michael closed the distance between himself and his partner. "I don't profess to understand everything that has happened. Not exactly. But I do know this: I still love you, you know!"

Witnessing the exchange, Barbara had never been prouder of her husband.

"Thanks, man," Mark said and then embraced him, awkwardly at first, but then both relaxed.

Together they walked into the house and closed the door behind them.

Nathaniel sat at the dining room table in the chair that Michael had vacated, and although Michael picked up on that fact right away, he did not allow it to linger. Michael knew how Nathaniel felt about his wife; he did not have to be told. It was the same thing he felt. However, he wasn't jealous anymore. In fact, he was thankful for knowing it because it would help him never take his wife for granted. He simply took another chair and sat down, then pointed at another chair beside Barbara and invited Mark to sit as well. He set the bundle down on the table.

Nathaniel watched the children. Jerod was still playing his PlayStation 2, but the room was in dim light now as Barbara had softened things up for their guests. The twins faced the dining room, Michael noticed. Following their gaze, he could almost detect a bit of a grin across Nathaniel's face.

"Yes?" Nathaniel said softly. "I see you studying me, Michael."

"You look happy."

The vampire turned to face the man. "I am. You have a wonderful family, sir."

"And I owe that to you."

The cell phone in Michael's left pants pocket began to vibrate.

Nathaniel seemed to want to shrug the notion off.

"It's true," Barbara added. She reached over and placed her left hand upon Nathaniel's shoulder. "Thank you."

The vampire said nothing further. He simply went back to watching the children at ease there in the living room. Earlier, he was not at all certain that this room would ever hold peace and happiness again.

Michael contemplated the name of the caller on the cell phone screen. He glanced at Barbara as he stood up and answered the call.

"Hello."

"Is Vanessa here?" Jackson asked. "We went to the house first, but it doesn't look like anyone's been home since we escaped this morning."

"Yes," Barbara said, turning to face him. "She's not well, Mark."

"Does she know what I am? What I have become?"

"We have not talked about that," she answered. "But, yes. I think she does."

"May I see her?" It was Nathaniel who asked the question as he continued to watch the children. It caught everyone by surprise.

"I don't know if that's a good idea, Nathaniel."

The vampire turned to face Barbara. "I understand."

Yet, Nathaniel immediately stood up and headed off down the hallway.

Michael was in the middle of the kitchen, and also in the middle of a very interesting conversation. "I'm flattered, Katherine," he said as he contemplated what she had just said to him. He was feeling mixed emotions. "I just don't know."

While he listened to the mayor deliver her sales pitch, Michael walked back to the mouth of the living room and stared at the couch. It was in a new location, parked directly in front of the sliding glass door. Its purpose, of course, was to hide what was left of the life of Chief O'Donnell. Barbara gave him a quizzical look. When he closed the cell phone and returned to the table, she got her answer.

"That was the mayor," he said deliberately, composing himself. "You're looking at the interim chief of police."

*   *   *

Nathaniel gently pushed open the door to Jerod's bedroom that Vanessa had been given to spend the night. Softly, he entered the room and approached the

365

bed. The woman looked lovely in the dark, but the sleep masked the pain that she was enduring. A heavy odor of saltwater hung in the air. She had apparently cried herself to sleep.

The vampire knelt beside the bed. Vanessa's right hand hung ever so slightly off the mattress. Most of her fingernails were broken. He took it lightly in his, allowing the chill of his flesh to bring her out of her slumber. Her reaction was immediate. She shivered and began to pull herself into a tight ball for warmth. He began to speak to her as she began to stir, hoping that his words would have a better effect while she was not yet so fully conscious as to reject him.

"Vanessa, it is I, Nathaniel. I know that you are hurting now, that you feel as if life itself is over for you. Part of it has, but not completely. Your husband was near death when he made the terrible choice to live. He did it for his friends and yours, and ultimately, he did it for you. Were it not for his sacrifice, we might all be dead now."

Tears rolled anew down Vanessa's bruised cheeks, pooling onto the bed linen, staining afresh the areas that had only begun to dry. Her eyes opened with a flutter and she brought her left arm across her face to catch more tears. It was then that Nathaniel detected another scent; a scent so faint that it was a wonder that even he had noticed it at all. A few days before and there would have been no way.

The vampire smiled. It was his first in a very long while and perhaps the most fitting of endings to a long, hard series of events. He let go of her hand, allowing her to warm back up.

"You have no children, is this correct?" Nathaniel asked.

Vanessa nodded, causing one hoop earring to swing. The other had come off sometime during Vincent's attack. Another solitary tear rolled down her left cheek, crossing over to her nose and then onto the bed. She allowed it to hang a moment and then fall.

"You thought you could *not* conceive, is this correct?"

Vanessa said nothing, but simply did her best to hold back the tears. He could sense her effort, as well as her growing indignation that Nathaniel was questioning her this way, making her feel worse... but he also knew she had very little strength left to fight back.

"You were mistaken."

"What?" Vanessa perked up.

"My touch is cold," Nathaniel told her. "Please allow it."

Vanessa stared at him, her eyes full of hesitant hope. He could see all of that anguish, those years of futile hope in those eyes, and the many prayers that she and Mark offered so they could one day have a child. So, at his words, her hands went out to him. Nathaniel took her hands in his and held them tight as he felt for the proof. Finally, a second smile crept over Nathaniel's face as he detected a second heartbeat within her. So new, so very scant, but it was there.

"You bear a child," he said simply and then pulled back his hand, patting her twice upon the clothed shoulder before standing back up and leaving the room to summon her husband. How the two of them were going to possibly maintain their marriage, Nathaniel did not presume to know. Perhaps it would prove to be an impossible weight to either carry or get beyond. It simply was what it was, and after that it was up to the two of them to figure out.

Michael was attending to the stove and the food that was cooking there when Nathaniel came back down the hall. Barbara was nowhere to be seen. Nathaniel did not ask of her whereabouts, but simply joined Michael in the kitchen.

"How is Vanessa?" Michael asked. "Did she speak with you?"

"Yes."

"How is she?"

Nathaniel glanced away for a moment. "I think I will allow her and Mark to tell you that. There is something, however, that we do need to discuss."

"Tiffany?" Michael asked.

"We could not find her."

"He told you that he killed her, right?"

"So he said."

"And you don't believe him?"

"Perhaps this time, in the end, he proves to be trustworthy. We could find no evidence of a body, however."

"Now that the beast is dead, will she be human again?"

"That is a myth, I am afraid."

"Should I be concerned?"

"No," Nathaniel said, getting up out of his chair. "I will be."

"Are you going somewhere?" Michael asked.

"I should go."

Nathaniel walked over to take one last look at the children. The twins were still standing. They turned to face him and he raised his right hand to give them the slightest of waves before turning and heading for the door.

"Nathaniel, my friend," Michael said, lowering the level of the burner that he was currently using and heading for the door himself. "Don't put yourself in the same category as Vincent. You and he were nothing alike." He offered his right hand. "And I am honored to have met you."

"My touch is cold," Nathaniel explained.

"Yeah," Michael grinned. "I got that! Just give me your hand."

368

When the vampire stepped out into the night, he found Barbara waiting there for him. Michael did not loiter in the doorway to see or hear what might take place; he quickly closed the door instead and gave them some peace. Barbara did not move from the bench, but motioned for Nathaniel to join her. He did not.

"I must go," he said.

"Not before I speak with you," she began. "I want you to know that you did a wonderful thing here."

"I caused all of this."

Barbara practically leapt out of her chair. "Don't you dare go there with me! This house is full right now of people that owe you their very lives. Their very lives! God brought both Vincent and you into our lives. He turned Vincent's evil into good. The Bible says that."

"Yes, I know," Nathaniel acknowledged. *"And we know that God causes all things to work together for good to those who love God, to those who are called according to His purpose."*

Barbara was amazed. "So how can you know the scriptures and not believe?"

"Oh, I believe. I believe that I am working outside of God."

"Still?" she pleaded, grabbing him by the arms. "After all of this, you still believe that God does not know you? That He has no use for you? That He did not use you this week for good?"

Nathaniel said nothing further. Barbara looked deeply into the vampire's eyes and waited for a response. When none was forthcoming she threw her arms around him. "You have answered wisely."

"I said nothing," Nathaniel whispered, greatly enjoying the embrace.

"By your silence you have given your answer." After nearly a minute she released him. "You may not be human anymore, but you are certainly no devil. The Lord Himself has convinced me of this. There is nothing that you can do or say to change my mind. And this may be too much for you to deal with, but I don't think you are lost, either. Seek God, Nathanlel! I believe He is making Himself known to you."

The vampire did not say another word that night. There was truth in what Barbara had said to him, but it was too overwhelming, too inconceivable for him to fathom. He had spent centuries hoping for a release from a cursed life, and the events of one solitary week, no matter how profound, were not going to easily eradicate that desire. However, there was something else present within him now; something that was not simply Barbara Lopez, but something else. Perhaps *someone* else.

Perhaps.

Dance on Fire: Flash Point

Five years after the death of their only child Tiffany, Steve and Angie Rosen receive an unexpected guest to their Morro Bay, California home: their daughter. She comes with a tale of having suffered a terrible head wound in the fire that took their Kingsburg home, causing her loss of memory and migraine headaches that force her to hide from daylight. Tiffany's reemergence is treated like Manna from Heaven; however, her story is only half true. Tiffany is a vampire and their daughter in name only. She sleeps during the day and hunts for human blood during the night, and has come back to enact a twisted revenge upon those who ruined the plans of her master, the notorious vampire, Vincent. More importantly, she is not alone.

Five years after the terrible events that reshaped the Swedish Village, Kingsburg lies unsuspecting as five vampires descend upon her with a great evil in their black hearts.

Five years after old wounds have finally healed and the old fires were thought extinguished, Police Chief Michael Lopez and Officer Mark Jackson and their families find themselves surrounded when fires blaze anew. The good vampire, Nathaniel, has pledged his service to these people, but he is no longer among them. He lives high in the Oregon Mountains near the California border, seeking whether God might have a place in His kingdom yet for him.

When Nathaniel discovers that Tiffany has returned, will he be too late to stop her? And will his desire to protect his friends destroy what God has begun in him?

It will all begin with a Flash Point.

Author's note

This is a work of fiction. The plot and characters are the product of the author's twisted imagination. Real persons, places and institutions are incorporated to create the illusion of authenticity.

I would like to thank the Kingsburg Police Department for their time and hospitality as well as my father, Lieutenant James Garcia (ret.), for answering many a law enforcement question over the twenty years that it took this novel to reach the light of day. Any mistakes are the fault of my own.

I would like to thank my wife and children for their support and encouragement.

Lastly, I would like to thank the Lord Jesus Christ for putting the pictures in my head and granting me the talent to put the images that I find there into words.

The characters that survived will return in *Dance on Fire: Flash Point.*

Author Bio

James Garcia Jr. was born in Hanford, California in 1969. In the mid 1970's James Sr. began a Law Enforcement career just up the road with the Kingsburg Police Department, taking the family there. It was not until junior high school; however, that anything of significance occurred. Discovering authors Stephen King and Michael Slade, as well as hard rock music, began to form a spark of creativity within his adolescent mind. He began to play guitar and pen song lyrics, but soon found himself confined in that tight medium, desiring to do longer works.

After graduation, he moved on to the local community college where he met his wife. By this time, he had written a handful of short stories, a couple of novellas and had begun writing the novel that would become *Dance on Fire*.

Career changes, building a family, and the busyness of life impeded his writing at this point. It wasn't until he came to the realization near his fortieth birthday that he did not want to go to the grave with any regrets that he plunged headlong into the dust-covered novel in earnest and completed it after nearly twenty years.

James and his wife, Aida, and their two sons make their home in Kingsburg, where he is an Administrative Supervisor for Sun-Maid Growers of California.

Made in the USA
Las Vegas, NV
11 April 2024